The SILENT SHIELD

THE KINGFOUNTAIN SERIES

BOOKS BY JEFF WHEELER

The Kingfountain Series

The Maid's War (prequel)
The Queen's Poisoner
The Thief's Daughter
The King's Traitor
The Hollow Crown
The Silent Shield
The Forsaken Throne

The Covenant of Muirwood Trilogy

The Banished of Muirwood
The Ciphers of Muirwood
The Void of Muirwood
The Lost Abbey (novella)

The Legends of Muirwood Trilogy

The Wretched of Muirwood
The Blight of Muirwood
The Scourge of Muirwood

Whispers from Mirrowen Trilogy

Fireblood
Dryad-Born
Poisonwell

Landmoor Series

Landmoor
Silverkin

The SILENT SHIELD

THE KINGFOUNTAIN SERIES

JEFF WHEELER

Published by 47North, Seattle
www.apub.com

Amazon, the Amazon logo, and 47North are trademarks of Amazon.com, Inc., or its affiliates.

ISBN-13: 9781611097535
ISBN-10: 1611097533

Cover design by Shasti O'Leary Soudant

Printed in the United States of America

To the Das family

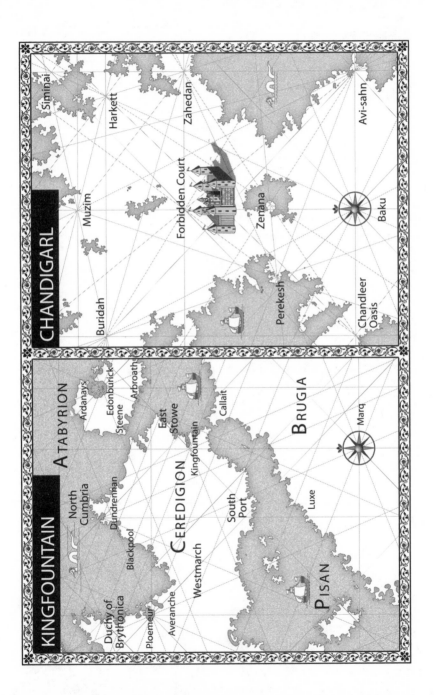

CHARACTERS

MONARCHIES

Ceredigion: Andrew and Genevieve (House of Argentine): the embattled young rulers of Ceredigion are in a desperate situation. The army of Kingfountain was crushed at the Battle of Guilme, and the king's chief strategist and champion, Owen Kiskaddon, disappeared mysteriously right before it began. Nearly a year has passed since that fateful day, without any word from the lost duke. The ruler Gahalatine vowed to invade Kingfountain again one year after the battle, and the time draws near.

Brythonica and Westmarch: Sinia (House of Montfort) and Owen (House of Kiskaddon): the disappearance of Sinia's husband has impacted her deeply. More secluded and reserved, she has pulled away from everyone who loves her best, including her own children. She is the king's advisor, his Wizr, but has been long absent from the palace of Kingfountain in her solitude. Her son, Gannon, has taken his father's title as the new duke of Westmarch. She has a new apprentice, Morwenna Argentine, whom she has been training in the lore of the Fountain-blessed.

North Cumbria: Fallon (House of Llewellyn): Fallon survived the Battle of Guilme. His rejected proposal of marriage to Tryneowy Kiskaddon has left him embittered and scarred but full of purpose. He is determined to win the vacant seat at the Ring Table known as the Siege Perilous and become the king's new champion.

Brugia: Elwis (House of Asturias): after his father's death at the Battle of Guilme, Elwis is a changed man, no longer full of the resentment and angst of the past. His renewed loyalty to the crown is reflected in his increased power in the court of Kingfountain. His kingdom is still vulnerable and lies in the path of Gahalatine's mighty armada. The enemy still holds the city of Guilme as a strategic foothold. There are rumors at court that Elwis has turned away marriage prospects from many rich and powerful heiresses. They say his eye is favorable to the Lady of Averanche.

Averanche: Tryneowy (House of Kiskaddon): only the queen knows Trynne's secret identity as the elusive Painted Knight, but the Lady of Averanche has openly turned her city into the main training ground for young women who wish to study the arts of war. Those who have taken up sword and shield to defend Kingfountain are known as Oath Maidens. Many knights of the realm resent that they will need to compete against female warriors in the upcoming Gauntlet of Kingfountain, but Trynne cares nothing for this rivalry. Her focus is on doing her queen's bidding, finding her missing father, and preparing for the return of Gahalatine.

Chandigarl: Gahalatine (Emperor of the East Kingdoms and Lord of the Distant Isles): this charismatic ruler succeeded in usurping the empire from the grip of his father, his overreaching uncles, and the Wizrs who supported them. He has coalesced power throughout the realms on his side of the world and seeks to increase his hegemony by conquering Kingfountain as soon as the terms of his temporary truce expire.

◆ ◆ ◆

I don't know who I am or how I came to be in this dungeon. My face is covered by a mask of black velvet. My jailor has said I'm too hideous to look at. It is dark and the cell is cramped. The only light comes from a brazier or something burning behind the door of my lonely cell. Two doors guard my prison—my cell door and the one leading to this moldering dungeon. My jailor comes to see me but once a day, when he brings me food and that awful sweet-smelling drink that I know is poisoned. I don't know how I know it's poisoned. I don't remember anything. Not my name. Not my childhood. All is lost to me.

Yet I know the door is made of iron and that the bottom hinges on the outer door are rustier than those on the inner door. I hear everything, from the scuttling of roaches and rats to the groans and cries of other prisoners. There are not so many of us. I feel loneliness and despair that I've lived in this cell for so long. I cannot remember anything before this smothering hood or these chains. My jailor says if I take off the hood, I will be executed. He says if I try to escape, I will be executed. I think I am mad or have done some terrible crime. The only things that soothe me are the pieces of broken stone on the floor. I stack them up in rows and then knock them down. I feel compelled to do this. If I keep doing it, maybe I will remember something. Or maybe I am truly mad.

◆ ◆ ◆

PART I

Wizr

CHAPTER ONE

Chandleer Oasis

Traveling the ley lines was like plummeting over a waterfall. It sent Tryneowy Kiskaddon's heart racing whenever she stepped into a fountain in one corner of the kingdom, only to almost instantaneously appear somewhere else. In the past, that mode of travel had given her a strong sense of queasiness that would not dispel for hours, but she'd practiced enough that she no longer grew sick to her stomach. No, what was disorienting Trynne was the fact that she'd left Averanche in the morning and arrived at her destination close to sunset.

She had appeared inside a fountain at the front of a palatial manor. As the mist dissolved around her and she heard the bubbling of the waters, she was struck by an oppressive heat that nearly took her breath away. The location was foreign to her, and her eyes filled with wonder as she stepped to the edge of the stone lip of the fountain. She didn't want to leave the protection of it yet, just in case her summons there had been a carefully laid trap.

With four equally sized quadrants, the fountain was designed to resemble a flower. There were glowing stones in the water—so curious to behold—which gave the water a strange aspect. She didn't know what made the light, but she knew Chandleer Oasis was part of the

Marusthali Desert, located along the major ley line going east and west. Her mother possessed a book of maps, which Trynne had studied all her life, imagining herself in places she'd only heard of by name.

This place was not on it.

She had never been so far from home, but she relished the adventure.

The fountain was in the middle of a paved courtyard. There was a thatch-roofed hut just in front of her. Extending from its side was a pyramid-shaped roof that was bolstered by sturdy stone pillars affixed with stones glowing as brightly as the ones in the water. Beyond the hut was the manor with its many spires and turrets. The courtyard itself was surrounded by a semicircle of pillars supporting timbers and beams and a latticework covered in a variety of grapevines and wisteria, all providing shade over the area. The nearby hedges were meticulously trimmed into square-shaped blocks.

When Trynne swiveled around, she saw a long path flanked by bizarre giant trees she had only seen before in her mother's books. They were very tall but narrow, like giant maypoles, and their bark bore a strange thatch-weave pattern. The tops of the trees burst into gigantic vibrant-green fronds.

The sound of sandaled feet slapping on stones caught her attention, and she turned again to see a dark-skinned man coming toward her from the shaded pavilion. The doors of the huge manor were being held open by other dark-skinned men wearing turbans.

The man approaching her wore a knee-length tunic the color of whey porridge. It was loose and breathy but embroidered with elegant stitches and patterns. He had a genial smile and bowed his head repeatedly as he approached, his hands pressed together in front of him, his fingers splayed.

"Worthy guest, you are most welcome," the man said in a heavy accent she'd never heard before, bowing his head yet again. He had a trimmed mustache and goatee and thinning hair on the top of his head. When he reached the edge of the fountain, he dropped to his knees and bowed before her, placing his hands on the ground and prostrating himself as if she were an object of worship.

"Please," Trynne said, feeling instantly uncomfortable. "Please stand. I didn't know you would speak my language."

The bearded man quickly rose to his feet, looking abashed. "I did not mean to displease you."

His reaction only made her feel more out of place. The oppressive heat had made sweat pop out on her forehead and shoulder blades. The water of the fountain didn't touch her skirts, but she would not have minded if it did.

"I'm not offended," she said, shaking her head. "I am unfamiliar with your customs. Are you King Sunilik?"

The man's eyebrows lifted. "Oh no, honored guest. I am but your humble servant, Samrao. Come with me, if you please, and I will take you to see him. He will be most honored that you came. If you would follow me?"

Trynne glanced again at the strangeness and beauty of the scene, but her head felt as if it were burning under the intense heat of the dusk. She could only imagine what the daylight hours felt like. She stepped over the edge of the railing, and the waters filled the gap she had left by standing in the pool.

She felt the presence of the Fountain all around her. Its magic thrived in this place, from the sleek vines and grape leaves to the polish on the stones at the edge of the fountain. There was a feeling of peace and serenity that made her less guarded and apprehensive.

As she followed the servant, he made a series of claps with his hands. Veiled maidens appeared from the doorway up ahead, each swaying an oversize palm frond. The air had been heavy and still, so the soft breeze came as a relief.

The interior of the palace bustled with servants and visitors who congregated inside to escape the daylight hours. The air was full of unfamiliar smells—spices and perfumes and the savory scent of dishes she'd never tasted. She followed Samrao across a polished tile floor that was made of marble with flecks of gold in the stone. The manor was not as large as Kingfountain, the royal castle in her realm, but it was impressive in its size and decoration.

Samrao paused to speak to another servant, who rushed ahead to announce them. As they moved through the manor, Trynne felt an increasing sense of self-consciousness. She was the only foreigner in the place. All the servants and citizens were dark skinned with black hair. Their form of attire was very different, the men wearing long tunics and boots and the women wearing brightly colored tunics with intricate patterns and covered by diaphanous veils. Trynne's hair was much lighter, brown instead of black, with a slight curl to her tresses she could never tame. She had always been diminutive, but she was not weak. As the strangers looked at her, she wondered how many had noted the paralysis that afflicted part of her face.

The main entrance hall backed into a high-ceilinged area that boasted a wall of wood-slat windows. Servants with long hooked poles were adjusting the slats to open them up now that the sun was setting.

Queen Genevieve had received a personal message from the King of Chandleer that Gahalatine had announced his intention to invade the small desert kingdom. He had not asked for Kingfountain to defend him. But he had asked if his youngest daughter could be brought to the relative safety of Kingfountain. The king was a disciple of the Fountain, and the magic had moved him to make his request of the queen rather than of King Drew.

Genevieve had showed the message to Trynne, and both had felt it would be an interesting opportunity to gain more knowledge about their common enemy. And since Trynne was training the Oath Maidens, the young women who would help defend their kingdom, the king's appeal had felt part of a larger design.

Two heavy wooden doors opened at the back of the hall, leading out to a veranda. It was there that she found King Sunilik waiting for her. Samrao gave a short bow and then slipped away.

Sunilik was not a tall man, only slightly taller than Trynne herself, and she was notably short among her peers. He was middle-aged and very fit and trim, with a touch of gray at his temples and thinning hair. He had a round face, and when he smiled at her, she noticed a gap in his front teeth. His expression changed into one of surprise.

"You are Lord Kiskaddon's daughter?" he asked with interest. His smile grew even brighter as he stared at her. "I am humbled that the queen sent you. My dear young lady, you are most welcome." He extended his hands in a tender gesture, and she took them, feeling their warmth. "I am a father of three daughters," he said. "Each is a treasure to my wife and me."

"You speak our language so well," Trynne said, feeling the Fountain's magic radiating from this man.

She glanced behind him and was dazzled by what she saw. The rear of the estate had a view of a jagged mountain that rose at a tilted angle before dropping precipitously down. There were no trees on the mountain, just red and brown rocks that reflected the fading sunlight in glints and colorful hues. More of the towering trees filled the rear of the palace, but they were eclipsed by the majesty of the pools and fountains spread out in front of her. The fountains were of different shapes and sizes, spilling and blasting beautiful plumes of water into the air. Walkways and bridges interconnected them.

"I can see you enjoy the fruit of our aqueducts," King Sunilik said with a smile, releasing her hands. He turned and extended his arm. "I did not build this, my lady. I am but the humble steward who inherited a kingdom that was formed centuries ago. This palace was developed by my grandfather, who visited the court of Kingfountain in your realm." He bowed his head humbly to her.

She shifted her gaze back to the oasis, marveling at the sight of the huge body of clean water amidst the parched desert wasteland. The Fountain could be felt in the trickling of the waters, but she realized it was also flowing from the man beside her. Intuition told her he was doing it deliberately to reveal himself to her.

"You are Fountain-blessed," she said.

Again, he bowed his head. He clasped his hands behind his back. "I have no chance of defeating Gahalatine," he said in a resigned tone. "I had hoped Chandleer Oasis would be too insignificant for him to consider. But he is running out of nations to conquer. And when one of his Wizrs arrived and emptied out our pools"—he said it with a shrug, but Trynne could sense the anger lurking behind the words—"I knew we would be overrun. He will give the oasis to one of his other leaders, someone from his spoke of influence. It will be a place where his people come to relax after their conquests. I have worked hard to maintain the oasis and protect its people. But Gahalatine will strip my position from me. That is what he does. I've heard too many of the stories to disbelieve it. And the strange thing is that since he, too, is Fountain-blessed, I will probably *thank* him for taking this away from me."

There was a hint of bitterness in his voice, not that he could be blamed for it. Trynne, too, had heard about Gahalatine's unique gift from the Fountain. It gave him such power of leadership that he had gathered to him a mighty host of kings who "wanted" to serve him.

"You said you had three daughters," Trynne said. "What of the other two?"

King Sunilik beamed proudly. "My eldest is already married and they have a child, my granddaughter. My second is far from the oasis, studying to be a healer. I will need someone to care for me when I reach old age, so I thought it wise to invest in her learning." He gave her a grin and a wink, but then his manner turned more serious. "It is my youngest, Sureya, who concerns me. The Fountain has whispered to me that I must send her away. I expected it would take a month for me to hear back from the queen. I wasn't sure Chandleer would even exist as it does by then. It calms my troubled soul to see you here so soon. Will you bring Sureya to safety? I have taught her about my gifts from the Fountain and how they are replenished. She may have the aptitude for it. She is only sixteen."

"So am I," Trynne whispered. King Sunilik's concern for his daughter reminded her of her own father—despite the many demands on his time, he had always made time for her—and her heart ached. She hadn't seen him in nearly a year.

"Then I feel better already, for you both will understand each other," he said with his gap-toothed smile.

"How did you know who I was?" Trynne asked him. "Did the Fountain tell you?"

"No," he said, shaking his head. "I have long wished to meet the legendary Owen Kiskaddon, so I learned all that I could about him. One of the things that I learned was that his eldest child, his *daughter*"—he said the word almost reverently—"had been attacked violently as a child. It was your expression that gave you away, dear one. The side of your face that is paralyzed." He gestured with his own hand across his left cheek. "If I hadn't heard the stories, I would hardly have noticed it. But my gift from the Fountain is a keen memory." He then tapped the side of his forehead playfully. "It has even been called prodigious. I knew that fact about you, saw a small evidence of it when you smiled in wonder, and the memory surfaced. If I have offended, I apologize sincerely."

Trynne let herself smile despite knowing it was lopsided. Though it had mortified her as a child, she had made an uneasy peace with it. Many suitors were seeking her hand in marriage, and while some were rude and stared at her, most considered her unusual smile an insignificant matter compared with the vast size of her inheritance.

"I'm not offended, King Sunilik," Trynne said. "And I will gladly take Sureya with me. How long ago did you receive the threat from Gahalatine?"

"Long enough that I've been dreading it more each day," he replied, turning back to the view of the mountains. "My soldiers are hidden in the desert and have been watching for signs of his advance. We will have ample warning before they arrive. That mountain behind us provides great protection."

Trynne looked back at the rugged, sloping shape. The sky had grown purple overhead, and the stars were winking into view one by one. Only a strip of orange painted by the sun's fire lit the eastern horizon. When she squinted at the mountain in the dusk, she had the queer sensation that she was being watched. Then she saw it.

There was someone standing on the tallest peak.

A feeling of dread blossomed in her stomach.

"You've grown more pale, if that were possible," the king said in a half-joking manner.

"That mountain isn't protecting you," she said. There was no direct sunlight to glint off the leaf-shaped armor. More and more spots appeared on the mountain, rising like ants coming out of a hill. She gripped his arm in concern. "They'll attack you tonight. Can you see them? Gahalatine is already here."

CHAPTER TWO

Lord of the Distant Isles

The tranquility of the oasis was shattered in moments.

Trynne was humbled by how quickly her warning had been heeded. King Sunilik had summoned his captains instantly, ordering them to bring Chandleer's defenders rushing to the palace. Although she saw fear in Sunilik's eyes, he did not panic; rather, he began to rearrange the defenses with a steady, confident voice.

"And Samrao," the king said to his servant after sending his captains off with their orders, "bring Sureya to me. These two must escape before Gahalatine arrives."

"It will be done," Samrao said with a hasty bow. The palace staff moved like a hive of disturbed ants, running to and fro in confusion. Sunilik paced on the veranda, gazing at the darkening mountain as it disappeared into blackness.

"I have little hope in this affair," the king confided to Trynne. "No other ruler has withstood the Lord of the Distant Isles, save one." He gave her a knowing look. "Your king."

Trynne shook her head. "We did not withstand him well," she answered. "The greater part of our army was wounded or slain. If you could have seen the field—" She stopped herself abruptly, not wanting to say more.

He looked at her from beneath lowered brows. "You speak as if you were there, my lady."

It had been an unintentional slip. Only her queen knew that she was the Painted Knight, the soldier who had joined Kingfountain's army in the Battle of Guilme to help protect the king. She did not wish to lie to King Sunilik, but she did not feel ready to impart the full truth either.

His eyes narrowed more and then he nodded. "Say no more, my lady. I will not pry secrets from you."

A tall man wearing a bronze breastplate and gripping a curved broadsword strode up to King Sunilik. The man, who was not quite middle-aged, towered over the king. "Master, I've left but a small force guarding the fountain before the palace. You wish for the rear gardens to be defended?"

"Indeed," Sunilik said. "See that your men are positioned along the upper and lower gardens." Then he turned to Trynne. "What would you advise?"

Once again, his deference startled her. "When we were attacked by Gahalatine, we were startled to discover that his warriors could . . . fly. Perhaps that's not the right word, but they could leap like insects and nearly hover in the air. Walls are not a protection."

Sunilik's eyes widened. "The Bhikhu. Then we have even less time than I feared."

"The what?" Trynne asked.

Sunilik clenched his fists and started to pace. "I had heard rumors of his alliance with the Bhikhu. They have the power you speak of. When he was driven from Imperial City as a young man, they say he sought refuge among the Bhikhu. That he became the ruler of their distant isle. You must away, Lady Tryneowy. You cannot be found here. Where is Samrao?"

Trynne felt her anxiety increase. She had never heard of the Bhikhu before, but she'd seen Gahalatine's men soar through the air. As she gazed back at the lights shining in the waters of the fountains, she noticed more of those strange tall trees again.

"My lord?" she asked, her eyes following one of the long trunks up into the sky. "Can your soldiers climb those trees?"

He turned and looked at her, then shot his captain a look. "Captain Ashok?"

The tall commander frowned. "Everyone can. We've all climbed the palm trees since we were children."

Sunilik smiled broadly. "Indeed. You are suggesting we hide soldiers amidst the fronds—"

"With bows or something else so they can strike from a distance," Trynne finished for him.

"Captain Ashok, see it done," Sunilik said.

Moments later, Samrao appeared in the doorway with a young woman dressed in the wrapped skirts and gauzy veils Trynne had seen the females in the palace wearing. This girl was dark skinned and dark haired, and elegant tattoos twined around her hands and forearms.

"*Piya!*" the girl cried out, rushing up to Sunilik and embracing him.

He clutched his daughter tightly, his brow furrowing into wrinkles of worry. "Sureya, this is Tryneowy Kiskaddon. You must go with her. Gahalatine is coming this very night."

"But how can I leave you, Piya?" the girl said with raw emotion. "I will stand with you. What happens to you will happen to me!"

Sunilik looked to be in great pain. He cupped his daughter's cheek, half-hidden by the veil. "I will bear what happens to Chandleer much better if I know you are safe. We must hurry, my daughter."

The girl was distraught, but Trynne could tell she was mustering her courage. She pulled away from her father, stood silently for a moment, and then nodded. "I will obey you, Piya. Though I would rather stay."

"You must go, child," Sunilik said. "Samrao, let us go to the fountain. Captain Ashok—see to the defenses."

"Yes, Master."

They walked briskly through the doors into the palace. Servants were hurrying from room to room, and soldiers wearing turbans and carrying shields on their backs jogged through the visitors' hall in columns from the front of the palace. The squawks of strange, colorful birds added to the confusion. Trynne was anxious to be gone.

"Have your king's spies had any success in locating your father?" Sunilik asked her as they marched through the palace.

"None at all," Trynne answered worriedly. It brought back a memory she would as soon forget. It was *she* who had found her father's severed hand in the grove in the woods outside of Ploemeur.

It had still been wearing the invisible ring that had marked him as the protector of Brythonica, Trynne's mother's duchy. That ring now graced the hand of Captain Staeli, whom her father had chosen as the new protector before his disappearance. The captain was also the man Trynne had put in charge of training the Oath Maidens in Averanche.

Despite the murmurs about his strange disappearance, the world believed Owen Kiskaddon had been abducted at the Battle of Guilme. Only Trynne and a few others knew the truth, that someone had summoned him to the grove by magic and then violently attacked him. The Fountain-blessed hunter they had brought to the grove to track him had found no trail.

"It is a shame, truly. Thank you for coming to see my daughter to safety. I owe Kingfountain a debt I cannot easily repay." He added in a melancholy tone, "I will miss this oasis," gazing back at the great hall of the palace. "It has been in my family for several generations. But what the Fountain gives us, it can then take away."

Samrao, who had preceded them out the door, came rushing back to them, his eyes wide with panic, his chin quivering with fear. "Master!" he choked out. "He's *here!*"

They all stopped in their tracks. Samrao pointed, his arm trembling violently, to the front door. "He's at the fountain!"

"Who? Gahalatine?" the king demanded.

Samrao nodded in abject terror.

Trynne felt Fountain magic surge through her. Someone had uttered "ekluo," the word of power that disarmed other magics. Distance limited the word's power, but she felt she was near the epicenter of its scope. The glowing stones in the palace dimmed, and shrieks of terror began to fill the air.

Trynne watched as the main doors of the palace were wrenched open. Her heart was beating violently in her chest, but the magic of the word of power had bypassed her. One of her own gifts from the Fountain, one that her father shared, made it impossible for other magics to affect her or those who stood near her.

"I need a veil," Trynne whispered to Sunilik. Large beads of sweat had popped up on his furrowed brow. He made a quick gesture to Sureya, who removed her own veil and hastily covered Trynne with it. Though Trynne could sense the invisible ley line just beyond the door, running east to west, she was not close enough to invoke its power to take them away. It was too late to get any closer.

Gahalatine entered the palace.

Sureya cowered behind Trynne as the Overking of Chandigarl strode into the hall. Trynne hadn't expected to encounter him on this visit, and it made her knees tremble with fear. She recognized his size and bearing, having witnessed his meeting with King Drew after the disastrous Battle of Guilme. He was not wearing battle armor this time, but a fancy knee-length tunic that was more suitable for Chandleer than her own garb. The collar was open, revealing the three leather straps around his neck. Just as she remembered, one was strung with a claw or fang, another with a circular metal device, and the last with a ring. Gahalatine was nicked with scars from a multitude of battles, and his dark hair looked almost like quills. His beard was trimmed close. He was remarkably handsome.

There was a huge, cavernous supply of Fountain magic inside him that radiated from him with intensity. He was flanked by a

Wizr, not Rucrius—the Wizr who had visited King Drew's council in Kingfountain and almost drowned the city by diverting the river—but another man with a sallow face and a pointed beard and darkened pockmarks across his cheekbones.

The Wizr pointed his staff at Sunilik and murmured something to Gahalatine.

Nodding in acknowledgment, Gahalatine marched up to Sunilik boldly. There were no guards with him, but he didn't look the least bit concerned about his safety.

"Lord Sunilik," Gahalatine said in a wary tone. He offered a polite bow of his head. When Trynne had last heard him speak, his voice had boomed like thunder. He was much taller than the ruler he faced and only half his age, but he had the presence and bearing of a man accustomed to being respected and obeyed. Trynne felt Gahalatine's magic begin to creep into the room, spilling out of him like slow syrup. She was standing near enough that she felt it too, but it split around her like a wave around a rock, not able to come near.

"Welcome to Chandleer Oasis," Sunilik said in a husky but controlled tone. He clasped his hands behind his back. "Would you care for a drink? I have a keg of Atabyrion uskebeaghe I bought from a Genevese merchant for special occasions."

A smile twisted the corners of Gahalatine's mouth. "You choose an interesting language to speak, Lord Sunilik. I had expected to address you in Hunjab."

"We can if you prefer, of course," Sunilik said offhandedly. "I speak it equally well. Have you come to enjoy the bathing pools, then?"

Trynne was impressed by the king's coolheaded response, which earned him another smile from Gahalatine. "I came seeking a glimpse of your daughter, Sureya. I hear she is quite beautiful. I also understand that *you* are Fountain-blessed. Did any of your three daughters inherit the gift?"

As he asked the question, Trynne sensed the subtle press of his will. He was testing Sunilik's power, measuring him, prodding him. Trynne noticed that Sunilik's fingers, still clasped behind his back, were digging into his own skin as if to repel the intrusive act.

"Alas, none of my three daughters have demonstrated aptitude as yet. My wife, Anupa, is not Fountain-blessed, and as you know, it does not always pass to the children."

"Where is Sureya?" Gahalatine asked, forcing another flex of his will on Sunilik. But because Trynne was standing nearby, it could not affect him.

"Well, to come to that point directly," Sunilik said, rocking on his heels a bit. "Since receiving your esteemed emissary"—he nodded to the Wizr standing at Gahalatine's shoulder—"I made arrangements to send my daughter to the court of Kingfountain."

Trynne was impressed by his bluff. He hadn't lied—he'd simply chosen not to reveal that his daughter was still standing there in the room.

A strange look crossed Gahalatine's face. There was anger there, certainly, but it was mixed with admiration. "You sent her to Kingfountain?" he repeated. He let out his breath in a chuff. "The one place I cannot follow her," he added in a low voice. He looked shrewdly at Sunilik. "Is Sureya Fountain-blessed?" he asked in a commanding voice. The power behind the words sent a pulse through Trynne's mind and she almost wanted to confess that she, herself, was Fountain-blessed. But the magic could not make her, nor could it affect Sunilik in her presence.

"As I said," Sunilik responded simply, inclining his head, "she has not, as yet, shown the aptitude. We are a small kingdom, my lord, well beneath the dignity of your esteemed presence."

Gahalatine's expression grew impatient. "I had hoped she would be," he said matter-of-factly. "I cannot always trust my *advisors*"—he gave a scolding look to his Wizr—"to be completely candid with me, and I often verify their reports with my own eyes. Well, if Sureya is visiting Kingfountain, I will have the honor of meeting her soon enough. I will give her your fatherly regards. She may not be what I came here to find, but you, sir, have more than impressed me. You've run your kingdom in a capable and compassionate manner. You have a reputation for integrity and honor. But I have greater use for your abilities in Chandigarl. I will leave a capable man to rule the oasis in your place. But your wife will be brought to you, and you will live together in luxury you cannot imagine." He flashed Sunilik a cunning smile before turning to his Wizr. "Take him to the Forbidden Court."

"As you command, my lord," the Wizr said. He withdrew a cylindrical object, something like a capped scroll case, from his belt and then reached out and touched Sunilik's arm. The two of them instantly vanished, as if blotted out of existence. They were not standing on the ley line at all.

There were gasps from the assembled witnesses. Worried voices began to titter in the semidarkened hall as Gahalatine stood there, brooding, gazing at the spot where the two men had stood. She felt his magic begin to seep out of him again as he turned and faced the large hall. She almost didn't dare to breathe, wondering how she had escaped his notice thus far. Slowly, she reached back and squeezed Sureya's hand.

"Please, do not fear for your lives," Gahalatine said, holding up his hand. "I do not seek vengeance on this place. Go about your work. Obey your masters. When I come to a defeated kingdom, I normally find the people in squalor." He turned as he spoke, his back now to Trynne and Sureya. If she were a poisoner, this would have been her opportunity to assassinate him. The temptation struck her suddenly, keenly, but she shoved it back.

Never take a life unawares or out of revenge.

It was one of the five oaths she had taken to become an Oath Maiden. The Wizr Myrddin had warned her that she would be tempted to violate the oaths. Adhering to them had given her great power and access to the wellspring of the Fountain's magic, but breaking them would bring grievous consequences.

"But I see that you have been treated fairly. There are no hovels or hunger in this place. You have truly made the desert bloom. It is a notable accomplishment. So far you have had a benevolent master. And you will have another in his stead. I give you my word."

As he finished his speech, he turned around completely and now faced Trynne and Sureya. In the darkness, he squinted a bit, looking at her more closely, and her heart began to clench with dread.

"You look familiar," he said. "You are not from these parts; your skin is too pale. You are from the West? Take off that veil. Have we met?"

Trynne didn't know what to say. She bobbed a curtsy, feeling vulnerable.

"My lord, might I entreat you kindly to speak to the captain of the guard?" Samrao said in a diffident tone, deliberately interrupting the exchange. "Captain Ashok has orders from my master to defend the oasis, but I wish to avoid bloodshed."

"Yes, bring him to me," Gahalatine said, giving Samrao a stern look. "Let me judge his character before deciding to replace him or not. He was loyal to Sunilik?"

"We all were," Samrao said with a humble bow.

Trynne took Sureya's wrist and whispered the word of power that would make them invisible. She was wrapped up in the magic instantly and felt her supply of it start to slowly drain. The princess gripped her hand back, almost hard enough to hurt, and Trynne led the way around the columns and furniture. They needed to get around Gahalatine so she could access the ley line.

The servants who had crowded into the hall to hear the speech could not see them, and a few bumped into Trynne, only to stare in surprise at the seemingly blank space before them. Many of them were visibly relieved, their countenances changed by Gahalatine's words. His magic had convinced them of his goodness and fairness, and now that the threat of destruction had passed, they were resigned to his victory.

"Who was that young woman?" she heard Gahalatine ask Samrao. "Where is she?"

"My . . . my lord?" Samrao asked in confusion.

"The one who was standing *right there*? Where did she go?"

"Whom do you speak of?" Samrao said. "The room is full of servants."

Gahalatine started after her, pushing his way through the crowd. He was clearly drawn to her use of the magic, which he could no doubt sense in the cavernous room. Since he was Fountain-blessed, he could follow her. Sureya, whom she was still pulling along, bumped into her, but Trynne didn't slow her pace.

When she finally glanced back, Gahalatine was looking in her direction, his eyes livid, his mouth pursed in a determined frown. She watched him lift the metal circle dangling from one of the leather cords around his neck. It was hollow in the middle, but the outside was covered in little spokes, like starbursts that went at odd angles from the round. The opening in the middle was the size of a forefinger and thumb connected into a circle. He picked up the medallion by some of the pointed ends and brought it up to his left eye as he walked.

Trynne felt the ley line just in front of her and tugged on Sureya's arm to hurry them both.

"*Stop!*" Gahalatine commanded. "I *know* of you. Stop!" His magic blasted at her in a hot spurt, but it rolled off her effortlessly. She knew then that he was looking at her through the hole in his strange medallion. He could see *her*. His eyes blazed with blue fire, and his cheek muscle twitched with desperation. He tried to reach out his hand toward her, but he wasn't close enough.

"*Kennesayrim*," Trynne uttered, holding fast to Sureya's arm as they both stepped onto the ley line and lurched away.

CHAPTER THREE

Zenana

Queen Genevieve listened intently to Trynne's tale of the narrow escape from Chandleer Oasis. When Trynne finally finished, the queen patted her own heart and pulled Trynne into a relieved embrace.

"Thank the Fountain," she murmured, stroking Trynne's hair and arm. "I could have sent Morwenna, but I did not want her knowing about this new alliance quite yet. I'm so thankful you are safe, Trynne. I had not realized I would be sending you to such a dangerous place. This Gahalatine can strike anyone, anywhere, it seems."

Trynne's heart had calmed enough that she could now look back on the narrow escape with a certain amount of excitement. It had been close. Perhaps too close. She worried that Genny would be more cautious the next time before sending her away.

"And you, Princess Sureya," Genevieve said. She gestured for the girl to come closer and join them. Sureya had edged away during Trynne's recounting of the details, likely because her father's defeat was still much too fresh for her.

As soon as the princess reached them, Genevieve took her hands, examining the tattoos that wound partway up her arms. In Chandleer, Trynne had felt out of place while wearing the fashions of her own people. She imagined Sureya had a similar feeling. The girl looked lost and uncomfortably cold. "You are most welcome to Kingfountain," Genevieve continued. "Only I don't imagine you are called a princess in Chandleer? What is your title?"

Sureya, still holding the queen's hands, managed a sort of curtsy. "*Rani*, Your Highness." Her voice trembled. "Does Your Majesty know what may yet happen to my father? To the other rulers Gahalatine has conquered?" There was a sheen of worried tears in her eyes.

Genevieve put her arm around the girl and guided her to the window seat, where she sat down with her. Trynne had known the queen her entire life and was one of the few who still called her Genny. The queen, who was originally from Atabyrion, had adopted the fashions of Ceredigion, although less ostentatiously than previous queens. She was kindhearted and generous, a true partner and equal to her husband, King Drew, who relied on her counsel and was completely devoted to her. Since the birth of their first child, the royal couple had been a bit beleaguered by the lack of sleep because they refused to let their many nurses share all their burdens. Genny had had an easy pregnancy and delivery, however, and she and Drew were pleased to welcome the little girl they had named Kathryn, after Drew's mother. Trynne gazed down at the babe, tucked into the soft downy blankets of her crib, wondering what dreams Kate could be having.

They were all deeply worried about the life awaiting the innocent child. A haze of despair and dread had settled over the realm after the Battle of Guilme. It had been a harsh teacher, showing them how unprepared they were to face such a mighty enemy.

Trynne could still remember the enormous treasure ships she had seen anchored off the coast of Brugia before the battle. They had brought a hundred thousand soldiers from Chandigarl, and the Espion had since learned that Gahalatine's full army was nearly ten times that number. He had more than a dozen Wizrs serving him, whereas Drew only had one left. Trynne's mother.

Gahalatine had called off the attack after learning that Owen had fallen victim to some sort of foul play—but he'd promised to return in a year to finish what he had started. He'd left a garrison to control Guilme, and they had learned much about their enemy from watching the goings-on there. What they had learned made their situation seem even more desperate.

"My dear," Genevieve said softly, stroking Sureya's hands, "since your father was taken to the imperial palace in the Forbidden Court, he will be chosen for some duty for the emperor. Our poisoner has been there, and she says the city is so massive that it is difficult to traverse it within a day. Gahalatine changed the capital of Chandigarl to the Forbidden Court after he started ruling his empire. Your father will likely live in comfort. That's what we know so far. From what Trynne just told me, it sounds as if Gahalatine was perhaps interested in you?"

Sureya nodded miserably. "Your Highness, it was my greatest fear to be taken to the Forbidden Court."

"Why is that?" Genevieve asked. "From our understanding, he is not yet married."

Sureya wiped a tear from her cheek with the back of her hand, and Trynne noticed that the tattoos smudged. "Gahalatine has been gathering his own *zenana*, my lady."

Trynne hadn't heard that word, and judging by Genny's baffled look, she hadn't either.

"I am sorry, our cultures are so different," Sureya apologized. "A zenana is a sanctuary for women, guarded by women. One can go there for protection. If a girl is abused or hurt by a family member or her father, she can flee there for shelter and no one can force her to come out. She is treated with dignity and honor. It is like the sanctuary of Our Lady.

"Gahalatine has created a large zenana, and the most beautiful and skilled daughters of all the rulers whose lands he has conquered have gone to stay there. They wish to win his heart, but there are so many of them, he cannot choose. The competition in the zenana is fierce, and the girls can be very cruel to newcomers. Gahalatine wants someone who is Fountain-blessed—and I am not. To be taken to that place, to be made to *stay* . . ." She shuddered.

Genevieve nodded slowly. "The idea behind the zenana is a noble one. There are many girls who suffer. But like everything Gahalatine has done, it is the sheer scale of it that causes the problem." She rubbed her mouth. "And the zenana is guarded by women, you say?"

Sureya nodded. "The *Urdubegis*."

"What does that name mean in our language?" Trynne asked.

Sureya thought a while. "Promise Keepers? That is near enough to it. They embody the Lady of the Fountain. The protectors of the home. I told my father that if I *had* to go to the zenana in the Forbidden Court, I would rather be trained as an Urdubegis. Gahalatine may *never* decide who he wants to marry because he doesn't stay in the Imperial City for long."

Genevieve gave her and Trynne a knowing smile. "Some men can be that way. You are here now, Sureya. And I think it's the Fountain's will that you are. Lady Tryneowy is an Urdubegis. In our language, they are called the Oath Maidens. She has been secretly training defenders of Kingfountain. When I heard of your plight, I thought you might wish to join them."

Sureya's eyes widened with eagerness. "Is this true? To become an Urdubegis is my greatest wish!" She turned to Trynne. "You are a warrior, my lady?"

Trynne nodded and offered a small shrug.

"Gahalatine believes in the power of the Urdubegis. After Gahalatine won his first victory, the Emperor of Chandigarl sent his general with a massive army to destroy him. The emperor—Gahalatine's father—had many children who were old enough to fight for him and was no longer accustomed to the rigors of war. His brothers ruled the court and the Wizrs ruled them. His general's reputation was one of ruthlessness, and the people hated him. Gahalatine summoned all the women in the city—the one that became the Forbidden Court—to defend himself. They did everything they could. Some even threw steaming potfuls of water down from the walls to injure his enemies. Many knew how to use bows and spears. Some fought with swords. Without the women who rallied to him, he might never have achieved his victory." She paused before continuing. "They say he is blessed so that people wish to follow him whenever he speaks. I felt the power of his words in my father's oasis. They stirred my soul, but I did not feel compelled by them as I feared I would. Why do so many others? My father stood up to him. I don't believe he was swayed. Is he losing his power?"

Trynne knew very well why it didn't happen, but she was not prepared to share her secrets so quickly. "Your father has a very strong sense of duty and integrity, I suspect," Trynne said. "And he has imparted that to you as well."

Sureya flushed and bowed her head respectfully.

"My thanks to you both. Trynne, can we speak on the balcony for a moment? If you'll excuse us?" Genevieve added, looking at Sureya, who seemed startled that a queen had begged her pardon.

Trynne retreated to the balcony with Genevieve. Outside, the air was fresh and cool, smelling of late summer. From her vantage point, Trynne could barely see the magnolia gardens. Her heart lurched from the memory of the last time she had been there. She'd not stepped foot in the gardens since Fallon had made his proposal to her—a proposal she had rejected despite her heart's desire for him. Her mother, whose visions of the future always came to pass, had seen her marrying someone else. Fallon was unreliable too, and despite her feelings for him, she couldn't trust him.

Any relationship between them would only end badly.

Kingfountain had always been a treasure to her, a place of childhood memories, a second home. But since their confrontation in the garden, those old memories were tinged with bitterness. She and Fallon

25

had hardly spoken since then, and whenever they *did* come face-to-face, her wounds felt raw and painful. Fallon had changed in the months that had followed. He was more serious, more circumspect and distant. She missed his quips and teasing now that they were lost to her.

"You've a faraway look in your eye," Genevieve said.

Trynne gave her one of her crooked smiles. "I left Averanche in the morning, arrived in Chandleer at sunset, and now it's midmorning again. I've been halfway around the world and back, and the day has hardly started. It was enough to make my head spin."

Genevieve knew she was being deflected—the look in her eyes said as much—but she didn't press. "I am indeed grateful that you are safe. Gahalatine is full of surprises. One moment he's in one place. Another he's gone. He's completely unpredictable."

Trynne nodded. "He's restless, I think. Full of ambition." Her brow furrowed. "But I'm concerned by something he shouted just as I was leaving." She looked into Genny's eyes. "He said, 'I know of you.'" A cold feeling welled up inside her, making her shiver. "He knew I wasn't from the oasis." She quieted, staring out at the river, at the sanctuary of Our Lady and the surging waterfall that could be heard in the distance like a soothing murmur. She imagined Kingfountain being attacked by that fleet of treasure ships. She imagined Wizrs turning the river backward and making it possible for soldiers to cross. The defenses of the city, which had once seemed impregnable, now seemed wholly inadequate.

"Yes, it's obvious he recognized you, but that doesn't mean he placed you."

"It doesn't help that I'm so small," Trynne muttered darkly. "I worry about King Sunilik. Gahalatine will likely question him at the Forbidden Court. Without me there to protect him, the king will no longer be immune to his powers. Gahalatine may learn that I was there."

Genevieve paled. "I hadn't thought of that. It also seems that his people can travel outside of the ley lines. That cylinder you mentioned . . .

what sort of device is it, I wonder? There's so much we don't know. I had assumed Gahalatine might be with his fleet."

"Has it been spotted since it set sail earlier this summer?" Trynne asked.

Genevieve shook her head. "None of the Espion hidden in the ports along the coast have seen it. But Lord Amrein has learned that fleet doesn't need a port. It can go for months without a harbor. What baffles me is how Gahalatine has accumulated so many vessels and conquered so much in so short a time! He's barely older than me, and look at what he's done! Ambition is certainly one of his gifts from the Fountain."

Trynne nodded, rubbing her palms along the stone lip of the railing. "Do you think he will attack Kingfountain first?"

Genevieve touched her shoulder. "Would that I knew," she answered with a sigh. "Your mother's visions are our only hope for a warning. I'm worried about her," she added, her voice dipping to a lower pitch. "Her grief is so consuming."

Trynne wanted to refute her, but it was true, and there was no sense in hiding it. "She's withdrawn deeper into herself. Morwenna has offered her some calming drafts to try and help her, but she refuses to be comforted by an elixir. When she's not here or training Morwenna, she walks at her favorite beach in Ploemeur. She'll be there for hours sometimes." Trynne's heart pinched with the pain of her own grief. Her father's loss had struck a terrible blow to the entire Kiskaddon family.

"Drew would like to see her as soon as possible," Genny said. "But please . . . don't hurry her if she's not well. We will abide without her for as long as we can."

"Very well, my lady," Trynne said, giving her another hug.

Genny kissed her cheek, then gripped her by the shoulders. "You haven't asked after Fallon in a while."

Fallon was Genny's younger brother. She reminded Trynne of him a little in the way she smiled. Sometimes it was comforting; sometimes it was excruciating.

"No, I have not," Trynne replied.

"He still cares for you," Genny said.

"It would probably be for the best if he didn't," Trynne said. Her own heart had been dashed to pieces in their last confrontation.

The queen folded her arms and stared out at the garden. "You are my friend, and he is my brother. I hate seeing you both hurting so much. I understand your reasons for saying what you did. He deserved it. But he hasn't come to terms with it yet. He's fighting it. I'm . . . worried about him. Worried he may do something . . . I don't know. He's another one who's difficult to predict."

Before the Battle of Guilme, Fallon had told Trynne that he suspected Severn Argentine, the former king of Ceredigion and Morwenna's father, was involved in a conspiracy to unseat the king. The men who were involved, he'd told her, dressed in black and wore silver masks. On the eve of the Battle of Guilme, Trynne had visited Fallon's tent while disguised as the Painted Knight. She'd found the exact outfit he'd described—silver mask, black coat—discarded on the floor. Despite her feelings for Fallon, and her desire to believe the best of him, it had filled her with suspicion.

Trynne had taken Genny into her confidence, and when her friend had asked Fallon if he was part of a conspiracy, not divulging her source, he had admitted to her that he'd donned the outfit that night to try to draw out the conspirators. He'd even told her that the Painted Knight had humiliated him and taken the mask away. His words lined up with Trynne's version of the events, which she was relieved to hear. But she didn't know if he was still dabbling with his Espion contacts or traveling in secret with Morwenna.

She could only hope he was not.

"Are you asking me to reach out to him?" Trynne asked with a wince.

Genny shook her head. "No, I wouldn't burden you with that. He should make the next move. I just hope that you wouldn't spurn his efforts to reconcile, even if they're clumsily made."

"Well said, Genny," Trynne replied with a small laugh.

Genevieve hugged her again. "We should learn more about this zenana. Are there true Oath Maidens there, the kind Myrddin taught you about? Or does it serve another purpose? I might send you there, Trynne. My heart says there is more for us to learn. Gahalatine must have a weakness. All this power, all this force. There has to be something we can use to turn the tide in our favor. We're running out of time."

Trynne nodded resolutely.

One of the queen's ladies-in-waiting pulled aside the curtains and appeared on the balcony. "I beg your pardon, my lady, but a visitor has arrived. The Grand Duke of Brugia."

Genevieve looked surprised. "He wishes to see me?"

The girl dimpled. "No, my lady. He came to see Lady Tryneowy."

CHAPTER FOUR

Elwis

Upon leaving the balcony, Trynne found the young grand duke of Brugia talking pleasantly with Sureya. His demeanor had transformed over the last year. Her first impressions of him had not been favorable. He had been rude and conceited, and the outfit he'd chosen for the king and queen's marriage was distinctly—and pointedly—Brugian in style: a fancy black tunic with white ruffs at the neck and cuffs. In the past, Elwis had always sported a sour frown while in Kingfountain, and he'd never acknowledged others as his equal. But his attitude had abruptly changed after his father was slain in the Battle of Guilme. He had come close to losing his precious kingdom, and it had not failed to make an impression on him that Drew's men had died in the effort to save his city.

He was courteous, though still a bit aloof at times. But he tried harder to be agreeable, and he'd tried exceedingly hard to be agreeable to *her*.

When Trynne entered the room, a small smile appeared on his mouth, one that reached his eyes. Leaning against the wall near the window seat, arms folded, he concluded his conversation.

"It was a pleasure meeting you, Rani Sureya. It has been a long while since I have seen fashions from the East. You speak our language exceedingly well. I bid you welcome to Kingfountain." He bowed graciously, and Sureya dimpled and smiled back in return.

How he had changed.

He was tall, his hair so blond it was nearly white. His rugged face still bore the fading scars he'd earned in the battle.

"I'm grateful I caught you ere you departed for Averanche," he said warmly, walking up and giving Trynne a formal bow. "I only just heard that you were at the palace."

He made no attempt to hide his regard for her. She was flattered by his attentions, naturally, but uncertain about how to respond to them. Her broken heart still pined for Fallon, even though her head told her that it was not to be. She had tried to wrest details from her mother about the man she'd seen Trynne marry in her vision. But Sinia had always refused to say more. It did nothing to comfort Trynne that her mother's look always had an edge of disappointment when they spoke about her future husband.

"I did not intend to stay for long," Trynne said, trying to be pleasant. "It is good to see you, Elwis. What brings you here?"

They were both members of the king's council and had seats at the Ring Table, so it was appropriate for them to discuss state secrets. Elwis glanced back at Sureya and lowered his voice.

"You brought her?" he asked. "I'm presuming you trust her."

"I do. Her father is an honorable man."

"Indeed, he is," Elwis said. "King Sunilik has a strong reputation among the spice traders of the desert. He is someone we've heard a lot about this past year. I was just very surprised to find her here. I came because we heard from a Genevese merchant that the fleet of treasure ships was seen at harbor in Jevva. They are coming for us once again. There can be no doubt of that. The Genevese captain is a canny man. He said the winds and currents put them about a month from our shores. I've tripled the numbers of archers in my realm. If they start falling from the sky again, you can be sure we will make it difficult. I came to relay this information to the king, along with other news."

"What news?"

"I learned that two years ago, when Gahalatine finished the work on his new capital, the Forbidden Court, he commemorated the celebration by inviting the rulers of the hundred kingdoms he's purportedly conquered. They were brought by his treasure ships and feasted and celebrated along the journey as well as in the capital itself. The ships were then stuffed to the bilge with trading goods for them to return to their kingdoms. Silks, jade, beautiful vases, plants of many varieties. Listen to this. The way Gahalatine does tribute is very different. People don't pay him for protection. He pays *them*. This Genevese captain I met said that there are over a hundred and twenty scholars in the Forbidden Court learning every spoken language so that they can be sent to negotiate terms of tribute. The scholars of Chandigarl have studied the stars for centuries and have maps more accurate than anything we possess. He saw the fleet at Jevva and was allowed to tour the vessels and gain this knowledge firsthand. They were boasting of their superiority."

Trynne's stomach turned sick with dread. "Can nothing stop them?"

Elwis looked equally helpless. "This Genevese captain asked the admiral of the fleet why Kingfountain had not been invited to the celebration. Do you know what he said?"

Trynne shook her head.

"He said we were too far beneath their notice. That we were nothing but a squabbling, rebellious land in need of a benevolent master." His voice bristled with anger. "I'm growing heartily sick of this Gahalatine fellow." She could see the depths of rage in his eyes and knew he still harbored revenge in his heart for the way his father had died.

"Thank you for sharing the news with me and not waiting until the council meets," she said. Worry had tied her up in knots. If only Myrddin were there to advise them. If only her father were.

"Of course," he said, waving aside her gratitude. He glanced at Genevieve and Sureya, who were standing over the baby's crib, before continuing. "When can I see you again?" he asked in a lower voice.

She blinked with surprise.

"I don't mean to startle you." He sighed, looking a little chagrined. Then he gave her a self-conscious smile. "Let me try to explain this delicately. I've been told that Averanche is inundated with suitors seeking to impress you. A veritable flood, as if the Deep Fathoms were trying to drown you. I have not, quite deliberately, attempted to press you in that way. But I did not want you to suppose I'm being inattentive either. You are not . . . like other women I know. Far from it. You are . . . I'm making a rather bloody mess of this, aren't I?" He laughed at himself, looking flushed and embarrassed. "Forgive me. All the little speeches I've rehearsed in my head have fluttered away like butterflies. I'm not very apt at wooing, Trynne. What I mean to say is that I would cherish the opportunity to spend more time with you." For a moment she thought he would touch her hand, but he didn't. "I would have no qualms about meeting you in Averanche, assuming I could get past all your suitors without being stabbed by one of them, or Ploemeur if you would prefer. You also have an open invitation to come to Marq. I've imagined taking you on a gondola ride and showing you the rich history of my state. There. I have said it. Clumsily, but there it is. I am far more confident with a sword."

She was touched by how flustered he was, how difficult it was for him to say such things to her. She did not have feelings for him, not the kind of feelings she had harbored for Fallon for so many years. But she respected him. Still, she could not help but wonder if Elwis was motivated more by her prospects than by her.

"I do have many visitors, it is true," she said. "Probably not as many as you fear. I've told them all the same thing. This is not the season to woo and marry. We are at war. I've also told them that if they seek my regard and notice, they should apply themselves more to their training. As you have." She gave him one of her crooked smiles.

Elwis took her compliment with a relieved grin and backed away from her. "As always, your counsel is wise. I'll not detain you further. By your leave." She could tell he wanted her to accept his invitation to visit. But he did not press her, which showed admirable restraint on his part.

As he turned to go, she called out to him. "Elwis?"

He stopped and turned.

"I have no plans at the moment for the Feast of St. Benedick. I should like to visit Marq again. Perhaps you can toss coins in the fountain at the city center until then?"

"I shall," he promised, looking at her fixedly. She gave him a nod.

It was time to bring Sureya home.

♦ ♦ ♦

Averanche.

Trynne loved the view of the sea from the upper balustrade. The wind fought to veil the view with her own hair, and she had to keep sweeping the strands away as she leaned against the stone railing, thinking about her conversation with the Grand Duke of Brugia. The sun was finally setting—the second time for her. She loved to watch the sun lower over the ocean, the majesty of the sight paired with the sound of the waves crashing so far below.

Located on the border of Westmarch and Brythonica, Averanche was a city that had surrendered to Trynne's father many years ago, after his successful surprise attack on the King of Occitania's army. She'd heard so many stories about his exploits that it sometimes felt as if she had lived them too.

Upon their return, she had given instructions for Sureya to be accommodated as befit her station. The girl was still adjusting to the change in climate, and the thin silks she'd worn in the oasis were not warm enough for Ceredigion.

There had been so many duties to attend to that only on her evening walk did she have time to process the grand duke's request to court her.

She thought about her promise to visit Marq for the feast day. She had not yet shown favor to any of the young suitors who had come calling for her. Some of them were not even young, like the prickly Count Bastian from Legault, who was making a ruckus down below since she'd refused a private meeting with him. He had attended dinner in the hall, for it would hardly have been polite not to invite him, along with five other would-be suitors, but she had ensured they were all seated far away from her. She pushed the thoughts from her mind and returned to a more pleasant one.

Elwis Asturias. It had taken years for her father to defeat his father, King Maxwell. Some wondered why Owen had hammered away at the defenses of Brugia's cities rather than pressing for a more decisive battle. But Owen did not treat his soldiers' lives rashly. He had known time was on his side. By besieging the cities, one by one, he'd strained Maxwell's resources enough to make his people desperate for peace.

Trynne wondered, in retrospect, whether her father had taken the long road in order to gain Maxwell as an ally. The Asturiases were a proud family. A quick victory would have caused more resentment than a hard-won fight.

Her father had always played the long game.

Perhaps she was destined to marry Elwis. If so, he would have to prove himself to her with consistency and determination—and not just because her heart still yearned for another. Trynne longed for adventure, and since her little brother, Gannon, would inherit both Westmarch and Brythonica, she did not feel the need to rush into marriage. She wished to visit all the places on her mother's map, and all of those beyond it too, including the Forbidden Court of Gahalatine.

There was noise on the battlement steps as the irate count jostled his way up the stairs. "I don't care! Stand aside, you old badger! I *will* speak with her!"

Trynne hung her head for a moment. Despite her position on the king's council, people still tried to treat her as a child, especially the most persistent of her suitors.

Count Bastian was a big man, at least thirty, attended by a whip-thin servant with groveling manners. The count was handsome and arrogant and very, very rich. He was also clearly used to getting his way.

Her herald, Farnes, could not keep up with him as he launched up the rampart steps.

Trynne turned and started walking toward them, bridling her anger.

"Ah, there you are!" Bastian said. He had clearly abandoned his composure down below. He threw up his hands. "I find it highly offensive that you have not only ignored me, but refused to see me, Lady Trynnwy. I've called for my carriage, and I will depart this miserable town at once. You did wrong to treat me so discourteously."

The beetle-eyed servant looked at Trynne with open hostility. Farnes, panting, finally reached the top of the steps. "How dare you address the Lady Try*neowy* in this manner," he huffed. "If you do not leave at once, I will summon Captain Staeli—"

Trynne gave him a covert gesture to remain silent and he did.

"Captain Staeli," Bastian sneered. "What can he do? I've seen your defenses, my lady, and they are woefully inadequate. You have perhaps a score of guards manning the entire castle. Twenty! I will not leave without taking what I came for." He lowered his voice, the boastful outrage vanishing. "This man is a poisoner from Pisan," he said, jabbing with his thumb toward the man, who had suddenly produced a dagger. "If you utter a word, he will kill your aged herald. And anyone who dares interrupt. I have fifty men concealed in the woods outside Averanche with orders to enter the city at nightfall. You are coming with *me*, Lady Trynnwy. Our women do not have such airs as you do. I've seen your little girls in the training yard." He spat with disdain. "Believe me when I say that you are not prepared for the world of men. But I will teach you obedience. Now, you will come with me quietly or your friends will get *hurt*."

He reached out and grabbed her arm.

She hit him in the fleshy part just above his throat so fast and so hard that his eyes bulged in shock and pain and he started choking.

Instantly she released the wellspring magic that had been building up inside her during his little speech. She had waited for him to make the first move because her magic always worked better in defense than in offense. As an Oath Maiden, she could draw on the experience of other Oath Maidens from a thousand lifetimes.

The poisoner gave her a startled look and dodged to the left to try to stab Farnes with the dagger. The poisoner's dagger had flecks of powder on it, and she was wearing a gown rather than the chain hauberk she wore while training. Still, Trynne got between them in a rush, catching the poisoner's wrist to stop the stroke. His elbow rocked back toward her chin, but she dodged to the side and kicked the back of his knee. He crumpled and then spun his other leg around to trip her, all while wrestling for control of the knife. She probed him with her magic, sensing for weakness. He was skilled with a dagger, very skilled, and he had the full accoutrements of a poisoner—vials, needle rings, and a cloth rag drenched with liquid that could instantly render someone unconscious. He was wire-thin but sturdy.

Trynne avoided the sweep of his leg. Though he was still struggling to regain his breath, Bastian grabbed at her from behind in a bear hug. Trynne ducked low, shouldered him in the stomach, and then rocked him over her back, sending him down hard onto the stone. The poisoner lunged at her next, and she had to arch her back to avoid the dagger slicing through her shoulder. As soon as his blow went wide, she flipped back up and kicked the poisoner in the face.

He pinwheeled away, but Trynne leaped at him, kicking him again in the middle with enough force that the air gushed out of his chest in a wheeze. She torqued his arm until he released the dagger and then brought her arm around his throat until he collapsed, unconscious.

Farnes stared at her in admiration, his knees wobbling, and gripped the balustrade for support.

She picked up the dagger, examining the dust on the blade. Vicarum, a poison that paralyzed its victims for several hours. Turning the blade over in her hand, she looked at Farnes.

"No more suitors," she said adamantly. "Send them all away. I don't have time for this nonsense. But put these two in chains. I think Captain Staeli will wish to talk to them."

♦ ♦ ♦

I think the poison affects my mind. It stops me from remembering. It's making me mad. My thoughts are muddled and sluggish. I've asked for water, but the jailor only gives me the sickly sweet drink. How can I stop drinking the cup? I think on it again and again. If I can figure out a way to stop drinking it, perhaps I will get my memories back. It's difficult to focus. There is no sense of time. Yet a strange idea came to me while I was stacking my little chips of broken stone today. Where did the chips come from? So I felt around the wall and discovered a broken section. Someone has chipped away at the stone. Did I do it?

As I felt the broken wall with my fingers, rough and jagged, I realized there's a pattern to it. The pieces are at angles. I'm so thirsty. I've tried not to drink for two days, but I can't die of thirst. It torments me. Water. I need water. I'm going mad. Because I hear water. Trapped inside the wall. It wants to come out so I can drink it. In my mind, I see a vision of a man with a crooked staff. A wild, ancient man. He hits a rock with the staff, and water gushes out. Water is in the stone. Water is in the stone.

♦ ♦ ♦

CHAPTER FIVE

Disciple

It was well into the night before all of Count Bastion's minions had been arrested and brought to the castle in chains. Torches flickered in the night wind as Trynne walked with Captain Staeli down the corridor to the balcony overlooking the yard. The evening was cool but not cold.

Staeli had been assigned as her bodyguard following Dragan's brutal attack on her, which had left half of her face paralyzed. A former soldier of Westmarch, he had been trained as an Espion because of his affinity for weapons and hand-to-hand fighting. Staeli was steady as stone and wholly committed to her and her family, and rarely uttered any nonsense. He had trained Trynne in secret before the Wizr Myrddin had made her swear the five oaths that had made her an Oath Maiden. Now, he was training the corps of Oath Maidens. He drilled them hard, sometimes to the point of vomiting, and felt that bruises earned in mock combat were badges of honor.

"Aye, lass, your hunters caught them assembling in the woods earlier this afternoon and kept watch on them. Mariette brought forty of the girls out to surround and capture them. I think they could have done it with twenty, the lads were so ill trained." He snorted in derision and pushed open the door to the balcony.

Trynne nodded to him as she walked through it, then planted her palms on the edge of the balcony and watched her warriors as they lined up the prisoners. Their armor and weapons had all been stripped away and were set in neat piles to one side. Mariette had proven to be one of the most capable of the Oath Maidens. The thirty-year-old widow was older than the rest. Tall, lithe, and blond, she was beautiful enough to be mistaken for an Occitanian princess. But Mariette was a leader, and while she'd enjoyed her position of power as the widow of a wealthy merchant, she'd always wanted to learn how to fight. Being taller than most men, she was intimidating to them. Trynne watched as she told the prisoners where to assemble, walking among them in a chain hauberk topped with a tunic bearing the badge of Averanche.

Staeli folded his arms and nodded with approval. "She'll make a good captain for you someday," he said, gazing at Mariette. "The new girl from the desert, I would put her under Mariette to start."

"Thank you, Captain," Trynne said. "I've had my eye on Mariette for a while. I wish I were that tall sometimes. She's going to compete in the Gauntlet of Kingfountain."

"Aye, and she'll do well," Staeli said proudly. "So will that hunter, Rhiannon. She's from Atabyrion, a tanner's girl. She knows more about hunting than most scouts I've known. She's the one who warned us about Count Bastian's knavery." His smile turned into a frown. "What would you like to do with him? His face is a little purple at the moment, and not from woad."

"Purple?" Trynne asked with a laugh. "I didn't hit him that hard."

"No, you did not. *I* did." He puffed out his chest a little, looking satisfied with himself.

Trynne wanted to hug him. Though he trusted her to take care of herself, he was still very protective of her. "If we let him go right away, he may not learn his lesson very well. I was thinking of holding him for ransom. He is from Legault, after all. There may be others he's treated poorly."

Staeli scratched his beard. "Very well, lass. It's better to kill a snake than release one, but skinning it first is helpful. The poisoner's name is Gawne. He's looking even more purple than the count," he added as an aside. "An ordinary chap from Pisan. Hired by Count Backstabber to kidnap you. That's his specialty—abducting youths. Capturing you was going to earn him ten thousand florins, of which he had already been paid half up front."

"So little," Trynne said, feeling sick.

"I'm offended he didn't demand fifty. This was not a royal conspiracy. Bastian was trying to do it on the cheap. He was woefully misinformed about your . . . your *vulnerability*." At this, he gave her one of his proud, fatherly smiles. By now, there were nearly a thousand Oath Maidens spread across the kingdom—women who had come to Averanche to be tutored in the arts of war by Staeli and to leave as warriors.

Trynne stared down at the yard again. The men who were gathered there had come expecting to earn a small pouch of coins for helping kidnap the Lady of Averanche. Instead, they'd been caught off guard, surrounded, and abducted by a group of highly trained women. She shifted her gaze to the Oath Maidens. There was Gillian from the Brythonican town of Passey. Haley from Dundrennan. That girl could throw a spear unlike anyone else. Maciel, who was the daughter of a sanctuary thief but had been raised by a kindhearted family. Brooke was one of the best fighters of the bunch. Emilia was a master archer. Savanne could throw down any boy her size. Camellia had shown aptitude to be an Espion, perhaps even a poisoner. There were dozens more, each with a story of how they had come to be there. They were not all equal in talent, but they had all defied tradition by seeking to defend their kingdom. She realized that they would soon be given that chance.

"What would you have me do with the poisoner?" Staeli asked in a low, meaningful tone. She recognized the tone of his voice, the implication wrapped up in his question.

She thought of the gaunt fellow she had captured and how ready he had been to stab her and claim his fee. How many girls had he abducted in the past? Where were they now? The thought filled her with such revulsion she couldn't prevent an angry frown.

Turning to Captain Staeli, she said, "I'd like the mayor to interrogate him, Captain. See if he can learn anything about his past victims. When he can no longer provide us with any useful information, have the mayor put him to death." She gave him a determined look. It was her right as the ruler of Averanche to invoke such a penalty. But if she could restore any of the captured children back to their families, she would.

"Aye, lass," he said, nodding at her in approval. Then, giving her a wry smile, he said, "You've had a busy day. What will tomorrow bring?"

"I wish I knew," Trynne said, rubbing the chill from her arms. "I'm going back to Ploemeur, though. There are things I must speak to my mother about, even if it pains me."

◆　◆　◆

Trynne walked down the quiet corridor of her mother's castle. It was the home of her childhood, and it caused her pain every time she returned. She loved the sculptured pillars with the symbol of the triple faces on them, the strong smell of eucalyptus, and the tall windows that let in light through gauzy curtains. But every room held ghosts from her past, invoked memories of her missing father. She knew the cadence of his tread, and her ears constantly strained to hear a sound that wasn't going to happen.

The rich history of Brythonica had played a large role in her childhood stories. It was an ancient place, one whose history went further back than Occitania or Ceredigion, and when Sinia was young, it had been a self-ruling duchy of Occitania. But the Occitanian king had tried to force Sinia to marry him, which had caused her to seek an alliance with Ceredigion. It had been a dangerous and delicate maneuver, but her mother had managed to pit the two kings against each other while retaining Brythonica's sovereignty.

The reason her mother had fought so hard to retain her position was because a Montfort needed to rule the duchy to maintain its boundaries against the Deep Fathoms. The line had almost been broken when Sinia's parents couldn't bring a living child into the world. Their grief had been shattering, especially since they'd known what it meant: their duchy would be swallowed up by the sea when the duke died. The grieving parents despaired, not knowing what they could do to save the kingdom. They were willing to do anything to appease the Fountain, to spare the population from drowning.

The answer was waiting for them one day on the shore of what was now Sinia's favorite beach. A newborn baby girl. An Ondine—a gift from the Fountain.

Most people were superstitious about water sprites. They could not be immersed in water, for their very skin repelled it, and the water rite had been developed in ancient times to prove whether a foundling had been naturally born.

Sinia's true identity was a closely guarded secret. Beyond her family, only the palace staff knew the truth of her sacred origins. As a water sprite, she had not possessed a soul until she kissed a human—Owen. Their marriage had changed her and made her human.

And now her grief for him was diminishing her.

"My lady!" chuffed the court steward, Thierry, when he rounded the corner ahead and nearly stumbled into her. He had served the Montforts for a long time, as had his father and grandfather before him. Thierry's hair was spiked forward in the Occitanian fashion, as usual, but it was well nigh all silver now. "I had not known you were coming today! Your mother will be grateful to see you. Let me alert her that you've arrived from Averanche."

"How does she fare?" Trynne asked, touching his arm.

Thierry's countenance shaded like a cloud blotting the sun. He had always kept a certain distance from Owen, but his devotion to Sinia was unquestionable. "Lady Tryneowy, she bears her suffering with great aplomb. She has been more distant lately. More introspective."

Trynne had feared as much. Her mother's visions had been bereft of glimpses of her husband, which had made all of them fear the worst.

"Thank you, Thierry. I would see her at once."

"Very well, my lady. She is with Lady Morwenna at the moment."

The news was like a blow to Trynne's heart. Morwenna had been in training as a Wizr's disciple since the Battle of Guilme. Originally, Trynne had been her mother's only student, but she had abandoned her studies in favor of training the Oath Maidens with Captain Staeli.

The daughter of Severn Argentine and Lady Kathryn, Morwenna was the king's blood-sister. She had an aptitude for Fountain magic and had demonstrated a quickness of mind in finding words of power hidden inside *The Vulgate*, an ancient text of legends about the famous King Andrew and his court. When she was studying the tome, Trynne had always found her mind wandering to the training yard and affairs of state. She was happier since she'd quit her Wizr training, but Morwenna's stunning beauty and multiple gifts had always made her feel self-conscious.

As they walked toward the study, Thierry kept up a steady stream of chatter. "There was a great shipwreck off the coast of Occitania in the last fortnight. A merchant ship, heavily laden, crashed against the reef and was destroyed. Bits of its cargo have been washing up on our shores for days since then and as far east as St. Penryn's."

"Were there any survivors?" Trynne asked without much hope.

"None, my lady. The manifest showed it was a Genevese merchant vessel. The crew all drowned."

"I'm so sorry to hear it," Trynne sighed. "What is the latest news about the Gauntlet coming up in Kingfountain?"

"They say the Grand Duke of Brugia and Duke of North Cumbria are favorites to win it. Wouldn't it be a trick if some lass beat them both?" He gave her a cunning smile and a wink.

Trynne had been training hard for it. She shrugged her shoulders, trying to look unconcerned.

"Let me announce you," Thierry said as they reached the door. He lifted his hand to knock.

Trynne caught his sleeve. "There's no need. I'd rather surprise her. Thank you."

Thierry nodded, bowed to her, and departed. Trynne stared at the polished wood, trying to gather her courage and resolve. Whenever Sinia traveled to Kingfountain, Trynne stayed in Ploemeur to await her return. If the stay ended up being longer than a few days, her mother would likely fetch her brother, Gannon, from Tatton Hall. He had been staying there, off and on, with their grandparents since being declared the Duke of Westmarch in their father's absence, but Sinia brought him home to Ploemeur for frequent visits. The child was a favorite with the palace staff, and Trynne found herself missing him when he wasn't around. She occasionally used the ley lines to visit him, but it wasn't the same as living together.

Gripping the handle, she turned it quietly and pushed open the door to the study. Just like the rest of the house, the room was achingly familiar. The walls were lined with bookshelves laden with dusty books, and the desk in the corner was covered in globes and charts. Trynne found Morwenna sitting there, scrawling on a rough piece of parchment covered in sketches of the diagonal spokes of ley lines. She appeared to be copying something from another map, and Trynne's stomach twisted with worry. Her mother's book of maps was a secret they hadn't shared with anyone.

Sinia sat at the window seat. The window was open and her golden hair rustled as the breeze wafted in. Her hand rested on the casement, her fingers limp. Her gaze was fixed on the endless sea on the horizon, and she did not seem to have noticed the sound of the door.

Morwenna lifted her head and turned. For a moment, there was a look of shocked surprise in her eyes. Almost a guilty look, as if she'd been caught stealing treats.

It was gone in an instant. Morwenna rose from the chair and quickly came to Trynne, embracing her briefly before pulling back.

"Has something happened?" she whispered, her brow furrowed with concern.

Trynne shook her head. "Nothing like that. The king wishes to see my mother."

Morwenna nodded. "That is no surprise. So she will be gone for a few days?"

"Probably," Trynne said. "What are you working on?" she asked, trying not to let any concern filter into her voice.

"Oh, that," Morwenna said, gesturing toward the maps on the table. "One of Lord Amrein's men managed to steal a map book from a treasure ship," she said. "It's all a great secret, but I can tell you. They already had the royal cartographers look at it. It goes far beyond anything we have seen in the past. Trynne, there's a map to the Forbidden Court. I've been trying to connect it to the ones we already have. As you know, the original capital of Chandigarl was on the east-west ley line. The Forbidden Court is farther north, off the main line."

"You've been to the Forbidden Court already," Trynne said.

Morwenna nodded. "Yes, but only through the ley lines. I haven't known *where* it was. This is a major clue to locating it."

"Have you heard of Chandleer Oasis?" Trynne asked. The two young women went to the map. Trynne glanced back at her mother, but Sinia was still staring fixedly at the sea.

"It's right here," Morwenna said, pointing to a spot on the map amidst the huge desert. "It's part of the spice trade."

When Trynne looked down at the map with all its hubs and spokes, she saw that it wasn't her mother's map at all, which relieved her for some inexplicable reason. She knew she shouldn't be jealous of Morwenna—after all, her father had trusted the girl—but she still had misgivings. There were markings on it in a different language, a foreign tongue that Trynne recognized but couldn't decipher.

"Trynne?"

It was her mother's voice. Trynne abandoned the map in an instant, hurrying over to Sinia. She squeezed her mother hard, wishing the pain would leave her.

"I have matters to attend to," Morwenna said discreetly, and then left the study, giving them some privacy.

Trynne joined her mother at the window seat, clutching her cold hands. Her mother looked queer, her face too pale, her eyes red rimmed. It was awful to see her suffering so nakedly.

"Mother," Trynne sighed, shaking her head, not knowing what to say.

Sinia's chest heaved. She was going to cry again. It bubbled up a bit before subsiding into trembling. "The Fountain . . . it believes I can handle . . . this. I don't want to falter. But I'm shaking under the weight." She took a steadying breath, tears glistening on her lashes but not falling.

Trynne bit her lip, feeling her own pain rising like a swell of the sea.

Sinia untangled their hands and then put hers on Trynne's shoulders. "There is something I must tell you. Before I tell it to the king."

Trynne stared at her mother in surprise. "Have you had another vision?" she asked with growing dread.

Sinia nodded firmly, her mouth pursed in a frown. She looked away from Trynne, shifting her gaze back to the sea. Her next words were cut off by a choked sob. She struggled to regain composure—dabbing her tears on her wrist—but her eyes were fixed on the scene outside.

"The Fountain bids me . . . that I must return. I must return to my origins. I must go back to the Deep Fathoms. The sea is calling me home."

CHAPTER SIX

Deep Fathoms Beckons

The words stunned Trynne and left her breathless with dread and confusion. The Deep Fathoms was the place where the dead went, where treasures from the past were hidden. Could the living go there and survive? Even if it were possible, she knew without question it would be dangerous beyond imagining.

She'd lost her father, and now the Fountain was reclaiming her mother. The cruelty of it was beyond her faculty to understand. She couldn't even imagine what Drew and Genevieve would say. They had lost the Wizr Myrddin on the eve of Kingfountain's woes. Then Owen. Now Sinia. It was too much. It was asking far too much!

Sinia pulled Trynne close, hugging her to her bosom, and began stroking her hair. "Grief and pain is part of this mortal coil. But no pain so sharp as that which afflicts a mother's heart. I think I can bear any sadness for my own sake. But seeing my children suffer . . . that is the worst pain of all."

Trynne only then realized she was crying. She lifted her head, gazing into her mother's face, seeing the turmoil there. Her mother had always been a source of strength for her.

"I don't understand," Trynne said. Never had she felt so frightened and alone.

"Neither do I, Trynne. Neither do I." Sinia smiled sadly, wiping a tear from Trynne's lax cheek. "I saw many things I do not as yet understand, but the vision was clear. It showed me boarding a ship in Ploemeur with Captain Pyne. We were outfitted for a long expedition, so we may be at sea for quite some time. The course we should take was not made known to me, but I saw that it would be revealed. I hear the Deep Fathoms calling to me even now." She turned and gazed out the window again, staring longingly at the sea. "It whispers to my heart to come."

Trynne felt nothing, not even the ripple of the Fountain inside her, but she trusted her mother's visions.

"Mother?" she asked, her voice trembling.

Sinia turned and looked at her.

"Mother, when you saw my marriage. I know you don't like speaking of it. But when you saw it, were you there? Will you *be* there?"

Sinia blinked rapidly. She reached down and took Trynne's hands. "No. I will not be. Trynne, when I go, Brythonica will be in peril unless the wards are maintained. You must make sure that it is done." Her look was keen. "You *must*, Trynne. This burden is on our house alone."

"But Gannon knows the words," Trynne said, feeling a yawning chasm opening and threatening to swallow her, to chain her.

"Of course he does. But he's just a child, Trynne. You are a woman. I know you have responsibilities of your own. I know that you do not want this burden." Her voice hinted at the disappointment she felt that her daughter had chosen not to follow her path. "You must see it done. The people will need the reassurance that a Montfort will always be near. Promise me."

The words were like shackles fitting around Trynne's wrists. She could feel the heaviness of them. Brythonica and Westmarch were her birthrights, her responsibilities. It was a relief to have Gannon, young though he was, to share the burden.

"I will, of course," Trynne said, though she could not completely mask the reluctance she felt. "The king asked me to summon you to court. That is why I came."

Sinia heaved a sigh. "This will not be welcome news."

"Indeed, it will not," Trynne said. "I think he is anxious for word on where Gahalatine will press his attack. We have too many vulnerabilities. The fleet of treasure ships is on its way. They are coming to invade us, and his Wizr is about to tell him that the Fountain bids her to leave." The panic and dread inside Trynne's heart threatened to consume her.

"The king has another Wizr," Sinia said, her voice flat. Although she was looking at Trynne, it was understood that she meant the king's sister. "Morwenna is powerful. She finds new words of power almost daily. She's drawn to them somehow, as if the books are trying to teach her quickly. I've never seen this before. She has surpassed where I was at her age." Her voice grew softer. "The Fountain has provided another to take my place."

It felt like another blow.

◆　◆　◆

Trynne had been there the day Myrddin had told King Drew and her father that he was leaving. The threat they had faced was less real back then; they had not been attacked by their enemies at that point, so Gahalatine had not yet possessed a foothold in their realm.

Trynne watched as Drew absorbed her mother's news in stunned silence. They were gathered in the solar of the palace at Kingfountain. Genevieve cradled their tiny babe in her arms, wrapped in the softest of blankets, and pressed little kisses against her feather-light tufts of hair. The babe's namesake, Lady Kathryn, was also present. She and Morwenna were standing side by side, and while Kathryn was clearly surprised by the news, a strange look had passed across her daughter's eyes. Perhaps Morwenna was thinking about being the realm's only Wizr. It was a powerful position, to be sure, and a dangerous one.

Drew was openly shocked. He was like an uncle to Trynne, and her heart went out to him as she witnessed him take the blow, as sharp and painful as a staff slammed into his gut. Tall and strong, he had the Argentine good looks, though he favored his grandfather, Eredur, more than he did his dark and severe uncle Severn. He was often serious, but had a habit of defeating tension with humor.

There was no humor in him now.

He stared at Sinia with confounded disbelief. "Surely," he said in a half-strangled voice, "the Fountain would not summon you when our need be so great. Myrddin assured me that the situation elsewhere he was summoned to was worse than our situation. Although I cannot see how."

Trynne ached at the tone of his words, for she felt the same way.

"My lord," Sinia said, "it is not my desire to abandon you. My visions have never explained why things happen. Only that they *will*."

"When I called for you," Drew stammered, "I had not expected such news. Forgive me; I need a moment." He walked over to Genevieve, who was sitting at a little bench near his mother. He put his hand on her shoulder, as if she were the rope that would save him from drowning. Genny looked up at him worriedly, gently rocking the babe, who was starting to squirm and mewl with hunger pangs.

Kathryn offered to hold Kate, giving Genevieve a sweet, comforting smile, and the queen handed the babe over. The queen dowager spent half of each year living in Glosstyr with her husband. Now that her grandchild had been born, Trynne imagined she'd be more likely to stay at court. Morwenna gave the infant a brief dispassionate look before returning her gaze to Sinia.

The silence in the room was uncomfortable and growing worse.

"I apologize for adding to your worries," Sinia said.

Genevieve took her husband's hand and squeezed it. "You have ever been our loyal friend and wise counselor, Lady Sinia. It would not hurt to remember that without your aid, this kingdom would have been buried in snow and ice over a decade ago. You have proven yourself a loyal ally of Kingfountain many times. May it always be so."

Trynne appreciated Genny's calming words. She was always so level-headed. As Trynne mulled over their predicament, she glanced again at Morwenna. The girl was struggling for composure—her lips were pressed into a flat line, and her eyes were glowering with some dark emotion.

Morwenna looked down, her cheeks a little flushed, before lifting her gaze to Trynne. Realizing her discomfort had been observed, she shook off whatever mood had gripped her—blinking rapidly and squaring her shoulders—and offered Trynne an apologetic smile.

"We must tell the council at once," Drew said, shaking his head. He put his arm around Genny's shoulder. "Send a summons. Sister, can you and Trynne help gather them all to the Ring Table?"

"Of course," Morwenna said, looking much less agitated than she had moments before.

"Whatever provisions you need," Drew said, looking at Sinia. "Name them. I will send you on my best galleon. If you go to the Deep Fathoms, perhaps you can seek aid for us. We are in sore need of it."

Sinia demurred. "We are going into uncharted waters. I need a sturdy merchant vessel of Genevese make. Indeed, I saw it in my vision. You will need all the ships you have. I do not wish to impose on Your Grace."

"Very well, then I will coax you no further." Turning toward Trynne and Morwenna, he said, "Duke Elwis is already here at the palace. Gather Iago and Elysabeth, Duke Ramey, Deconeus Stellis, and Fallon, of course. Best if they all hear the news straightaway. See it done."

His tone was one of command, and both girls bowed in deference. Morwenna hooked her arm through Trynne's as they left the solar. Trynne was uncomfortable, wishing she hadn't seen that look on the other girl's face. But Morwenna was ever one to plunge into dark waters and dive to the heart of the matter.

"I'm sorry you caught me in a moment of self-pity," she said as they walked. "I know it's childish, but it pains me to hear my father's defeat mentioned so casually or as a point worth celebrating." She squeezed Trynne's arm. "It shattered him, Trynne. He was the King of Ceredigion. This was his castle once. It might have been mine under different circumstances." She sighed. "Well, there's no use fretting about a coin lost in a river. We have all lost things that were important to us." She gave Trynne a knowing look, full of sympathy. "Or will yet lose. Your mother has surprised us all. Had you suspected this would happen?"

Trynne and Morwenna had once been friends, but they'd slowly grown apart once the poisoner had begun studying under Trynne's mother. It was painful hearing about her accomplishments and progress, especially since Trynne had struggled so much to learn the craft. Then there was the fact that Morwenna was tall and darkly beautiful, capable of turning heads just by walking into a room. While she was Fountain-blessed, Trynne did not know what her powers were, only that she got a cold feeling in her presence at times. Still, in many ways, Morwenna was practically the reincarnation of Ankarette Tryneowy, Trynne's own namesake.

"No, I was as surprised as everyone else," Trynne answered truthfully.

"I've never seen my brother so distraught. Don't you find it strange that his strong pieces are all being swept from the board? I don't mean to be brash, but this feels like a game of Wizr. The set that Rucrius broke when he came to deliver his warning. You remember it?"

"Of course I do," Trynne said, trying not to sound peevish. "It was the ancient set played by the original King Andrew. The one that helped the Argentines stay in power all these years."

"One by one, our pieces are falling," Morwenna said as they walked toward the closest fountain to travel on the ley lines. "You don't think . . . ? No, I'd best not say it."

Her refusal only made Trynne more curious. Which was probably her intent.

"What?" Trynne pushed.

"I was just wondering," Morwenna said, letting her words trail off as she came to a sudden stop next to a large glass window with a spacious view of the gardens below. The sky was roiling with storm clouds. "Just wondering," she continued in an almost absentminded way, "if the Fountain heeds those with the strongest will. Does not Gahalatine serve the Fountain as well? And do not we? How can we both be serving the same power? Perhaps it has chosen one of us."

Their conversation was interrupted as heavy drops of rain began to lash against the glass. They both stared at the glass as the surprise squall opened over the city. It had been a cloudless day when they'd arrived. The limbs of the magnolia trees beneath them swayed and jerked as the wind started to gust.

It was the very garden where Trynne and Fallon had argued. Was it coincidence that had brought them there?

"I will go to Edonburick," Morwenna said, putting her hand on Trynne's shoulder. "I've not seen *my* grandfather in some time and should like to. Why don't you go to Dundrennan to fetch Fallon?"

Trynne gritted her teeth, her feelings tangled and tender. "I would rather not," she muttered.

"I know," Morwenna said with one of her lovely smiles. "Which is all the more reason that you should. Fallon is a dear friend. You really hurt him, Trynne. I think it's time the two of you mended the breach."

Trynne believed she was right. But it didn't make her eager to do it. She sighed, trying to summon her courage. It would be painful to see him. But she would try. "Very well," she said.

"How strange that it's raining so suddenly," Morwenna said, cocking her head. A white flash exploded outside the window, blinding them both. Thunder boomed heavily over the castle, shaking the stones.

"I think it struck the rod atop the poisoner tower," Morwenna said, her voice shaking from the sudden thrill of danger. "I'm glad I wasn't up there just now!"

Trynne wondered if the sudden storm was a freak of nature. Or if the king's brooding had invoked the secret power of the hollow crown.

CHAPTER SEVEN

Dundrennan

It was cold in the North. Even the hissing torches lining the walls could not ward off the chill. Even the air smelled different. There was an inescapable scent of crushed pine needles, of mountain air so clean and cold it made her chest burn.

Dundrennan was a spacious fortress, nestled in a mountain valley in the highlands with an incomparable view of an enormous waterfall. It was nearly the headspring of the river that ended at Kingfountain. Memories of the place flittered through Trynne's mind. Her father had been raised in this place after spending his boyhood in Tatton Hall, and while she had not visited the North often as a girl, she'd always loved imagining her father playing with his tiles by the hearth, or chatting with Fallon's mother and her grizzled grandfather, Duke Horwath. The standard of the Pierced Lion still dominated the tapestries. It made her heart flutter to realize she was now in Fallon's domain.

As soon as she'd appeared in Dundrennan, a servant had seen her and hastened to fetch the master of the castle. It was not uncommon to receive strange visitors from the chapel, but Trynne could tell they were used to someone else. *Morwenna.* The servant's eyes had widened with surprise, and she'd stammered her name as she hurried away.

Fallon's herald, a man by the name of Stroud, arrived shortly thereafter. He was tall, nearly fifty years old, with thinning, graying dark hair and a serious set to his mouth.

"Lady Tryneowy, this is an unexpected pleasure," he said in a deferential yet formal tone. "Lord Fallon will attend you at once. Please follow me."

"Thank you, Master Stroud," Trynne said. He was tall, and his stride was much longer than hers, but she followed him as best she could. They approached an open door leading to the solar, from which she saw and heard the crackling hearth fire, but to her surprise, they walked past it.

Stroud brought her through several twisting tunnels before stopping in front of Fallon's personal chamber. If she had been nervous before, it was eclipsed by his decision to meet her in his private space. The great hall was for meeting strangers. The solar for more intimate friends. What could she make of this?

Stroud rapped on the door and opened it without awaiting a response. He bowed stiffly, gesturing for Trynne to enter first.

Trying to quell the wild feeling in her chest that made her want to flee, Trynne forced herself to step into the chamber.

There was a flurry of movement to her left and she saw Fallon emerge from behind a changing screen, fastening a belt and scabbard around his waist. He had a rushed and agitated air about him. When he saw her standing there, he gave her a glance and hurried to a massive desk full of scrolls and papers and things. He picked up a signet ring from a gold plate and twisted it onto his littlest finger.

She had not seen him in months, and the changes in him immediately struck her. He was bigger, his shoulders broader, his gait and posture more robust. He was even more impossibly handsome than she had remembered. Fallon had always been tall, but now he seemed to fill the room with his presence. Grabbing a towel from the desk, he mopped his neck and brow.

"I was training in the yard," he said, by way of excuse. His voice was wary, with none of the warmth or friendliness that they had once shared. There was no humor in his eyes, no mischievous grin just for her. "I needed a moment to make myself more presentable for the palace. I'm assuming you came to bring me there. Have we been attacked by Gahalatine?"

Their estrangement pained her deeply, but they could not undo what had happened. She could only hope time would heal them both.

"No, it's not that," Trynne said, trying to find her way through the dangerous waters between them.

He rifled through some of the papers on the desk, picked up several, and stuffed them into his pocket. It did nothing to hide the pain in his eyes. "Then why did you come?"

She wondered at all the correspondence on his desk. It would appear he was still dealing in secrets. His obsession with the Espion was one of the chief reasons she had difficulty trusting him.

"I did come to bring you to the palace," she said. "There is news, just not the tidings you were expecting. We did receive word that Gahalatine's fleet is on the way. Part of it was sighted by a Genevese merchant."

Fallon nodded in a way that implied he already knew of it. "What news, then?" he asked. "If you can tell me." The way he said it reminded her of another wall between them. The last time he'd asked her to share a secret with him, it had not been hers to tell.

Trynne licked her lips, feeling the discomfort of the moment yawn between them. Stroud stood in the doorway behind them, a silent observer, but Fallon gave him a dismissive nod, and the door quietly shut, leaving them alone together.

"I am sorry it has come to this, Fallon," she said. "I am sorry to have lost your friendship. I never wanted that."

He stood by the table, his arms folded guardedly. They were so much bigger now. She could see the scars on his hands, along with one on his cheekbone. She wanted to hold him, to comfort him, to soothe the anger she saw churning inside him. There was so much she wished for, so much she could not have.

Where once he had been glib and spontaneous, now he seemed to be struggling for words. Gazing down at the mess of correspondence, he sighed, favoring her with a sidelong look. His mouth twitched, reminding her of her old friend, the one who had never tired of teasing her. But the look was swept away like a cloud on the wind. "It was my own fault," he said in a formal, self-deprecating tone. "I acted against my better judgment when I approached you that day. You were so kind as to point that out to me." Again, the formality of his speech hurt her. "So, must I wait for this news until I get to Kingfountain? Has it to do with the Gauntlet? Is the king canceling it?"

"Not at all," she said, shaking her head. Her legs felt locked in place, so she took a hesitant step closer to him. She pressed her thumb in circles across her palm, fidgeting slightly. She knew that Fallon was preparing for the Gauntlet of Kingfountain. He had made no secret of his wish to take her father's seat at the Ring Table, the one known as the Siege Perilous. It was the seat of the king's champion. Gahalatine had given Drew one year to choose a replacement for Owen if he could not be found. The winner of the Gauntlet would win that title.

What Fallon did not realize was the Fountain had whispered to Trynne that *she* must sit in the chair.

He was looking at her pointedly now, his gaze penetrating. He had the clearest gray-green eyes she had ever seen. Memories of their childhood together buffeted her.

"The Fountain has bid my mother to depart Ceredigion," she said at last. The anguish of the feeling was still fresh and raw. "She will be leaving imminently to seek the Deep Fathoms at sea."

His eyes widened with disbelief, and she took some small satisfaction in having shocked him. She took advantage of his stunned silence to continue. "She saw this in a vision. Drew and Genny are just as surprised as you are. As we all are. The king has summoned his council to the Ring Table to tell them. Morwenna is fetching your parents. She . . . suggested that I come for you."

"Trynne," he breathed, a look of pain and anguish on his face. "How can this be? How can the Fountain even . . . ?" He stopped short of speaking blasphemy. "You must be devastated. Both your parents?"

She bit her lip, not letting herself take too much comfort in his sympathy. "It is not what my mother wishes. Her visions show what will happen. Not why."

"And she has not seen Gahalatine's invasion yet? It means we'll have no forewarning of where he will strike." He shook his head in wonderment, gazing away from her, hands on his hips. "This is grave news indeed. I am sorry for you, Trynne." When he returned his gaze to her, his eyes were full of compassion.

She took another step closer to the desk.

"I believe in the Fountain," Trynne said softly. "Even when I don't understand its will."

"You have more faith in it at the present than I." He chuffed, shaking his head. She reached the edge of the table, adjacent to where he stood. So many papers. So many secrets. It was like Lord Amrein's desk in the Espions' Star Chamber in Kingfountain. It would be easy for her to return and rifle through them, using her magic to make herself invisible. Where did his true loyalty lie? Would she find evidence here to incriminate him in a conspiracy? Or was he truly seeking to unmask the king's enemies by pretending to be one of them?

"So Morwenna sent you," Fallon said coolly after the silence became uncomfortable. He pursed his lips. "I had *hoped* you'd come of your own accord. But it matters little. I understand you have been very busy of late." He gave her an arch look. It reminded her of his frustration that the king didn't use him for important assignments.

"Fallon, let's not argue," she said.

"It's not my intention to argue," he said, folding his arms again. "I have no wish for another drubbing. When Stroud told me you had come, I had thought your news might be . . . well, that's not really important now. I was wrong."

"What were you wrong about?" Trynne asked, more confused than ever.

"It's of no consequence. Shall we go to the chapel, then?"

"Fallon," she said as the familiar pain rose. "Will we ever start trusting each other again? I told you the truth about why I came here."

"I know; I understand," he said curtly. He was growing more agitated. "I had thought you were here to deliver other news."

She blinked at him, trying to discern his meaning.

"As I said, it's of no matter. But I see I'm in the wrong again. I've failed you before by not saying what's on my mind. Let me say now, and you can call me a fool." He leaned forward and planted his palms on the table, gazing at the heap of papers. "One of the questions that has been plaguing the Espion for months is the true identity of the Painted Knight. This *person* fought near the king at the Battle of Guilme. This *person* entered my tent the eve before the battle and took something from me." He looked at her with knowing, accusatory eyes.

Trynne felt her heart flutter in a sudden panic.

"I think I've known for some time who it is," Fallon said in a low, confident tone. "The woad is a clever disguise, but I believe I've solved the riddle. I think my sister knows too, but the king certainly does not. I had hoped, Trynne, that I would not have to unmask the fellow myself. I'm the only person who even knows his name. Sir Ellis. *Fidelis.* A nickname you once teased me with, and a virtue you claim that I lack."

He sighed and looked away from her. "I'd hoped you would tell me yourself, Trynne. But I figured it out eventually. That is something else that I am good at." He gazed across the heap of scrolls. "That's all these really are. Clues. Pieces of paper." He lifted one and flung it aside. Then he gave her a sidelong look and she caught another glimpse of the old Fallon. "I won't ask you to deny it. Or to affirm it. You've probably bound yourself to an oath you cannot break or some such foolishness."

His astute statement twisted a smile from her. She stood silently, gazing at him, grappling with the news that he had finally discovered her. He had suspected her before, of course, but she'd thrown him off.

"You've always been clever, Fallon," Trynne said, her voice husky.

He shrugged off the compliment. "I'm also incorrigible, incomprehensible, infallible, impassible, and incontrovertible as well." He gave her a sidelong smile, then he turned away and sighed. "I had hoped you were here to tell me your secret. Of course, I can think of many reasons why you wouldn't, including the most obvious one. We'll be competing against each other at the Gauntlet of Kingfountain. I admire your courage and skill. You've bested me before. You also bested Elwis. He doesn't know, does he?"

Trynne shook her head no.

"I didn't think so," he added. There it was again, the twinkle in his eye that reminded her of the way they used to be together. "Well, I don't intend to reveal your secret, Trynne. As I said, I'm quite confident my sister already knows, and if she hasn't told the king, there must be a good reason for it. I'm still loyal to him. I always have been. Well, I guess we should be on our way?"

He straightened and gestured for her to precede him. As she started to walk, she saw him slip another letter from the desk into his pocket. After opening the door, Fallon turned to Stroud, who was standing outside it like a sentinel.

"Stroud, be a good man and clean up my mess, will you?" Fallon said, gesturing to the disheveled state of the room. "Lady Trynne and I are going to Kingfountain."

They reached the chapel shortly thereafter, the air still ripe with the fragrance of pine. She stepped into the fountain water and Fallon joined her. They needed to be touching for the magic to work, and she was reaching for his arm when he took her hand instead.

Her confusion must have shown on her face because he immediately said, "I'm sorry, that was presumptuous of me. It's just that I've always held Morwenna's hand when we traveled together. I thought that's how it was done."

They both stood there awkwardly for a moment. Trynne felt a searing flash of jealousy at the realization that Fallon had traveled the ley lines with Morwenna many times before.

"It's all right," she said dismissively, trying to keep her voice calm. She kept his warm hand in hers, feeling her heart give a lurching jolt that wasn't entirely due to the magic she invoked.

CHAPTER EIGHT

The Ring Table

Trynne rubbed her palm across the smooth grooves of the massive table in the great hall of Kingfountain. The round of trunk had been cut from an enormous tree, and she could see the individual rings marking the generations that had passed. Only great power could have summoned something of that enormous size into the hall. But it was more than just a slab of wood. The Ring Table was a conduit for the Fountain's magic, and it possessed powers none of them truly understood. But Trynne sensed that its chief function was to bring together disparate people from different backgrounds and customs, unifying them in one purpose. It was the symbol of ancient King Andrew's fallen realm, a kingdom that had been riven by infidelity, and it had disappeared after his fatal injury over a thousand years earlier.

The new ruler of the court of Kingfountain sat at the table beside Genny, their hands interlocked. Drew looked careworn and burdened. He was a young father, a young king, and the trusted advisors who had supported him over the years were falling away. As Trynne cast her gaze around the table, her eyes found the conspicuously empty seat her father had occupied.

The room was silent, save for the hiss of the torches. The king had just revealed that Sinia would be embarking on a journey to a distant shore. The council was still reeling from the news.

Drew rubbed his bottom lip, staring across the table at each of them in turn. "Our enemy is coming," he said, his voice serious and wary. "I have no doubt that Gahalatine will make good on his promise to invade us. Whether or not we are prepared, he will come. Where will he strike first? Advise me on how best to defend our borders."

Duke Elwis was the first to speak. He leaned forward in his chair and said, "He started his attack at Guilme. He has a foothold that he can use to land ships and his forces. We have dug a series of trenches throughout Brugia. We've spent the last year training new archers to defend against attacks from the sky. Brugia will be the chief battleground, my lord. Let us defend your kingdom there."

Lady Evie, Queen of Atabyrion and Fallon and Genny's mother, spoke next. "I've read the accounts of many wars and battles. The one thing they have in common is that they have nothing in common. Lord Owen was successful as a battle commander because he was always unpredictable. I do not think Gahalatine will strike us twice in the same place. I mean no offense, Grand Duke Elwis, nor do I minimize the preparations we've *all* made in defending our borders."

Trynne watched Elwis's cheeks flush. But despite his natural inclination to bristle whenever contradicted, he controlled his expression and, even better, his tongue. He did not speak up against her.

"Say on, my lady," Drew said to Lady Evie. "If he does not attack Brugia, where do you think he will strike?"

Lady Evie looked at her husband, Iago, who gave a quick laugh. "Go on, love. Everyone here already knows you are wiser than I am." He chuckled again. "I'm not cheapened by that."

Trynne smiled at the honest remark and cast a quick look at Fallon, whom she caught smirking.

"I believe, my lord, that he will strike at the heart of your realm. He will attack Kingfountain first. One of his Wizrs has already revealed that they can access the palace through the fountains. There is no doubt in my mind that they have seen our defenses and feel confident they can overcome them. The river has always been a protection to us." She shook her head. "Rucrius proved it cannot shield us."

There were murmurs of agreement and disagreement from others at the table. The king looked as if his mother-in-law had clubbed him. He cast a furtive look at his wife, and Trynne saw their fingers tighten. The rumble of thunder sounded in the distance.

"I cannot abandon Kingfountain," Drew said, shaking his head. "It is the seat of my power. This castle has never been vanquished by a foreign enemy. Why would he start by striking the heart of our realm?"

Lord Amrein spoke up. "We have prepared the docks to be burned and have gathered enough supplies for the city to withstand an extended siege. The cistern is full and we have barrels of water to provide for our needs."

Lady Evie sighed. "My lord, you asked me what I think Gahalatine will do, not whether I think it wise. If he does start by attacking Kingfountain, we could close in and surround him on all sides. The court historian told me a story of an enemy ruler who plunged into the heart of a kingdom and murdered the king, only to find himself fenced in and destroyed. Yet Gahalatine is ambitious. He is crafty. Like any leader, he will strike where we least expect him to."

"Who is to say he will only attack *one* location?" Fallon said in a low, serious tone during the lull that followed.

That comment caused even more dissension. Duke Severn was the first to address the suggestion. "You're a raw youth," the old king snapped. "Gahalatine knows that we are defending our homeland. Coordinating multiple attack points would be too perilous for him, especially since the populace is likely to rise up against him. You carve up your army in the face of your foe to outwit and outflank him, not before you have even attacked. No, he's more likely to concentrate his force on the position where our army is the strongest." His voice was full of ire, and Trynne shuddered as he spoke, for she imagined what it must have been like for her father to serve under such a disagreeable man. "I have always been struck by Lady Elysabeth's wisdom." He tapped his gloved finger on the table forcefully. "Defend Kingfountain, or lose it all."

Fallon scowled at the rebuke, his eyes narrowing coldly as he stared at Morwenna's father. But he made no attempt to save face; he only stroked his bottom lip and remained quiet. Trynne's heart went out to him, but she respected that he didn't argue his point.

"And how would you advise defending the palace?" Drew asked in a deferential tone.

Severn sneered. "The palace will not be difficult to defend. I would move half of your army to Beestone castle. You don't want everyone to be trapped inside the city during a siege. You'll need a solid force outside to coordinate attacks. If it were *me*," he added in an aggrieved tone, "I would stay at Beestone myself. Let him throw away lives trying to attack a landlocked castle. Then hit him hard from the sides. Remember, lad. *You* are the kingdom. Taking the capital won't make Gahalatine king. Only you can give him what he seeks."

As much as Trynne hated to admit it, she saw wisdom in Severn's words. He had spent his entire reign clutching the hollow crown, defying those who sought to wrest it from him. Drew didn't have that kind of experience. How much was he willing to wrestle to preserve what the Fountain had given him?

"Lady Trynne," Drew said, shifting his gaze to her. "How would you advise me?"

She was startled by the sudden attention to her and her ideas. Her stomach began to fill with butterflies, but Genny smiled at her husband's question and patted his arm approvingly.

"Well, I know for a fact that Gahalatine is not with his fleet," Trynne answered, feeling her voice tremble a little. She had received Genny's permission to share her story with the council. "The queen recently sent me on a mission to Chandleer Oasis, which lies in the desert along the trade routes to Gahalatine's domain. He attacked it while I was there, striking from the mountains to the east of the oasis. No one expected it, least of all the king. I agree with Duke Severn," she said, giving him a respectful nod. "The kingdom is where *you* are, my lord. And that means you should not be where Gahalatine can easily reach you."

A few murmurs of assent followed her words.

The king breathed heavily. "I do not relish the idea of leaving my wife and child unprotected."

Genny leaned forward. "Your grandfather once sent his wife and children to the sanctuary of Our Lady during an invasion. I don't think Gahalatine would harm a woman deliberately. It's you he wants."

Drew's eyes narrowed. Trynne could see he was wrestling with the decision. "Lady Sinia?"

Her bearing was very solemn. "Morwenna knows how to invoke the protections that will defend the sanctuary from a flood. My visions have all been about the journey I must shortly make. I'm sorry to be of no use here."

"Maybe your use," the king replied with great respect, "will come from assistance in other quarters. May the Fountain guide your sails, my lady of Brythonica."

Sinia bowed her head to the king.

Drew rose from his chair and planted his hands on the table. "You think I should go to Beestone, then?" he said to Trynne.

She narrowed her gaze. Something didn't feel quite right. She trusted each person in the chamber, for all had proven their loyalty to the king. But what if Gahalatine had a way of listening in on their conversation? What if he could know of their plans?

"I think, my lord," Trynne said, "that you must choose with care where you will go. Choose—and tell no one."

Genny nodded. "That is good advice, Trynne. My lord husband, I will begin preparations to set up my household in the sanctuary. I will defend the city if we are attacked."

Drew nodded, his mouth turned down in a frown. "So be it. The Gauntlet of Kingfountain will be held following the Feast of St. Benedick, less than a fortnight away. That is when I will name my new champion."

Grand Duke Elwis sat up straight, his gaze on the duke of the North.

Fallon met his look unflinchingly.

♦ ♦ ♦

Trynne was only too grateful to be back in Averanche. There was no need to bring Fallon back to Dundrennan. He had decided to stay at Kingfountain to train until the Gauntlet. Sinia had departed to Tatton Hall to bring young Gannon to Ploemeur, where he would reside during their mother's long absence. Sinia wanted her children to be together while she was away, and the presence of both heirs would be a salve to the people of Brythonica—a reassurance that there would always be a Montfort in Brythonica.

Trynne knew she only had a short time to spend in her city, and she wanted to make the most of it.

At noonday, she was in the training yard of the castle. Captain Staeli stood back-to-back with her, wearing his armor and holding a sword defensively. The two of them were hemmed in on every side, completely surrounded by the Oath Maidens. Each held weapons of various sorts.

"This is what I am asking you," Trynne said, wearing her hauberk and tunic, feeling the gauntlets and greaves groan as she moved. "Do not hold anything back. Do not let up until we are both knocked down. Our enemies will not hold back. Our foes will not hesitate. You must fight until you fall. Then get up and fight again. And again. You are Oath Maidens. Captain Staeli stands proxy for your king. You stand proxy for our foes. Fight with all you have in you. So will I."

Staeli rocked on his feet, preparing for the attack. Trynne's heart beat faster as she registered the looks of determination on the faces of the girls and women surrounding them. She had both her swords out, one in each hand.

It was no surprise that Mariette led the charge. Trynne's mouth went dry as she and Captain Staeli were rushed from all sides. Her magic flooded over, rising in response to the threat she faced. During the last months, she had trained with multiple foes, increasing the number by one every week. At the Battle of Guilme and before, she had felt limited by her supply of Fountain magic. The only way she had found to increase it was by self-discipline and practicing against more and more foes. In the months since the battle, she had increased her store of magic considerably and could fight without stopping for nearly an hour. Sometimes, she was so at one with her magic that it felt as if time itself slowed to a crawl and she alone could move while her enemies labored to attack her.

These tests always wore her out, sapping her magic until it was gone, and even then she'd continue to fight until she was physically exhausted and could barely stand.

The girls could not all attack at once, and she could defeat any of them individually. The test came from protecting someone else, in this case Captain Staeli, which was what she had trained to do. She was the king's protector. She was going to become his champion.

As the magic swept through her, she reacted on instinct alone. She blocked not only the attacks aimed at her, but also the attempts at Captain Staeli. Hers was defensive magic, and she could sense every person coming against them. She did not wait until the attackers got close, but came forward and blocked and countered with crisp efficiency. Her magic pinpointed her enemies' weaknesses instantly, allowing her to disarm them or knock them back. After training for so many months, they had all gotten better and better.

But it was impossible to face multiple foes without getting hit. Her armor protected her from fatal wounds, but every thrust that made it past hurt, and she wished she had her father's magic scabbard to heal her wounds. Grunting and breathing hard, Trynne swiveled and pitched and kicked her way through the women attacking her and Staeli. The captain was not a docile defender himself, and the two of them together were a formidable pair.

Yet wave after wave of girls kept coming, most of them fresh and eager for a chance to prove themselves, and Trynne's arms started to grow heavy and tired. She could feel the edges of her magic shrinking, pulling in tighter and tighter.

Suddenly five organized themselves to launch a simultaneous attack on her.

"*Tychos!*" Trynne shouted, invoking a word of power. The attackers struck an invisible wall and crumpled against it, falling to the courtyard floor.

"How're you . . . feeling, lass?" Staeli said with a gasp.

She could hardly breathe and uttering the word had left her winded.

"Quite well," she managed to say. "You?"

Staeli punched one of the girls in the stomach, twisting his leg around hers before throwing her down.

"Never better!" he shouted with a defiant grin.

Trynne's face was dripping with sweat. But she wondered what she would do if there were no end to Gahalatine's soldiers.

Even her magic had its limits.

◆ ◆ ◆

My mind is much clearer now that I've stopped drinking the sugared poison. I still cannot remember who I am or how I came to be in this cell. But I have learned some things from the clues around me. I can summon fresh water from a carving I made in the stone wall. I don't know how I do it, but I feel there is power inside me. My left hand once bore a ring. The skin on my ring finger is callused where it used to be. I feel an empty ache inside of me, a longing for people I cannot remember. I was married, or used to be. I know how to fight. Every time the guard comes to feed me, I am tempted to wrestle him for control of his dagger. He has some gout in his left knee, and even with these chains, I think I can overpower him. He refuses to answer my questions, but he's worried that I'm so lucid. I think he realizes that the poison isn't affecting me anymore.

Someone is coming. Not enough time has passed since my last bit of food. What is happening? I can feel the power the visitor is using. The door squeals as it opens. My jailor has brought a man wearing a silver mask.

◆ ◆ ◆

CHAPTER NINE

Turandokht

As Trynne fastened a bracelet onto her wrist, there was a knock on the door. She gazed at herself in the mirror, feeling clean from her bath, fresh in a gown, and confident. She had not depleted all her magic during the test with the Oath Maidens. Far from it. After some delicious peaches and salted nuts, she felt replenished and invigorated and ready to leave for Ploemeur.

"Enter," she said, pulling out a pair of earrings as the door opened and old Farnes entered, wheezing, with Rani Sureya behind him.

Farnes gave her a formal bow, struggling with his breath. "A carriage arrived at the gate with a nobleman from the Occitanian city of Lionn seeking to meet you. I . . . sent him away. You wished to speak to the princess." He straightened and shut the door as he left.

Sureya, who had taken to wearing the fashions of Kingfountain, had also bathed and changed. She looked on nervously as Trynne fastened the earrings to her lobes.

"You fight very well, Sureya," Trynne said, turning around and smoothing her dress. "I thought you came here to be taught, but you are more capable than many of the girls who have been training for months."

Sureya blushed and bowed her head. "I am not nearly as skilled as you are, Lady Trynne."

"Who taught you?"

"My father has only daughters. He made certain we were trained to defend ourselves. There was a man, a mercenary of Genevar who had gone to live among the Bhikhu. My father hired him to train us."

Trynne wrinkled her brow. "Your father mentioned the Bhikhu previously. They are the ones who fight for Gahalatine."

Sureya nodded. "I cannot float as the Bhikhu do." She wrung her hands together. "You fought today like Turandokht, Lady Trynne. I am honored to serve you."

Trynne approached her, appraising her further. "You fought very well yourself. You use your elbows and feet as deftly as you do your weapons. Who is this Turandokht you mention?"

"You have not heard of her?" Sureya said in surprise. "She was the most famous Fountain-blessed of her generation."

"In our histories, the most famous Fountain-blessed was the Maid of Donremy. She was a girl from an obscure village in Occitania who led her people to victory against Ceredigion. Could we be using different names for the same person?"

"No, Turandokht is from our part of the world," Sureya insisted. "She was from Chandigarl. Her uncle was the Emperor of Chandigarl three centuries ago. Her father's name was Turan. In that country, *dokht* means 'daughter.' She had brothers, but she was the best fighter and horse rider in all Chandigarl. She fought with hook swords. Two of them. They were Turandokht's specialty."

Trynne nodded. "While I am gone, please speak to Farnes about them. He will have the castle weaponsmith make them. Thank you for sharing her story with me."

Sureya beamed at her with pleasure. "Even your name sounds like it comes from Turan, Lady Trynne. She was famous in our lands. She refused to marry anyone who could not outwrestle her. It was said that if a man challenged her for the right, he had to give her three horses if he failed. There was grazing land dedicated to the herd of horses she'd won. No one ever did defeat her, although she did choose to marry eventually. After Turan died, her brothers fought over the inheritance. People said that she should have inherited all of her father's wealth, for she was very wise."

"Whom did she marry?" Trynne asked. Her father had always said that certain roles were played over and over throughout history. He had described it as being trapped on a waterwheel in a river of destiny that one could not easily escape. She knew better than to ignore coincidences.

"A man who tried and failed to murder her father," Sureya answered with an impish smile. "The history of the East Kingdoms is lavish with intrigues."

The words sent a tremor through Trynne, as if some heavy stone were being dragged across the floor, rumbling the entire castle. It struck her forcibly, stealing her breath.

"Are you well, my lady?" Sureya asked.

"I am," Trynne said, though she felt slightly dizzy. "I must be away. Thank you for sharing the history with me."

"I've offended you," Sureya said, her face growing worried.

"No, you haven't," Trynne said, touching the girl's arm. "My father is missing. I worry about him every day. Your words struck me, that is all. It would be . . . it would be very *difficult* for me to love a man who'd hurt him." Fallon's face flashed inside her mind, along with the remembrance of the silver mask she had taken from his tent in her guise as the Painted Knight. If Fallon had had *anything* to do with her father's disappearance, whatever his reasons, she would lose all respect for him.

Sureya nodded in understanding. "I should have been more cautious in my words. Forgive me. I share your pain, Lady Trynne. I too wonder what has become of my father." Her brow furrowed with worry. "I would give anything to know."

Trynne found herself liking the princess more and more. The two embraced, a simple gesture that strengthened their connection. Trynne gave her new friend a smile. "I will look forward to training with you when I return."

"Is it near the Feast of St. Benedick?" Sureya asked. "Are you going to meet your lover?"

Trynne's eyes widened with shock. "Grand Duke Elwis?"

Sureya nodded, but her eyes were guarded.

"No!" she replied, laughing a little. "No, he . . . I am not going to see him yet. And he and I are not . . . attached. I promised him that I would visit, but I need to go to Brythonica first to see my mother. She is leaving on a great journey."

Sureya blinked with surprise. "You do not care for the grand duke? The one whom I met?" A little flush crept onto the princess's cheeks.

Trynne shook her head no. "He is much changed from what he was. I admire him, but no . . . things are more difficult for me." She swallowed. "I'm in love with another duke. But I know that I cannot be his. My mother is a Wizr, and she sees things that will happen in the future." It felt good to speak about it with someone who wasn't directly involved in the situation. Genny was understanding, but she was also Fallon's sister.

Sureya's jaw dropped. "There is no more powerful gift from the Fountain," she whispered.

"That is true," Trynne said. "She told me she has seen a vision of the man I will marry. And he is not the man that I wanted him to be."

Sureya blinked in understanding. "How difficult for you," she said, taking Trynne's hands. "I'm sorry."

Trynne shrugged. "My family is used to swimming in deep waters, you could say."

"And your mother is leaving the court of Kingfountain?" Sureya said. "Isn't she the king's Wizr?"

"Yes. The king's blood-sister will stand in for her while she's away. My mother had a vision of the future. She will be departing by boat."

"She seeks Fusang," Sureya whispered reverently. "I am sorry. In your religion, it is called the Deep Fathoms."

Trynne cocked her head. "Yes. How did you know?"

Sureya grew more excited. "There is a legend in our culture. Over a thousand years ago, a traveler came to the emperor's palace claiming to have crossed the sea. He had discovered Fusang, the place between the worlds. One can only reach it by sea. The dead go there. But so can the living, those whom Fusang summons. There is a tree there full of different fruit. One of them grants immortality. When the emperor learned of it, he sent his chief Wizr, Xu Fu, with a fleet of ships to discover it. He never returned. They say that Xu Fu did find it and that he took the fruit of immortality for himself. That he is still *alive*. That he serves the people in secret and travels the world in disguise, advising kings and emperors and warning them to hearken to the Fountain. They say the tree with the fruit is the source of the Fountain. That water gushes from its roots."

Trynne had never heard these tales, but they ignited her imagination.

"Thank you, yet again," Trynne said, feeling brightened by the news. Maybe the Deep Fathoms was trying to help them? She had feared her mother wouldn't return from the journey.

Sureya cast her eyes down. "The other girls have said that Grand Duke Elwis is the best warrior in all Ceredigion now. Many have cast their eyes on him, and it is said he is not unhandsome." She swallowed, growing more subdued. "Is he . . . is he *pleased* that women are becoming warriors? Many men frown upon us."

"I will have to ask him when I meet with him," Trynne said with a sly smile. She suspected that Elwis had left an impression on the princess.

◆ ◆ ◆

The smells on the beach of glass beads were familiar and soothing. The wind tousled Trynne's hair, and she brushed aside the strands as she watched her mother and Gannon walk hand in hand. Her mother's blond hair fanned out, so lovely and full. She was still heartbreakingly beautiful. There was so much Trynne admired her for—her gentleness, how quickly she responded to the needs of other realms, and her conviction in the Fountain's direction.

Trynne would miss her sorely.

"And what kind of bird is that?" Sinia asked Gannon, nodding toward the white-breasted birds running back and forth along the shore.

"Plovers," Gannon said excitedly. "Look, Mama! Pelicans! Five of them! That one is going to dive. Look! It did!"

"Yes, it did," Sinia said, her pleasure at his enthusiasm evident in her tone. "They must catch a lot of fish with those big beaks."

"And those over there are puffins. The bills are so orange."

"And what about that one? With the long, pointed beak?"

"A curlew. Their beaks are as long as swords." His memory had always impressed Trynne. Her heart filled with love for the little boy who was as happy and carefree as their father hadn't been in his own youth. Owen's absence made the child melancholy at times, but he knew how deeply he was loved, and Trynne was grateful that he had never grown tired of holding their mother's hand.

The salty smell of the ocean, the sound of the waves crashing against the shore, and the cry of the seagulls overhead—all of it flooded her with memories of other times she'd visited with her mother. It was Sinia's favorite place, but though it was beautiful, it was also a reminder of the inexorable power of the Deep Fathoms. The tiny beads of polished glass they trampled in the sand were relics of Leoneyis, a kingdom that had been swallowed by the sea. Her mother had often described to her visions she'd seen of Leoneyis at its prime—the enormous palace full of huge glass windows and glass chandeliers, dangling prisms that spun rainbows everywhere when the sunlight struck them. Yet the great wealth of the king had corrupted his heart. In time, he had forsaken the Fountain and destroyed all the Oath Maidens, ultimately depriving his kingdom of everything. Only those who had gathered in the sanctuary of St. Penryn had been spared the tidal flood that had destroyed the realm.

They walked for some distance along the shore, hidden by the huge rocks and land that formed the edge of the coast past the beach. Only at the harbor was the water deep enough to permit boats during high and low tide. Any fleet that tried to bottle in Ploemeur would end up being dashed against the rocks if it anchored too close.

Trynne's mother had taught her the magical defenses of the city multiple times. Yet Sinia had insisted on bringing both of her children to check on them one last time.

The first of the caves could only be reached during low tide. At high tide, the low entrance was submerged, concealing it from others. The jagged stone cliff was green with moss that dripped constantly as if shedding tears. Small gnats floated in the air, and the loamy smell of decaying vegetation filled Trynne's nose as they walked up the crisp sand to the cave. Gannon dashed ahead impetuously, grinning with excitement as he rushed into the dark entrance. The hissing surf came nigh to the mouth of the cave.

There were guards posted at the beach to prevent people from stealing the beads of polished glass, which were sold in pieces of jewelry. Guards patrolled it at night as well. But their purpose was not only to guard the ancient glass; they also guarded the caves along the shore.

Sinia ducked her head and followed Gannon into the cave, grazing the sharp rocks with her hand as if she were petting an animal. Trynne was shorter than her mother and barely needed to dip her chin to get past the opening. Gannon's laughter echoed through the confined darkness.

"*Le-ah-eer,*" Sinia whispered, invoking the word of power for light.

The interior of the cave began to glow. The light emanated from various stones, but the sources were hidden beneath skeins of moss and lichen. Gannon scrambled up onto a taller rock and dug his fingers through the moss to try to see it better, grinning at the magic on display.

The ground was full of sand and shells that crunched beneath their boots. It was tall enough for even Sinia to stand straight up, but the cave was pretty small. Roots from trees up on the cliffs dug into the cave, but none so deep as to penetrate the stone. Fresh water dripped from the walls, tinkling and splashing in little waterfalls to join the sand and empty into the beach.

"This is where one of you must always come," Sinia said. The words had been spoken quietly, almost in a whisper, but they echoed off the close walls of the cave, sounding firmer, more somber. Gannon's expression turned serious and he turned to face her, listening carefully. They had both heard this speech many times, but it felt more solemn now.

Sinia's eyes shone in the radiance of the glowing green moss.

"Since I was very young—your age, Gannon—I have always come to these caves to invoke the magic that protects Brythonica. We will go to each of them. It doesn't take long to come here and utter the word of power. In fact, it is sufficient to even *think* the word. These stones can hear you. As I've shown you, beneath the moss are faces carved into the rock—"

"They don't *look* like faces," Gannon interrupted.

She was not upset by it. "Not anymore, my son. We don't know who carved them, only that they are very old. The sea has rubbed away at the stone for centuries and more. Maybe one day the protections will fail because time itself has robbed them of their faces." She looked up at the walls with an air of reverence. "All it takes is a thought, and the protections are extended for another season. I have never forgotten my duty, nor lapsed in it in all the time since I was a little girl. Sometimes very small things have terribly large consequences." She bowed her head, breathing in through her nose. Then she looked up at Trynne. "I am leaving with the tide. I have never before been away from Brythonica for an entire season, but this time I might be. You both know how to extend the protections. I don't mind if Gannon does it. But Trynne, *you* need to ensure that it is done. Please do not let your other duties and responsibilities crowd your mind enough for you to forget." Sinia shook her head. "You *must* do this, Tryneowy. I give the charge to you until Gannon is of age." She reached out and ran her fingers through Gannon's hair. But her eyes were riveted on Trynne.

"I will, Mother," Trynne promised, blinking back tears.

The cave loomed above her as if it would crush her beneath its bulk. She did not want the responsibility. She did not want to be shackled for the rest of her life to Ploemeur. But neither had she made the promise lightly. She knew what was at stake.

But there was a dark part of her, a small whispering doubt as tiny as an insect, that warned her that she might not be able to fulfill her vow.

CHAPTER TEN

Upon the Feast of St. Benedick

Brythonica had long maintained a sizable navy and had standing ties with the Genevese to ship the duchy's berries to distant realms. As Trynne stood on the stone quay in Ploemeur, she watched the sailors crawling up and down the rigging of her mother's ship. It was a beautiful, solid galleon that could brave the open ocean.

Gannon was dabbing his tears on his sleeve, but there was a look of trembling courage on his face that hearkened to the man he would become. Trynne's heart was heavy as she watched Sinia speaking gently with Owen's mother and father. Morwenna had come to Ploemeur earlier to say farewell, but only family members had come to the dock. They had been gathered there for some time, and it was obvious the Genevese captain of the vessel, Captain Pyne, with his stubbled head and cheeks, was ready to leave. He kept rocking back and forth on his heels and glancing at the ship.

As soon as she finished speaking with Trynne's grandparents, Sinia lowered herself down to Gannon's level. She was smiling, trying to project confidence and motherly assurance, but Trynne saw the pain in her eyes. "Now you, little duke, must obey your grandparents and your sister while I'm away."

Gannon threw his arms around her neck and kissed her cheek. "But if *I'm* a duke, then must not *they* obey *me*?" He said it in his teasing way.

Sinia smoothed the hair from his forehead before kissing him there. "You can only have the authority of your station when you're older, *after* you've proven yourself. But remember, my son, that leading means serving. You serve the people of Westmarch. You serve Brythonica." She tugged and straightened his tunic front. "I will take so many pleasant memories with me on my journey. You are a wonderful son, and I love you with all my heart."

"I feel sorry for Trynne, then," replied Gannon with a grin. "There's none left for her!"

Trynne arched her brow at him, but his smiles were infectious.

"There is room in my heart for both of you," Sinia said, tapping his nose. She hugged him fiercely then, squeezing her eyes shut with such a look of pain that Trynne's throat caught.

Brushing away a tear, Sinia rose and came to Trynne. They hugged each other, saying nothing. Trynne felt the warmth of her mother's breath against her hair. For so long she had worried she'd disappointed her mother by not becoming a Wizr, and the secrets the Fountain had bid her to keep had created a gulf between them.

The biggest of those secrets was the one that Fallon now knew—that Trynne was the Painted Knight. Rumors abounded about the knight, about *Trynne*, as the Gauntlet of Kingfountain loomed nearer. The legends were vastly different than the truth, each story growing grander as it was passed along. Someone had seen the Painted Knight in Atabyrion defeating twelve men at once. Some said the Painted Knight was a ghost from the drowned kingdom of Leoneyis. Others said his face was painted because a poisoner from Pisan was trying to kill him. Each tale was a fabrication, but that did not stop them from spreading like wildfire. Everyone expected the Painted Knight to come and compete against the best knights of the realm.

She wanted to tell her mother before she left, but the Fountain had told her it was not yet time.

"Trynne," Sinia said, pulling away from the hug. She stanched tears on her sleeve cuff. "The king will still need you. I know that he will. There are dark days ahead for him. This war with Gahalatine will test his mettle, his confidence, and his will to rule. I know that you will need to go to Kingfountain. I just ask that you make sure Brythonica is watched over. Owen's father is a wise man and has served me for many, many years. He must play the role of father to his grandchild." She sighed, looking down. "It is so difficult for me to leave you and Gannon. It will take courage to find the Deep Fathoms. Or the land of Fusang, as the Oasis princess described it to you. It goes by many names. It calls to me still." She looked out toward the sea, her expression suddenly distant, as if she heard a voice at that very moment.

"I'm glad you chose Captain Pyne," Trynne said. "He's one of the best sea captains in Genevar."

Sinia nodded, then pressed a kiss on Trynne's cheek. "I love you, Tryneowy Kiskaddon. You have not been a disappointment to me. I love you with a mother's heart. Nothing can change that, no matter what choices you make. The Fountain has work for you to do." She smiled tenderly. "I don't know what it is, for the Fountain has not revealed it to me. But I sense its importance. You are my greatest treasure."

Her words made Trynne's heart shudder and tears spill from her eyes. They embraced again, holding each other tightly.

"Ahem," Captain Pyne murmured, coughing into his fist. "The *tide*, my lady."

Sinia ignored him, holding Trynne and stroking her hair while she wept, but she finally stepped away. It hurt to watch as the captain escorted Sinia up the gangplank. There were sailors and servants, archers and knights, all wearing white tabards decorated with the Raven badge of her mother's house. There were ravens in the rigging, she noticed, birds that would go out to sea with the ship. Trynne felt a hand on her shoulder and noticed her grandmother had sidled up next to her. The tears in the older woman's eyes reminded her that she was not alone in her grief. Hugging her grandmother, Trynne watched as the boat left the pier, the wind filling the small sails as the captain barked orders.

It grew smaller and smaller until it was gone.

◆　◆　◆

The feast day of St. Benedick had finally arrived, and Trynne was at once nervous and excited to spend the afternoon with Elwis Asturias in Marq. Her mother's ship had been gone for nearly a fortnight, and the palace at Ploemeur had already begun to feel like a prison. Trynne still started each morning at the training yard in Averanche before bathing and changing into a gown and returning to Ploemeur in time for breakfast. She had never been more thankful for the ability to use the ley lines to travel.

Today, she wore the gown she had purchased with Captain Staeli on the trip they'd made to Marq. Her stomach was full of butterflies as she stared at herself in the mirror, making sure the lacings were all fastened and tidy. The white blouse was bunched together with garters at the upper arms, elbows, and wrists. The black velvet hat with the silver edging was still waiting at the table. It wasn't fashionable to wear such hats in Brythonica, so Trynne hadn't put it on yet. She had enjoyed strolling the city and seeing the canals and gondolas. What would it be like to ride in one with Elwis handling the oars? Her stomach did a little turn.

It occurred to her that they would both be competing at the Gauntlet of Kingfountain shortly afterward. She and the Oath Maidens had been preparing for the event for months. Would she be able to reveal herself at last? She smiled at her reflection in the mirror, but the crooked part of it seemed to mock her.

It was in this very room that Dragan had attacked her.

Just thinking about her father's enemy kindled a dark, evil feeling in her heart—along with the fear she had long sought to control. She was no longer a helpless child. She remembered sensing Dragan in the room that day. He had the uncanny gift of being able to turn invisible. Well, she knew the word of power that could expose him. And he knew that she *could*. The last time she had seen him was on her first, fateful trip to Marq. She wondered, darkly, not for the first time, if he had been involved in her father's disappearance.

A rap at the door startled her, making her heart quicken with a spasm of dread.

"Enter," she called, fussing over her skirts once again, feeling herself hideous and unworthy of any man's love.

The door opened and Benjamin entered.

"My lady, there's a messenger here from Brugia. A captain by the name of Abinante. He says he bears a message from Grand Duke Elwis that he's to deliver to your hand alone."

Trynne pursed her lips. "Is he with you?"

"He is waiting in the solar, my lady."

"You can bring him here," Trynne said.

Benjamin nodded and quickly departed. A moment later, the door opened and Gannon came in with their grandmother.

"It's time to go to the House of Pillars," Gannon said, holding their grandmother's hand and swinging it eagerly. "Are you coming with us? Grandpapa has the carriage ready."

Trynne shook her head. "I have a messenger from Brugia to see first. Why don't you go ahead and I will meet you down there. I'll probably get there before you will."

"Very well," Grandmother said, tugging at Gannon's hand. She shot Trynne a conspiring look. "You are leaving for Brugia at noon, my dear?"

Trynne nodded, but she could barely pay attention—her heart was thumping as she considered what news the messenger might have brought. Her family left, and shortly thereafter Benjamin returned with a tall, barrel-chested man who was bald and bore earrings. With a crinkled white collar that fanned out at the throat, his outfit was distinctly Brugian. The fabrics were of the very best quality, she noticed, and he wore a sword at his side. Still, it was the medallion around his neck that caught her attention most. She'd seen that kind before, a circle with several rays shining from it. Gahalatine had worn something similar, and the sight of it put her immediately on her guard.

"Captain Abinante," Benjamin said with a bow, but he did not leave.

"Lady Tryneowy," the captain said with a gregarious smile, "it is a pleasure to meet you. I believe that was your younger brother I passed on my way in?"

"It was," Trynne said, feeling her anxiety grow.

"A charming lad. I have been in Ploemeur for two days, my lady, and will leave with the turning of the tide today. I have served House Asturias for many years. My lady, the grand duke is a changed man, and I attribute that to your influence and his father's untimely demise. He is one of the most determined men I know. None of this has he commanded me to say." He smiled in chagrin. "I just wanted to speak his praises myself. He gave me this note, fixed with his seal, to deliver to you on the morning of the Feast of St. Benedick. I don't know what it contains, but I have discharged my duty." He withdrew a folded and sealed note from his wide belt, offered it to her, and bowed with a flourish.

Trynne accepted it graciously. "Thank you for taking the trouble, Captain."

"It was no trouble at all, my lady," he said with a smile. "I hope you will grace our fair kingdom soon with your presence. Good day to you." He bowed again and departed. Benjamin escorted him to the doorway and out, but paused and looked back at Trynne as she examined the letter addressed to "My Lady" in an elegant hand.

She wondered if the letter were from Elwis at all. Poisoners were deceitful people, capable of anything. She opened herself to her magic, letting it test the paper, the seal, and the contents for signs of danger. There were none, which relieved her, but the dread she'd felt earlier, from the mere memory of Dragan, lingered. Her heart began to beat faster and she was overcome by the sudden urge to flee. Determined to face her terror with courage, she walked calmly and deliberately to the balcony and stepped outside into the fresh air.

There was a wall of fog out at sea, but it had not come ashore today. The air was flavored with eucalyptus and salt. Standing at the balcony edge, she suddenly felt vulnerable. The cliff down to the city below was sharp from her vantage point. She heard the jangle and clack of the carriage carrying her brother and grandparents as the horses started down the road leading to the House of Pillars, the place of judgment in Ploemeur, which her mother had long presided over.

To dispel her nervousness, she broke the wax seal and carefully unfolded the paper. The breeze tousled her hair as she leaned back against the railing and read the short message.

My Lady Trynne,
If my messenger has found you, then you are reading this on the morning of the Feast of St. Benedick. I will be awaiting you at the sanctuary of Our Lady of Marq. I have no expectations of you. I am filled with gratitude that you condescended to meet me. I would be lying if I said I was not looking forward to showing you the wonders of this great city where I spent much of my childhood. There is a beautiful fountain amidst the waterways that I am most eager to share. I think you will like it. I pray to the Fountain this will not be our only opportunity to grow better acquainted.
With great respect,
Elwis

Trynne blinked, feeling a rush of relief. Elwis had calmed her worries about the visit in one simple note. There were little clues throughout his message that his feelings for her were deeper than he'd expressed them to be. But he was determined to woo cautiously and allow her behavior to guide him. So unlike the daft nobles who had pressed for interviews with her in Averanche.

She read the letter again quickly, admiring the steady hand and penmanship. Had he copied the letter several times to get it right? She assumed he had not delegated the writing of such an intimate matter to one of his scribes.

It made her smile, and she pushed away from the railing and turned to look over the city once more. A sunrise in Averanche. A sunset in Marq. She was so grateful to have the ability to traverse the kingdom in a mere moment. It would be a memorable day, an opportunity that would not come again now that the threat of war was on the horizon.

There was a cracking noise in the distance, followed immediately by the screams of horses. Trynne's heart lurched as her eyes went to the source. A plume of dust churned into the air, and she watched in horror as the carriage carrying her brother skidded off the side of the mountain, dragging the terrified horses with it.

CHAPTER ELEVEN

Mortain Falls

There were no majestic, towering waterfalls in Brythonica. But Mortain Falls was just on the outskirts of Ploemeur, nestled in one of the beautiful hunting woods preserved by the house of Montfort. It was forbidden to hunt in the woods except by leave of the duchess. The falls were a series of steplike rocks, full of moss and fern, down which water fell steadily, radiating a comforting sound. Part of the stream was diverted around a larger outcropping, breaking the falls into two, around a cluster of fern and gorse. An ivy-covered shrine dedicated to Our Lady sat at the head of the falls, but there was a wooden deck built lower in the grotto that permitted visitors to come and throw coins into the water. Tarnished coins sparkled in the depths.

Mortain Falls was where the bodies of the dead rulers of Brythonica were sent to rest in the Deep Fathoms. The woods were thick and teeming with life, but the birds sounded less exuberant than usual as they observed the silent throng assembled at the falls.

Trynne stood in mute agony, wearing a black gown and a matching veil. The small canoe bearing her brother, Gannon, was carried by pallbearers. The body was covered in blankets to conceal the injuries that had inflicted his death. Sometimes it felt like a nightmare. If only she could pinch herself awake. She was broken to pieces inside, a boulder that had fallen off a cliff and shattered on the rocks below. Her grief came in waves that left her drowning. She clung to the rites of the Fountain for comfort as she assumed the roles she had inherited from both her parents. She had two vast realms to rule because there was no one else.

The pallbearers stood at the edge of the wooden platform, overlooking the small pool that emptied into a stream that would carry the body away. They stood silently, awaiting her orders. A nod was all it required. But she could not bring herself to give it.

She clung to a desperate hope that the Fountain would intervene, that one of her parents would arrive at the last instant, sent by the Fountain to speak the word of power that could revive Gannon. Trynne knew the word just as they did, but her mother had taught her never to use it against the Fountain's will. It wouldn't work, and the effort would likely kill her. In her grief, she had nearly risked it. She had waited to fulfill the funeral rite for two full days, hoping the Fountain would send her the message she so desperately wanted to receive. Hoping that someone or something would intervene.

She could still feel the Fountain magic. It offered a measure of solace in her darkest hours. But it did not grant her deepest desire.

Her eyes were sore from crying. She felt hollow. Her father's eldest brother, Gannon's namesake, had been strapped to a canoe and executed by waterfall following the Battle of Ambion Hill years before. It felt as if that horrible legacy had come full circle.

Trynne's grandparents had also both died in the accident. Their bodies were being taken to Westmarch to be mourned after by the people who had once honored them as rulers.

The carriage had been demolished in the fall, but there was evidence that someone had tampered with the rear wheel. Trynne had not been the only horrified witness. Many people had watched the carriage plummet off the downward descent as it was making a turn. The momentum had carried it over the edge, and the weight had pulled the horses with it. Her mind instantly went to the thief Dragan. Had he sabotaged the wagon? Was he still intent on punishing her house in another act of grim revenge? Oh, if only she had caught him that day in Marq. She hoped she never saw him again. She was afraid if she did that she would violate one of the five oaths she had sworn.

The pallbearers grew restless, but none of them dared look her in the eye. The stillness of the grove was impressive. A few insects clicked, and a snatch of birdsong sounded through the trees. Trynne approached the canoe bier one last time. Her mind flashed to the thought of facing her mother someday. The idea filled her with misery. She reached out and laid her hand on the foot of the bundle. She could see where his nose pressed against the fabric. She would have gladly given her life to summon his back. In her mind, she pleaded with the Fountain, begging it to take her instead.

She waited, listening to the silence, tears gathering in her stricken eyes. *All will be well in the end. You are needed here.*

The thought in her mind was so soft, so fleeting, she wondered if it were her imagination. The thought brought a measure of comfort, but it was so small compared to the vastness of her grief. She stroked the blanket tenderly and walked around to the head of the canoe. Bending down, she pressed a gentle kiss where his forehead was.

"Go in peace," Trynne whispered, her voice choking on the words. She stood back and nodded to the pallbearers. It was the hardest thing she had ever done.

The pallbearers climbed down the wooden steps leading to the edge of the platform and gently set the canoe onto the water of the pool. With its feathery tendrils of water, its verdant smell, and its lush greenery, Mortain Falls cast an idyllic scene. This was a gentle place, much more appropriate for her gentle brother than the violent rushing of a massive waterfall.

Thierry approached her as she watched the current drag the canoe away. He had doted on Gannon more than her. But the look of anguish in his eyes was tempered by pity.

He stood next to her, hands clasped behind his back, his gray hair combed forward in the Occitanian fashion. "I stood nearby when Lady Sinia watched her father put her mother to rest in the Fountain." His composure started to waver. "And I was there when Lady Sinia did the same for him, the grandfather you never knew. This peaceful grove has seen its share of sorrows, child. It is fitting and proper that we should weep for the loss of those who die. It hurts because we loved them so much." He sniffed, trying to maintain his composure. "I loved that little boy. It was not your fault, Lady Trynne. I will do everything in my power to continue to serve the Montfort line. *You* are the last of that line. You are the only thing standing between Brythonica and annihilation. Take care of yourself. We look to you as our savior."

Trynne already felt the awful weight of that burden. She turned her head slightly. "I will do my best to deserve that trust."

Thierry nodded, rocking backward on his heels. "Lady Sinia told me of her vision. That you will soon marry."

She turned to him, startled. "Soon?" she asked with an edge of panic in her voice.

Thierry nodded. "Praise the Fountain," he said, then kissed the edge of his forefinger. "Would you like to be alone for a while?"

"Yes, Thierry. Send the others back to the castle."

She gazed up at the ivy-covered shrine to Our Lady—a stone arch suspended over the waters—and then, making her decision, took the small side trail leading up to it. The falls looked almost like white bridal veils. She ascended the path slowly, climbing the rocky steps. The ferns brushed against her skirts, and she parted some of the taller ones with her hand in order to pass. As she crested the top of the hill, she saw the stream that fed the falls.

Walking around the little shrine, she ran her fingers through the tangled ivy, feeling the waxy petals glide against her fingers. Grief came in waves. It was subsiding, but she knew it would swell again.

As she circled around the back of the shrine, she saw someone standing at the edge of the pool below her. Someone who hadn't left with the others.

Her breath stopped when she recognized that it was Fallon Llewellyn. He was dressed all in black, looking almost like Severn Argentine. He was staring up at her, his expression full of sympathy. After their eyes met, he began to ascend the steps, taking them two at a time with his long stride.

He was before her in a moment, up near the shrine. His face showed the torture of his emotions. He was suffering deeply, and it moved her.

"How are you even here?" she asked him, shaking her head in confusion. "Morwenna?"

Fallon shook his head no. "I came as soon as I heard. I was in Blackpool, so I took the first available ship."

"But how did you hear so quickly?" she asked him.

His lips pressed together. "I have a man in Ploemeur," he said softly.

Trynne bristled with anger. "The Espion are only permitted as messengers," she said.

He shook his head, and she could see him grow defensive. "He's not part of the Espion, Trynne," he said, holding up his hands. "I grew up here, remember? There are people in Ploemeur who still remember me as a boy." He licked his lips. "He knew that I would want to know about Gannon's death, so he sent me word." His voice was thick. "I'm so sorry, Trynne. I can't imagine how you're feeling. I just wanted to . . . I wanted to comfort you. I knew you'd be hurting."

It was exactly what she needed to hear. She rushed to him and buried her face against his chest, wrapping her arms around his waist. He hugged her back fiercely, protectively, holding her and swaying until it felt like she was floating. Another swell of grief started to build, coming at her with all the intensity of a tidal wave.

"Oh no, oh no," she started to wail as the feelings slammed into her. She sobbed against him, her shoulders shaking, squeezing him so hard, digging her fingers into his tunic, clinging to him as if he were driftwood and she were drowning. She couldn't breathe, the veil was stifling her, and she yanked it away.

"I'm so sorry," he murmured, stroking her hair. His presence was such a comfort, and she was grateful she did not have to stand against these crushing waves all alone. His chest felt so warm, his hands gentle and soothing. She wished deeply that it could be some other way, that *he* could have been hers.

The pain started to recede, much sooner than it had in the recent past. Fallon had helped lighten the burden. Squeezing her eyes shut, she listened to the murmur of the waterfall, and then she heard the even softer sound of his heart beating.

"Thank you for coming, Fallon," she said, her voice raw. She clung to him, nestled close, enjoying the feel of his arms around her shoulders. She felt as weak as a newborn puppy.

"I'll take you back," he said, patting her shoulder. "We shouldn't be alone like this. I have my reputation to maintain, you know."

She laughed softly, though the sound was thick with tears. He always could make her laugh. "Thank you for considering *your* reputation." She craned her neck, looking up at him. He was the most handsome man in the world to her.

"What?" he asked, seeing her expression but not understanding it.

"Thank you, Fallon. Thank you for being here." She hooked her hand around his neck, pulled him down, and gave him a kiss on the cheek.

It was obvious he was a little startled by that, but he gave her one of his appreciative smiles. With her arm still around his waist, they walked together down the rocky steps leading to the base of the falls.

"Is the Painted Knight coming to the Gauntlet of Kingfountain?" he asked as they maneuvered down, side by side.

Trynne felt a shudder ripple through her. She knew she couldn't leave.

"She can't," Trynne whispered darkly.

PART II

Knights

CHAPTER TWELVE

Genevar

Trynne sat facing Fallon across the Wizr board. They were in the solar of the castle in Ploemeur, sitting on two wooden chairs in companionable silence. She cast surreptitious glances at him as he brooded over the board, deep in thought. It was her father's set, the one King Severn had given him as a child.

He reached out his hand, took a deconeus piece, and moved it diagonally to block a move she had been preparing to make. His interception abruptly ruined her plan. His abilities in the game had increased over the years. In their youth, he had played impatiently, often making quick errors that she had exploited to her advantage.

His arrival in Ploemeur had been a source of much-needed comfort to her. It did not change the terribleness of the situation, but it did soothe part of her misery. He leaned back in the chair, waiting patiently for her to make her next move.

"Are you going to take a ship to Kingfountain for the Gauntlet?" she asked him. "It's in three days."

Fallon rubbed his chin and then shook his head. "No, I'll be riding directly. I think an overland route is safer, considering Gahalatine's fleet is still at sea. Chandigarl may be to the east, but that doesn't mean he can't strike from the west." He sniffed, stroking his upper lip. "I've seen some of the latest Espion maps that Kevan commissioned. Our world is like this fruit," he said, leaning over to a nearby table and snatching up a large orange. He rubbed his thumb across the peel and slowly rotated it with his wrist. "The Genevese sail to many foreign ports. I think they know much more about Chandigarl than they are letting on." He wagged his eyebrows at her. "It's your move."

She had already planned her next three and adjusted one of her pawns forward to begin her attack.

"Genevar has been a trading nation for centuries," Trynne said. "They go to great lengths to keep their secrets."

"Who can blame them?" Fallon replied with a snort. "Without their ships moving things back and forth across the seas, we'd all starve. Well, except for Brythonica. You'd survive on your berries, but only just. That was a good move. I see what you're trying to do."

"Do you now?" Trynne asked in a teasing voice. *You can't get used to this*, the voice in her head reminded her, *he's not yours to keep.*

"Yes, it's as obvious as the sunrise. Your plan won't work."

"I think you are just trying to trick me into revealing something."

He smirked. "You've already given yourself away." Then the smirk faded into a sweet smile as he glanced around the room. "I have so many fond memories of this place. Hiding in the larder to sneak fresh-baked tarts. Watching your father stare at the fireplace. Finding your mother's shoes in odd places."

They were both quiet for a moment, lost in thought about how things used to be, and then Fallon heaved a sigh. "I should leave. This game could last awhile and I'm tempted to linger." He leaned forward, planting his elbows on his knees. "If there were some way I could take this pain from you, I would. My sister is preparing to flee to the sanctuary of Our Lady, trusting in the integrity of a foreign emperor to protect her and my niece. I'm not certain we can trust Gahalatine's integrity. If he had any, he would not have attacked us in the first place."

"He did call off the attack at the Battle of Guilme after what happened to my father," she reminded him. "How many battle commanders would have done the same?"

"None that I've ever read about," Fallon said with a chuckle. "But his ambition defies all belief. He's determined to conquer the world. What happens after he does? Have you ever heard the tale of Prince Jeffrey? It's one of the stories from King Andrew's time."

Trynne wrinkled her brow and then shook her head. "I don't think I've heard that one."

"Really?" Fallon said in surprise. "It's about the brother of the King of Bremen. The king's brother was made chancellor after his brother was crowned, and he was given the keys of the treasury. I think he was Fountain-blessed at spending other people's money," he added with a grin. "The treasury was depleted and taxes were constantly being raised because Prince Jeffrey could not stop spending. The royal harbor was full of boats that were never used. The stables full of horses that were never ridden. The paddocks full of carriages. The prince bought and he bought until the king finally had to remove him from office because the people were rebelling. The horses and boats and carriages were sold at a fraction of their value." Fallon chuckled to himself. "What a debacle."

Trynne laced her fingers together. "That's why he made it into a book, though. If the prince had been a responsible chancellor, there would have been no story to tell."

"I heard that story from my mother," Fallon said, his voice becoming softer. "While she's always loved a juicy tale, the lesson she took from it was that greed is a hunger that will never be satisfied." He was still leaning forward, his eyes finding hers. "She shared that story with me after I returned to Edonburick after our last . . . conversation in *our* garden. Mother said my hunger to be recognized and appreciated was like Prince Jeffrey's greed. It would never be satisfied. So why should I be surprised that others saw in me what I was blind to? Mothers have an interesting way of rebuking wayward children, but they do it so

nicely that you have to forgive them. Even better, learn from them."
He breathed out a long sigh. "I have learned a great deal since that
day, Trynne. I want to thank you for speaking the truth, even though
I wasn't ready to hear it." He paused, judging his next words carefully.
"My mother—and *you*—are very wise. I still wish to earn your father's
seat at the Ring Table. But only because I too would sacrifice my life
for the king's."

The door of the solar opened and Thierry entered, walking up to
her briskly. He gave Fallon a weighing look.

"My lady, I've just spoken to a ship captain from Genevar. He has
news from your mother."

Trynne quickly rose, her heart fluttering in her chest. Her worried
look prompted Thierry to continue. "My lady, the captain encountered your mother's ship in the open seas. He hastened to Ploemeur
after unloading his cargo in Genevar to share the news. Firstly, that
he did encounter her ship. He had not heard of her departure and was
surprised to find her so far from Brythonica. Secondly, he warned her
that he had encountered an enormous fleet at anchor in the Myristican
Islands and had discovered, while trading there, that they were preparing to sail toward our shores. The captain feared your mother's ship
would encounter them. He also wanted to hasten here to warn us to
prepare in case they strike at Legault or Brythonica."

Fallon rose instantly, his expression grave. "Attacking from the west,
not the east," he said, nodding his head. "This is timely news."

"Indeed," Thierry said, his head bobbing in agreement. "I can have
the captain brought if you would like to speak with him yourself."

"I would," Trynne said, also rising. "Fallon, I can take you to
Kingfountain. The king must be told at once."

His eyebrows wrinkled. "Thank you for offering, but there's no
need. I will ride to Kingfountain straightaway."

"But I can bring you and return instantly."

"You are needed here, Trynne. I can be there in three days. If Gahalatine attacks Ploemeur, I will come to your aid. North Cumbria is ready to defend our shores."

"I know you will," Trynne said. She reached out and took his hand, squeezing it. It was a little strange that he'd refused her twice, but she didn't wish to question him. There'd been too many misunderstandings between them.

He stared down at their hands, his mouth twitching as he wrestled with his feelings. "I must go."

If Thierry hadn't been standing there, she would have hugged Fallon good-bye. Her heart was still at war with her destiny, now more than ever. Fallon squeezed her hand and then rushed from the room. The moment he left, the emptiness of the room was palpable to her. She decided to leave the Wizr board untouched.

◆　◆　◆

It wasn't even dusk, yet Trynne was wearied by the day's labors. The sudden news about Gahalatine's fleet heading toward their shores had given her a new purpose, a distraction from the anguish of her brother's and grandparents' deaths. Knowing the massive fleet could easily blockade Ploemeur, she had ordered the Brythonican navy to set up a defensive ring around the coast and to keep watch for approaching vessels. There was enough food to withstand a siege, and the castle was full of defenders armed with bows in preparation for an enemy that could fly up to its walls. She was considering sending for Captain Staeli when Thierry arrived with news that he had come of his own accord.

"Please, bring him to me!" she said. She had been studying maps in her mother's library, but she cleared some space on the table.

Captain Staeli arrived, looking like the soldier he was at heart, his cloak and tunic begrimed from the journey, his boots scuffed and weather-beaten. He stood in the doorway a moment, wringing the leather hood in his hands. His beard was mussed, his balding head spotted with sweat. He looked grief-stricken, and she realized that he had come after hearing the news of Gannon's death. He was not a talkative man by nature, but he cared for her like a daughter. His lip twitched as the silence deepened between them.

"I am so glad you came," Trynne said, coming around the table.

He stuffed the hood into his belt. His eyes were fierce. "I only heard the news yesterday," he said, then sniffed. "Mariette is in charge while I'm gone. She's a clever one, that lass." He gave her a small smile. "Rani Reya's not far behind her. She's forged these strange hooklike swords. Very unnatural way to make a blade."

Trynne laughed. "Yes, compared to our ways," she agreed. She reached out and gripped his hands. "Thank you for coming. We're about to be invaded, I think. Death has struck my family. I could use a friend at the moment."

Staeli's cheeks reddened at her words. "I've watched over you since you were a wee lass," he said. "If Dragan has done this ill deed, as I suspect he has, then I will bring him to justice." He sniffed. "I swear it by the Fountain." The smoldering rage in his eyes was frightening—or it would have been had it been directed at her.

"I must bear the loss as best I can," Trynne said. "But I would caution you against seeking revenge. I need you to help me fight a war, my friend." She went to the table and pulled him with her. Unfurling one of the maps, she pointed along the coast. "I've ordered the fleet to patrol these waters. I've set up riders to relay messages back to the king along the main roads here, and also here to alert Occitania. Westmarch is close and can be ready quickly to come to our aid. So can the army of Pree. Fallon said that Dundrennan will come, but that's much farther away." Her finger glided to that spot on the map, her heart tightening at the thought.

"Duke Fallon means well," Staeli said with a nod. "I encountered him and his hunter on the way here."

Trynne looked up from the map, her nose wrinkling. "He was alone."

Staeli sniffed, shaking his head. "No, he was with a hunter from Dundrennan. I recognized the lad, although he's older now. I fought with your father and Captain Ashby at the battle that deposed Severn Argentine. The lad is in his thirties now, a man grown. Carrick. He's Fountain-blessed. The lad is famous for his tracking."

A feeling of dread opened inside Trynne's chest. Both she and the captain knew what mission had brought Carrick to Brythonica in the past. He had been sent to search the grove where her father had disappeared—to no avail.

"Where did you see them?" she asked, her voice suddenly hoarse.

"They were leaving the road that cuts through the woods with the grove," Staeli said, folding his arms. "I take it they didn't have your permission to be there."

Unfolding his arms, he stretched out his hand and tapped his finger on the forest that held the magic bowl and the stone altar. It was labeled as a royal hunting wood on the map. There was no other marking to give it significance, but of course the captain didn't need to be told. Her father had assigned him to be protector of Brythonica—and the grove—should anything happen to him. While she didn't like to think of it, the captain wore the ring that went with the station.

The one that had been found on her father's severed hand.

◆ ◆ ◆

I must get away from this prison. The man with the silver mask's body is crumpled on the floor. I did not intend to overpower him, but the thought came to me so forcefully, especially when he used an artifact of magic on me. I felt its power emanating from him like a storm. He was frantic, muttering something about the need to move me in the next few days. The dungeon where I'm being kept is about to be overrun. I must be moved and moved quickly. He tried to use his power to make me submissive and afraid. But it could not affect me. It was strange, because I felt its force and understood his intent, but it did not compel me to do his bidding. The jailor had left us alone together.

When he saw his power did not move me, the man in the mask grew frightened of me. How did I know? The mask hid his expression. It's just that I knew his weakness, knew that he was intimidated by me. So I struck him with the chains. He crumpled to the floor. If I could remove these chains, I could take his silver mask and cloak and make him wear my meager clothing and mask. The jailor wouldn't know that he was being deceived. It might give me a chance to escape, to find help from whoever is coming. The jailor has the keys. How can I remove them?

There was a whisper. A single word. The chains have opened. But there is no one else here with me.

◆ ◆ ◆

CHAPTER THIRTEEN

The Breaking

It was the day of the Gauntlet of Kingfountain and Trynne longed with all her heart to be there. But she knew it was the Fountain's will that she remain behind. She didn't understand it, but she accepted it. She gazed out the window of the solar, ignoring the plate of food that had been set before her as the evening meal. She'd lost her appetite completely after the carriage crash. Every mouthful was difficult, and she found herself doing little more than picking at the plates set before her.

One of the reasons she wanted to be at Kingfountain was to confront Fallon, to demand to know why he had spied on the sacred grove of Brythonica. After Captain Staeli had told her of their encounter, she had traveled to the grove through the ley lines. The silver dish, which she'd feared would be missing, was chained to the marble slab. The stone table was littered with detritus from the oak tree. She had searched the entire grove, including the cave set into the boulders where Myrddin had been trapped for centuries. But there was no evidence that either Fallon or Carrick had removed anything. Still, the intrusion had once again damaged her confidence in him.

She had since received letters of condolence from the king and queen, written personally by them and not by scribes. She recognized their handwriting and appreciated the comforting words. There was also a note from Morwenna, expressing her deepest sympathies and shared grief. She wrote about how fond she'd always been of the little one and how she knew Trynne must be suffering.

Gazing out the window, Trynne stared at the wall of sea fog out in the harbor past the beach of sea glass. This was not unusual in Brythonica. The rich sea mists regularly flowed inland and helped provide moisture for the thriving plants in the fields. But something about it reminded her of the night her father had disappeared, the night of the Battle of Guilme, and a feeling of nervous agitation grew inside her. She sent for Thierry.

He arrived, looking wearied by his duties, and his face fell further, if that were possible, when he saw her nearly full plate. "My lady, you *must* eat!" he implored.

"I will, Thierry. I want you to make sure the night watch is vigilant tonight. It looks like there will be fog."

Thierry nodded. "Fog is a good thing. The shores of Brythonica are deadly to seamen who are unfamiliar with them. If you get caught in the wrong tide, a ship will crash on the rocks."

Trynne was not comforted by his words. "I have no doubt that our enemies have extensive maps of our coastline. They may have even gotten the tide schedules from the Genevese."

"Genevar would never betray us!"

"Not willingly, perhaps. In the House of Pillars this morning, it was reported that no vessels from Genevar have landed in Ploemeur in the last two days. Did any arrive today?"

Thierry looked at her blankly. "I don't know."

"When you give the order for the night watch, please see if you can find out."

"As you will, my lady. Please . . . eat some food." He said it with a look of worried tenderness.

Trynne nodded, but she rose from the table as soon as he left and paced by the window, watching the wall of fog. It would mute a dazzling sunset. She went back and took a morsel of bread and slowly bit into it, forcing herself. Then she opened the balcony window and stepped out, feeling the chill of the sea breeze cut through her gown.

Had the Gauntlet been completed yet? Who had won? Part of her wanted Fallon to win the role he coveted so much. Part of her hoped one of the Oath Maidens like Mariette had claimed it instead, just to spite him. The sun was probably setting over Kingfountain at that very moment. Should she steal away through the ley lines just to find out the news?

A heavy, strangling feeling followed the thought. It felt wrong—very wrong. Trynne frowned, folding her arms and leaning against the door frame, and shivered.

And that was when she saw the first row of ships emerging in a line from the bank of fog.

◆　◆　◆

The main hall of the palace in Ploemeur was thronged with people. The citizenry who lived down below were hunkered in their homes, doors bolted. They were all praying to Our Lady to save them from the invasion that had started on the very eve that King Drew had named his new champion.

Gahalatine was striking Brythonica first. As soon as the ships had been sighted, messengers had rushed eastward to deliver the ill tidings. It was up to Trynne to protect her people, and she felt frightened for them, for her realm, and for herself. Her battle captains had gathered, as well as the captain of the night watch. Her herald stood by listening. There were so many ships sailing toward them, Trynne suspected the first part of the battle would happen on the beaches. She was not going to sit still. As soon as the meeting was finished, she intended to garb herself in armor and fight for her duchy as the Painted Knight.

"My lady, our scouts have counted a massive squadron," the navy commander said. "They are not concealing their approach. There are six treasure ships and over a hundred support vessels. They are coming en masse!"

"And why did we have no warning?" Trynne said angrily. "I thought our fleet had encircled the area to give us advance word?"

The commander looked stricken. "I can only surmise that our defenses were insufficient. They are coming in with the night tide. They could not have chosen a more advantageous moment to attack."

"Of course not," Trynne said, thinking of Gahalatine's cocksure expression when he had launched his attack on the oasis. Was he part of this attack? Would she have to face him sword to sword?

"This squadron is only a portion of Gahalatine's fleet," Trynne said next, shaking her head. "He has many more ships than this, enough to attack our entire coast. This is only the first wave. I am certain of that." Her stomach twisted with worry. "Keep the citizens indoors. I do not think they will be harmed if they stay away from the fighting. I will not surrender Ploemeur without a contest. Send word to Pree and see how soon they can send soldiers to relieve us."

"Aye, my lady," replied her herald, Farnes.

A commotion erupted from the hall as the doorway was thrust open. "The castle! They're in the castle!" a serving girl shrieked in panic.

"What? How?" barked one of the captains. "Where are they?"

"They came from the chapel," the girl said through her sobs.

The sound of weapons and clanging armor lit up the corridor.

Benjamin grabbed Trynne's arm. "My lady, you must flee!"

She shook herself free. "I will not abandon Ploemeur so quickly. Bring me my swords."

He stared at her incredulously. "My lady?"

"They're in my chamber. Now hurry!"

Her mother's aging battle captain, Marshal Soeur, ordered the guard to assemble at the door and shut it. He drew his heavy greatsword while they rushed to obey, but the doors were flung back when they tried to close them.

The noise of metal scraping against stone filtered in from the hall, the grinding shriek of it stinging their ears. Four of the soldiers at the door skidded into pillars, as if slung by giants. None of them got up. Trynne felt a building tide of Fountain magic from beyond the corridor. More soldiers ran forward to help their fallen comrades. Their boots thumped against the tile floor, and Trynne watched in shock as all of them suddenly flew sideways into the nearest wall, brushed aside by invisible arms.

Three men strode down the corridor toward the audience hall. All three were Wizrs, and Trynne recognized the first among them. It was the Wizr Rucrius, who had almost destroyed Kingfountain by diverting its mighty river.

A tall man with very long pale hair and dark eyebrows, he wore an elegantly braided tunic that went down to his knees. An equally extravagant sword was belted to his waist. As he walked toward her, she noticed that the staff he clutched had a nick in it from where her father had attacked him with his sword. Rucrius looked confident and smug as he passed the fallen soldiers. One of the men tried to reach out and intercede, but he lacked the strength to rise.

As he approached, Trynne noticed that his eyes were glowing like a cat's, reflecting the light of the palace's lamps and torches. She shifted her gaze to the other Wizrs, whom she did not recognize. One had a black beard streaked with gray and a bald head. He had a menacing look. The third Wizr was younger, in his thirties perhaps. Clean-shaven like Rucrius, he wore very costly apparel with medallions and bracelets and a turban-like hat sewn with pearls.

Benjamin had rushed out the side door toward her chambers and had not yet returned. Another group of soldiers, including the aging marshal, yelled in challenge and rushed at the Wizrs.

Rucrius gave them a look of disdain as he began to whirl his staff. When it struck the first soldier, the man flipped over and struck the tile floor hard. Rucrius was a skilled warrior, and he used his weapon to clear away anyone who dared engage him. The other two Wizrs put their fingertips together and began muttering words of power.

Trynne sensed the ley lines knotting together and realized that they had come for her—they were trying to prevent her or anyone else who was Fountain-blessed from escaping.

The Brythonicans would not give up their daughter without a fight. More soldiers came forward to defend Trynne, who was momentarily stunned—she'd never done battle with one Wizr before, let alone three—and uncertain what to do. Rucrius extended his palm at the aging marshal, who suddenly froze, unable to swing his sword. He stood there, his muscles bulging, his eyes wide with terror as he was forced to hold his sword suspended over his head, unmoving.

Rucrius smirked at the older man as he passed him, closing the gap to Trynne even as more soldiers continued to charge at him. She could not believe this was happening. Then she saw Benjamin rush into the room, holding her twin swords.

"Enough of this foolishness!" Rucrius snapped impatiently. He brought his staff down on the tiles hard and the floor jolted. A huge crack split the floor from one end of the hall to the other, and the earth bucked, knocking everyone to the ground except for Trynne and the three Wizrs. She felt the magic from the earthquake, but it passed around her harmlessly.

Benjamin had fallen with the rest, stunned by the display of magic. But even though he'd tumbled down to the floor, he shoved one of her swords toward her, sending it skidding across the tile. The sight of her weapon jarred her back to her senses. She reached down to grab it.

"*Please*, Lady Tryneowy," Rucrius said with an ungracious smile. "Have the grace to accept your defeat. You are Fountain-blessed, and my lord and master Gahalatine sent me to escort you to his capital. He desires to meet you. Your people will not be harmed if you submit to us now. Already our fleet is nearing the shore. Unless I give the proper sign to halt them, they will commence their attack, and many will needlessly perish. Brythonica has always been the weakest of the duchies of Ceredigion. Now I ask you, plainly, to set down that sword and accept your fate. Perhaps Gahalatine will choose you as his consort? Though I think he may prefer someone else." He gave her an oily smile, staring at the left side of her face in a manner that made his meaning all too clear.

"I will not surrender my duchy," Trynne said, her voice trembling with passion. "And our people and my king will fight Gahalatine's aggression."

Rucrius snorted. "Your king is being attacked in four places at once, young lady," he said. "You cannot flee from me by the ley lines, and you lack a Tay al-Ard to travel without them. I commend your bravery, my lady, but do not be a simpleton. I will take you to the Forbidden Court by force if I must." He gave her a mocking bow. "You won't be the first who came unwillingly."

She saw the lord marshal straining, the sword held helplessly over his head. The others were still on the ground, staring at her, and she could see the look of devotion in Thierry's eyes, his outrage at the foreigner's insult.

And then an idea struck her as clearly as a ringing bell. The Fountain whispered it to her; she knew it had.

"I thank you for coming all this way," Trynne answered, walking forward. "By tangling the ley lines, you have made it difficult for *you* to leave as well."

"Do you think that I fear a wisp of a girl such as you?"

"No," Trynne answered. "But you should."

CHAPTER FOURTEEN

Defending Ploemeur

Trynne's idea came from the staff the Wizr Rucrius held. It was clearly his strongest weapon, and she could sense the nature of the Fountain magic it possessed. It could shatter stone and split rock. She sensed its power was from the Deep Fathoms itself. Having been raised in Ploemeur, she knew the power that earthquakes held over water—and what a tidal flood could do to a host of ships caught in its path. Her own fleet was out at sea, so they would not be dashed onto the rocky shores of the coast. The Chandigarli fleet would be.

She needed to get the staff from him.

Facing three Wizrs at once would be madness.

Her only hope was to distract Rucrius enough that she could wrench the staff from him. The idea came to her at once: the word of power that could restore life also had other uses . . .

"*Nesh-ama*," Trynne breathed softly, invoking the power while her strength was at its fullest. She directed the spell at the tunics of the castle soldiers, each bearing the Raven sigil.

There was an awful croaking noise as the ravens lifted off the fabric, first fluttering flatly and then coming to life, turning into enormous birds. The black plumage and raking claws rushed to the center of the audience hall, the birds' beaks snapping at the turbans and hair of the three Wizrs of Chandigarl. Trynne used the sudden commotion to rush forward, spinning her blade in the circular pattern she had practiced for years, forming a whirlwind of steel.

Rucrius's mouth contorted into a snarl of anger. He met her, swinging the staff down at her to interrupt the movement of her blade. She felt the jolt of the staff as it struck her, felt its power bunch up to throw her back across the room, but its magic could not be used against her. Next, the Wizr reversed the blow and tried to strike her stomach with the other end of the staff. She knew the reversal move well and blocked it with her blade. Then, turning in a corkscrew move, she flipped around and kicked him in the face.

Rucrius staggered backward, stunned that she had struck him. A splotch of red appeared on his lip and dribbled down his chin. He touched it, confused, then saw the blood on his fingertip. His dark eyebrows knitted with fury, and he came at her fast and hard, spinning the staff over his head and knocking ravens out of the way as he whirled and struck at her. Again and again. Trynne ducked, dived, and rolled, trying to keep away from the staff. She was immune to its Fountain-enhanced power, but a blow to her skull would still knock her unconscious.

From the corner of her eye, she saw the ravens had started to drop from the air, their bodies suddenly gray and stiff as stone. The Wizrs had overcome their shock and were fighting back.

"*Eliac!*" one of the Wizrs shouted, a word of power Trynne didn't know, and a flash of blinding light exploded in the hall.

Trynne couldn't see.

Rucrius struck his staff against the floor and the entire castle shuddered. The floor heaved and buckled, and chips of rock and stone began to fall from overhead.

"Must I bring this entire palace down to convince you?" Rucrius shouted. "Must innocents perish for your stubbornness, waif? I command you, yield!" The staff struck Trynne's ribs and she bent double.

She hadn't seen it coming because of the spots dancing in her eyes. "Grab her!" he ordered.

One of the Wizrs seized her from behind, pinning her arms to her sides, making the sword useless. She arched her head back and smashed it into his nose. Pushing her arms out to loosen his grip, she dropped low and elbowed him in the groin. The Wizr collapsed in a heap on the floor, writhing in pain.

"You fool!" Rucrius barked in frustration. He swung the staff down at her and she twisted, feeling the wellspring come to her aid. Rucrius's staff hit the fallen Wizr, exploding with power and knocking him unconscious.

There were two left.

Trynne lunged at Rucrius, arcing her blade toward his greatest vulnerability, his throat. His eyes widened with fear as he jerked backward, then countered with the staff and caught her on the shoulder with it. He was incredibly quick and skilled. She'd never faced someone who could meet her reflexes. The blow sent her spinning, and she had to roll to prevent the staff from striking her again. As it hit the tiles, they cracked apart. She swept her leg out to trip him and he deftly evaded her before twirling the staff around and bringing it down at her again.

Trynne rolled once more and the staff struck a decorative urn, shattering it. She rushed forward and grabbed for the end of the weapon. Rucrius tried to pull it away, but she managed to close her fingers around it. Raw power raged inside of it—a supply that far outstripped her own. The two of them careened, wrestling for control of the staff. As they lurched, the end of it struck one of the supporting pillars of the room and shattered it.

"Rucrius!" the other Wizr shouted in panic. "She's an Urdubegis! We must flee!"

Rucrius kicked her leg, swinging the staff around to shake her off, but she would not yield. She brought her knee up into his stomach. His teeth were bared with rage and pain, and his long hair whipped around, slapping her face. He was stronger than her and swung the staff up and over, trying to force her onto her back. Clinging to it, she put her weight on it and kicked him with both feet.

He lost his grip on the staff as he fell backward. Trynne landed on the broken ground on her shoulder—a painful fall—but she had what she needed.

The other Wizr blanched when he saw Trynne holding the staff of power. She sensed him untangling the ley lines hurriedly, and she rolled on her feet and swung the staff around in a full circle, trying to hit his head. The Wizr vanished along the ley line just before the end of the staff made contact with his skull.

It left Rucrius alone to face her. Trynne whirled and brought the staff up behind her, locked against her arm and her shoulder blade, preparing to swing it around to attack him.

"That is *mine*," he snarled.

The magic of the staff had revealed the hidden layers of the world around her. She could sense the fissures in the mountain on which the castle stood. Feel the ridges and clefts of stone far beneath it that opened into the harbor of Ploemeur and a vast underground chasm full of the ocean. This was an ancient weapon of destruction, as powerful as any she had ever seen. It was of the Deep Fathoms. In her mind, she felt the rifts in the land beneath the water. She could jar them loose, causing an earthquake.

"No," Rucrius uttered in horror as he stared into her eyes.

Trynne twirled the staff overhead and struck the ground with it. She directed the magic to the underwater rifts.

And the earth *moved*.

Rucrius's eyes widened with utter fear before the first tremor even struck. He reached to his waist and grabbed a brass cylinder, the twin of the one Trynne had seen at Chandleer Oasis.

Then he vanished.

Trynne stood still, breathing hard, as the ground bucked and swayed. She wobbled, nearly falling, but remained standing. Her magic was still not depleted, although it was starting to drain more quickly. She stared at the people sprawled across the floor, the warriors who had watched her face down and defeat three Wizrs. Their expressions were full of fear and joy.

"You *are* the Duchess of Brythonica," Thierry breathed, rising to his feet. He bowed.

"Sound the horns," Trynne said, knowing they didn't have long before the tidal flood came. "Everyone must flee to higher ground."

◆　◆　◆

The horns and trumpets of Ploemeur were still bleating when the waves rushed in. It was already high tide, and Trynne watched mutely as the moonlight revealed the monstrous series of waves that had engulfed the piers and razed the shores. Most of the homes of Ploemeur had been built on higher ground. The desolation of Leoneyis had persuaded the ancient rulers of Brythonica to take certain precautions.

There was a certain irony to Trynne's situation—to fulfill her duty to protect her realm from floods, she had summoned one in an act of defense. But it was the Fountain itself that had given her the idea. While her mother undoubtedly knew the word of power that could have caused an earthquake, Trynne did not, but Rucrius had unwittingly brought her the very tool she'd needed to do it.

She shivered as she watched the ocean rush across the horizon from the balcony window, surrounded by the guards who had witnessed her confrontation with the Wizrs. Shops that had stood on the lowland for generations were completely submerged. The cracking noise of snapping timbers and debris was followed by screams and cries of terror from the people of Ploemeur. Trynne squeezed the staff, hardly able to bear watching the devastation she had unleashed. *This* was the power of a Wizr. It horrified her.

"The ships," Marshal Soeur exclaimed. Trynne looked up and saw Gahalatine's fleet, lit up with lamps and torches, bobbing and bucking as the waters dragged them into the coast of Brythonica. Trynne stared helplessly as the ships were crushed against the rocks. One of the massive treasure ships struck the Glass Beach head on, wedging into the sandy surf, its hull breached and torn apart. It was the worst series of shipwrecks that Brythonica had ever experienced. The shrieks of the doomed warriors filled the night sky.

Trynne's heart wrenched with compassion. These warriors had come to defeat her people, but they'd done so on the orders of their emperor. They deserved a better fate than this.

Too many had already died.

"Thierry," Trynne said, nearly sobbing as her emotions overwhelmed her.

"Yes, my lady?" he whispered, staring awestruck at the wreckage below. One of the ships had rolled upside down before crashing into the shore.

"Summon all the people," she said. "We must search for survivors. We must bring them into our homes." She put her hand on his shoulder. "All of us."

"But what about the water?" Thierry replied. "It will take days for it to subside!"

She remembered how Rucrius had overturned the river outside Kingfountain. How he had used his staff to destroy the ancient Wizr set. Her mother had summoned the excess water into the sanctuary of Our Lady.

Trynne shook her head. "No, it will not. Mother taught me how to calm the sea."

CHAPTER FIFTEEN

Wreckage

The rising sun revealed the full extent of the devastating wreckage. Trynne was exhausted from the all-night labor. Not only had she pushed her body to the limits of its endurance, she had used nearly all her reserves of Fountain magic to drain the floodwaters from the city. There were carrion birds circling overhead, as well as flocks of screeching gulls. So many had perished in the night. But even more had survived.

She walked along the beach of sea glass, now strewn with crates, debris, and broken planks of teak wood from the treasure ships. It would take weeks to clean up the mess. The horizon was full of ships, the ships of Brythonica, which were still rescuing survivors who had fallen into the water.

The receding tide had made the rescue effort easier. Dinghies ferried the survivors to the shore, where they were wrapped up in blankets, fed soup and berries provided by Trynne's generous people, and taken to shelters to rest. The able-bodied soldiers of Gahalatine's army had immediately joined in the rescue efforts, working side by side with Trynne's knights to save as many as possible.

Trynne had hidden Rucrius's staff in the waters of a palace fountain. It radiated so much magic that she couldn't hide it anywhere else without it being discovered, and she didn't want it to be stolen. Horrified though she was by its magic, it had been the means of saving Ploemeur. She rubbed her weary arms as she trudged through the sand and debris. The foodstuffs that had been stored aboard the vessels were likely all ruined, but they were salvaging whatever they could. They would need extra stores to help feed everyone.

Thierry marched up to her, winded from a long walk. His sleeve was torn and his face was haggard. He'd been helping all night as well.

"My lady," he said with a wheeze. "Come quickly. We found him."

"Who?" she asked in concern.

"The Wizr who attacked you," he answered. "He was among the survivors."

Trynne looked at him in confusion. "He didn't return to Chandigarl?"

Thierry shook his head. "Apparently not. He was found comatose next to a corpse—a woman in very fine attire who looked to be of his own race. They're both unnaturally tall and pale, unlike the rest of the Chandigarli we've seen wash up on shore."

"Take me there," Trynne said. Then, turning to one of her captains, she gave orders for her people to continue clearing debris from the beach before the next tide came in late in the afternoon.

They walked together briskly, Thierry leading the way. "One of the soldiers brought a series of maps to me," he confided as they went. "They had navigation charts that show the entire coastline of Brythonica, including the secret coves. There were even charts revealing the tides based on the moon phases of the year. They knew exactly when and where to strike. I do not know how they obtained such detailed maps, my lady. They were written in a foreign hand but show an intimacy with our seasons and borders that no foreigner should have been able to access."

The implications sent a chill down Trynne's back. "What you are saying is that the maps were copied from ours."

Thierry nodded. "My lady, it implies there is a traitor among us."

"The Espion don't have any maps of Brythonica," Trynne said. "They've never been allowed inside the duchy other than to deliver messages." Though she hated to suspect him of something so ugly, Fallon had been raised in Ploemeur as a boy. He knew her people and had won their trust. He had also recently visited her. Another possibility was Morwenna. Hadn't Trynne spied her copying something from the library? What had it been? Her mind struggled with the memory. Would the king's sister have betrayed them?

Trynne's mind shot to something Gahalatine had said to her in the oasis while trying to stop her.

I know of you.

That statement had troubled her. What did it mean? Had Gahalatine heard rumors about a Fountain-blessed girl at the court of Kingfountain? As far as Trynne knew, she and Morwenna were the only two. Had he heard of the poisoner or the duke's daughter? What did it all mean? If Rucrius was captured, there was a possibility he could provide some much-needed answers to her questions.

"I hadn't considered it being the Espion," Thierry said. "The Genevese come here often enough. Surely they have created their own maps."

"That's true," Trynne said, walking more briskly. Would that the maps had come from them. "How far is it?"

"See that treasure ship?" he said, pointing. "He was found near it. It's almost exactly where a whale was trapped on the beach when your mother was a child."

The massive ship with the shattered hull hulked before them. There were carpenters at work dismantling it, and the commotion of their hammers and saws could be heard against the rush and hiss of the waves. A group of knights wearing the Raven stood in a circle, and it was toward these men that Thierry took her.

As she approached the group, she recognized Marshal Soeur among the gathered men. He had the Wizr's sword scabbard in one hand and his brass cylinder in the other. He offered them both to Trynne.

"My lady, we took these from him. He's unconscious, not dead."

The soldiers parted and Trynne saw the crumpled Wizr resting on the sand, his chest rising and falling. His long hair was bedraggled and his fancy clothes were ruined. One arm was draped across the stomach of the dead woman. A fly came and touched down on the lashes of her open eyes. They didn't blink. Her skin was pale. She'd been a beauty in life, her hair dark and luxurious.

Trynne approached the Wizr and knelt by his side. He wore a medallion similar to the one Gahalatine did, the circle with the sun-rays coming from it. Gahalatine had looked at her through that circle.

"Take off the medallion," she said, nodding to one of the soldiers. She summoned her magic, what little she had left, and felt it flicker to life. When she reached out to Rucrius, her suspicions were confirmed. His reservoir was completely empty. He must have passed out using the last of it. From the way his arm draped across the woman, even in sleep, she deduced the answer well enough. Rucrius loved this woman and had tried to save her from drowning. After finding her, he'd probably tried to bring her back to life by using the word of power even though it was against the Fountain's will.

The soldier lifted Rucrius's head, pulled free the medallion, and handed it to her. Accessing the dregs of her Fountain magic, she held the circle up to her eye. When she looked through the circle, she saw the weblike ley lines that stretched all around them. They were like strands of spider silk crisscrossing in the air. People walked through them, unseeing, as they worked on the rescue effort. The strongest of the ley lines stretched all the way from the island sanctuary of Our Lady at Toussan to the castle on the nearby ridge. It was awe-inspiring to physically see something that she'd only seen written on a map. This device was one of the ways the Wizrs traveled the ley lines. And by taking it from Rucrius, she was depriving him of an easy escape.

"He's rousing," Marshal Soeur said blackly.

Trynne gripped the medallion in her hand, staring at Rucrius as he rolled slowly onto his back. His energy was completely wasted. "I hear you," he said in a guttural tone.

Trynne knew through her magic, which had probed him, that he'd struck his head on a timber and swallowed too much seawater. He was injured enough to not be a threat to them. Yet. She wondered how he regained his power. Was it through games of strategy, skill with the staff, or some other habit he possessed that was unknown to them?

"We saved as many as we could, Rucrius," Trynne said.

He opened his eyes and stared at her with eyes full of loathing. "You. Won."

Trynne felt a shiver of fear, even knowing he was helpless. "Well, if this is but a game of Wizr, then *your* piece comes off the board, I suppose. One of your fellows escaped. The other you killed with your staff while trying to strike me. You are our prisoner, Rucrius."

He turned his chin away from her and his head lolled to the side. He blinked, staring at the dead woman lying beside him.

"I will have my revenge for this," he whispered thickly, his cheeks quivering with grief.

◆　◆　◆

It wasn't until later that day, after Trynne had some time to rest, that she decided to face Rucrius again. Her mind still felt as thick and tangled as fleece from lack of sleep. The tide was starting to come in again, bringing with it more debris from the wreckages. The navy of Brythonica was on full alert, for some Genevese ships had arrived that day with news that Legault had been conquered and a squadron of treasure ships and support ships were anchored in the harbor there. The victory at

Ploemeur had not ended Gahalatine's threat. Trynne dispatched ships and riders to Kingfountain immediately with the news.

The palace had no murky dungeon full of torture equipment. Though infrequently used, the cells were clean and well kept by the palace staff. Trynne had never considered it before, but they were positioned away from the ley lines that ran through the palace.

As she walked to the place where prisoners were kept, she fingered the brass cylinder. She remembered Rucrius had called it a Tay al-Ard and she surmised from his words that it worked without the help of ley lines. It was a piece of curious workmanship, very similar to the type of looking glasses sea captains used on their vessels to spy distances. But instead of curved glass at the end, there were brass fittings bedecked with gems. The cylinder contained Fountain magic. She knew how to break the bindings of the device, but while it could be unmade very easily, she had no idea how to recreate it. The talents of the Wizrs of the East were clearly superior. Stuffing the cylinder into her girdle, she nodded to the guardsmen at the door and they opened it for her.

Inside, there was a corridor lined with cells. None were occupied except for Rucrius's. After claiming the armor and weapons of Gahalatine's army and bringing them to the palace, she had made sure that each survivor was assigned a place to stay. She had entrusted the leaders to the noble families in Ploemeur, who would keep them separated but treat them with courtesy and respect. But Rucrius was an enemy who needed to be kept nearby.

As she approached, she found him pacing in his cell, hands clasped behind his back. There was a stack of folded clothes on a chair, a new tunic and pants in the Brythonican fashion, but Rucrius still wore his ruined vestments. His jewelry and weapons had all been taken away. She summoned her magic and reached out to him, trying to sense his stores.

He noticed her prodding immediately and rushed up to the bars, gripping them with his hands.

"You *dare* test *me*?" he growled, his face contorted with anger.

Trynne was grateful he was in a cage. He had no weapon, but her instincts told her that he was dangerous.

Even so, she ignored his angry remark and continued to prod him. His reserves were still depleted, but they were growing again. Somehow, though he was doing nothing more than pacing in his cell, something was feeding him.

Trynne stood apart from him, far enough that she was out of reach. His eyes went from gazing hotly at hers to glancing down her body to the cylinder in her girdle. His eyebrows twitched with fury as he stared hungrily at it. He wanted it back with a fierce desperation. She had no doubt he would kill her to get it.

She wondered what sort of power his access to the magic gave him, but doubted he would reveal the truth to her intentionally.

"Where did Gahalatine strike? You said last night he would strike in four places at once. Brythonica obviously. Where else?" She knew about Legault, of course, but she wished to see if he would be truthful.

His hands squeezed the bars until his knuckles were white, his brows narrowed scornfully. "Connacht in Legault, Marq in Brugia, and, of course, Edonburick. I tell you this not because I am disloyal to Gahalatine. I am not. I say this because it takes your kingdoms pitifully long to communicate, and you will undoubtedly hear this same news later."

He was trying to provoke her, and she knew it. "Then no doubt news of *your* defeat will also travel quickly."

His teeth clenched and his body trembled with rage. "You will not have power over me for long. Do you intend to execute me? You would be wise to release me. If you give me that scroll, I can be of greater service to you than you can possibly imagine."

"I doubt you would keep your word," Trynne said. "I have some questions for you."

"Give me that scroll," he said more intently. She felt a push of magic, but it was no more forceful than an infant tugging on her arm.

"I think I'll keep it," she answered. "Do you know where they took my father? Do you know where Owen Kiskaddon is being held? I know he's alive."

She saw it in his eyes. There was knowledge, there was truth, there was the information she desperately sought. But the low, cruel smile he gave her told her that he would never reveal it to her. That he would rather die than help her.

"Why should I know such a thing?" he said. "My lord Gahalatine did not abduct him. How dare you suggest it."

"I didn't suggest that Gahalatine did. I asked you a question."

"And what would you do to get the answer?" he said smoothly, his voice full of cunning. "Would you betray your king?"

His words cast a shadow on her soul. She wanted to save her father, and she believed that Rucrius knew where he was. But she could do nothing to force him to tell her.

"Tell me," Trynne said, barely able to control her anger.

"I can bring you to where he was taken," Rucrius said. "Hold out the Tay al-Ard. We will both touch it together. You cannot go there alone. But I can. I know the way. I will take you there. Hold out the scroll."

Again, she felt his thoughts pushing against her. They were pushing stronger this time.

Their silent stalemate was broken by the noise of steps coming down the corridor. Trynne turned and saw her father's herald approaching rapidly.

"My lady. Morwenna Argentine is here."

CHAPTER SIXTEEN

Revenge

When Trynne reached the audience hall, she found Morwenna walking amidst the debris of cracked floor, gouged pillars, and detritus from the battle with the three Wizrs. The king's poisoner had a look of wonder and astonishment as she surveyed the damage to the once-tranquil room. None of the palace servants had begun cleaning yet—all their focus had been on rescuing the survivors along the shore.

Morwenna's hand stretched out and touched one of the fragments of broken stone on the floor. After hefting it in her hand, she set it down and turned as Trynne approached.

"You're safe," Morwenna breathed out with a sigh of relief, reaching out and embracing her. "When you did not come to Kingfountain straightaway, the king worried that you too had been abducted. He and the queen bade me to bring you back to the royal castle if you were here."

Trynne caught her meaning immediately. "Too? Who else has been taken?" She still harbored doubts about Morwenna's loyalties after seeing the maps and was more interested in gaining information than in sharing it.

Morwenna shook her head, looking saddened. "The Queen of Atabyrion."

"No!" Trynne gasped in shock.

"Fallon knows," Morwenna said with a suggestive tone. "He's beside himself with worry. Gahalatine attacked Edonburick personally. The defenses were no match for him, and the heights were overpowered in short order by those flying troops of his. Queen Elysabeth was snatched away by one of the emperor's Wizrs. She's probably already been taken to the Forbidden Court."

Trynne felt as if her broken heart had been wrenched from her chest. "What happened to Iago?" she pressed.

"He was taken aboard one of the treasure ships. There is a governor of Edonburick now, assigned by the emperor. He has brought gifts— more like *bribes*—to pay off the nobles. Some fled and returned to their own lands. With Iago *and* Elysabeth gone, only Fallon has a chance to rally any defense for Atabyrion. But he's still at Kingfountain." She reached out and touched Trynne's shoulder. "He was chosen, you know. He's the king's champion."

The Gauntlet had been the furthest thing from Trynne's mind. So Fallon had won after all?

"I'm glad for him," Trynne said, her feelings still very conflicted.

"Yes, there was hope that someone else would compete. You know the people keep talking about the Painted Knight." She gave Trynne a conspiratorial smile. "They were surprised *he* didn't come to Kingfountain."

Did Morwenna know? Trynne kept her expression guarded, but suspicion writhed inside her like a nest of snakes. Had Fallon told Morwenna?

"I had not heard the latest news. Thank you."

Morwenna looked around at the rubble. "When I arrived, I was surprised to hear that you were not also captured. They must have sent someone to take you?" Her tone urged Trynne to confide all her secrets.

"Yes, and they learned that Brythonica was not as helpless as they had supposed. We were not easy prey."

Morwenna looked startled. "I am impressed, Trynne. The king will wish to hear of your success from your own mouth. Shall we go now?"

Trynne had the feeling that Morwenna was more surprised than she was letting on. Despite the bonds of the past, she felt more wary of her than ever. Severn's daughter was a dangerous person, a Wizr in her own right, and Trynne's own stores of magic were perilously depleted. If Morwenna's loyalties lay elsewhere, she would be walking into danger if she left with her.

"I will come shortly," Trynne said, deciding to trust her instincts. "Please tell the king and queen that I am safe. Ploemeur is unconquered, and our navy is still intact. There is other news I must bring them as well." Trynne wasn't going to share what she had learned with Morwenna. Nor was she going to tell her that Rucrius was being held in the dungeon.

Morwenna looked at her eagerly, her eyes wide with interest.

Trynne patted her arm. "Thank you. Tell Fallon that I'm sorry about his parents. He must be very worried."

"I will," Morwenna said, unable to hide the disappointment in her voice.

♦ ♦ ♦

It was nearly midnight and the fire burned low in the hearth. Trynne sat on one of the couches in her bedchamber, her legs tucked beneath her. She still hadn't changed out of her gown, and it was tattered and filthy from the events of the day and preceding night. Weariness had made her nod off, the Tay al-Ard still clutched in her hand. She had examined it, trying to understand how it worked and the magic that had formed it. If only she had her mother's memory. No doubt there was some ancient legend divulging the history of these magical devices. She brushed some hair behind her ear and chewed on her lip, deep in thought.

An idea had been simmering in her mind since Morwenna had returned to Kingfountain. She was so tired, she wasn't sure her plan was particularly wise. She tapped the cylinder against her palm. When Gahalatine thought someone was useful to him, he took that person directly to the Forbidden Court. He had done so with King Sunilik. The Wizr who had brought him to Chandigarl had used the Tay al-Ard to do so. It sounded like Queen Elysabeth had been moved the same way, to the same city. That meant Gahalatine respected her and thought she might prove useful to him. Iago had been put on board a ship, which meant he was of little value to the emperor. Gahalatine had also sent three Wizrs to Ploemeur to capture Trynne. Perhaps they'd feared Sinia would return to defend her ancient duchy. Or maybe they'd feared Trynne.

She pinched the bridge of her nose to try to stay awake. She'd never felt so tired and spent. Hundreds had perished in the attack on Ploemeur. But most of the deaths had been among the invaders, who were now stranded in Brythonica. The Chandigarli leaders she had spoken to throughout the day had been humbled by her mercy and generosity. They didn't see Trynne as an enemy. They had set sail for Kingfountain under the impression it was a benighted realm with corrupt leadership. That the people were living in misery.

They saw for themselves that it was not true of Brythonica. Was Gahalatine just as misguided? Or could he have knowingly given his people a false pretext for the invasion?

Gahalatine was young and handsome, perhaps ten years older than her, full of energy and vigor. There was no questioning his ambition, and his successes and his power with the Fountain had emboldened him. He'd taken over the oasis despite knowing the king was good and true, something that bothered her, but he'd also shown signs of fierce intelligence. Nobility. Was he truly the enemy? Or were the men who were guiding him the problem?

She remembered something her father had taught her years after the first lessons he'd given her in the game of Wizr. Father had told her that the enchanted Wizr set, the one whose pieces represented real people, had been a gift of the Wizrs of old to the King of Ceredigion. The Argentine family had been playing the game for centuries by the time Rucrius came to Kingfountain and destroyed it with his staff—the staff she now held. What was it her father had told her? She had only been a child, but the words had struck her even back then.

Trynne felt a ripple from the Fountain magic, stirring her memory.

The Wizrs of old had made the rules. They were the ones who had lived to witness the rise and fall of several kingdoms. They were the ones who had offered the magic game of Wizr to a man who was *ambitious* enough to rule.

Her throat constricted, her eyes widening. That word described Gahalatine perfectly.

Had the Wizrs of Chandigarl run out of patience with the Argentine family at last? Had the game gone on too long? The king piece was not the most powerful piece on the board; the Wizr was. But the game ended when the king was defeated. Perhaps they'd feared King Drew was becoming powerful enough to usurp them?

She pushed her legs off the couch and rose. Little pinpricks of pain tingled in her feet. She feared falling asleep, afraid of what might happen to her land if she rested at a time like this. Rucrius was a dangerous man. She didn't know what fed his power, but she'd sensed it growing even in captivity, faster than her own was growing. Knowing his powerful will, she had ordered that he be left alone, without being able to speak to his guards.

After pacing a moment, she stuffed the Tay al-Ard into her girdle and opened the door of her room. The four guards on duty were startled by her sudden appearance.

"My lady, you're not abed?" one of them asked.

"I'm going to the dungeon. Come with me."

"Yes, my lady."

The palace was quiet, but there were soldiers patrolling the corridors night and day. Torchlight shone off the mirrored floors. Someone had swept them after the events of the day. She shook her head in amazement at the diligence of the palace staff. When she reached the dungeon, the captain of the night watch bowed to her and unlocked the door. She was afraid that she'd find the cell empty. She dreaded it.

"Wait here," she bid the soldiers. "I'll speak with him alone."

They looked at her with concern, but they obeyed. As she walked down the dimly lit corridor, she reached out with her magic. No, Rucrius was there. She sensed him as she approached, feeling the rippling well of magic seething behind the bars of his cell. He had been sitting on the cot, but he rose and walked to the door, his pale, strong hands encircling the bars and squeezing them. His eyes were full of wrath. They glowed in the darkness, reflecting the torchlight.

"Your eyes glow," Trynne said as she advanced, keeping well clear of him.

"That is common for my race," he said disdainfully. "I am not like you." He still had not changed his clothes either. They stood facing each other, Trynne's heart quailing in the face of his power. He'd been utterly spent that morning, and now it seemed like his power was filled to the brim. *How?*

She felt him reach out with his magic and test her, poking and judging her supply. A mocking smile creased his face. "You're tired, Tryneowy Kiskaddon. Are you afraid to sleep? You have me locked in a cell. Why should you be troubled? These bars don't make you feel safe?" His eyes flashed in the darkness.

She felt her fear of him deep inside her bones, but she would not let it control her. "If you try to escape, my warriors have orders to kill you."

He pulled one hand back and examined his fingernails. "We both know that your soldiers cannot stop me from escaping if I choose, just as we both know that my Fountain magic is stronger than yours. I have permitted myself to be your captive. And I am certain you are clever enough to discern why."

She wished her father were there. *He* could match wits with Rucrius. She felt young and naive. But she was also determined.

"You know where my father is," she said.

"And *you* took my staff and my Tay al-Ard. But even more important, Tryneowy, you are protected from my magic. Just like your father." His voice was oily and cunning. "I didn't know that you'd inherited that gift from him. How curious. What Gahalatine would do to know that . . . Do you know how *powerful* you are, Tryneowy? He has long wished to heave off the yoke of the Mandaryn. Do you even know what they are? I doubt it."

She felt chills shoot through her. The Wizr was toying with her, manipulating her, saying things to make her desperate for information.

"Where is my father?" she asked, keeping her tone calm and measured.

"You want to barter? How quaint. Give me the Tay al-Ard and I will take you to him."

"Assuming you have him imprisoned, then your offer to take me to *share* his prison isn't acceptable."

He gave her a lazy smile. "We both have what the other wants. But time is on my side, Tryneowy. Your father wears chains and is being kept in the dark." His face turned cruel as he spoke. "His face is sheathed in a hood that makes it difficult to breathe. He reeks of his own filth. And best of all, he has forgotten you completely. Yes, my dear. He *cannot* remember you. He *cannot* remember his wife. He doesn't know his own name. You have no comprehension of the power that we possess. You will not find him on your own. And if anyone tries to free him, he will be killed without mercy. Even to attempt it risks his life."

He pressed his cheek against a bar of his cell, his glowing eye glaring at her like a cat's. It made him seem inhuman. Everything inside of her wanted to react to him, but she tried to stifle her horror. Clenching her teeth, balling her hands into fists, she stared back at him.

"Why?" she demanded hotly.

"You might be wondering how I've managed to add to my store of power in this cell," Rucrius said. "Revenge. You, my dear, deeply underestimate the force of that motive. I do not need to stack tiles. I don't need to stitch or play a harp. Revenge is the power of thought. And you cannot stop me from *thinking*. You stole from me the only woman I loved. I tried to get her back. You will never live up to your potential, Tryneowy, until you embrace revenge in your heart and in your will. You've had so many chances to learn that lesson. That disgusting slack cheek of yours started it. You've shied away from the truth, but you'll find that revenge endures forever. Like it or not, you are already becoming one of us."

He smiled at her through the bars and it made her sick.

The infection of his words had begun to shake part of her loose inside, rattling her to break apart like a . . . like a wagon wheel. Her eyes widened with horror at the thoughts.

"My brother," she gasped.

And the knowing look on Rucrius's face made her shrink.

CHAPTER SEVENTEEN

The Fault Staff

Not since taking the five oaths had Trynne been so tempted to break one of them. She wanted to punish Rucrius, to inflict pain on him and force him to reveal where her father was being held prisoner. But she would not. She knew she could not trust what he told her; his words were infectious and subtle, and she knew that he was trying to manipulate her and her emotions. So she left without a word, giving her guards the order that if he tried to escape, he should be executed immediately. His death would be in his own hands.

But as Trynne fitfully tried to sleep that night, she could not purge the words that continued to haunt her mind. Her father had been stripped of all sense of himself. How could they do such a thing? Owen had always been immune to the Fountain magic of others. Perhaps it had been managed with another relic of the Deep Fathoms. It was hard to banish the image of her father in a cramped, dark cell wearing a mask. The memory of her little brother's wagon going off the side of the cliff. The feeling of helplessness was anguishing.

She had to return to Kingfountain to speak with the king, but she dared not leave Rucrius behind in Brythonica. There was no end to the havoc he could unleash on her people. With his power, he could seek out and dismantle the barriers that kept the tides at bay. No, he could not be kept in Ploemeur.

As sunrise finally began to cast away the shadows of night, she sat up in her bed in her nightclothes, staring at the brightening sky, arms crossed and resting on her knees. The realization struck her that she had defeated a portion of Gahalatine's forces. The other three locations he'd attacked had been lost. What would Gahalatine do when he discovered the attack on Ploemeur had ended in failure? It was likely his first. A small smile twitched on her mouth, bringing with it a little shiver. Would he come for her himself next time?

Once again, her mind turned to the conundrum of Gahalatine. Though there was no doubting his ambition or his pride, there was goodness in him. Surely he had sensed that Rucrius was evil. Perhaps many of the Wizrs in his court were, but he lacked the power to overthrow them. He had sought her father's guidance—and it seemed as if the Wizrs had kidnapped Owen to keep that from happening.

Was Rucrius right? Was Gahalatine in search of a consort? Would the emperor wish to make Trynne, who shared her father's power, his queen? A small flush started on her cheeks.

Where was Gahalatine at that moment, she wondered. On one of his massive treasure ships? Back at the Forbidden Court speaking to his new hostages? Trynne imagined Lady Evie standing up to him in her outspoken way and the thought made her laugh.

She rested her cheek on her arms, wondering what to do. If she could not leave Rucrius in his cell, then she would need to take him with her to Kingfountain as her prisoner. She would not give him access to the staff or the scroll, both of which she'd hidden.

Rising from her bed, she quickly changed into a new dress and brushed the tangles out of her hair. If only there was a way to get Rucrius to *volunteer* the information she wanted. Her arm stopped midstroke, still holding the brush.

A poisoner could do it. Her father had told her of the properties of nightshade and how Ankarette had used it to learn information from people. Afterward, he'd said, the people who had divulged their secrets did not even recall doing so.

Morwenna. Even though Trynne did not trust her, she might still be useful.

◆ ◆ ◆

The rush of the Fountain swept through Trynne as she left Ploemeur with Rucrius. As they shot through the ley lines, she felt the Wizr battle her for control of the destination and experienced a wrenching feeling that tried to pull her along the southern line instead of the eastern one. His will was strong, but his magic could not force her to abandon her desire or her goal. She could not be brought off course by his disruption.

They appeared inside the gurgling waters of one of the palace's fountains.

As they stood in the waters, Trynne wrenched Rucrius's arm behind his back at an angle that was excruciatingly painful. His brow wrinkled, but he kept himself from grimacing. She could see that he resented the indignity of being roughly treated by her.

"You will submit and walk with me side by side," Trynne said, "or I will knock you unconscious myself and have soldiers drag you in front of my king in a heap."

Rucrius glowered at her, but he could not speak. His mouth was gagged to prevent him from uttering any words of power. There was no torchlight in the small chapel, so his eyes no longer glowed like a cat's. He inclined his head submissively, but his cheek twitched.

Trynne stepped over the rim of the fountain and they were immediately met by knights wearing the livery of the Sun and Rose.

"Lady Trynne!" one of them said, gawking in surprise when he saw her prisoner.

"Where is the king?" she asked, starting to march down the corridor, her hand gripping Rucrius's fingers. It was easier to control someone that way; she could immobilize the Wizr quickly if he tried another rash act. Her heart was still palpitating from their struggle along the ley lines. Had she not been anticipating such an act, she may have found herself in the Forbidden Court.

"He's at the Ring Table," the soldier answered. He barked a quick command, and one of the knights ran ahead.

Being away from Ploemeur gave Trynne a feeling of vulnerability. She had warned the palace staff to keep her departure a secret. While the other survivors of the shipwrecks did not seem like a threat, she worried that the fleet from Legault would swoop down on them next. The protection she owed her people weighed heavily on her.

As they approached the audience hall, muted murmuring could be heard from the open doorway where the guards were stationed. As soon as Trynne entered the hall, the conversation cut off. Duke Ramey's jaw went slack at the sight of the captured Wizr. Queen Genevieve was there, cradling her baby in her arms, and she looked at Trynne in wonderment. King Drew was standing, his fists planted on the table, his mouth still open to deliver whatever remark he'd intended to make to Duke Severn. Fallon was seated in the chair called the Siege Perilous, his elbows on the rests, his fingers splayed. He watched her enter, his expression brooding and somber, and then his gaze shifted to Rucrius, whom he regarded with open enmity.

Elwis, who had been pacing around the table, halted when he noticed her. He looked relieved to see her, but also very agitated.

Drew spoke first. "We were attacked by Gahalatine's forces in four locations at once. To execute such a precise strike across such great distances must have required knowledge and power beyond anything we have yet experienced from our enemy. Three lands have fallen to the might of Gahalatine. But one of ours prevailed. My sister brought me the good news, Trynne." He smiled and shook his head. "So it is true? Brythonica has not fallen?"

"We stand ready to defend the hollow crown, my king," Trynne said humbly, bowing her head. "I have brought the Wizr Rucrius as a prisoner. He is dangerous still and his words are powerful."

Duke Severn straightened, folding his arms. "Then let's be done with him," he offered with a cold look. "Send him to Dundrennan, my lord. Chain him to the rock. Let him speak to the ice and wind."

"I will gladly take him there if you bid me, my lord," Fallon said. He had not stopped staring at Rucrius, his eyes burning with anger. "I suspect he knows where Lord Owen is. And my mother."

Genevieve continued to rock from foot to foot, patting the babe's back gently, but there was a thoughtful look in her eyes.

The Wizr's gaze was disdainful as he looked on his captors. He did not seem like a defeated enemy, even with the gag in his mouth.

"Take him to Holistern Tower," the king ordered. "He will only be ungagged in the presence of my sister *and* Lord Amrein to eat his food. Death will be your reward if you defy me, Rucrius," Drew said with a stern and hard edge in his voice. "When you last troubled us with your presence, I ordered Lord Owen to arrest you. I am grateful his daughter has fulfilled that command. Take him away and alert me when my sister returns."

"I am here," Morwenna said, shutting the paneled door behind her. She had just entered the room from one of the secret Espion passages, her hair windblown. She gazed at Rucrius in surprise. "Where is your *staff*, Wizr?" she asked, despite his inability to respond.

"I took it from him," Trynne answered. The way Morwenna had asked about it disturbed her.

Severn's daughter blinked as she turned. "Well done, Trynne. In my errands to the East, I learned that Rucrius was the Wizr entrusted with the Fault Staff. It is a relic with great power."

"It is safe where I have hidden it," Trynne answered vaguely. She did not mention the Tay al-Ard. She did not trust Morwenna to be alone with Rucrius and would have objected if the king hadn't demanded that Kevan also be present at the inquisition. Her father had always trusted the master of the Espion.

"What would you have me do, Brother?" Morwenna asked, smiling at him. "You were going to send for me?"

"Go with Lord Amrein and take Rucrius to Holistern. See that he is fed, but do not allow him to speak. We will discuss his fate in council."

"As you will, my lord," Morwenna said with a bow. Lord Amrein summoned a group of knights, and together they left through the door of the audience hall. Trynne saw Fallon rise from his chair and whisper something to Morwenna. The poisoner nodded briefly before leaving with the group that had fallen in around the prisoner. Rather than sit down, Fallon leaned against the back of his chair. As Trynne stared at him, she felt distrust welling up from deep inside her.

"Trynne, how did you do it?" Genevieve asked, coming toward her, concern nakedly evident on her face. "The fleet . . . Gahalatine . . . how? All the other places that were attacked crumpled."

She was still weary from all the work they'd done to rescue the survivors, exhausted from the lack of sleep. She met Genny with a gentle hug, careful not to press against the baby.

"Gahalatine's fleet was disrupted by a rogue wave that struck our shores," she said, not wanting to reveal the full truth in front of the gathered audience. Of those present, the only people she felt she could trust without reserve were the king and queen. "Our navy was patrolling outside the cove when it struck. I consider it a blessing from the Deep Fathoms that protected us." What she said was truthful. But she withheld the rest to be told later in confidence.

Turning to face the king, she said, "Rucrius confessed that Gahalatine struck Atabyrion, Legault, Brythonica, and the capital of

Brugia . . . Marq. How did those other attacks happen? Marq especially, as it is accessible by river, but not by an entire fleet."

Drew's exultant look diminished. "Lord Elwis?" he said, waving his hand with a gesture of weariness.

Elwis looked chagrined. "What we did not know, Trynne, was that for weeks prior, Gahalatine had been sending confederates into Marq. They were Brugians from Guilme, men and women who had been living under his rule for the last year. Apparently," he added, scratching his neck with discomfort, "they were convinced of the justness of Gahalatine's cause. Guilme has prospered this last year, enjoying an uncommon surge of wealth."

"They've been bribed, you mean?" Trynne said, frowning.

Elwis shrugged. "Yes, it could be called that. Gahalatine has showered riches and treasure on the city, opening it to ports and splendors they never had access to previously. Even the lowliest merchants became wealthy . . . nearly overnight. Gahalatine appealed also to their dissatisfaction with how long the war with Kingfountain lasted. Our treasury was nearly emptied to pay for the war. Times have been hard. Suddenly, every man jack is rich." He shook his head. "Let's just say there was no shortage of willing confederates who were eager to conquer Marq. My forces were patrolling the coast with a minimal guard at the capital. I truly expected he'd bring his fleet to Guilme again. Retaking my city will not be easy."

Genevieve touched Trynne's shoulder. "The same pattern has happened in Atabyrion and Legault. When faced with a choice of fighting to the death or accepting unbounded wealth? Gahalatine is winning their hearts quickly through their purses. If he were murdering innocents and burning fields, it would give the people something to rally against."

"But where is he getting all this treasure to hand out these bribes?" Trynne asked, feeling conflicted by the news. She respected that Gahalatine was not using cruelty to conquer their land. He'd claimed all along that his goal was to depose corrupt leadership and improve the living conditions for the common people. But what would happen once he'd conquered the world and couldn't use the riches of one kingdom to bribe the next?

"We don't know," Drew said, shaking his head. He glanced at his wife and then back at Trynne. Genevieve kissed her baby girl's cheek before returning her gaze to Trynne.

"Perhaps you can find that out for us," Drew said in a low, steady voice. "I would like to send you and Morwenna to the Forbidden Court. Gahalatine's fleet is raking our borders. I cannot even imagine the vastness of his resources. His army will continue to grow as he finds those willing to believe in his vision and leadership. We need to find his weakness." He glanced at his wife once again and Genevieve nodded. "And to rescue our lost friends."

Trynne saw Fallon start, his brow furrowing with worry and concern. He clenched his fists and opened his mouth as if to demand that he come with them. He was the king's champion now. He had won the Gauntlet of Kingfountain.

But he surprised her by saying nothing.

CHAPTER EIGHTEEN

The Greatest Power

There was a special kind of magic in a baby's laughter, Trynne realized. She watched from the entryway to the nursery as the queen rubbed baby Kathryn's feet together and then nuzzled them with her nose and lips until the little giggles erupted spontaneously again. The emotions Trynne felt surge inside her were so akin to the rushing feeling of Fountain magic that it filled her heart and added to her reservoir. She leaned her head against the doorjamb, soaking in the tender moment, watching the pure joy of a mother who loved her child. In that moment, Genny was like any mother in the kingdom. Her child just a child, not a princess. The simple beauty of it overshadowed the looming threat of Gahalatine's invasion.

"How does it *feel* to be a mother?" Trynne asked softly from the doorway, enjoying the moment—hungering even for it to happen someday to her.

Genny was startled, but she didn't stop showering her baby girl with kisses. "Trynne, it is the most wonderful thing in the world. And the most frightening. I haven't decided which feeling is stronger." She gently wagged the babe's foot, giving it one more kiss. "I adore everything about her. Her eyelashes. The little nails that fit so perfectly. So tiny. And yet I fear for her. What sort of world will she inherit? Will it be Gahalatine's? Or her father's?" She sighed.

"She'll inherit the world we leave her," Trynne said. It made her feel fraught with purpose.

"And what kind of world will that be?" Genny said, not really posing it as a question. She reached out and ran her thumb down Kathryn's little nose and the baby squirmed.

"I didn't truly understand what love was before she was born," the queen continued after a long pause. "I love my mother and father. I've always loved them. I loved your father for saving me from being swept away by the river. He risked his life to save mine, and I've never forgotten it. I've also loved my husband since we were children ourselves. I didn't know what that feeling was at first, but Drew always fascinated me, even when I was too young to understand why. As we grew older, I hoped he would choose me as his bride, but I did not think it possible." She flushed a little at the confession, casting a vulnerable look Trynne's way. "Then I learned that he *had* chosen me over so many others, others who would have brought peace to his realm sooner. Others who would have brought him more beauty. More refinement." She pursed her lips. "Isn't it tragic how we women always compare ourselves to one another? Comparing our faults to others' perfections? When Drew chose me, I thought I knew the meaning of love." Then she shook her head and caressed the babe's cheek with the edge of her knuckle. "I didn't think my heart could grow any bigger, but it did. It wasn't until this little girl wriggled out of my body amidst the greatest pain I've ever felt that I realized how *big* love could be. My heart swelled and swelled and it hasn't stopped swelling yet." She blinked away tears and dabbed them against her wrist. "Look at me, I *am* a mother! I'll be weeping over sunsets ere long."

She turned to face Trynne with a serious air. "I have a mission for you."

"I assumed that is why you summoned me," Trynne answered, feeling her heart twist with a little tug of envy. Genevieve had found her love. Trynne worried if she ever would. So many of the people she loved had been taken from her.

"I am so sorry about your brother," Genny said, as if reading her thoughts. "Words fail me. I cannot imagine how Lady Sinia will feel when she returns to Brythonica. How you must feel. I'm sorry that we must ask you to leave your home at such a perilous time. I know you are responsible for maintaining the protections of Brythonica, and that your duchy is still at risk from the fleet in Legault. I wish we could send more soldiers to defend your lands, but all our forces are stretched impossibly."

"Loyalty binds me," Trynne whispered thickly, repeating the motto her father had inherited from Duke Severn. Her family and Genny's had always been close. She couldn't remember a time when she hadn't known Lady Evie and Iago. Fallon had been a young boy when Trynne was born, and they'd spent a good part of their childhoods together.

Genny shuddered at the words. "I need to speak with you about something I didn't dare mention in front of Duke Severn."

"What do you mean?" Trynne asked, leaning away from the wall and stepping closer to her friend.

"Let me just say that I've come to doubt Morwenna Argentine's loyalty. Fallon has shared some facts with me. Some suspicions."

Trynne's eyebrow arched. "Like what?"

"Things he has already confided in you," she answered. "He's my brother first and foremost. We have always been close. He was right, you know. He was the one who predicted how Gahalatine would invade."

Trynne bit her lip, wondering if she would speak the words, but she decided she must. "*Did* he predict it? Or did he already know?"

Genny looked at her seriously, not startled by the accusation. "Sometimes little doubts whisper to me. Like when I learned that your little brother died in that accident. It kept . . . it kept the Painted Knight from competing in the Gauntlet." Genny wrung her hands. "But I cannot believe it of him, Trynne. No, I *cannot* believe he would stoop to murder. He still carries such a burden of grief about your childhood injury. He blames himself for leaving the castle that day, for being greedy about pies. Even now, he still thinks if he'd stayed with you . . . well, it's so easy to torment ourselves with what might have been. The Fountain could have prevented Dragan's attack against you. The Fountain could have healed you. Yet it did not. We all must play a purpose in this world, Trynne. I think you are here to protect and defend my husband and his throne. You are truly the king's champion. But at this moment, you must be your queen's."

Genny sighed and gave Trynne a look of pure determination. "I want you to do the king's bidding and go to the Forbidden Court with Morwenna. I need you to try and rescue my mother. But more importantly, I need to know if Morwenna has been telling us the truth about her visits there. My heart tells me there is a spy among us. I suspect Morwenna, but perhaps I'm wrong. She's proved her loyalty over and over. However," she added, tapping her lip, "she is also an Argentine. Her father used to be the king. I cannot help but wonder if her loyalties are conflicted. Still, the spy may be Fallon or someone we haven't even considered. I only know that someone has revealed our secret councils to Gahalatine. Someone has prepared his army for this invasion. There is a saying that Myrddin often repeated. 'If you know the enemy and know yourself, you need not fear the result of a thousand battles.' That was how your father kept winning. He took the time to understand his opponents. I think our enemies have been studying us for many years."

Trynne felt a shiver go through her. "I think you are right."

Genny nodded firmly. "Be careful, Trynne. Morwenna doesn't know you are an Oath Maiden. She has possibly become *too* powerful."

Trynne let out her breath. "If I must go, then I think you should summon some of the Oath Maidens to Kingfountain to protect you. None of the others are Fountain-blessed, at least not that I've sensed, but they are skilled fighters. I would advise choosing Rani Reya or Mariette."

"Mariette, merchant Barton's widow, correct?"

"You have an excellent memory."

Genny smiled. "Thank you. I will summon Mariette to wait on me. Any others you should send to Brythonica to ease your worries. Trynne, my husband believes his sister is loyal. I've shared my suspicions with him, but he cannot bring himself to believe it. He does not know what I'm asking you to do. Once you get there, you may be cut off from the ley lines. Remember how Reya told us that the women are kept in a compound called the zenana? That is where you will likely find my mother. You have a ring that can disguise you, the one that Morwenna originally gave Fallon. But there may not be any ley lines to help you escape. If Morwenna is planning you any harm . . ." Genny bit her lip and shook her head helplessly. "I know it's a great risk. I hate to ask this of you, but I must. You're the only one I can trust with such a mission."

Trynne gave Genevieve a fierce hug. "Don't you worry about me, Genny. I'm confident that I can get away if I need to. I didn't only take the staff from Rucrius. He was also carrying a device the Chandigarli call a Tay al-Ard. It's one of the magics of the Deep Fathoms, I think, and it allows the user to transport from place to place without using the ley lines at all. Morwenna doesn't know that I have it." She paused, then added, "I don't think Rucrius is truly loyal to Gahalatine. When I interrogated him, he said he knew where my father was. That he's been held prisoner, forced to wear a mask. Somehow his memories have been stolen from him. If Morwenna wants to prove her loyalty, then perhaps she can help us get information about where he's being kept."

Genevieve nodded. "While you are in the Forbidden Court, learn what you can about our enemy. We need to understand Gahalatine. We need to understand how he can afford to pay such exorbitant bribes. His wealth cannot be unlimited. Find that out, if you can. Then perhaps we can discern where he will strike next."

The conversation with the queen had filled up Trynne's reservoir of magic. She had always loved discussing politics with her father, plotting and planning maneuvers that would help them achieve their ends. A memory struck her in a flash that could only have come from the Fountain.

She smiled eagerly. "I think it was Ankarette who said that the best way to predict the future is to make it happen. Why wait to see where Gahalatine strikes next? We know what he wants. The hollow crown. He will go to wherever Drew is to get it. Some say Castle Beestone is the most defensible fortress because it is in the center of the land, but I know from my father that it is riddled with tunnels and caves. No, the strongest fortress is Dundrennan. It is the source of the river that flows down here. Fighting a battle in a winter storm would make any soldier quail. Even ones who can fly."

The smile that came onto Genevieve's face made Trynne flush.

"I am so grateful," the queen whispered tenderly, "that you are on *our* side."

♦　♦　♦

Trynne stood in her room at the castle of Averanche, holding the Tay al-Ard in her hand. She had forewarned Mariette that the queen would summon her to the palace. The beautiful widow had bowed graciously, failing to conceal a look of eager excitement. Trynne had also spoken privately with Reya.

Trynne was prepared for her journey, dressed in the outfit Reya had worn while fleeing Chandleer Oasis, with two of the hook swords that Reya had commissioned from the blacksmith concealed in a long lute case strapped around her shoulder. She had used them in the training yard with Reya and liked how light and fast they were. She'd also had a scroll case brought to her to conceal the Tay al-Ard.

It was Trynne's plan to avoid setting a time for their departure from Kingfountain. She did not want to give Morwenna the opportunity to plan an ambush.

Trynne stared at the device in her hand, then at herself in the mirror. The disguising ring was on her finger, but she had not yet activated it. One of her ideas was to make herself look like Reya until she reached the zenana. Then she would wander around the place until she found Lady Evie and dropped her disguise. But she hoped Reya's outfit might be enough to help her blend in with the local populace.

Only at the end, if Morwenna proved trustworthy, would she reveal she had the Tay al-Ard. The betrayal, if it happened, would likely occur as soon as they were away from the protection of the ley lines.

After examining her costume in the mirror, she turned the device in her hand. There were no buttons or symbols on it. Her whole plan hinged on it working. When the Wizrs had used it in her presence, none of them had uttered a word of power aloud. Perhaps the device was sentient and could know her thoughts?

She fixed her thoughts on the queen's private chamber, imagining it in as much detail as she could muster. Before she could think the word of power that allowed her to travel across the ley lines, there was a jolt, followed by a searing spasm of movement, and then an instant of nausea and dizziness. She had just finished blinking when she realized it had worked. She was in the queen's private chamber. The rod tingled in her hand, and she felt the ebbing of Fountain magic. Not from her stores, though. The journey had taken nothing from her at all.

Smiling in triumph, she strapped the device to her forearm, covering it with the sleeve of Reya's loose garment. Everything she had prepared for the journey had come with her. There was no one else inside the chamber.

When she left Genevieve's room, she startled the guards who had been standing at attention. She smiled at them, nodded politely, and then started walking down the corridor toward her intended goal. She passed servants, who gave her strange looks, and found her way to the iron door that was always locked. Standing at the door, she gripped the handle.

"*Ephatha,*" Trynne uttered, and the lock twisted open on its own.

She was headed up to the poisoner's tower.

CHAPTER NINETEEN

The Forbidden Court

Trynne's heart was full of trepidation and excitement as she mounted the steps to Morwenna's tower. She reached out with her magic, just a little trickle to avoid any dangers or traps that might block the way. The tower well was dark, but there were arrow slits in the wall that served as little beacons of light. Her heart beat wildly, both from the climb and from nervousness. In her mind, she pictured her father as a young boy, following Ankarette Tryneowy up the cold steps.

Her breath was coming quickly by the time she reached the top of the winding staircase. She sensed the presence of magic coming from the room and slowed her steps. Cautiously, she knocked at the door—a sound that echoed all the way down the tower shaft. Her insides twisted with concern as she waited.

When no one answered, she reached out and tried the handle. It was locked. The word of power released the mechanism and the handle turned without Trynne touching it. Taking a breath and holding it, she pulled the door open, her senses taut, ready for action.

The room smelled of dried flowers. The curtains were open, providing sufficient light to see the tower's simple furnishings. It would not be easy to carry a bed and feather mattress up and down stairs, so it came as no surprise that the bed against the wall matched the one she'd seen when her father had brought her up the tower's winding stairs years before. The embroideries that Ankarette had made were all gone, save one. It was an embroidery of the White Boar, Duke Severn's sigil, done by an expert hand.

Morwenna was not in the room.

"Hello?" Trynne called out as she entered. She stepped in cautiously, feeling the soft carpet absorb the noise of her steps. There was a brazier stocked with blackrock, but it wasn't lit. The desk showed a beautiful mirror, Genevese craftsmanship, with a series of brushes and paints and lotions. Strands of black hair clung to the brushes. Trynne felt she was invading a private sanctuary.

The source of the magic was in the room. It had beckoned to her while she climbed the steps. Trynne hurriedly examined the contents of the table—an assortment of vials, mortars and pestles, and the accoutrements of the poisoner craft. There were concoctions already made, little vials full of amber, red, and purple ichor. Her magic warned her of the danger emanating from them. Looking at them made her skin crawl.

Would Morwenna have left any incriminating evidence in her tower? If so, where would it be hidden? It was probably still true that none of the palace staff came up there. The other entrance to the poisoner's tower was in the kitchen, which was how Ankarette had always received her meals, left on the counter by Liona. There was a bottle of wine on a small stand by the bed, half full.

Beneath the bed, she spied a chest. Trynne listened at the doorway and heard nothing. She might not get another chance like this. Kneeling by the edge of the bed, she dragged the low chest out. But there was no magic emanating from the chest at all. There were not even any locks on it. Biting her lip, she flipped the latch that sealed it and lifted the lid.

The chest was full of men's clothes. A tunic, a shirt, a pair of boots. But it was a badge on one of the tunics that made her heart sink like a stone. The badge of the Pierced Lion. The badge of the duke of the North. Tears pricked Trynne's eyes as she lifted the garment to her nose. Jealousy made her feel like that pierced lion. The tunic *smelled* like Fallon. There was a change of his clothes in a chest *beneath* Morwenna's bed. Her hands started to shake, and that's when she heard the sound of footfalls coming from the stairwell. It was a light step. It was an urgent step.

Trynne hardly had time to consider the implications of her discovery. Her time had run out. But even as she hurriedly put the tunic back into the chest, she thought back on the clues she had witnessed before. Morwenna always told the story of how she'd accidentally appeared in Dundrennan the first time she'd used the ley lines—and then immediately fainted. She had claimed that she was trying for Kingfountain and overshot it. But Trynne realized that had probably been a lie. Morwenna likely lied a lot.

The bitter taste in her mouth was stronger than any poison. Fallon had confessed his love for Trynne. Said that he had always loved her. But had her rejection of him estranged him enough that he'd sought solace in the willing arms of another woman? She hated where her thoughts had taken her and the feelings they were breaking loose. She slid the chest beneath the bed and hurriedly sat on the edge of the mattress, trying to mask her emotions and feelings in preparation for Morwenna's arrival.

The Argentine girl slowed her steps as she approached the landing. Trynne leaned forward, entwining her fingers, summoning her magic to defend herself if necessary. She felt Morwenna's magic as well, spilling into the room to test for intruders. They were both aware of each other, as they had been that day in Marq. The day that Trynne and Captain Staeli had chased Dragan through the city. The day she'd first learned that Morwenna had been seeing Fallon.

Morwenna appeared in the doorway, a dagger in hand, a look of wariness on her beautiful face.

"Trynne?" Her voice was low, almost accusatory.

"I'm here," Trynne answered, rising and clutching her bosom. "I was winded after the climb up the stairs. I've not been here long."

Morwenna paused at the entry, looking suspiciously at either side of the doorway, as if anticipating an attack. She slowly lowered the dagger.

"I barely recognized you in your Eastern garb," Morwenna said. "Where did you get it? It's very authentic."

"I borrowed it from someone," Trynne answered, deliberately vague. "I think we should go to Chandigarl now. It is nearly sunset. What time of day would it be in the Forbidden Court?"

"I hadn't heard you'd returned to Kingfountain. No one sent for me." Morwenna glanced around the room surreptitiously, as if trying to see if any of her things had been rifled through.

"I just arrived."

"Apparently so." Her wariness was softening. "I'm sorry for my lack of courtesy, Trynne. I don't entertain visitors up here . . . very often. You startled me."

Was there a double meaning in her words? A test to see Trynne's reaction? She wrestled with her feelings.

"I'm not surprised to hear it. It's quite a climb."

Morwenna shrugged. "Sunset means it is nearly sunrise in Chandigarl. I've found the timing to be quite opposite whenever I've gone there. This works well for two reasons. Firstly, the corridors will be mostly filled with servants, so we will not seem out of place. Secondly, I've just given Rucrius a sleeping draft. He'll be unconscious for a long time. Some poisons impede magic. I'm sure you've probably guessed that. It would be better for us to leave while the potion is still working. Shall we go to the fountain, then?" She finished her words with an encouraging smile.

"Will you need to change your clothes?" Trynne asked.

Morwenna shook her head. "I have a ring that alters my appearance and radiates very little magic. There are so many treasures in the

Forbidden Court, so many relics of the Deep Fathoms, ours will hardly stand out. Have you had any word from Lady Sinia? I do miss her guidance."

Trynne had to breathe deeply to endure the stab of pain in her heart. She shook her head no.

"I pray to the Fountain she is well," Morwenna said graciously. The two young women started down the steps together, and Morwenna linked arms with her as she'd done so often in the past.

It made Trynne cringe inside.

♦　♦　♦

There was nothing in Morwenna's demeanor or attitude that hinted she was about to perform trickery. After walking together to one of the palace fountains—each was guarded by Espion day and night—Morwenna stepped into the waters without any hint of ceremony, her arm still linked with Trynne's. Trynne followed and they both stood together.

Into the cistern, Trynne thought, her stomach full of butterflies. It was a motto of courage she'd learned from her father. He'd feared heights when he was a child, but Lady Evie had grasped his hand and jumped into the water of the cistern at Kingfountain with him—an experience that had awoken his bravery.

"First, we go to Pisan," Morwenna said. "It intersects the east-west ley line. Normally I would have brought us to Marq or Guilme, but both are controlled by Gahalatine." She uttered the word of power in a low voice, "*Kennesayrim*," and the magic pulled them away on the ley line. It was a familiar sensation now, and in an instant, they were standing in a small circular fountain at the poisoner school. Night had just fallen, and Trynne saw the torches on the walls, flickering orange light. The stone sconces were sculpted into the form of twisting snakes and the walls were made of wood and plaster. An old, mildewy smell of waterways and damp corners filled the air.

Morwenna wrinkled her nose, still clutching Trynne's arm. "Have you been to Pisan before?" she asked.

"Never," Trynne replied.

"I would offer to show you around. The training yard is unlike anything you've seen, I'm sure. But perhaps another time would be better."

Trynne nodded.

Morwenna smiled impishly. "I've gone to Chandigarl many times, Trynne. There are so many people, you couldn't possibly imagine it." She gave Trynne a coaxing smile. "Now be ready. It's a *long* fall."

The poisoner uttered the word of power again, but this time the feeling of falling down a waterfall persisted for much, much longer. Trynne's stomach roiled with sickness and nausea as the magic swept them away. Would the journey never end? There was a fear that it might not, that she was trapped beneath some enormous cascade of water that fell into oblivion. She felt Morwenna's arm tighten against hers.

Suddenly, they arrived. Trynne wobbled, wanting to fall down, but Morwenna held her up and uttered the word, "*Anthisstemi.*" It was the same word Myrddin had used when he had taken her to make her oaths.

Trynne straightened, feeling her strength instantly return.

"Thank you," she muttered, disentangling their arms. The very air felt different, full of humidity and moisture and strange smells. She was used to the noise of morning birds chirping, but this land was full of clicking insects mixed with a different kind of birdsong.

Even the fountain was different. Instead of it being a circle, it was made of a series of half-circles at odd angles to each other. The porcelain tiles were a rich blue, and the waters had a greenish cast. No coins were resting in the basin.

Morwenna stepped outside of the fountain and her image shimmered as she disguised herself in courtly dress. Her hair was still black, but now it was done up into intricate ringlets that cascaded down from a series of headdresses. Her skin was darker, her eyes slanted, but Trynne could still tell it was Morwenna. The disguise could not shield that truth from Trynne's magic.

"These are the ceremonial robes of a Shaliah," Morwenna explained, gesturing to her pale silver gown and high girdle. "They are sacred healers in this society. I adopted the disguise because it allows me to wander wherever I wish. Come, we're at the edge of the zenana. We cannot get there through the ley lines."

Trynne adjusted the strap across her shoulder, feeling the bulk of the weapons in the lute case thump against the small of her back. She also stroked her arm, feeling the straps holding the Tay al-Ard beneath the garment, grateful for its reassuring presence.

The little shrine with the fountain sat amidst a park full of willow-like trees with deep green foliage and fragrant blossoms. The plants and flowers were unlike any she had seen in Kingfountain, and the enormity of the park was very striking. Everywhere she looked, there were people walking, exercising, and enjoying the beauty of the place. Some were even playing musical instruments. There was no debris anywhere along the grass-lined path. The grounds were immaculately kept, and extended almost as far as the eye could see.

Morwenna walked along a paved footpath that led toward a long wall of trees. Trynne had no idea what kind of trees they were, but the leaves were red and jagged and looked like fire. It was lovely beyond anything she'd seen before. Beyond them, Trynne could smell a lake and hear the ripples of the water lapping against the shore.

"The zenana is over there," Morwenna said, pointing toward the enormous lake through the trees. "They're still building a bridge to connect the island to the mainland, but that will take years. You can see the part they've completed over there." She gestured to it, and Trynne saw the sweeping archways extending into the waters. It only went partway across, but the portions that had been completed were intricately carved.

"How do we get there?" Trynne asked, glancing backward to see if anyone was following them. The garden had dozens of people, but it was vast enough to feel empty.

"There is a harbor right there," Morwenna said. "They have stone boats. That is the only way to cross. Men are not permitted to enter the boats without a scroll showing the royal seal. Women can come or go as they please, or so I've been told. Do you know the word of power for languages?"

"Yes," Trynne answered.

"Good. I thought so."

They agreed to wait until they crossed the waters of the lake, as some magics did not work over water.

"How can their boats be made of stone?" Trynne asked. "Don't they sink?"

Morwenna smiled. "Not this kind. They are powered by Fountain magic. You will see them shortly, just past the trees. Follow me."

They passed the row of fiery-leaved trees before reaching the calm, placid lake. It was like a huge mirror, and she felt it radiating magic like the grove in the woods in Brythonica. It was a hallowed place, a place of great power, and forbidding. The water ripples were small, for there was very little wind. An octagonal tower rose in the center of the lush, green island, and the multiple levels were bedecked with curving, slanted roofs. Each layer of the tower grew smaller as it went up, ending in a sharply sloped roof crowned with a steeple of gold. The columns supporting the roof were painted red and the windows were of colored glass. Farther down the hillside, there was a wall that encircled the entire island, level with the shore. There were a couple of small square stone huts with similarly shaped roofs perched atop the walls, and Trynne could see guards standing there. The same fiery-red trees lined the walls, each placed a measured distance from the others. The spacing and detail were impressive.

"That's the zenana," Morwenna said, pointing to a nearby dock. "See the boats? There is one always coming and one always going. See how they float on the water?"

Many passengers dressed in silks were getting into the boat from the dock, and if Trynne craned her neck, she could see another vessel skimming the surface of the lake from the island. The boats were more like barges, except longer, and they were indeed made of sculpted stone. The prows jutted up in a circular design, carved with images of waves and the crashing sea. Two layers of compartments were constructed atop the stone platforms, made of a series of arches, and the whole structure was topped with a triangular roof. The arches were open and the sturdy pillars provided support.

"Amazing," Trynne whispered, shaking her head.

"They glide on the water like ducks," Morwenna said. "You can *feel* the Fountain magic coming from this place."

"Where is Gahalatine's palace?" Trynne asked.

"You can see it better from the lake," Morwenna said. "If we hurry, we can get on that one before it leaves. There are no rowers. It is powered by magic. If we go to the upper level, you'll have a perfect view."

The two young women hurried their steps until they reached the pier. The sun was just starting to appear on the horizon. It was dawn, not nightfall. It felt a little strange, but it was also thrilling.

Only women were at the dock, and no one gave her or Morwenna a second look or even asked them a question as they boarded the vessel. All of the guards protecting it, Trynne realized, were women too. They had an array of weapons, including broadswords, staffs, and long-shafted spears. Some of the women making their way to the barge looked frightened. Some looked eager. Others were nervous.

Trynne remembered that it was a sanctuary for women, that Gahalatine offered his protection to any women who sought refuge. How difficult would it be to find Lady Evie amidst so many?

So far, Morwenna had proven herself to be a reliable guide. There was nothing in her manner to suggest there was anything untoward about her motives. She boarded the barge ahead of Trynne and took the narrow steps to the upper deck. Trynne was fascinated by the paintwork on the stone columns. From a distance it had seemed like ivy vines, but she realized on closer inspection that the leaves were all painted. There were benches in the interior of the barge and less than half were filled. The warrior protectors walked among the girls, gazing beneath the benches to be sure no one was hiding there.

Trynne mounted the steps and joined Morwenna and several other maidens at the upper level.

"That is the Forbidden Court," the poisoner murmured softly, nodding toward the north side of the lake. The view was better from the second level of the barge, since the boat was taller than most of the trees lining the lake. Trynne's mouth gaped a little. The main palace was enormous, a dozen times larger and grander than Kingfountain. And the city that hunkered beneath the shadows of its massive walls was larger than any city she had seen. It glittered with gold as the buildings' roofs captured the flaring sunlight. Pree and Kingfountain pressed together could only have occupied a tenth of the space of this one city. There were homes and palaces and manors and buildings all crowded against one another, arranged in orderly sections of rows that crisscrossed the view. From the distance, she could see specks of movement, little ants that in fact were people. She had never been to so grand a place.

"Gahalatine *built* this?" Trynne whispered in awe.

Morwenna stood near her. "The imperial palace used to be south of here. All of this has been built since he became emperor. He is the greatest king who ever lived," she said in an almost reverent tone. Then she smirked. "Or so they would have everyone believe."

The barge lurched as it began its journey across the lake. There was no noise, no grunting of oarsmen. The barge just glided from the docks at an even pace, as peaceful as a swan.

Trynne stared at the massive city, comprehending at last the vastness of Gahalatine's resources. And this was only a portion of Chandigarl's wealth. He had claimed dominion over dozens, if not hundreds, of other kingdoms. And he had turned his eye at last on Kingfountain, determined to overthrow the Argentine dynasty.

How could they hope to defeat him?

Morwenna crossed to the other end of the seating area, hands clasped behind her back, staring at the magnificent city. A woman bowed her head respectfully to Morwenna, as if she were a great dignitary. What was Morwenna thinking about as she gazed on the court?

Gahalatine was in search of a Fountain-blessed wife.

Wasn't that what Reya and Rucrius had said? Perhaps that was the only motive Morwenna needed. Trynne could not imagine being the lady of such a vast empire. Averanche was more than satisfactory to her. But perhaps Morwenna craved what she did not.

It was while she was staring at the poisoner that they passed a barrier of some kind. It was invisible, but Trynne felt it rush past her. It was insubstantial, like smoke, but Trynne recognized it as magic. There were other protections surrounding the island and the lake, and they had crossed them.

Trynne blinked, seeing Morwenna's disguise had been stripped away. She stood as her true self, hands behind her back, her hair falling down around her shoulders.

"*Mofa!*" someone shouted in warning, pointing at Morwenna.

Two of the warrior maidens were already on the upper deck on patrol and both whirled around. They drew weapons and rushed the poisoner.

I've discovered my prison was on an island. After I overpow-ered the man sent to question me, I stripped away his silver mask and cloak. His face was painted over, and the sight of it nagged at my memory. I've known people who could disguise themselves, but I cannot recall what or who they are. The man is dangerous—I could sense that just from staring at him. So I switched clothes with him, locked him in my irons, and put my mask on his painted face. I left the dungeon without being stopped and now find myself in a palace of some kind. It is very opulent, and everyone's clothes are rich and decadent.

There are many women here, but I do not feel safe. I feel at any moment I will be discovered and killed. I need to get off this island before they discover I've escaped. I cannot trust anyone. This place feels wrong.

I look at my face in a mirror. I don't know myself. Why do I have a patch of white in my hair?

CHAPTER TWENTY

Zenana

The two guardswomen rushed Morwenna, and before Trynne could react, the poisoner struck the first in the throat with the edge of her hand. The second leaped at Morwenna with a flying kick, but the poisoner ducked the blow. The two became embroiled in a battle of punches and kicks that lasted only a few moments before the second guard collapsed, dazed from a blow to her stomach.

The sound of another guard vaulting up the steps filled Trynne with a feeling of panic. Morwenna vaulted off the railing, catching hold of the pillar that held up the roof overhead, and twirled down as she descended to the lower level. Several passengers rushed to the railing, shocked by the poisoner's sudden flight, and Trynne wondered what she was supposed to do. Should she flee as well?

Had Morwenna known that her disguise would be dispelled crossing the lake? Surely she should have after her many visits to the Forbidden Court. Trynne felt more confused than ever by the poisoner's motivations.

The two fallen guardswomen struggled back to their feet, their expressions full of pain and anger. A third reached the top of the steps, and one of the passengers spoke to her in a foreign tongue, gesturing down the ramp.

Trynne heard a commotion down on the lower deck, followed immediately by the splashing of water. Rushing to the nearest railing, she looked overboard and saw Morwenna's dark hair against the green water, sinking lower and lower as she swam. Another guardswoman jumped in the water after her. It was obvious that they were not going to let Morwenna escape so easily. Trynne's heart beat wildly. She had the Tay al-Ard, so she would hopefully be able to escape. Had Morwenna abandoned her, knowing she'd be captured? Or was she trying to save her own skin and allow Trynne to continue with their mission to save Lady Evie?

Most of the girls who were sharing the deck with her were shaking with worry—some talking amongst themselves, others isolated and fearful. Trynne did not have to try very hard to look agitated. She continued to watch from the railing, trying to see what would happen to Morwenna and if she'd be caught. The stone barge did not halt or change direction, even though one of the guardswomen was overboard.

Surprisingly, no one had accused Trynne of being in league with the girl who had jumped off the barge. No one had tried to speak to her. After several more moments, Trynne began to calm down. She was grateful she'd relied on Rani Reya's clothes to disguise her. If she'd used the ring, she too would have been discovered.

As the barge approached the island, Trynne observed how the guardswomen gathered together near the lead end of the craft. They were talking furtively amongst themselves. The woman who had jumped overboard was still missing, and their voices were edged with worry. As Trynne and the other passengers approached the dock, they found servants, all female, waiting for them. At least one was dressed as a Shaliah, which Trynne recognized as being like Morwenna's disguise. The barge slowly glided to a halt at the platform. Water lapped against the stone hull. None of the passengers were allowed to disembark until the leader of the guardswomen explained the situation to the warriors on the platform. After a few moments of discussion, the women were permitted to leave.

Once Trynne was on the stone quay, she followed the others toward the outer wall of the island, which she had seen from a distance. She invoked the word of power *xenoglossia*, so that she'd be able to understand and communicate. The spell worked instantly, and she suddenly understood the conversations of the girls around her. They were discussing the disruption on the ride, weighing the possibility that the girl who had jumped overboard had been sent to try to kill someone in the zenana. Most of the girls were uncommonly pretty, Trynne noticed, and through their hushed conversations, she could tell some had come to try to win Gahalatine's heart.

"Have you seen Gahalatine at the Forbidden Court?" one of them asked. "He is the most handsome man. He still has not chosen a wife."

Another voice said excitedly, "He must choose one soon. The Mandaryn demand it. If he does not choose for himself, then one will be chosen for him from the zenana."

"I hope he chooses me," whispered a shy girl, eliciting peals of excited laughter.

Each step along the wharf toward the wall filled Trynne with excitement and dread. She did not know where she was going. She did not know how she was going to find Lady Evie. But she felt a growing confidence that the Fountain would guide her. Even though one wrong step could kill her.

◆　◆　◆

The path toward the tower at the summit of the hill was sheltered by enormous trees bedecked with green spear-shaped leaves. Colorful birds with curved beaks perched in the branches, squawking incessantly, and the buzz of insects filled the air. She saw clouds of mosquitoes just off the side of the road, but there were none on the trail itself. The path was bracketed with stone obelisks carved into faces, and she sensed Fountain magic flowing from them.

Chandigarl felt like another world, and she was reminded of stories she'd heard as a child from Myrddin of other worlds that he had visited. None of the other girls craned their necks to see the monkeys clambering in the branches. But Trynne could not stop watching their antics as they pried fruit from the trees and hunkered down to devour them.

The air was so heavy with moisture that Trynne was sweating openly as she walked, but the loose silks of Reya's clothes helped prevent her from overheating. The massive tower at the top of the hill loomed ahead, the decoration and carvings gilded with pure gold that dazzled the eye. She saw no men along the way, only women who bowed and greeted the newcomers as they passed.

As they came nearer to the tower, the noise of the birds and monkeys was joined by a sorrowful melody of flutes and lutes. Voices joined the instruments in song, though they didn't sing words—they simply matched the pitch of the music.

A series of majestic fountains converged at the top of the hill, in front of the tower. Trynne stared with surprise as she watched shoots of water spurting up from the floor, forming pillars like upside-down waterfalls. There was an open pathway through the pillars, but the sound and the size of the display was impressive. The grounds of the zenana were larger than the palace of Kingfountain.

As she entered the tower, she felt the richness of magic, but there was also something strange in the air. It was difficult to define, but it made her wrinkle her nose. The opulence of the decorations was beyond imagining. Glittering chandeliers hung from the ceilings, and the marble floor shone with light. Trynne arched her neck, gasping when she saw that the tower was open in the middle, all the way to the sky overhead. On each floor, the rooms had been built around the open space, layer by layer, floor by floor. There were plants and birds inside the tower, man-made waterfalls, and decorative fountains more elaborate than anything in Kingfountain.

There were women everywhere she looked—most bent in conversation or showcasing some skill or other. Some of the women were hurrying about, delivering chalices and cushions and trays of fruit. The servant girls wore rich garments and displayed obsequious courtesy to those who had come to the zenana for sanctuary. But her first impression lingered. Something was wrong there. The sense wasn't coming from a specific person or from an object, but it was persistent and undeniable.

The place had been built as a sanctuary for women. Reya had told her that the noble daughters of the realms Gahalatine had conquered had been brought there, and she could see that many of the women in the zenana were indeed of noble birth. There were girls with outlandish headdresses, some literally burdened with necklaces and bracelets that lined their arms from wrist to shoulder. An air of haughtiness, pride, and splendor pervaded the tower. Trynne saw women coming in and out of rooms on the higher levels. There were people everywhere. Her heart sank as she realized just how difficult it would be to find Lady Evie.

The servants offered warm greetings to the newcomers. One of them, a matronly woman who was beautiful and proud, approached Trynne. "Welcome, daughter, to the zenana of the Forbidden Court. You are from the deserts, if I judge you well by your appearance."

"Thank you," Trynne said, pressing her hands together and giving a little bow as she had seen Reya do.

A sudden whoosh of power and magic filled the air, and a Wizr appeared in the center of the fountain on the lowest level, his hand gripping a girl's arm. Both the Wizr and the girl were unfamiliar to her, but she saw how very few of the people around her paid them notice. Everyone was talking, their conversation filling the air with noise and laughter.

"A new arrival," the matronly woman said, noticing Trynne's attention had been drawn away. "The Wizrs bring in girls regularly. You will get used to it."

And then Trynne saw a figure dressed in a black cloak and a silver mask. He was walking along the outer edge of the room, away from the center, gazing at the women assembled, keeping to the shadows. Her heart quailed when she saw him, pricked by that sense of wrongness.

"Is that a Wizr?" Trynne asked, gesturing surreptitiously to the man in the mask.

The matronly woman turned, gazing out at the room. "Who are you speaking of?"

"The person over there. With the mask."

The woman scowled a little. "Oh, he is one of the Mandaryn. They oversee the zenana. The only other males you will find here are guests invited by the emperor. There is nothing to fear."

"Why do they wear masks?" Trynne asked.

"To keep their identity concealed, of course," the woman said. "Please don't trouble yourself about them. They will not hurt you. One of their duties is to find suitable brides for the emperor. They observe the girls, nothing more. Some of you will be selected to meet Gahalatine. Now, since you are new here, you will stay in one of the dormitories on this level. You may come and go as you like. But to become noticed, you must display some form of talent. A talent for conversation, music—such as the lute," she added, gesturing to the lute case Trynne wore over her shoulders. "Poetry, languages. If you impress the Mandaryn, you will be chosen to advance to the next tier." She gestured toward an upper level. "There are more private rooms and higher rewards for those who are deemed exceptional. Some girls come here to heal after they have been . . . mistreated." She gave Trynne a sympathetic look. "You may stay as long as you desire. Gahalatine blesses this place with food, leisure, and opportunity. Some of his generals are permitted to come here to choose wives. Listen for the sound of the trumpet. That is the signal that a dignitary has arrived. That will be your chance to impress them. If that is why you came. If not, well, perhaps you can learn new skills while you are here. Improve upon your talents."

Someone was approaching them. Trynne turned toward the sound of footsteps and nearly gaped in shock. It was King Sunilik.

"I recognized your clothing from my beloved oasis!" Sunilik said in a charming voice. He was looking at her face, but his expression betrayed nothing. "You must be one of the minstrels who used to serve me. I think I may even recognize you. Welcome!"

The matronly woman looked pleased. "I thought you would want to know about her," she said, bowing and flushing. "I was going to tell you straightaway."

"You are always so thoughtful, Jenaya," Sunilik said, pressing his hands together and bowing to her. "Thank you." He turned to Trynne graciously, still not revealing even a hint that he knew her identity. "You must be missing the delicious fruits of the oasis! I have some brought here regularly. The zenana grounds are being expanded, you see, and I'm overseeing the undertaking. Follow me. It will give you a taste of home."

"Thank you," Trynne said, swallowing. She bowed to Jenaya, who excused herself and walked away.

"Well, my dear," Sunilik said in a low voice. "When I first saw you, I imagined you were my daughter. As I drew closer, I recognized you for who you are." He shook his head in disbelief and his voice dropped. "How is Reya?" he asked with a throb of concern. He gestured for her to keep following him.

"She is safe," Trynne said, her stomach bubbling with excitement. "I had not expected to find you here of all places."

"I'm relieved to hear it," Sunilik said. "My heart feared you brought ill news. We won't be able to speak privately for long without attracting unwanted eyes. I understand that the invasion of Kingfountain is under way. I'm privy to some court secrets now, but not many. If you had been captured, a Wizr would have brought you here."

They walked slowly, and he kept his expression neutral and made little gestures at plants and trays as if explaining the place to a newcomer.

"No, I came here seeking someone who was captured."

"The Queen of Atabyrion, perhaps?" he asked, giving her a broad smile.

"Indeed. Do you know where she is?"

"She is on the upper levels." He gestured upward. "I will show you where. First, I must thank you for what you did for me and for my daughter. Somehow, I have not fallen sway to the emperor's magic. Mayhap it is because I'm Fountain-blessed, as I told you, but when Gahalatine arrived at Chandleer Oasis, I felt him use his power on me. It didn't work the first time. I've since seen him use it on others who are Fountain-blessed, and it's completely overruled their minds. The same has happened to me since then. So I have deduced that perhaps it had something to do with you." He glanced around furtively, looking to see if anyone had noticed them yet. "I learned of your escape after I was taken to the Forbidden Court. I was thankful to hear that my daughter wouldn't be held hostage for my good behavior."

He clasped his hands behind his back as they stopped at a tray laden with small fruit slices. "Try some of this one, my dear. It is quite impressive." He took a slice and bit into it himself, but then continued his story in an undertone. "When Gahalatine returned after you thwarted him, he brought me to a private interview. I thought I was a dead man. He asked me pointed questions. I gave him pointed answers. I told him what I'd done—how I'd written to the Queen of Ceredigion for help. I said that someone from court had come to help bring my daughter to safety. He asked who you were and I told him the truth, Lady Tryneowy. And because I told him the truth, he has rewarded me extensively."

He gave her a serious look. "We do not have much time, so I will tell you what I can. The emperor has put me in charge of the construction and running of his palaces. It is a position far vaster than what I held in Chandleer. He heard of my reputation and sought me out to serve him. I meet in private council with Gahalatine regularly. Because I have continued to speak honestly with him, he has begun to trust me. Lady Tryneowy, I have been brutally honest with him regarding his situation. His expenditures have far exceeded his income and his resources. The treasury is nearly barren. He commissions new projects with no ability to fund them. The fleet of treasure ships has stripped his land of wood and trees, which will require another generation to replenish. Only his continued success in subjugating other kingdoms has allowed him to continue. If he fails to conquer Kingfountain, there will be a revolt inside his own empire when he can no longer pay the tributes his people have grown accustomed to. This empire that he's built is an illusion of power, though it may yet work—for if enemies believe in his power, they will continue to yield."

Sunilik shook his head. "We have all been persuaded that Gahalatine is unstoppable. But it is not true. His success is also his greatest weakness."

Trynne's ears burned eagerly. The news was vastly important. And not only because it confirmed what she had suspected. "And you have learned this for yourself?"

Sunilik nodded. "I have spoken to the various treasurers. They do not speak to each other. No one else knows how precarious the situation is, I think. Well, no one except for the Wizrs. There has been a power struggle between Gahalatine and the Wizrs of Chandigarl ever since he claimed the throne and usurped authority over the empire. While he controls the army, they still control the finances. But the Wizrs want to wrest the power back from him. They have employed the Mandaryn to look for a bride that *they* can control. He's been given an ultimatum to choose a bride and sire an heir or one will be chosen for him. The leader of the Mandaryn is a Wizr named Rucrius." Sunilik's eyes glittered with enmity.

Looking past Sunilik's shoulder, Trynne spied a man with a silver mask approaching them swiftly.

CHAPTER
TWENTY-ONE

The High Tower

"And these Mandaryn wear silver masks?" Trynne asked in a low voice, nodding subtly to Sunilik as she took a cluster of huge purple grapes from the tray of fruit.

Beads of sweat popped on Sunilik's brow. "Yes, in fact. They do." He turned just as the man drew near.

"I must speak with you," the man said in a curt, angry voice. His only greeting to Trynne was a dismissive jerk of his neck. "You have an audience coming up soon with Gahalatine over the palace enlargement project he intends to begin. What will you advise him?"

Sunilik gave Trynne a helpless smile and motioned for her to stay near. "I was just finishing my conversation. If I could speak to you in another moment?"

Trynne felt power radiate from the man in the silver mask. It exuded from him like smoke, sending tendrils spilling from his robes in a noxious haze.

"I would speak with you *now*," the masked man insisted. "Are you going to recommend that he cancel the expansion? I insist you tell me."

Trynne felt the gusts of magic parting away from her and Sunilik. The man in the silver mask radiated authority and power, but Trynne could tell it was emanating from some magic artifact he wore. She would have reached out with her own power to discover more about it, but she did not want to risk revealing herself.

"I was going to recommend holding off on the project for a while," Sunilik said, rocking back on his heels. "It seems premature to build an extension of the palace dedicated to a queen who has not, in fact, been chosen yet. The proposal that I looked over from the chief builder was quite extravagant considering the . . . ahem . . . state of the treasury."

The man in the mask clenched his fists. He was much taller than Sunilik and seemed even more aggravated that the man wasn't sniveling before him. There was another jolt from the magic, but it diverted around them and had no effect whatsoever.

"The emperor will choose his bride soon. I assure you, I have it from the highest authorities that the decision is imminent. The expansion of the palace must begin at once. To the specifications that were given to you. You would be wise to heed my counsel."

Again there was a throb from the magic.

"I will certainly take your *recommendation* under advisement," Sunilik answered in a carefree manner. "How long does the emperor have to decide before you force—*insist* that he marry someone chosen by the Wizrs?"

"You speak boldly," the Mandaryn said in a low growl.

"I speak the truth. Which is, I believe, why the emperor put me in charge of construction. Good day. I would like to continue my conversation with this young lady, so newly arrived."

"Watch yourself," the Mandaryn snarled. "I assure you that the treasury is not as depleted as you fear. Another shipment is due to arrive soon. Others will come afterward. There are additional . . . sources of wealth still untapped. The palace must be built to honor a queen. See that it is." He turned and scrutinized Trynne, gazing at her face and her mode of dress. She couldn't see his expression because of the mask, but there were dark lines painted beneath his eyes. He stared at her as if she were an insect waiting to be crushed under his boot. Then he stormed away and she felt herself begin to breathe again.

Sunilik watched him go with a dark look. "*That* sort of exchange happens rather frequently here, unfortunately. It's unsavory. I would give up this new position to return to the oasis. But while I serve Gahalatine, I will do so with integrity."

Trynne felt her courage building and her respect for King Sunilik as well. "What I have learned here is important. The emperor cannot endure a prolonged war. He will be forced to marry if he does not choose soon. Do you know who the Wizrs have chosen for him?"

Sunilik shook his head. "I do not. But I would expect him to choose someone from the noble houses of Ceredigion. Much could be gained from such an alliance."

Trynne swallowed, feeling her heart race. "Can you take me to the Queen of Atabyrion?"

"I have no pretext for visiting her, but I will tell you how to find her. If you look up the center of the tower, do you see the gardens near the top? That is the level where the highest-ranking women of the zenana stay. There are only a few suites up there, as rich as any palace. Look for the one with the door handles shaped like magnolia flowers. She is there."

"I cannot thank you enough for your support, Sunilik," Trynne said.

"You have kept my daughter away from this place," he replied with a bow. "This is not a shelter for women. There is something else here." His eyes narrowed. "Something dangerous. If you can disguise the queen some way, it may be possible for you to get out on the barges. They are the only way on or off this island without a Wizr."

Trynne smiled and touched his arm. "Thank you."

He mustered a grin for her, bowed formally, and left. Trynne craned her neck, staring up at the hanging garden high above.

◆　◆　◆

Trynne walked cautiously higher up the tower levels. She listened for the sounds of the female guardsmen—the Urdubegis—patrolling the halls, and often stopped and concealed herself behind a corner, an extravagant piece of furniture, whatever was available. At the top level, there were perhaps two dozen of the guards, continually walking along the main corridor. There were side corridors that opened to the air outside, and in one attempt to hide, Trynne found a monkey who had stolen a skein of grapes and was devouring the buds of fruit greedily. It glanced at her, chittered in warning, and continued to gorge itself. The din of the commotion down in the courtyard below could barely be heard at the heights of the tower.

Trynne walked down the hallway, nodding deferentially to the guardswomen as she passed, studying the doors leading to each of the suites. The doors were intricately carved with murals showing the fashions of Chandigarl. Everything was new and shining, and the marble tiles on the floors reminded her of a new Wizr set. Her thoughts were all awhirl: Would the Tay al-Ard work in the tower? Had Morwenna been caught? Was the poisoner a friend or foe?

Then she found it. The door handles were shaped like magnolia flowers, causing a prick of memory from the gardens of Kingfountain. The arch of the doorway was bedecked with extravagant gold flourishes, and the columns she passed were wide and full of grooves. Huge urns full of green plants decorated the sides. The details of the place were exquisite, and they were intended to show the lifestyle that wealth could purchase.

Trynne stopped and stood before the door. A guardswoman could be heard approaching from down the way, and Trynne knew she'd likely be challenged if found standing there. She needed to know if Lady Evie was alone. Using her magic would reveal herself, but it was a risk she had to take.

Trynne sent a trickle of magic into the room. She felt the presence of another Fountain-blessed inside. Was it a Wizr? She knew if she probed too much, it would alarm them, so she gripped the handle of the door and opened it. It released easily and quietly despite its heaviness.

Everything was bright and full of light. The interior of the suite was furnished with couches and decorative tables holding an assortment of flowers she'd never seen before. There was a lush balcony with gauzy curtains that reminded her a little of Ploemeur. Lady Evie stood beside it. She had a worried look on her face. She was dressed in a gown from Atabyrion, a simple thing made of green with a golden girdle. Her hair was dark and braided and she was fidgeting with her wedding ring. Lady Evie turned as Trynne entered the room and then her eyes widened with surprise. The worry deepened.

"I told you she would come," said a voice from behind the curtains. There was a shadow there she hadn't noticed before, but she recognized the voice.

Gahalatine.

CHAPTER TWENTY-TWO

Threat and Mate

The curtain rustled slightly and Gahalatine emerged from the balcony. The sun shone on him from behind, illuminating the emperor's decorative tunic, which was similar to that of Rucrius—full of painstaking detail. There was a belt that went around it and three familiar necklaces hung around his neck. The medallion she'd seen before along with the claw or tooth. His hair was askew and tousled, and he had a small beard, trimmed very close. He stopped next to Lady Evie, whom he towered over.

"You were expecting someone?" Trynne asked, feeling her heart flutter with fear. Gahalatine was standing too close to Evie. She had been the bait for this trap. Trynne bit her lip, feeling herself a fool.

"I was and you didn't disappoint me," he answered smoothly, giving her a wary but interested look. He brushed his finger along his upper lip. "I recognize the outfit from Chandleer. When we *last* met. It suits you, but I think you'd be more comfortable in an outfit like the queen's. We were speaking about you, Tryneowy Kiskaddon. I was learning what I could from the queen, but she is very strong-willed. She is also deeply loyal to you."

"Loyalty binds me," Lady Evie said.

Trynne took a step deeper into the room, glancing to either side to see if they were truly alone. She had only felt the presence of one Fountain-blessed in the room.

"Did you have to use your gift on her?" Trynne asked in a challenging tone.

"Only a little," Gahalatine answered. He stepped away from Lady Evie, putting himself between the two women. "I know it won't work against *you*."

Trynne's mind was whirling fast. How much did Gahalatine know or suspect about her? What had Lady Evie told him? What had he learned from others?

"Lady Evie, are you well? Are you all right?" She gave Gahalatine an accusing look. "What did she tell you about me?" she asked, locking eyes with him as she edged a little closer.

"How you were injured as a child," Gahalatine answered. "I admire how you've overcome your challenges." His tone told her he meant it. He clasped his hands behind his back, studying her. "She told me you're the Lady of Averanche, a very small port city on the border between Brythonica and Westmarch. It's on my maps. I've gazed at it from St. Penryn's. I've *heard* that you stopped entertaining suitors."

He gave her a pointed look that made her throat catch.

It felt as if the warmth of the room was closing in on her.

"You've invaded my kingdom," she said, trying to gather her wits to her. "You've threatened my king."

Gahalatine shrugged. "Yes, I tend to do that. Tryneowy, I implore you to hear my side. I'm sure you realize that I've caught you in my little trap. There are no ley lines from the High Tower. My guardians allowed you to wander in here. I didn't want it to be too easy, for fear you'd fly away like you did the last time. So much of what I've learned about you fascinates me." He swallowed, taking several steps closer to her, not in a threatening way, but like someone curious to know more. It put more distance between him and Lady Evie. One thing he *didn't* seem to know about was the Tay al-Ard she had strapped to her arm. He might not have even heard about the destruction of his fleet at Ploemeur.

"I have heard much about you as well," she said, matching his tone and a little of his haughtiness. "But what I've learned has only deepened my concern about the kind of man you are."

His brow furrowed. "It is not unjust to claim authority over a kingdom by right of conquest. The history of Kingfountain is ripe with such tales. Surely that cannot offend you."

Trynne shook her head. "You have that right, as does any king." She paused and added, "We once had a king whose words could influence people. He was known as a tyrant."

Gahalatine looked offended. "Are you comparing me with Severn Argentine?"

"No, I fear you may be worse," Trynne replied, jutting out her chin. She stepped deeper into the room, approaching him but keeping Evie within her field of vision. "You can tell a lot about a man by the dogs he keeps on a leash and the ones he lets roam free."

Gahalatine's look changed to one of surprise. His eyebrows lifted. He tapped his heart with his finger. "*I* am the one on the leash," he growled. He stepped closer to her. They were still far enough apart that he could not touch her. "And I cannot achieve the vision I have without a strong, courageous woman at my side. I seek, Tryneowy, to *change* the game that has been played out since the world was new and the boundaries of the Deep Fathoms were first established. The people truly suffer with hunger, blight, and disease because of the squabbling of their leaders and those who crave coin more than they do the well-being of their fellows. And you cannot tell me that such tortures do not happen in *your* kingdom. I pity the weak and the dispossessed. And I firmly believe that the populace of Kingfountain would welcome my benevolent hand if someone they trusted and respected stood at my side. Think on it, Tryneowy. Together, we could remake the world."

He was using his magic on her. She saw it was not deliberate—he wasn't trying to manipulate or coerce her. His convictions were so much a part of his character and his nature that the magic simply spilled out of him when he spoke about them. He was utterly confident that he was meant to rule the world.

But the power of his words, his convictions, could not pierce her heart. The magic of his words swept around her, leaving her with a strong sense of herself and what she believed. And she believed that it was King Drew's right to rule his own lands. That the Fountain had established him as the benevolent ruler who would—and had—brought peace, slowly, bit by bit. Gahalatine was a like a flood that threatened to sweep everything away. Drew was more patient, steadier. His Wizrs had always served him willingly. Gahalatine obviously wrestled with his own.

"You cannot make me believe you," Trynne said softly, piercing him with her gaze.

"I know," he said, a smile on his face. "Do you have any idea how far I have searched for someone like you? There are two young women from the Ceredigion Court who are Fountain-blessed. You and another. The Mandaryn have tried goading and coaxing me into taking the Argentine girl." His nostrils flared. "The daughter of a king. That is who they would choose for me. But I will not heed the Mandaryn or take a wife of their choosing." He paused, looking into her eyes, then said, "I fear they have abducted your father. I have had my trusted allies searching for him this last year, and if he were in my domain, I would know of it. So I suspect they are keeping him somewhere in your king's lands. When I attacked at Guilme, I had hoped to negotiate a marriage treaty with your father for your hand. And now you are here and within my power. Do not flee from me, gentle Tryneowy. You may be the only one who can save me from them."

Trynne swallowed, her ears ringing from his declarations. Was this the husband her mother had foreseen for her? Was that why Sinia had looked so sad whenever Trynne had asked about the vision?

The door of the chamber was yanked open and guardswomen stormed inside, swords drawn. A man with a silver mask stood amongst them.

"That is her!" He pointed at Trynne. "She is the poisoner from Pisan! She will kill the emperor!"

"Stop!" Gahalatine shouted angrily, holding up his hand. "Be silent!"

Trynne had been so caught up in the rush of magic pouring out of Gahalatine that she hadn't sensed another source of power building up outside the room. The Mandaryn with the silver mask was using the magical device in his possession to control the guardswomen. They were convinced Trynne was a dangerous threat.

"There are blades in her bag!" the Mandaryn shouted. "Kill her!"

The guardswomen flew at Trynne in a savage fury, rushing at her to defend the emperor they served and cherished. They seemed completely oblivious to his shouted commands.

"Trynne!" Lady Evie shrieked in terror.

"No!" Gahalatine raged, stepping between her and his own guards.

Trynne rushed toward the queen as she fumbled with her sleeve for the Tay al-Ard. She sensed a sword swinging toward her from behind and her magic responded to protect her. Trynne swiveled just in time, and the blade struck the lute case. The strap was severed and the case thumped to the floor. Whipping her leg around, Trynne kicked her attacker in the jaw, knocking her to the ground in a single blow. The next two attackers were almost upon them, but Trynne backstepped toward Lady Evie, pulling the Tay al-Ard free from its bindings.

Gahalatine had heaved two of her attackers away and he turned to gaze at her. His eyes were filled with panic and desperation. It was obvious he thought she was going to be murdered right in front of him, and just as apparent that he was powerless to stop it. The emperor of the Forbidden Court was powerless.

Trynne put the Tay al-Ard between her and Evie, grabbed the queen's hand with her own, and summoned the magic to take them away as swords slashed down to kill her.

The sound of a blade ringing against the stone lingered in her ears as the magic yanked them away.

CHAPTER TWENTY-THREE

Midnight

Trynne's heart was still racing when they appeared inside the fountain at the small chapel in Kingfountain. A couple of torches flickered from wall sconces at their sudden arrival, and Trynne felt the water soak into her skirts and boots. She didn't normally get wet when she traveled the ley lines, but the Tay al-Ard was a different magic, and it had brought her exactly where her frantic thoughts had imagined.

She was still clutching Lady Evie's arm, and the two stared at each other in the shadows for a moment, the stillness of the night such a contrast to the blazing day they had left on the other side of the world.

"That was terrifying," Lady Evie said at last, releasing her panicked grip on Trynne's arm. "I thought we'd both be killed." She stifled a sudden yawn.

Trynne was about to reply when she became aware of the presence of Fountain magic. It permeated the very air she breathed, whispering through the corridor like a breeze. It was as if an enormous shroud had fallen over the entire palace. It felt like fog on a misty morning.

Everything was utterly silent.

Trynne's brow furrowed and she walked to the edge of the fountain and stepped over. The waters sloshed and splashed as she and Lady Evie extricated themselves from it. Water dripped onto the polished marble floor.

Only then did Trynne see the two crumpled bodies that had been concealed by the edge.

Lady Evie gasped, seeing them at the same moment. "Look! Are they dead?"

Trynne knelt by the two bodies that were wearing Espion rings on their right hands. They had been stationed to guard the chapel fountain at all hours, day and night. Her insides quickened with fear and dread, but she heard the men breathing. Both were in a deep slumber.

"Something's wrong," Trynne whispered, once again sensing the magic that hung in the air. She jostled one of the men by the shoulder.

The Espion didn't move; he just rolled onto his back, his mouth parted. It was a magically induced sleep.

"This is unlike Kevan's men," Lady Evie said, shaking her head. She stifled another yawn. "They're supposed to be guarding this place."

"I think they are under a spell," Trynne whispered, holding up her hand. She was tempted to reach out with her magic, to divine the source of the shroud. The magic was trying to make her fall asleep, but it could only billow around her and Lady Evie. Trynne realized that her presence was the only thing keeping the Queen of Atabyrion awake.

"It's so quiet," Lady Evie whispered. Her look grew more concerned.

Trynne licked her lips. "The Wizr Rucrius was being held prisoner here," she said. "Morwenna claimed she'd drugged him to sleep before we left to find you."

"Morwenna said that?" Lady Evie answered in a distrusting tone.

Trynne nodded. "We must go to the king. Let's make sure he is safe."

"*And* my daughter," Lady Evie said.

They started walking down the dark corridor together. Trynne immediately felt the presence of multiple Fountain-blessed in the audience hall where the Ring Table stood. She discerned there was other magic at work as well. Fear churned inside her. What was happening? Had Rucrius broken free in the night?

They walked as quietly as they could, but without any other sound, their steps seemed loud. There was another knight crumpled on the ground, fast asleep, ahead, hidden by the shadows. Another was sitting up against a pillar, his head lolling to one side. Trynne's anxiousness grew with each step.

The main door to the audience hall lay just ahead. There were voices coming from it, but the thick door was too heavy for her to understand what was being said. They were the first sounds of life they'd heard since arriving in the fountain.

"My heart is full of dread," Lady Evie whispered, but her eyes were more angry than fearful.

They stopped outside the door. There were four knights collapsed in front of it, spears splayed out haphazardly. Trynne gripped the cold handle with her free hand, the other still gripping the Tay al-Ard. She was so tempted to reach out with her magic, but she knew it would immediately reveal her to whoever lurked on the other side of that door. Much better for them to crack the door open and take a look. Carefully, she and Lady Evie pulled on the heavy door, Trynne praying all the while the hinges wouldn't squeak.

The door resisted at first, but then it relented and opened, bringing a crack of light from the audience hall. There were torches lit inside and people were moving around urgently. Trynne blinked and pressed her eye to the slit.

Rucrius stood in the center of the room, his hand resting on the king's empty chair. He was still wearing the clothes in which he'd been rescued, but he was no longer a prisoner. He was the one barking orders.

"Change into their tunics quickly!" he said impatiently. Trynne saw that there were several warriors in the hall, quickly donning tunics of the Sun and Rose. She recognized their leaf armor from the Battle of Guilme. Her heart shriveled as she realized the palace was being stolen right under their noses. "Then return to the guard posts and pretend to be asleep like the others. When dawn comes, the people will see the treasure ship moored in the harbor. It will cause panic."

Another Wizr spoke up. Trynne hadn't noticed him because he was standing before Rucrius, who was much taller. "You know Gahalatine would not wish to win this way."

"Gahalatine will conquer Kingfountain as he desires," Rucrius snapped. "Is that not what matters? Their confusion will give us an easy path to victory. The city will fall. Then the king's champion will lose to our champion, and Gahalatine will challenge the king in combat. Without the Kiskaddon brat, the king will succumb to our power and relinquish the hollow crown."

"But this is sooner than we agreed upon, Rucrius!" the other Wizr said. She could not see him well, but she recognized him from the Battle of Guilme. He was one of the three Wizrs who had brought Gahalatine to King Drew on the hilltop.

"Events are already in motion, Astorel," Rucrius said dismissively. "The game goes on. The poisoner is in the Forbidden Court as we speak. She brought our enemy with her."

The other Wizr chuffed. "Maybe we should just kill the king now and be done with it."

Trynne's heart filled with a burning rage. Were they speaking of Drew or Gahalatine? There was a fallen spear on the ground in front of her, only a couple of steps away, and she felt a powerful urge to seize it and hurl it through Rucrius's back. The temptation was painful. But it was against one of the oaths she had taken as an Oath Maiden, and she would not give in to it. Still, she promised herself Rucrius's treachery against his own king and hers would be punished.

The sound of boots came from the corridor behind them and she felt the power and presence of Fountain magic once again. Trynne whirled around just in time to see more soldiers marching down the hall, all of them wearing the leaf armor. Lady Evie did the same. Another Wizr was with the warriors, and when they turned the corner, they saw the two women at the door.

The Wizr's eyes widened in surprise. "Who are you?" he demanded. She felt something in his eyes, some look of recognition.

The door behind them was shoved open by invisible hands, knocking them both away.

"Rucrius!" the Wizr shouted. "It's her!"

Trynne summoned her magic to defend herself. She had faced three Wizrs before, but not while fighting so many soldiers—that would be impossible. The magic revealed to her that the power of the sleeping spell was coming from high above the castle. She grabbed Lady Evie by the wrist and used the magic of the Tay al-Ard to bring them to the poisoner's tower.

◆　◆　◆

The rush of the magic spilled them both to the floor of the tower room, and they landed on their hands and knees. Trynne's head swam with dizziness, and the force of the magic blasting down from the staff above her rang in her ears. She had sensed the magic coming from the tower earlier, but it had not been activated at the time. It was certainly active now. The power radiating from it was so immense, it had rendered the entire palace asleep except for those the Wizrs had made immune to it.

Trynne kicked open the balcony window and stepped outside, knowing her time was measured in moments. She gazed out at a sea of fog shrouding Kingfountain's lower harbor beneath the falls. The fog was thick and unnatural, most unusual for the season, but she still saw the hulking treasure ship coming up the river. The crews and ships stationed at the harbor would not be able to see it coming. She heard the rush of the waterfall and realized with despair that the city was lost.

The Wizrs were controlling events, not Gahalatine. Trynne's hasty visit to the Forbidden Court had merely accelerated the plans they'd already been brewing.

Morwenna was involved in the plot. Trynne was certain of it. The Wizrs had chosen Severn's daughter to be Gahalatine's queen. Was she wittingly part of it, or a pawn in the scheme?

At that point, it didn't matter. Trynne had to get the king away from the palace. She was the only one who could. Gazing at the peak of the tower, she saw something crackling with power. A staff had been bound to the steeple, strapped with leather. It was the source of the magic.

"*Anoichto ekluo!*" Trynne commanded, gazing up at the staff bound to the tower spike. With her words, she unmade the fastenings of the straps and the staff fell from the spike, hurtling and spinning as it fell from the heights and cracked to pieces on the cobbles far below.

The fog of magic in the air vanished.

Save the king.

Her heart quailed with dread when she heard the whisper from the Fountain. She was still dizzy from using the Tay al-Ard, but she rushed back into the chamber. Lady Evie's face was ashen with concern, but she looked determined.

"We've lost the palace," Lady Evie murmured darkly. "Haven't we?"

Trynne nodded. "Their game does not end until they have the crown," Trynne said. "I need to take the king to shelter. The people will rally to fight for him. I think Dundrennan would be the strongest defense."

"It *will*," Lady Evie agreed passionately. "It is the strongest castle we have. I know it is. The ships cannot reach it, and the soldiers there will be loyal to the king. More so than to my own son."

Trynne nodded. "I will take us all there. Come!" She locked hands with Lady Evie and quickly envisioned the king's private chamber. They vanished, wrenched away by the magic.

The room was dark save for the burning embers still glowing from the brazier. Trynne stumbled, her legs turning to jelly from having used the magic so many times in such a short while. She was nauseated and felt like vomiting, but she uttered the word of power to restore her strength, feeling the power sip from her magic stores.

"Who's there?"

It was Drew's voice. He stood at the side of the bed, the sword Firebos in hand. The blade was glowing, illuminating his face, his tousled hair. He looked haggard and tired.

Trynne reached out with her magic and sensed Rucrius coming down the hall.

"Trynne," she answered hurriedly. "I'm here with Lady Evie. The castle is overrun, and I must take you to safety. Where's Genny?"

Drew rubbed his eyes, still clenching the blade. "Something made everyone fall asleep. I couldn't get up. I couldn't move until just a few moments ago."

"Where is Genny?" Trynne repeated more urgently. "Where's the baby?"

"The nursery, I think," Drew said. "She never came to bed last night. I think the baby was ill."

Save the king.

Trynne felt frantic, but the warning pounded through her, even more urgent that time. She tried to see how she could get all of them to safety and realized it wasn't possible.

Suddenly Lady Evie touched Trynne's shoulder. "I'll get them," she promised. "I know my way through the Espion tunnels. I'll get them to the sanctuary of Our Lady through the cistern. Go."

Trynne felt a pang of relief and nodded. Evie rushed to the wall and tripped the latch that opened the secret door. She disappeared into it and shut it behind her.

"My lord, we must go to Dundrennan," Trynne said. She marched up to him and seized his arm. The hollow crown sat next to the bed. The king stared at it as if it were a wolf spider, a bane. Then he took it up with his other hand, holding Firebos to his chest. He looked worried, heartbroken, and furious.

"Take us there," he ordered.

The door flew open, revealing Rucrius and several guards wearing the Sun and Rose. But they were imposters and she knew it. The Wizr's eyes were glowing, reflecting the light from the torches held by his lackeys.

Trynne pictured in her mind the castle of Dundrennan. She invoked the magic of the Tay al-Ard.

She felt the magic murmur.

Nothing happened.

A foul smile spread across Rucrius's face. "All magic has its limits."

The Wizr reached out his hand, the one with the beetle-sized ring, and the Tay al-Ard wrenched from her grasp and flew to him. He caught it triumphantly.

Then his visage shifted, his body altered, and suddenly Rucrius was King Drew, flanked by his knights. "Now give me my crown!" he snarled.

His eyes were still glowing.

♦ ♦ ♦

I made it off the island in the disguise of a gardener. There is a great war under way. The king of this land is seeking all available warriors to join the cause. I don't know how I know this, but I am skilled in the arts of war. I saw a knight riding his steed, and when I saw his sword, I knew that I could use it. I have neither money nor a weapon of my own. They say the king's army is across the sea fighting an ancient enemy. More warriors are needed. Perhaps I was a mercenary. I wish I could remember more.

♦ ♦ ♦

CHAPTER
TWENTY-FOUR

Scattered

"Stand behind me," Drew said to Trynne, gripping the pommel of Firebos with angry determination. "He may mask himself, but I am the true king."

Trynne felt the throb of worry and fear. She had no weapon, and the Tay al-Ard, which had failed her, had been wrenched from her hand. Rucrius had soldiers with him and she had no doubt they were here to murder her king. When the king tried to come before her, she held out her arm, barring him. Her magic reached out, looking for vulnerabilities in their enemies, searching for a way they could escape.

"You cannot take the crown," Trynne said defiantly to Rucrius. "It must be earned."

"You have been meddlesome long enough," the Wizr snapped. "Take the girl, she has useful information. Slay the king."

Trynne's magic saw that there were only three ways out of the chamber: through the door that Rucrius was blocking with his men, through the Espion tunnel that Evie had just used to flee, and another, which Rucrius would never suspect. There was a garderobe closet behind where she and the king stood, connected to the cesspit at the base of the castle. Her magic sensed that the shaft was wide enough for a single person. No ley lines passed through the room.

She needed to buy them some time. "My lord," she said over her shoulder. "Through the privy. Now! *Aspis!*"

She invoked the word of power to create a shield around her and the king, backing toward the privy doors as the warriors rushed forward. As soon as they reached the boundary of her shield, the magic flung them backward violently. She only had a moment or two, though—Rucrius could rip her shield apart. The king looked at her in confusion and then realized what she meant. A look of disgust twisted on his face as he turned and flung open the door to the garderobe.

She felt Rucrius's power throb against hers, but she maintained her hold on the shield.

"Quickly, my lord!" Trynne panted.

King Drew flung the wooden seat up and gazed down the black shaft.

"Into the cistern!" Trynne said, invoking her father's words.

King Drew's face twisted with revulsion, but he jumped down the shaft, holding his sword in one hand and the hollow crown in the other.

"Stop her!" Rucrius roared in fury.

Her shield unraveled. One of the soldiers rushed her, trying to club her on the head with the pommel of his sword. She caught his wrist, kicked him in the knee and then the groin, and wrestled the blade from him by flipping him onto his back. Spinning the blade around her back, she struck one of the knights in the chest as he charged at her.

There was no time to spare. Still holding the sword, Trynne rushed to the garderobe and jumped in after the king.

The black stone walls of the shaft rushed past her, and it felt like traveling over the ley lines until she hit a curve in the stone. She had to scrape her front until she began free-falling again.

She landed in a heap of muck just as the king pulled himself free from it. His sword glowed a brilliant blue.

"This is awful," Drew said through clenched teeth. The smell of the cesspit was unbearable, and he started retching uncontrollably.

Trynne knew a word of power to help fight the feeling, so she invoked it and quickly scanned the darkness. They were in a large stone box, and the opening they'd slid down was on the ceiling just behind them. On the other side of the room was a series of deep stone steps leading upward. She hurried over to them, and when she looked up, she saw an iron-barred hatch. Moonlight and fresh air were pouring in from above. The cesspit was hot, and the sound her shoes made in the filth sickened her. Another body landed in the muck pile behind them. Trynne, who had made her way up the steps, whirled around and watched King Drew kill the attacker with a single blow of his sword.

Trynne pushed on the iron hatch, but it was locked by an iron ring fastened to a bar. "*Anoichto!*" she said, and the lock slid open. The hatch groaned as she pushed on it.

"Up here!" she called to Drew, straining her shoulders to lift the hatch. The king rushed up the steps and helped her push it up. The hatch rattled and clanged as it fell away. Trynne's heart was still in her throat at the narrowness of their escape. The others were coming, or would be.

The king set down his sword and hoisted Trynne around her middle to lift her up through the hole. He handed up the crown and both blades, which she set on the edge of the opening, and then he reached up to grab her hand. She planted her foot on the side of the wall and helped pull him up as he clambered out.

The sound of another body landing in the cesspit alerted them that their time was nearly done. There was cursing and grumbling followed by the sound of someone vomiting. Trynne and Drew slammed down the hatch lid together, and then she worked feverishly to secure the lock while he claimed his weapon and crown.

There were stone walls on three sides of the hatch, the kind of rough-hewn stone that was not meant to be decorative. The edges were blunted and the pieces held together by mortar.

"By the Fountain, Trynne, what's going on?" the king whispered to her. "Where is the Espion? Where are my knights? How was I left so vulnerable?"

After locking the hatch, she gripped the sword she'd commandeered and led the way out of the inlet. She gazed both ways, searching for movement. They were in the gardener's paddock, where the rakes and shovels and wheelbarrows were stored. When she craned her neck, she saw the castle rising up behind them, dark and skeletal.

"My lord, there is a plot afoot," she answered, rubbing her hand along her arm to quell the shivering. Her clothes and skin reeked of the cesspit, but the stench was no longer so overpowering. "Morwenna and I went to Chandigarl. I brought back Lady Evie, as you saw."

"Where is my half sister?" Drew demanded intently, his eyes narrowing.

"Back in Chandigarl, for all I know," Trynne said. "Her disguise failed while we were going to rescue Lady Evie from the zenana. My disguise wasn't caused by magic, so no one suspected me. But no, that's not true. Gahalatine set a trap. He *let* me come into the tower, hoping to capture me. My lord, I'm sure there are more layers to the situation than what I understand." She gazed at the abandoned yard and then motioned for the king to follow her to the arched doorway leading to the gardens.

A rattling at the hatch behind them startled her. She did not believe Rucrius would jump down the shaft after them. He was too proud, too powerful for such a scheme. Reaching the doorway, she listened and heard the tread of boots coming toward it.

"Someone is coming," the king whispered, hearing the sound.

"There is a fountain that way," Trynne said, pointing toward the door. "I know this part of the grounds well. If we can reach it, I can take us through the ley lines." She motioned for him to stand on the other side of the door. She pressed her back against the stone, holding the sword up. Drew mimicked her and waited breathlessly on the other side.

The door handle jiggled and then it opened, but it was not Rucrius or any of his men on the other side. Drew, the castle's woodsman, entered the gardener's paddock, gripping an axe in his hand. His snowy white hair nearly glowed in the moonlight.

Trynne sighed and let the sword drop.

"Drew?" the king asked in surprise.

"Your Majesty!" the woodsman said with a chuff of surprise. "What are you doing here? You smell like the royal hog pens, my lord."

The king let out a short laugh. "They say a pig is happiest in its own filth. I assure you, that is not my emotion. Where is Liona?"

The woodsman lowered the axe. "She's abed. I awoke with a start and had a strong feeling that I needed to come to the paddock. It's an ill omen, my lord. The grounds are too quiet. I heard some strange noises."

"The castle is overrun," Trynne said, shaking her head. "The Wizr Rucrius is impersonating the king."

The snowy-haired woodsman shook his head angrily. "By what black art is he doing that? Are you escaping Kingfountain, then? I think the Fountain woke me to help you."

Trynne felt certain it was true. She turned to the king. "We have to get away from the palace. There was a magic staff in the poisoner's tower that made everyone fall asleep. I broke it before coming to you, so it cannot harm anyone now. It's my belief that the Wizr was planning to harm or imprison you and then pretend to be you to disrupt our defenses. I don't think Gahalatine would condone his actions."

King Drew nodded in agreement. "Master Woodsman—we share the same name. Right now, you must act on my behalf. Find Lord Amrein of the Espion. Tell him that we've escaped and that there is an imposter in the palace. Tell him to rally our forces to Dundrennan. We will fight for Kingfountain from the North. Then get you and your wife to safety. Can I entrust you with this mission?"

The woodsman nodded sternly. "I will not fail you, my lord."

"Thank you. I depend on it."

They would away to Dundrennan, and Drew would send warriors to meet them. Lady Evie would try to bring Genevieve and the baby to the sanctuary of Our Lady. Trynne told herself that it would all work out as planned. She had to believe it.

The woodsman hefted his axe and returned to the garden. Trynne and the king emerged into the immaculate grounds. In her heart, Trynne believed Gahalatine was not part of the ploy. He intended to win his victory on the battlefield, not through trickery. But his own servants were actively plotting against him as well.

Together, Trynne and Drew hurried across the gardens. Trynne looked at the shadowy magnolia trees. The reminder of Fallon struck a bitter chord inside of her.

"Where is your protector?" Trynne asked. "Where is Fallon?"

"He's still at the palace. I ordered him to summon his army and bring it to Kingfountain," Drew said, shaking his head. "His messenger has probably just arrived at Dundrennan."

Trynne sighed. She saw the fountain ahead. The waters were stilled at night, so there wasn't the sound to guide her to it.

"I can't thank you enough, Trynne. If you hadn't returned when you did, all would have been lost. I can imagine someone like Rucrius *pretending* to be me." His voice was swollen with anger and resentment. "Genevieve will see through the disguise if he tries to lure her out of Our Lady. He might pretend, but he cannot be me. Now I regret that we didn't execute him the moment you arrived with him as your prisoner."

"Wizrs are the most powerful piece on the board," Trynne said. "Your Wizrs have always served you and the interests of Kingfountain.

In Chandigarl, it is a different culture. Men like Rucrius feel they are above the king."

Drew nodded. "I never felt that from Myrddin," he said. "Or your mother. Or from you, for that matter. Do you think that my sister was part of this plot, Trynne? Do you think she was trying to dethrone me?"

"Yes, my lord," Trynne said honestly. "Yes, I do think she is part of it."

As they approached the quiet fountain, the panic she'd felt earlier began to subside. She had feared the waters would be guarded. Glancing around, she reached out with her magic, knowing full well that Rucrius would be able to feel her doing so. She wanted him to know she had escaped with the king. She wanted him to worry about what they would do next.

At the center of the fountain was a series of sculptures depicting scenes of the Deep Fathoms, including a representation of the Lady of the Fountain. As Trynne stared up at it, she wondered where her mother was at that moment. Was it dark where she was, or daybreak? A breeze washed the scent of the magnolias over her. Trynne closed her eyes and stepped over the edge of the railing. The king followed her, gazing back at the castle he was abandoning. His mouth was pressed into an angry frown. The sword Firebos dipped down toward the waters as he held it in a loose grip.

"To Dundrennan, then," he said to her.

Trynne shook her head. "No. To Averanche first. It's time you met your other protectors, my lord."

CHAPTER
TWENTY-FIVE

The King's Defense

There was not even a pale glimmer of dawn in the horizon yet. But the Oath Maidens were already up and training fiercely. The noise of staves clacking against each other was mixed with the din of steel blades. Trynne had brought King Drew through the garden fountain to her castle and had walked to the upper battlements, which offered a view of the yard. True to form, Captain Staeli was drilling the girls hard before the dawn, and he would continue to drill them throughout the day.

For a long while, the king stared dumbfounded at the action below in the yard. There were easily a hundred girls wearing padded tunics and leather arm bracers. Some trained with shields, others with spears. A row of girls with bows practiced relentlessly with the archery butts. Those with long hair had it tethered back into braids or bound with straps. They were all dressed like warriors. Trynne couldn't suppress a smile as she leaned over the wall, gazing down at the assembled group.

"I'd not imagined there were so many," the king whispered in amazement. "This is what Genevieve has been supporting?"

"There are even more," Trynne said. "Those who have completed two months' training are sent back to their homes with the skills they have honed and the weapons they have trained with, but some have stayed on to help train more. Each of these girls has been trained to battle Gahalatine's knights. That girl, the one with the dark hair, is the daughter of King Sunilik of the desert. She trained among her own people and has been a friend to me." She turned to him and added, "There are nearly a thousand Oath Maidens throughout the realm as we speak."

"A thousand," Drew gasped in wonder, shaking his head. He pressed his hands against the edge of the battlement wall. "I'd never imagined there would be so many. Who is that overseeing the training? I think I recognize him. He was one of your father's captains?"

"Captain Staeli," Trynne said.

"Yes, Staeli. He was there at Guilme. When I was a lad, he became your father's captain after the Battle of Dundrennan." Clenching his fist, he tapped it on the stone of the battlement. "I should like to meet them, Trynne. But not looking and smelling like this. Can I borrow some clothes from the Lady of Averanche? I should be very proud to wear your badge."

◆ ◆ ◆

It was daybreak when Trynne and Drew returned to the training yard. The king was outfitted as one of the guardsmen of Averanche, wearing the badge of the Tower Moon. A suitable scabbard and belt had been furnished for the blade Firebos, and the weapon of kings was strapped around Drew's waist. Beneath the tunic, he wore a chain hauberk. The hood was down around his shoulders. Trynne had also provided a leather satchel for him to keep the hollow crown on his person at all times.

Trynne also wore the garb of a warrior, and her two blades were strapped behind her. She had sturdy boots and pants, both of which were well worn and had served her well in her own training as a knight. When the king saw her, he startled a bit.

"I suppose it hadn't dawned on me fully that you also made the time to train with Captain Staeli," he said with a sheepish grin.

Trynne hooked her thumbs in the broad leather belt. For an instant, she thought he had figured out her secret, that he'd recognized her as the Painted Knight. But in most of her appearances as the knight, she'd used her magic ring to alter her looks. "I was the first to train with him, my lord. And I have for several years." She had the urge to tell him about Myrddin and the oaths she had taken, but just as she was about to speak, she felt the power of the Fountain stiffen her tongue. It was still not time to reveal it to him.

She gestured toward the door, and they walked together along the hall. Farnes had gone ahead to warn Captain Staeli they were coming.

When they reached the door leading to the battlement wall, from which they could take the stairs down to the training yard, Trynne paused, gripping the handle.

"The crown, my lord," she said, nodding to the satchel. "Let them feel that you are their true king."

Drew nodded in agreement and undid the straps of the satchel. His expression was conflicted as he drew out the ancient, tarnished crown. He stared at it for a moment, the light of the day glimmering off the metal band, but he did not put it on.

"What's wrong, my lord?"

He glanced from the symbol of his power to her face, meeting her gaze. "I'm impressed that you've assembled such a force willing to fight for me, Trynne. I'm humbled, actually. You were the most prescient of us all." He paused, gathering his words carefully. "But I'm struck by the realization that some of those maidens will die for me." His free hand clutched at his tunic front, as if his heart were paining him. "How can I ask that of them?"

He gave her an imploring look. There was no doubt that he needed the additional support, but he was still reluctant to use it. Part of him still saw these warriors as innocents in need of protection.

Trynne felt a splash of insight in her mind. She turned to face him fully, her back to the door.

"My lord, let me try and put your mind at ease. Many women fear that they will die in childbirth. Yet despite that fear, we still willingly choose to bring life into this world." Trynne turned her shoulder and gently patted the door. "Each one of these women who came to Averanche made the choice to be here. None were compelled. None were forced. If they die giving birth to your kingdom, is that not just as worthy a cause? They have chosen to be here, my lord. They have chosen to sustain you as their king. Their rightful king. I have been to Chandigarl and seen the opulence and riches there. But there is also a foulness to that kingdom that I don't comprehend. I choose to fight for you, my true king and sovereign lord. And so do *they*."

She could tell her words had struck him to his heart. Drew was silent for a moment, then he nodded to her and put the crown on his head. She felt the power of it radiating like sun melting the slush of snow.

"Thank you, Trynne Kiskaddon. A simple village maid once offered her help to the Prince of Occitania. And look what she accomplished." He gave her a grateful smile and a nod. "Open the door."

Trynne beamed at him as she tugged open the door. With one hand on the hilt of Firebos, Drew marched ahead of her and was greeted by a thrum of cheers from the Oath Maidens assembled in the yard below. An even louder cheer sounded when she appeared behind him.

King Drew marched down the steps of the battlement wall and entered the throng of warriors who gathered around him eagerly. Haley from Dundrennan stood near the front, taller than many of the others. She'd be helpful in securing assistance from the garrison. Maciel, the thief's daughter. Gillian of Passey. Brooke was grinning as if she were ready to rush an army all by herself. The group of them gathered together, anxious to see the king up close.

"Stand at arms!" Captain Staeli roared, his command breaking the spell of adoration.

At his command, all the women separated into even rows and columns, legs spread in a martial stance, one hand behind their backs, their faces at attention.

Staeli walked slowly and deliberately, pausing to gaze sternly at the girls who had not fully stifled their excitement.

"My lord," Staeli said with a sniff, bowing before the king, "I present to you the Oath Maidens of Averanche. All have been trained and will serve you faithfully. There is not a one of them whom I wouldn't trust your life with, my lord king. They will fight to the last. Every single one of them."

King Drew nodded his head at the little speech. He began to stride in front of the first row of warriors. "Last night, I was driven from the palace of Kingfountain by treachery," he said. "My wife and daughter, I presume, have made it to the sanctuary of Our Lady. I know not for certain. I have no Espion to give me reports. I have none of my knights or captains. You," he said, pausing in his walk and gazing at them, "are all that I have. We go to battle, my friends. I will not relinquish this crown willingly. Our enemy has magic in his words. He has persuaded many to bend the knee and serve him. He has replaced kings with men of his choosing. But our most dangerous foes are his Wizrs, who scheme and plot and murder. They do not know us or our customs very well. And they do not know that our people will not be ruled by a stranger."

He unsheathed the sword Firebos, and a shimmering blue light emanated from the naked blade as he held it aloft. "The Fountain gave me this weapon just as it gave me this crown." He lowered his sword. "And it has given me all of you." Drew paused, his voice becoming thick with emotion. "I may not deserve such blessings, but I am grateful for them. I accept your oath of service. Serve the Fountain, and you serve me. We ride to the North. I will defend my kingdom at Dundrennan. Ride with me, my sisters. Fight with me. You each have the courage of a hundred men."

A shout of energy throbbed in the air as the Oath Maidens united their voices in a thunderous cheer.

◆   ◆   ◆

The army of Averanche camped that night in a meadow beside an ancient grove of yew trees. Everyone would sleep out of doors on blankets, including the king. While the men from Trynne's garrison in Averanche had chosen to camp in the meadow itself, the women had sought the shelter of the yew trees. There were no cookfires to reveal the army's position. The horses were being tended to.

Trynne stifled a yawn on the back of her hand, her body weary from the hard riding that day and from the events of the last few days.

"You're exhausted, Trynne," Drew said as he walked alongside her. They had just visited the camp of the men, where Drew had spoken to the soldiers. They had fought at the Battle of Guilme, and some were anxious at the prospect of facing Gahalatine's forces again. They had invited the king to camp amongst them, but he had declined, saying that the Oath Maidens were charged with protecting his royal person. A gibbous moon hung in the sky, bathing the meadow in silver light.

"I am fine," Trynne answered, struggling to conceal another yawn.

"How long has it been since you last rested?" he asked her pointedly.

She couldn't even remember. The previous night had been a flurry of nonstop action, from her journey to the Forbidden Court to their return to Averanche. The army of Oath Maidens had begun its march immediately, and couriers had been sent out to summon the rest to Dundrennan. They had ridden hard and changed horses at Beestone castle, where they'd put the castellan on alert and sent out word via the Espion that the true king was on the march. Part of the garrison had ridden with them.

"I may have dozed a bit in the saddle," Trynne said.

"Well, let's remedy that. You'll be of no use to anyone if you're too tired. I'd like to send one of the maidens to Grand Duke Elwis. I know he wishes to reclaim Brugia, but I need his help defending the realm. Whom would you trust on such a mission?"

Trynne thought about it. "Rani Reya. I will ask her to go."

"I trust your judgment. Send her in the morning. We all need to rest."

Several Oath Maidens were standing guard around the grove, including Emilia, the master archer. She lowered her bow when she saw who it was.

"If any of the *other* men try to visit our camp during the night," she asked the king with a sly voice, "do we have your permission to rebuff them . . . sharply?"

Drew chuckled. "Indeed. They won't make the mistake twice."

Trynne grinned as she led the king to the edge of the woods, where blankets had been gathered around the gnarled roots of a tree. There were so many bedrolls around, it was difficult to step over them to reach the vacant space at the center of the area—the spot they'd reserved for the king. Drew nestled down next to a tree, leaning back against it instead of lying down.

Trynne found her blanket and settled into it after unstrapping her sword belt. The smell of the dirt and loam was intoxicating. Her eyelids were getting heavier just from being near the ground.

"Won't you sleep, my lord?" she asked, propping herself on her elbow.

"I will," the king answered softly. The sound of breathing and the quiet murmur of voices mixed with the noise of crickets and cicadas. Oath Maiden sentries ghosted in and out of the trees, keeping watch while the others slept. There was excitement in the air, as thick and palpable as the yeasty smell of the gorse.

Trynne laid her head on her arm, her mind spinning with fatigue. She would fall asleep in moments, she had no doubt of that.

"Trynne?"

The king's voice was just a whisper.

"Yes, my lord?" She lifted her head again, staring at him in the darkness. The massive yew shadowed them. There was no glint of light coming from him at all.

"A thought struck me just now," he said, shifting a little to get more comfortable. "I just wanted to share it with you."

"Please do," she said.

"For the last year, I have felt so . . . so forsaken by the Fountain. It felt as if everything was being wrenched away from me. First Myrddin. Then your father. Your mother. Some of my dukes. Now my wife and daughter. One by one, those most important to me have been taken away. I've been disheartened, Trynne. Why would the Fountain allow this to happen? Why would it give me the kingdom and then painfully strip it away from me?

"You've experienced such evils too. Misery and grief that surpasses my own. Have either of us ever deliberately acted against the Fountain's wishes? Not that I can think of, anyway. Yet still this has happened." His voice sounded forlorn, yet there was a spark of hope in it still.

"And what have you decided, my lord? What have you realized?" She gazed at the dark shadows, unable to see him. But she heard his steady breathing.

"Your father taught me that history repeats itself over and over. And so a thought struck me. My own grandfather, King Eredur, had his kingdom wrested away from him by his uncle Warrewik. He had to flee to Brugia with his brother, Duke Severn. He had to win his kingdom a second time. It was Genevieve's mother who told me the story, and then Polidoro confirmed it when I asked him about it. Eredur lost everything and had to live by the means of the King of Brugia. He had no soldiers. He only had his brother. His wife and children were in sanctuary. Does this not sound familiar?"

Trynne felt a ripple from the Fountain in her heart, warming her against the cold of the night. "Very," she answered with a smile.

"Then Polidoro told me something that filled me with hope. Eredur never would have reclaimed his throne all alone. The people wanted him to be king, not Warrewik. Not an Occitanian prince. The one who helped my grandfather win back his crown was his poisoner, Ankarette Tryneowy. Sometimes I forget that you were named after her. I'm glad you are with me, Trynne. Good night."

His words warmed Trynne more than her blanket. He was a kind-hearted man—a good and true leader—and she had to believe that he was right, that they would prevail.

"Good night, my lord." Trynne laid her head down on her arm again and fell asleep immediately.

She wasn't sure how long she slept before being jostled awake. It was still dark, in the fullness of night.

Drew's hand was on her shoulder. A man stood by the king holding a small shielded lantern. She didn't recognize him, but she noticed the Espion ring on his hand.

"Trynne," the king whispered. She rose quickly, her muscles aching and weary.

"What's wrong?" she asked, trying not to groan.

"This man is an Espion from Glosstyr. He says Gahalatine's fleet, the one that sacked Legault, has landed at Blackpool. Duke Severn is under attack. The battle started at sunset."

CHAPTER
TWENTY-SIX

Trapping the Boar

It was a bruising ride from the yew forest to Blackpool. Trynne wished the old Wizr board had never been destroyed, that they could observe the pieces and see which were black and which were white. The kingdom was besieged and what they lacked most was information. Drew had asked for Trynne's advice on whether she thought Severn had joined his daughter in betraying them. If they hastened to Blackpool, would they be greeted with a trap?

In Trynne's mind the solution was obvious. Speed was essential. If Severn were loyal, their arrival might aid him. If he were false, knowing sooner would be better. Either way, an enemy army could block the road to Dundrennan, and it was critical that they reach the mountain fortress as soon as possible.

Going to Blackpool would only help their cause.

They had roused the sleeping troops with word of the conflict. The marching soldiers were told to move quickly, to abandon their camp and to get on the road under the pale moonlight. Riders from the

Espion were dispatched to bring the duke word that support was on its way. The king's presence was to be kept a secret.

Trynne was still weary, but at least she'd managed a little sleep. Despite her dwindling reserves of magic, she was ready for a fight.

Dawn found them on the road. As Trynne rode alongside the Oath Maidens, she could sense the tension that hung in the air. They had trained to go to battle. Blackpool might be the first opportunity to face their enemies. There was excitement. There was also fear.

The small army from Averanche marched up the road. This was the army of Captain Staeli, a proven battle commander. His eyes were radiant with emotion. He looked eager for a fight, to prove the mettle of the women he had relentlessly trained and the men who had served under him so courageously.

Midmorning, a rider from the Espion arrived with news that the battle was still under way. Severn would not quit the field even though he was overmatched. His soldiers had fought hard all night long, refusing to quit. The field was littered was corpses, it was said, and the enemy had nearly encircled Severn's forces. The town was occupied by Gahalatine's army, but Severn would not quit the battlefield.

Trynne's stomach roiled with worry as they rode hard toward Blackpool, trying desperately to arrive in time. When they crested the hill that spread down to the plains surrounding the city, Trynne could see the shore and the fleet in the harbor. She was reminded of the story of how Lady Evie had once set a trap for Eyric Argentine in that very place. This battlefield was much larger.

It was clear to her from the vantage of the summit that this was a one-sided battle. Severn's army was going to lose. She could see that more soldiers were still unloading from Gahalatine's ships. There was a never-ending flood of them, like the surf that hammered the shore. The stains of death were everywhere. She could see the strewn bodies in the field below, the snapped battle standards, could hear the moans of the wounded and the dying.

Duke Severn was down to his last hundred men, if that. His army was surrounded, and she thought she could spy the old king in the thickest part of the fighting. He had no horse. None of them did.

Severn was trying to stem the tidal flood by himself and she thought she knew why. Before the Battle of Guilme, her father had confronted him about the men in silver masks—the Mandaryn, she now realized—who had been infiltrating Glosstyr. Surely Gahalatine had determined that this was a weak point of the realm. But Severn would not have it said that his duchy had been won through treachery. He would rather die than be remembered as a traitor.

"By the Fountain," King Drew said hoarsely as his stallion rested next to hers, panting and lathered from the hard ride. "We've come too late. Too late!" There was a hard anger in his voice.

Trynne examined the battlefield. Even with the troops they'd brought, there were not enough of them to stem the advance. What would her father do in this situation?

She stared down at the fierce fighting, at the men of the White Boar surrounded by their enemies. Should they abandon their countrymen to their fate?

The thought struck her forcibly. No. The men had held their ground against impossible odds. Their king had come to rescue them. And even if they could not drive away Gahalatine's forces, they could save the wounded survivors. She knew what her father would have done. He would have ridden down there to rescue Severn himself.

"My lord," Trynne said, her voice choked with emotion. "By your leave, let me take my maidens into the fray. Raise your banners and wear the crown, and hold aloft your sword. Have the soldiers make a clamor on their shields. They do not know how many soldiers we have brought. Let's give them a fright."

Drew stared at her in surprise and then a grin brightened his face. "A deception."

"A ruse, my lord," she said, nodding. "It may not work."

"But then again, it just may," the king said, full of confidence. "Take your maidens. Go!"

Trynne nodded and quickly rode up to Captain Staeli. "Protect the king. I'm taking the maidens into battle."

His expression told her what she already knew—her plan was risky, no, insane—but he was a soldier first and foremost. He obeyed. The look he gave her was full of worry. "Don't be rash, lass. That's all I will say."

She gave him a crooked smile. "Are you worried about me, Captain?"

"Aye," he answered like gravel. "And always will be."

◆　　◆　　◆

Trynne fed part of her magic into the stallion she rode, invoking the word of power that would banish fatigue and weariness. The ground thrummed with the noise of horses' hooves as the host of Oath Maidens charged down the hill. The enemy had turned to face the onslaught of horses. Trynne saw rows of archers lining themselves up in front of the leaf-armored knights. They were disciplined and calm, row after row of steel and fletching and death. Trynne's heart hammered in her ribs. Was this foolishness? How many of her sisters would fall? She dared not think on it.

A shout of command was given and the archers drew back their arrows, kneeling in the trampled grass, elbows pulled back, fists by their cheeks. The order was given and a hail of arrows arced skyward before plummeting like daggers. Before the first volley had fallen, a second was launched.

Trynne felt the magic of the Fountain sweep through her as the arrows began to land in the grass all around her, sticking like quills on a porcupine. She gritted her teeth, hearing the screams and cries of horses stumbling and falling.

The throb of magic swelled in the air as a cloud of arrows hammered down at them. Then it dawned on her why she hadn't heard any screams from the maidens. And it thrilled her to her core. One of the five oaths they had sworn was never to kill a man by spear or arrow—and in return, they would not be slain by one. The magic of the oaths they had taken had been extended to the Oath Maidens riding with her, forming a shield of sorts that was invisible but real. But it had not protected some of their steeds.

She was close enough to see the archers, close enough to see the fear bloom in their eyes when they realized their bolts hadn't harmed a single maiden. Their discipline shattered, they tried to claw their way through the leaf-armored knights to escape the front lines of the battle. Trynne had a sword already in hand, the reins tight in her other, and watched as the archers abandoned their lines.

Trynne's horse was in front, but she heard the thunder of her companions' charge, felt them coming as a scythe to mow the wheat. She heard the tumult coming from the army behind them, the clatter she'd asked the king to make. When the maidens screamed a furious war cry as they leaped into the ranks of the enemy, it felt as if a tide had swarmed the enemy. Trynne surrendered to her instincts, to the wellspring magic that flooded her with knowledge and experience from hundreds of similar battles.

Their foes wilted before them. Some were running, some were trying to fight, and a few were attacking their own forces in the confusion and chaos. Trynne charged ahead, swinging her blade on both sides of her horse as she went, fighting her way through the ranks.

Trynne's magic enveloped her as she fought her way toward the beleaguered soldiers. Attacks from the glaives glanced off her hauberk, but she countered viciously and fast, and so did her sisters. The ranks of Gahalatine's soldiers broke apart, and the warriors began to flee, creating an opening to the stranded knights of Ceredigion. There was a cheer from the men of Glosstyr, a throaty roar of triumph.

In that moment, Trynne felt the urge to invoke the ring of disguise she still wore on her finger. The power came over her, almost without her bidding it to, and she felt it transform her and her steed. She could see the illusion of it—she was wearing the armor of the Maid of Donremy, disguised as the Painted Knight—even though she knew it was not real. In the commotion, she butted forward, using her sword to carve a path through the dense melee.

Finally they reached the haggard knights, their black tunics drenched, the white boars now crimson. She saw Severn, ashen-faced, bleeding from multiple wounds, barely able to stand. He leaned against a spear, gripping a battle standard in one hand and a bloodied sword in the other. Men had fallen all around him. There were perhaps less than fifty remaining.

Trynne saw the duke's eyes on her. He had no Fountain magic left. His stores were completely depleted. But she felt the presence of another Fountain-blessed. A Wizr.

As she approached Severn Argentine, the man she had sensed stepped out from amidst the fleeing soldiers, his face twisted with rage. He was brimming with magic—until now, there'd been no reason for him to use it. The only armor he wore was a helmet buckled beneath his chin. His robes were ornate, in keeping with the customs and fashions of his people. He was dark-skinned, nearly coal black, with a nose ring and jeweled bracelets. The eyes of the Wizr were full of wrath as he stared at her, although she knew he saw the Painted Knight.

He gave a cough of command, the word of power to dispel magic and reveal that which is hidden. "*Apokaluptis!*"

She felt the blast of it strike her, radiating from him like a rock thrown into a pond. The Wizr's eyes widened with surprise and realization when it did not affect her. Had her very immunity to the magic revealed her to him?

Slapping her steed's flanks with the flat of her blade, she charged him. He spat spell after spell at her, trying to bind her, to thwart her, but none of them worked. His magic was powerless against her, and she watched his eyes widen in terror as she bore down on him with her horse, sword raised. Her magic revealed, once again, his vulnerability. As she'd sensed with the other Wizrs, his neck was his weakness. It was why he wore a helmet into battle.

That helmet bounced twice on the ground before his body slumped to the ragged earth. The dark magic in the air vanished.

Trynne yanked on the reins, watching as the warriors of Gahalatine fled toward the city. Other soldiers were coming; pikemen wielding long spears with hooked flanges were rushing in to defend the invading forces against the mounted knights. The poles could be fixed in the earth, forming a wall of spikes that even the bravest of horses would shy from. The response was quick and efficient. Despite the euphoria, she knew that they were still vastly outnumbered.

It was time to leave.

She rode back to Severn. He was rallying his men as the Oath Maidens helped them up onto their horses, the men riding behind the women. Severn refused to accept a hand, insisting that each of his warriors should be rescued first. He hoisted the battle standard and waved it in the faces of the onrushing pikemen, shouting defiance at them in a hoarse voice.

"Come on, you blackguards! I spit in Gahalatine's eye! Where's your bravery now! You bleeding cowards! Come and fight us! Fight our Painted Knight, you craven fools!"

One by one, the surviving knights of Glosstyr were pulled up onto the saddles of the Oath Maidens. Trynne gazed around the field, and her heart grieved at all the lost lives, the wickedness of war. It was Gahalatine's ambition that had started it.

All the surviving knights had been rescued. Only Severn was left. Trynne rode up to him, her face impassive.

"My kingdom for a horse," Severn croaked, a sneer on his face as he gazed at the oncoming warriors. Once again he had faced the odds and prevailed.

Trynne said nothing but reached her hand down to him. "I think we can spare one," she said gruffly.

◆ ◆ ◆

I joined the king's army. There are rumors that the foreign war is not going well, that more soldiers are needed to join the attack. They are seeking older men now and training us in the arts of war. I keep quiet and to myself. It's better to sleep in the barracks than in the brush. There is plenty of food. I have this feeling that I need to keep silent. To not reveal that I don't remember my name. I call myself Stiev. I don't know why. There was a man in the barracks the size of an ox. He thrashed anyone who stood up to him. I tried to stay out of his way, but he sought me out and tried to intimidate me. A feeling came over me. I knew his weakness and hit him there. I hit him hard. Now he stays away from me. They all do. The training yard is my favorite place to be. I know more than the weapons masters. But I don't let on that I do. Maybe I used to be one? They say we might be put on a boat soon and sent to the enemy's kingdom.

◆ ◆ ◆

CHAPTER
TWENTY-SEVEN

Dundrennan

Following the battle, there was no time to attend to the dead. Chandigarli reinforcements began to march toward the field from Blackpool, and Drew issued the order to continue north to Dundrennan. Trynne had released Severn near the king and transformed back to herself amidst the press and confusion. Another knight had offered his horse to the duke.

She rode up next to the king after he gave the order.

His face brightened in relief when he saw her. "You're safe!" he said. "Captain Staeli lost track of you, but said you were in the thickest part of the fight. Did you see the Painted Knight, Trynne? He joined the battle and rescued Severn."

"Yes, I've heard," Trynne answered, not wanting to lie to him outright. She felt a compulsion to keep quiet, to withhold the secret a little while longer.

"Everyone expected him at the Gauntlet," Drew said, shaking his head in wonderment. "I had thought to name him champion. Some say he hails from Atabyrion, but no one knows who he is. It's a mystery, truly. But he was here on the battlefield today."

The king gazed at the crowd, looking for a soldier with a stripe of blue across his face. Trynne stifled a smile.

Severn rode up, his armor battered and stained with blood and dirt. "My lord," he said curtly, trying to settle the fractious mount. "They are marching quickly from the city, and more soldiers are disembarking from the ships. How many soldiers did you bring? If we rally now, we can fight them back to the shore. Do not let them gain a foothold here. Dundrennan is a mighty castle, but it is leagues away. Fight them now!"

Drew shook his head. "My lord duke, we have barely a thousand warriors with us in all. Just the forces from Averanche under Lady Trynne and Captain Staeli and part of the Beestone garrison. My army will gather in the North. We don't have the ability to stand and fight here."

Severn looked surprised, but he recovered quickly. "It was only a ruse, then," he said with a cough and a chuckle. "I thought you'd ridden from Kingfountain when you got word of the invasion."

Drew chuffed. "We've been driven out of Kingfountain, my lord. My wife and daughter are in sanctuary at Our Lady. Many of the nobles have scattered. If I'm to fight Gahalatine, then I want to choose the ground. I choose Dundrennan."

A strange look came over Severn's face. It was the very place where *he* had lost the crown of Ceredigion. Trynne wondered how he was feeling. His hand grabbed the dagger hilt at his belt and clenched it hard. His cheek muscles twitched and his nostrils flared. "The men of the North are strong, my lord," he said at last. "They'll defend you."

"I'm counting on it," Drew answered. "Captain Staeli!" he called. When the captain approached him, he asked, "How many have you lost?"

"Twelve of the maidens," he replied, his voice thick with anger. "So far. If we don't hasten, then all will be slaughtered."

"I agree. Form a rearguard to protect us as we go. We've lost Blackpool. But we got what we came here for." He gave Severn an honored look and then nodded at Trynne. "Ride with us, Uncle. The winter has not yet started."

"Aye," said the duke, tugging at the reins of his steed. Then he nodded toward the hollow crown, his eyes glittering. "But maybe it *should*."

♦ ♦ ♦

They did not stop until they reached Dundrennan. Fresh mounts were taken from the cities and towns that they passed. Trynne was so used to using the ley lines to travel that it felt strange to be going at such a slow pace. Not knowing what awaited them at Dundrennan, she felt it would be better for her and the king to arrive with an army at their backs instead of alone.

The mountain air grew colder, the trail more rugged and steep as they trudged into the hinterlands of the realm. She saw the icy peak of Helvellyn, where the Maid of Donremy had been executed by being chained to a rock. Severn had once ordered her father to be killed that way, but Fallon's parents had prevented it. She had always wanted to visit that place but never had, having spent so many of her days in Brythonica and at the palace. Her few visits to Dundrennan had been spent at Dundrennan.

Fallon was likely still at Kingfountain. Did he believe the Wizr's disguise? Or had he helped arrange the ruse himself? She wanted to believe that he was loyal to Drew, but she kept seeing that change of clothes in the chest beneath Morwenna's bed.

Her shoulders and thighs ached from days in the saddle, but as they crested the final hill, the view of the fortress banished her fatigue.

Dundrennan stood as tall as a mountain itself. There was a huge waterfall behind it, the noise of which could be heard even from a distance. They stopped at the ridge, admiring the breathtaking view of the valley.

She noticed the king had a faraway look.

"What is it?" Trynne asked Drew softly, drawing up beside him. He slumped a bit in the saddle, a puff of mist coming from his mouth. It was getting dark and they hoped to find warmth and shelter before nightfall.

"It's the castle of my childhood," Drew said, turning and giving her a friendly smile. "When you grow older, the places you remember from childhood can begin to seem very small to you. But not Dundrennan." He rested his hands on the pommel. "This place only grows grander." The smoke rising from hundreds of chimneys offered a thin haze. The valley was pristine, crowded with enormous pine and fir trees and huge boulders cleft from the mountains. It was a place that had been untarnished by war since before Trynne was born.

As if he shared her thoughts, the king suddenly sighed. "But we bring trouble wherever we ride." He turned in the saddle. "I want all the Oath Maidens with me when we enter. This is where we will fight."

"Would you like me to go on ahead to make sure the castle is safe?" Trynne asked.

Drew frowned. "No. If I'm not safe here, I'm safe nowhere. The people here remember me. We go together, Trynne."

An Espion rider fought through the crowded road to join them at the crest of the hill. His stallion was beleaguered, and the man looked as if he'd been riding even harder than they had.

"News, my lord," the man panted. "From Lord Amrein. He said I would find you here. I'm glad he wasn't mistaken."

"Tell us," Drew said patiently, watching the man gulp down some wine from a flagon to clear his throat.

"I've ridden ahead from Kingfountain. I was with Lord Amrein two days ago at the sanctuary of Our Lady. Your wife and mother be safe, my lord. And your daughter."

"Thank the Fountain," Drew sighed out. "What else?"

"Lord Amrein bid me warn you. Gahalatine has taken Kingfountain. Your blood-sister returned to the palace just before he rode into the

216

castle. She warned that there was an imposter pretending to be you. It put the whole castle in an uproar."

Drew and Trynne exchanged a look. She felt a sliver of doubt at the man's words.

"Morwenna?" Drew asked.

"Aye, your poisoner. We already knew the truth by the time she arrived, and we'd been working with Lord Amrein in secret. He ordered that we collapse the bridges to separate the palace from the city and the sanctuary. But Gahalatine doesn't need bridges to move around. We were overrun and everyone fled. Most are heading upriver, to the North. Gahalatine's ships can't come this way because of the waterfall, but his army is marching on the other side of the river. And as I was nearing North Cumbria, I had to slip past another army blocking the road."

"That's the army from Blackpool," Trynne said. "How many did you count?"

"Nigh on fifty thousand between the two of them," the man said, scratching his throat noisily. "Word has it that Duke Fallon withdrew his army from Dundrennan to bring it south. I was told to turn it around and return, but I've not seen any sign of it. Have you, my lord?"

The king glanced back at Trynne again, his expression brooding. "No, we have not."

The Espion bit his lip. "I'll ride ahead, then, my lord. Mayhap the Espion at the castle will know what's what."

"On your way, then," the king said curtly. He stared at the fortress below, his brow furrowing. "I don't like this, Trynne," he said as the man rode away. "We have two armies behind us. And likely one ahead."

"But whose side is it on?" she murmured softly. She tapped the flanks of her horse with her spurs and they both started down toward Dundrennan.

◆　◆　◆

Cheering greeted them as they rode through the streets leading toward the castle. The people of Dundrennan were hanging out of windows, wagging lanterns, and shouting ebulliently. Everywhere Trynne looked, there were knights wearing the badge of the Pierced Lion, joining in the ruckus and holding aloft their swords as they welcomed King Drew to the North. Trynne and her Oath Maidens surrounded the king and cleared the path for him.

The throngs followed them, offering drink and food, blankets, and warm garments to the weary soldiers of Averanche. There was nothing but pure joy in the air, and they were greeted with respect and courtesy.

Trynne gazed up at the castle on the bluff ahead, wondering what they would find there. The castle was lit with torches and bedecked with banners, but trickery had been used to win many battles.

Haley, who had been sent on ahead, met them on the road. She rode through the crowd, making her way to Trynne.

"My lady," she shouted, trying to be heard over the commotion. "We heard you might arrive during the night. The maidens have been flocking to Dundrennan daily. The people here are loyal to the king. So are the guards at the castle. Duke Fallon has ordered them to make preparations to welcome everyone. The women and children have been gathered into the castle. The menfolk are going to stay outside. The castle is on alert day and night."

"Fallon is here?" she said, feeling a shudder of anticipation go through her. The news was unexpected.

"Yes! He arrived earlier today."

"How many soldiers defend the castle?" Trynne asked.

Haley shrugged and frowned. "I heard some were called to defend Kingfountain. We have about five thousand. The duke can explain better than I can. Come to the castle."

Trynne nodded, still not allowing herself to feel relieved. The king was waving to the crowd, looking regal despite his weariness from the punishing ride to the North. The cheers grew louder. Still, Trynne needed to be sure. She reached out with her magic, searching for any threats to the king. Her magic responded as it usually did in such moments. There were armed soldiers everywhere. The danger was real. But at the moment, there was no imminent threat.

The sharp clash of the horses' hooves against the flagstones changed when they reached the wooden drawbridge of the fortress. Trynne craned her neck, looking up at the ramparts patrolled by knights holding spears and pennants. She was worried about meeting Fallon, but determined to speak openly with him. She needed to know about his connection with Morwenna. Needed to know what he knew.

The inner bailey was teeming with servants who led their weary mounts away to feed them fresh provender. A few young boys with shovels stayed behind to scoop up the filth left by some of the horses.

There he was among his men, giving orders and seeing to the needs of the arrivals. Fallon stood a head above his fellows, and it struck her anew how very tall and manly he had become. He looked as if he hadn't shaved in days. When he glanced her way, their eyes met and she felt a jolt in her heart at the look he gave her—one of utter relief. She felt the same way. Despite all her questions, it soothed her heart to see him unharmed.

"My lord," Fallon said as he came forward and bowed before the king's horse. "Welcome back to Dundrennan. Although our food is being rationed in preparation for a siege, I'm sure we can find something to please you. Many people are waiting to speak to you, but you must also be very weary from the journey. The state rooms have been prepared for your arrival."

"Thank you, Fallon," Drew said with a sigh. "I would appreciate a moment of quiet. My ears are still ringing."

"Cousin Trynne seems to be in good health," he said blandly, giving her a mocking smile.

But the pleasure of seeing a glimpse of his old self passed her like a shallow wave. She felt and sensed the presence of another

Fountain-blessed, one with enormous power, and a feeling of deep foreboding made her hand reach for her sword pommel.

Morwenna strode into the bailey from the castle. She was no longer wearing the same gown that Trynne had last seen her in. This one was an eye-catching silk brocade with a low neckline. Morwenna's face was flushed as she pushed through the crowd, her eyes wide with panic until she saw him.

"Father!" she called worriedly, rushing up to Duke Severn as he led his horse by the reins. She clung to him, burying her face against his chest, her shoulders heaving with emotion. Severn murmured gently to her, stroking her black hair in a tender gesture that made Trynne feel helplessly conflicted.

Trynne felt Morwenna's magic ebb as she calmed herself. Trynne shouldn't have been surprised to find the poisoner there, yet she had been. How else had Fallon gotten to Dundrennan so quickly? Once again, she thought of the little chest of clothes beneath Morwenna's bed in the tower.

But the painful thoughts were pushed away when she sensed the presence of another Fountain-blessed, one within the castle itself. Was it the hunter Carrick? she wondered.

Or was there someone else waiting for them?

CHAPTER
TWENTY-EIGHT

Prisoner

The fortress of Dundrennan felt more familiar to Trynne than it should given the few visits she'd made there. But so many of her father's stories had taken place *there*. It made her feel connected to him, and despite her discomfort, she couldn't resist the urge to run her hand along the wall as she walked down a torch-lit corridor. The air held the aroma of baking bread and pine sap, and her boots crunched on the green needles as she crossed the threshold into the royal residence, the room where the king and queen always stayed. Fallon was a considerate host, and food was arranged before them, invoking the pangs of hunger she'd suppressed on the journey. But she could not forget the other Fountain-blessed she'd sensed in the castle, and when she reached out with her magic to make sure the food was safe to eat, she felt the person's power again. It was like hearing the distant chord of harp strings. It unsettled her. It made her want to investigate.

Fallon spoke while the king ate, although he cast a quick glance at Trynne and her plate. She had not started eating yet.

"My lord, I have no doubt that Gahalatine is coming to attack Dundrennan," Fallon said. "I've sent word to rally as many of your knights as possible. The Duke of East Stowe is on his way with ten thousand. I sent a summons for Grand Duke Asturias as well."

"As have we," Drew said, wiping his mouth with a napkin before he spoke. He had removed the crown and returned it to the satchel that never left his possession. "We sent word from Averanche."

"If we can hold off the siege," Fallon continued, "it will give our allies a chance to flank him."

"How many soldiers do you have defending the castle?" Trynne asked pointedly, staring at him, unable to get over the nagging doubts that assailed her. Morwenna was there, after all, and there was still no explanation for the person whose presence she sensed.

"Fifteen thousand men, all loyal, to a man," Fallon answered.

Trynne frowned. "I heard some of your soldiers were marching south."

He gave her a sharp look. "Who told you that? It's not true."

She clenched her fist under the table. "Maybe I misunderstood."

Fallon nodded curtly. "I think defending Dundrennan will be much easier than trying to recapture Kingfountain. We just need to hold out and let Gahalatine lose men and nerve hammering away at our walls. He cannot dock his ships nearby, so he'll need supply lines to feed and equip his men. I don't think he's prepared for a long siege."

There was an urgent rap on the door and Fallon scowled, having left instructions for them not to be disturbed. The door opened and Morwenna entered. Her face was flushed, her hair disheveled. Trynne felt instantly wary.

The king turned to look at his younger sister as she approached his table. Although they shared the same mother, he had inherited his mother's looks whereas she had inherited her father's.

"Morwenna," the king said. "Would you join us?"

"I won't stay for long, Brother," she said a little breathlessly. She looked at Trynne, as if only now recognizing her in her rough soldier's garb. "Who are these women in the castle? All these maidens with swords and shields?"

"They are my protectors," Drew answered, his voice guarded. "You had something of importance to say. What is it?"

Morwenna fidgeted with a ring on her finger. She cast a sidelong look at Fallon and the flush in her cheeks deepened. "I haven't had the opportunity to speak to you. I heard that the Painted Knight saved my father's life in battle."

"Indeed," Drew answered. "I saw it."

"But where is he now? Was he riding in your company?" Morwenna gazed at Trynne with a hint of suspicion.

"I have no idea," the king replied. "He comes and he vanishes, often without saying more than a word. He said nothing when he appeared at Guilme. They call him the Painted Knight, but I think of him as my silent shield. When I am in danger, he is there."

Trynne felt a shiver of warmth at his words, but she kept her expression neutral, her eyes focused on Morwenna.

"How did you escape Chandigarl?" Trynne asked suddenly, breaking the silence. She heard the accusation in her own voice, and Morwenna assuredly felt it too, for she bristled.

"I was going to ask you the same question," the poisoner countered. "There are no ley lines coming or going from the zenana. I heard you *attacked* Gahalatine."

The tension in the room was growing palpably. "No, I was the one who was attacked while rescuing Fallon's mother. I brought her back with me to Kingfountain." She looked at Fallon and added, "She helped sneak Genny away. They are safe, I believe."

Fallon looked dumbstruck. "You found my mother?"

"And brought her back," Trynne answered with a nod. "Morwenna, you have been to Chandigarl multiple times. Surely you knew that your disguise would be unmasked as we crossed the waters to the tower?"

"Are you implying that I am in league with our enemies?" Morwenna asked, her face betraying a look of fierce anger. She turned to her brother, who had stopped eating and was staring coolly at her.

Taking a reflexive step backward, she said, "My lord, I must warn you to be wary. I believe you are in very real danger. When I last saw Trynne, we were both on a stone barge crossing the waters to the zenana. I had no idea that my illusion ring would cease working as we crossed. When the guards attacked, I had no choice but to leap off the barge into the water and swim to safety. My lord, I have contacts in the Forbidden Court, people I have bribed for information. I was told that Gahalatine has sworn an oath to marry Trynne Kiskaddon and make her Empress of Chandigarl."

The king pushed away from the table and came to his feet. "That is quite an accusation to make, Morwenna!"

The poisoner nodded. "When I learned about it, I returned hastily and discovered the Wizr Rucrius had invaded the palace of Kingfountain. He was disguised as you, but I saw through his little trick. I found Lord Fallon and brought him here immediately." She turned to face Trynne. "Do you deny this? Did not Gahalatine offer to make you his empress?"

Trynne felt the ground beneath her had turned unstable. One wrong step and she would fall. Her stomach writhed from the confrontation, from the baseless accusations. "He did," she answered softly. Then she turned to the king. "That part is true, my lord. He did offer to marry me. And I soundly rejected him. There is a struggle for power between Gahalatine and his Wizrs. He will not be controlled by them as other emperors were. His financial state is nearly ruined—"

"Only the Wizrs and the Mandaryn know that," Morwenna said. "This proves you are in league with them."

Trynne turned to her calmly. "I did not learn this from them. But it begs the question of how you know it?"

"She brought Rucrius to Kingfountain," Morwenna said with a hint of triumph. "Wasn't he the person who spelled everyone in the castle to fall asleep?"

"The spell came from a staff fixed atop *your* tower," Trynne shot back.

"My lord, I *caught* her in my tower the eve we were departing to Chandigarl."

"Enough!" the king said forcefully. He looked back and forth between them with growing incredulity. "You cannot *both* be right."

"Brother, you must listen to me," Morwenna pleaded.

"I have listened to you," he said, holding up his hand to silence her. "The greatest gift from the Fountain is the blessing of discernment. I cannot pretend that I understand the intricacies of this situation, but I trust Trynne with my life. If she were in league with Rucrius, she could have delivered me into his hands. You have always claimed to be loyal to me, Sister. Now is your opportunity to prove where your loyalties lie. Choose well. Lord Fallon, arrest her and confine her in the dungeon."

Morwenna drew a dagger.

Where she'd concealed it, Trynne didn't know, but her magic screamed a warning at her. There was a look of utter hatred in the poisoner's eyes. Trynne was about to step forward and block the king's body with her own, hoping she was fast enough to deflect the dagger if it was thrown, when the weapon suddenly thumped onto the floor.

Morwenna's eyes had cooled. "As you command, my lord. I plead my innocence in laying down my knife. I will suffer the indignity of a cell to prove myself to you. I knew you would take her side over mine." She turned to the duke, whose eyes were wide with shock, and said, "Fallon, you know I'd never hurt you. I will go willingly."

Fallon's cheek twitched as he stepped forward. "Morwenna Argentine, I arrest you on command of His Majesty."

Morwenna held up her hands to him, wrists held together. Fallon gripped her by the arm, not gently, and escorted her from the room.

◆　◆　◆

Drew leaned back against the table after they had left. "By the Fountain," he said with a gasp, clutching his throat as if he'd just escaped being strangled. "I scarcely know what to say or think."

"Poisoners are trained to be clever," Trynne said with a small laugh. She was trembling inside at how close it had come to violence. She'd felt danger moments before Morwenna had dropped that knife. The lack of food had not only made her famished but light-headed as well.

"So it's true," Drew said with a mocking smile. "Gahalatine proposed to you?"

She shrugged, tilting her head to one side. "Yes, I could say that he did."

"You could have told me."

"I think jumping into the cesspit with you may have distracted me," Trynne countered. She wrung her hands, beginning to pace. Was Fallon loyal? He had arrested Morwenna, but was he just as compromised as she was? She knew what she wanted to believe, but she couldn't let her feelings for him blind her.

"While secrets are being laid bare," she went on, "I have also sensed another Fountain-blessed here in the castle."

"Duke Severn?" the king prompted.

"No, I already knew about him, and his power is mostly spent for the time being. There is someone else. I feel it nagging at me. I'm conflicted, my lord. Can we trust Fallon? One of the maidens, who is from Dundrennan, told me ere we arrived that the garrison had been marched away to defend Kingfountain. An Espion told us the same. Fallon has flatly denied it." She turned her head, trying to conceal her confusion. "I did go to Morwenna's tower before we left. I found . . . I found some of Fallon's clothes—with his badge—among her belongings."

"That does not bode well," the king said with a weary sigh. "You suppose they are lovers?"

"I don't know what to suppose," Trynne said. "Fallon is very . . . complicated."

Drew snorted, and when she looked at him, he was nodding in agreement. "I've never fully understood Genny's brother. In the last year he has changed for the better. I named him my champion and defender, but only because the Painted Knight didn't come to the Gauntlet. I had hoped . . . almost expected that he would." He rubbed his temples.

"Well," he said with a sigh, "the truth will out, as they say. Owen thought keeping Morwenna close would be the wise course of action. She's still very young." He gave Trynne a pointed look, acknowledging that the two were of an age. "I hope she hasn't betrayed me. I forgave her father. Could I forgive her? Could I chain my own sister to a rock on the mountain yonder and watch her freeze to death?" His voice broke and he shook his head.

Trynne felt sorry for him. The decision, ultimately, was his to make.

"My lord, perhaps Morwenna is driven by ambition and not revenge. I heard in Chandigarl that the Wizrs are forcing Gahalatine to marry. If he does not choose his own bride, they will choose one for him. Perhaps Rucrius's plan is to put Morwenna on the throne. She looks like a queen. She's the daughter of one."

Drew pursed his lips and gave Trynne a tender, sympathetic look. His face was calm and peaceful. "But Gahalatine is wiser for having chosen you, Trynne. My grandfather always valued Ankarette's advice above all others. Now I can see why. Discernment is as important as she always said it was. I trust your instincts, Trynne. I believe in you. Now," he added, shifting to a more playful tone. "I would normally ask this of my poisoner, but she's indisposed. You said you felt the presence of another Fountain-blessed in the castle. It's probably Carrick, the hunter. But just in case, I'd like you to take some of the maidens and go find this person. Let's be sure they are on *our* side."

Trynne bowed in obeisance and left the king's chamber after the servant they had sent in search of Captain Staeli returned with him and six maidens. There had been no chance to eat amidst the commotion of the day, so she nibbled a bread roll as she led two of the girls through the halls. The castle was still in commotion from their arrival. The common hall was filled with rows of trestle tables, and the maidens sat eating the provisions that had been set out for them. There was a feeling of good spirits now that they'd reached the protection of the mountains, but there was also worry in the air. Everyone knew Gahalatine was on his way. Some of the serving girls were talking to the Oath Maidens, admiring their armor and weapons, and intrigued to hear the tales of their training.

Trynne could feel the call of the magic reaching out to her still, those musical notes playing over and over. She left the great hall and found a passageway leading to a set of spiral stairs in one of the tower turrets. Grabbing a torch from the wall sconce for light, she led the way down to the lower level. The noise and commotion from the common hall receded. Below she found the armory, where soldiers were grinding axes and swords while blacksmiths fixed and repaired armor. The smell of men's unwashed bodies was everywhere and some were smoking pipes and speaking in the Northern accent.

The soldiers they passed were unused to seeing women in their domain, and Trynne and the maidens were given a few leers as they passed. She ignored the rudeness and followed the strain of magic down another corridor. At the end, she found a heavy iron door with torches bracketed on either side of it. There were two guards posted there, arms folded.

"Back up top, lasses," one of them said dismissively as Trynne approached.

"What's through the doors?" she asked, ignoring the command.

"This be the wine cellar," he replied stiffly. Even without her power, she would know it for a lie. "Not a place for visitors."

Trynne gazed at both men. "My name is Trynne Kiskaddon," she said. "Lord Owen was my father. He grew up in this castle."

The two guards exchanged surprised looks. "I beg your pardon, your ladyship. Our master has given instructions that you are permitted to go anywhere you choose. I meant no disrespect." He turned and yanked the door open. It took both men to do the job because of its weight.

As Trynne passed, she caught one of them giving the other a knowing look. She stopped and held out her hand to the maidens. "You both wait here. I should return promptly."

"Yes, my lady," they said, nodding. She could tell that they understood her meaning, that they were to wait behind to prevent the guards from locking her in.

Holding the torch, she continued down the steps, feeling the swell of the magic growing stronger. The stairs were short and ended in front of another door watched by another set of guards. They wore Fallon's badge, the Pierced Lion. They asked no questions as she approached, only turned and pulled at the heavy doors for her. She nodded to them both, feeling her unease growing with each step.

The presence of magic was growing stronger. She could sense it filling the corridor. She reached out with her magic and sensed a single person waiting for her ahead. Her heart pounded in her throat. Was it Gahalatine? He was making no effort to hide his power at all. In fact, quite the opposite. His power was luring her there.

They were belowground in the bowels of the castle. The noise of the grinding stones had faded, and all was quiet other than her footsteps and the hissing flame of the torch. The smell of pitch was strong.

As she walked carefully ahead, she saw an iron gate blocking the way. The darkness and her weariness descended on her, making her fearful. There were several iron doors farther down the corridor, beyond the gate, but no one was standing guard. She approached the gate, watching the light play off the round bars. There was someone in the corridor, though not behind any of the iron doors. Someone she could sense but not see.

When the magic dissolved, all the air huffed out of her in a gasp. Dragan stood leaning against the bars, his cheek pressed against them.

"Hello again, lass," he said by way of greeting. There was a look of cunning and cruelty in his eyes as he stared at the left side of her face.

CHAPTER
TWENTY-NINE

Lost

Once again Trynne found herself facing the man who had harmed her as a child. Even with the bars separating them, she felt part of herself plunge into a dark abyss. Her childhood had been shattered by this man. She wanted revenge. The oath she had taken would be tested again.

Somehow she found the courage to speak his name. "Dragan." She stepped forward, holding the torch higher to get a better look at his face. He winced, his eyes not adjusting well to the stabs of light.

"Put it down or put it lower; I can see ye well enough," he said with a growl in his voice.

"Why are you here?" she asked, keeping a good distance between them. She reached out with her magic and tested him. His reserves were running low. How did the thief lord usually supply his needs? Was it through stealing? If so, his cage was preventing it. Then again, there was no reason for him to be invisible in his prison.

"Even a clever rat gets caught by a trap," he answered, wagging his eyebrows at her. He gripped a bar with one hand and slid his palm up and down, taking the measure of it. Then he shook the bars roughly, impotently, furiously. His teeth were bared. "I was not expecting ye, lass."

"Then who were you expecting?" she demanded, trying to keep her voice from quavering. She probed his weaknesses. He was not a threat to her physically. His heart beat in quivering, irregular thumps, and his other internal organs were tender from hard drinking and complacency. He'd be winded in a trice if he tried to run—and that was if his knees held him.

"Someone else," he answered with a shrug of one shoulder.

"Well, I'm the one who found you. The king is here. Did you know that?"

Dragan blanched. "Well, I daresay he didn't leave Kingfountain on a pleasure jaunt, did he? His time be almost up. There will be a new king soon."

Trynne glared at him. "Not if I can help it."

He chuckled roughly. "And what can *you* do, lass? You're not half as clever as your *papa*." He said the endearment with loathing in his voice. "Naught like your mam, neither. She was powerful. I heard about the day she saved the sanctuary from flooding. My ilk still pay homage to me. You swooned when ye tried to help her. If the other lass hadn't come, you would have faltered and they'd all have drowned."

He was plying her with his words, trying to manipulate her emotions. She was tempted to thrust the torch through the bars to burn him. *No!* She reined in her feelings sharply.

"You want revenge on me," Dragan said. "I see it in your eyes. Your kind like to strut and mince and make a tinkling with your fancy jewelry. You say 'as it please you, Father' and make a little curtsy. Your papa got my daughter killt." His eyes blazed with animosity. "I tried to be revenged on ye in turn. A daughter for a daughter. Right is right. But it didn't satisfy. I made ye ugly, but it's your father I wanted to destroy. Do you know where he is, lass?" He leered at her.

"Tell me," Trynne said in a low, dangerous voice.

Dragan shook his head. "First, ye open this little rat trap. I swear I won't harm ye further."

"You think I trust you?" Trynne said with annoyance. "*You* got your daughter killed. I know the stories. She died saving my father's life. It was your fault."

He clucked his tongue. When he resumed speaking, his accent was less affected. He was comfortable speaking to any class, it would seem. "I know what I know, lass. A daughter's duty is to her father, is that not the way of things? Now let me out of this cage. You can help me. And then I will help you. There are answers I can give you. Answers worth a king's ransom, I should think, if you only knew them. It won't save your king's life. Nothing can do that now. But it could help *you*, lass. It could bring back your father."

Trynne stared at him. He was desperate for any way to escape the punishment he knew was coming. He had stolen all his life and he knew his life would be forfeit now that he had been caught.

"I couldn't believe anything you told me," Trynne said with a shake of her head. "You're a liar and a thief. You're not acquainted with the meaning of truth."

He pressed his face against the bars, his eyes burning into hers. His lips quivered with rage. "I'm a liar, am I? The secrets I know are valuable."

"Prove it."

"Your father was summoned to a grove of trees in Brythonica," Dragan said. "How would I know that except if I was there? He had a little ring . . . a ring on his finger. No one could see it, but it was there."

Trynne's stomach twisted with dread. Dragan knew.

"I see by the twitch of your cheek that you know I'm right. There's more, lass. I know where the ring is."

Trynne narrowed her eyes. "How could you know that?"

He grinned at her, his teeth rank and rotting. "Lass, open the gate and I'll tell you all. My stash means nothing to me if I'm trapped in here. I was the one who captured him. But I was paid to do it by someone who knew about the grove. Who knew about the silver dish and what would happen if water were poured from it onto the slab. That was the trick, you see. That was how we got him. I had some sanctuary men with me."

"You cut off his hand and left the ring in the grove," Trynne said, barely controlling the fury she felt as she stepped forward again, gazing into his green eyes.

He shook his head. "No, lass. That wasn't his hand!" he said. "It was only made to look like it. It was meant to throw you off the trail, looking for a one-handed man. But I kept the ring, sez I. And I know where it is. You have a decoy. A copy. She's very good at copying."

Trynne jumped on the clue instantly. "She?"

Dragan's cheek twitched. He'd revealed more than he'd intended. "I will be killt for what I know, lass. Come, little dove. Open the gate. I'll tell you all. You've a spider in the corner. A spider with fangs."

Morwenna.

The grating of an iron door startled her. Her heart raced as she turned toward the sound of approaching bootfalls. Dragan tried to gaze past Trynne, but the light had made it impossible to see.

Trynne turned sideways, shifting enough to watch the newcomer's approach but not enough to lose sight of Dragan. She recognized the sound of the stride. From the shadows of the corridor, Fallon emerged.

"What are you doing down here, Trynne?" he asked. He had a dark countenance, a brooding look.

"Hello, Master," Dragan said.

"I'm tempted to reach through those bars and throttle your neck, thief," Fallon said grimly. "I am not your master, as you well know. Trynne, come with me."

"If you leave me here alone, I'm a dead man," Dragan said to Trynne, his eyes widening with fear.

Fallon glowered at him. "Your death is already a foregone conclusion." He had reached Trynne and stood by her, almost in a protective stance. "I hope you don't give too much credence to anything he's said to you. He's liable to say anything to save his skin from frostbite."

Trynne looked up at Fallon, feeling the familiar feelings at war inside her—the desire to trust him and the fear that she could not. "Why is he even here, Fallon?"

"I will gladly explain it to you," he said, gesturing for the exit. "But I'd rather not say more in front of such a man. He has a thousand tricks. I had no doubt that you would sense him when you arrived. I might not be Fountain-blessed, but I know that one Fountain-blessed can feel the presence of another. I was going to tell you about him before . . . well, you know what happened. Let's speak now. Come with me."

"She *will* kill me," Dragan said softly.

Fallon snorted. "Not likely," he countered. "She's behind bars herself and I had the blacksmith melt lead into the lock. Just as I did with this one. When I open this gate, it will be to drag you to a donkey and haul you to Helvellyn to freeze to death." He took another step toward the locked gate, as if he couldn't help himself. "I know you were at the grove, Dragan. I know you were part of the abduction, and I've already found the horde of coins you were bribed with. You have no further information I desire. The only thing I want from you now is your sorry carcass. But it will be done by the Assizes or by the king's command. Not my own. But rest assured, Dragan, if your life is ended sooner by other means, I could hardly care less." Then he turned and bowed to Trynne. "My lady, if you would come with me?"

Trynne nodded, feeling her heart flutter as Fallon's words sank home. He gently took her arm and offered to carry her torch. As they walked away together, Dragan began to shake the bars in a fit of rage and screamed violent oaths.

Neither of them turned to look at him.

◆ ◆ ◆

The stairwell leading up to the highest spire of the castle seemed unending. It was wide enough that they could climb it side by side, but soldiers wearing the badge of the Pierced Lion were coming down from above and they had to hug close to the wall to make room. Trynne craned her neck, peering up the dark shaft, unable to see the top. The noise of their steps and heavy breathing mingled to drown out any other sounds, save for the patter of distant steps and the noise from the wind every time they passed an arrow slit.

The climb was long but invigorating. By the time they reached the highest level, coming to a stop before a ladder leading up to a trapdoor, Fallon had a sheen of sweat on his brow. Both of them were a little winded.

"I don't think Farnes would care to serve in Dundrennan, do you?" he asked.

Trynne smiled a little as she thought of her aging herald scaling the steps. Fallon climbed up the ladder and pushed open the trapdoor. A brisk, knifelike wind came rushing down, cutting through her tunic instantly as she started to climb up the ladder. He emerged first and then reached down to help her up.

The tower was the highest point of the castle and the view nearly made her dizzy as she stared down at the bailey. The sky was thick with clouds, though they parted to show a sliver of brilliant moon that shed its light across the woolen veil. The noise of the waterfall was much louder up there, a constant murmur against the howl of the wind. Fallon quickly removed his cloak and draped it over her shoulders. It was warm from his body heat and the exertion of the climb. The gesture sent a little shiver through her, and she smiled up at him.

There were four soldiers already up there, each one looking in a different direction, their eyes piercing the gloom. There were no torches, but each man had a hooded lantern. The bailey yard below was still teeming with people.

"What's the latest news, Captain?" Fallon asked, half shouting to be heard above the screech of the wind.

"My lord," the captain shouted back, putting his arm out and gripping Fallon's shoulder. "The forefront of Gahalatine's army has reached Doublebrook. They'll be at the walls before dawn by our reckoning."

"That soon?" Fallon answered, shaking his head in amazement.

"Aye, my lord. His army never stops, not fully. A part of it is always in motion. There are now two supply lines. One from Blackpool. Another from Kennit, one on either side of us. They seemed to know the king would be here."

"Seems so," Fallon responded gravely. "I'd like a moment with this young lady, if you wouldn't mind, Captain."

The captain, a large man with a full beard and whiskers, grinned a toothy grin and motioned for the others to join him. "Let's wait out of the wind for a bit, chaps. What do you say?"

"Aye, Captain." There was no disagreement, and soon Trynne and Fallon were alone at the top of the tower. The howling wind whipped her hair across her face.

"I'm sorry to have brought you up this high, but it is one of the few places I can be assured a private conversation," he said with a chuckle. He stood in front of her, leaning back slightly against the wall of the parapet. She was afraid the wind was going to suddenly shove him over the edge, but she was close enough to grab his sword belt if that happened. She gazed up at him, feeling a surge of warmth for him when she noticed how his unruly hair was being ruffled by the wind.

"I owe you some answers," he said, folding his arms.

"I think you do," Trynne agreed.

"I can't tell you how many times I've imagined us being here together," he said, shaking his head. "There's so much of the North that I long to show you. The falls. The ice caves where our parents found Drew's sword. There's a man here named Carrick. He's Fountain-blessed—a hunter. I learned that he was called on to investigate your father's disappearance. I was wroth that he kept the secret for so long, but eventually I wheedled it out of him. Don't blame him, Trynne, he was forced between his duty to me as his duke and to his loyalty to your family. When I came to Gannon's funeral, I brought him with me so he could show me the place where he'd found the evidence. He stayed at a farm outside Ploemeur.

"That's why I didn't want you to bring me back to Kingfountain when you offered. There were no more bootprints, obviously. I just wanted to see it with my own eyes. There is something about that cave, Trynne." He shook his head, gazing downward, his arms still folded.

Then he looked at her, meeting her eyes without flinching. "I should have told you. My heart was hurting because of what happened to your brother. I was sure Dragan was behind it, and it made me sick to think of him walking free after everything he's done. But how does one catch a thief who can turn invisible? Well, I've thought about that for a long time. The answer was greed. Dragan loves to steal, and the harder the target, the more it interests him. So I built a trap for him in my treasury. I commissioned a very expensive champion's medallion and hired someone to build a trapped box to contain it. I kept it a secret, but I knew that workmen talk. I counted on it. The gate was installed so that if someone lifted the box, the trap would be sprung and the gate closed. I couldn't care less about the treasure. I wanted to capture Dragan. I knew he would strike while I was at Kingfountain participating in the Gauntlet. He's been trapped here for days, his power dwindling because there is no one to steal from. I only found out I'd caught the rat in my trap after arriving here with Morwenna. We've fed him prisoner's rations through the bars so he won't die, but it's not expected he'll live long now."

Trynne gave him an encouraging smile. "That was fairly clever, Fallon Llewellyn."

He shrugged but seemed to enjoy the praise, as his cheek twitched. "There's more. I think Morwenna was behind the plot to kidnap your father. I've often wondered how she became so powerful so quickly. She knows things that a young woman her age . . . shouldn't possibly know. While she says it comes from reading *The Vulgate*, I've had my doubts. I think she's allied with the Wizrs of Chandigarl, and the men in the silver masks were coming here at her bidding. I even disguised myself as one to try and ferret out who was behind the plot. That ended disastrously," he said with a snort, shaking his head with embarrassment. Then he looked at her. "When I heard she was taking you to Chandigarl . . ." He stopped again, sighing. "I cannot tell you how it tortured me. I feared I would never see you again. I had to trust that you'd remember the warning I gave you about Morwenna before, and that you'd be on your guard because of it. Now, there are two more reasons I wanted to bring you up here." He reached out and took her shoulders, and for a dizzying moment, she thought he was going to kiss her. Instead, he turned her around until she was facing away from him.

"You are too clever by far, Trynne," he said, lowering his voice but bringing his mouth near her ear. "One of your maidens must have told you about my soldiers. She told you correctly, and I disavowed it because it needs to be a secret still. I have ten thousand men up in the heights with a hundred thousand spears. Probably not that many, but it's sufficiently vast. They're awaiting my orders to start hurling them down at Gahalatine's army after it arrives."

The pieces fit together in her mind. "That explains why you were so coy about it," she said, nodding and turning around. "Can they see us?"

He shook his head. "It's too dark. They are living in snow caves they've dug themselves. They can't stay up there forever, but hopefully long enough to strike hard at Gahalatine and throw him off. The lanterns are to be the signal. They let them shine at the changing of every watch, always from a different place. That way we'll know they are still there and they are ready."

"You're brilliant," Trynne told him, feeling her heart swell with pride. She turned and hugged him, grateful that he had finally revealed himself to her. Part of her longed to question him about the clothes she'd found in Morwenna's room, but she could not bear to ruin the moment by mentioning it.

He seemed surprised by her sudden embrace, but after another moment passed, he put his arms around her shoulders and rested his cheek against her hair. She felt so short compared to him, yet so warm and protected too. She savored the moment, drowning in it.

"I've told you this because I trust you completely, and I know that you are truly loyal to the king. I've harbored doubts about Morwenna for some time, and she proved herself a traitor this evening by accusing you of her treachery. *My* Trynne."

He pulled back a little and lifted her chin so she could look up at him. The silver moonlight revealed his expression of hunger and torment and fierce protectiveness. The wind blew hair across her face again, and this time, he cleared it away before she could.

"Trynne," he whispered urgently.

Her heart was aching. It hurt down to her deepest core. She loved him still. She had always loved him.

And when he started kissing her cheek, her nose, and then her mouth, she lost all control of herself and kissed him back, clinging to him to keep from flying away on the next gust. He pulled her against him as she gripped the front of his tunic. Warmth and giddiness tore loose inside her. She wanted to be his. She wanted to be his always.

The sound of the trapdoor slamming against the flagstones behind her caused her to flinch and pull away. She hastily parted from Fallon, still feeling the memory of his mouth on her lips, her legs trembling with exhilaration.

When the aging captain poked his head up, Fallon looked at the man as if he were sorely tempted to blister his ears with curses.

"Unless the battle has just started, you'd better have a good excuse for interrupting me . . ." he said.

The captain shrugged helplessly. "The thief is dead."

CHAPTER THIRTY

Rage

Silence followed the captain's pronouncement. *Dead? The man who'd hurt her family so much was dead?* She wasn't sure how to feel.

A scowl crossed Fallon's face, and he said, "I will be down shortly. Do not touch the gate. It could be a trick."

"Aye, my lord," the captain said, ducking back down. He left the trapdoor open for them to follow. Fallon stood there for a moment, one hand on his side, the other gripping his furrowed brow. Trynne's heart pained her. Their situation buffeted her worse than the wind.

"We should go back down," she said, knowing it was wise but not wanting to be wise at that moment. She gazed up at the tortured look on his face.

"Trynne," he said, stepping forward. She retreated, keeping space between them, holding up her hand. He looked at her hand as if it were a stone wall.

He shook his head at her. "Please don't push me away."

"I must," she whispered, but she doubted he could hear her over the wind.

He reached out and pressed his palm against hers, then entwined their fingers. "I will never stop hoping," he said.

The heartsick look on his face worsened her own pain. "We have a duty, Fallon," she said, squeezing his hand. "You cannot play in the river near the falls without the risk of being pulled into the current. Please, we must go down."

He nodded in agreement and, holding her hand still, guided her to the edge of the trapdoor and the ladder.

They both halted at the same time. A snake made of a thousand torches wound all the way down the valley road toward Dundrennan. It shimmered in the black, stark night against the stone and trees. Gahalatine's army would arrive by midnight.

Fallon's expression turned dark and severe. "He won't wait for the dawn," he said with conviction. "He will attack tonight."

♦　♦　♦

Captain Staeli finished the final buckle of Trynne's armor—the Maid of Donremy's armor, which Trynne had found in a sanctuary in Occitania. The captain had carried the heavy armor with him, uncomplaining, on their journey. Once it was on, he stood back and appraised her with a frown. His chain cowl was down around his shoulders, but he had on the battered breastplate she'd seen him wearing at the Battle of Guilme. His belt was equipped with a throwing axe, several daggers, and a glaive. His sullen expression and bearded mouth looked so familiar to her, so dear.

"The woad, then?" he asked.

She was wearing the spelled ring under her gauntlets. She had felt the Fountain's subtle suggestion that she should dress the part of the Painted Knight and then use the ring to hide her distinctive armor and painted face.

Tonight, she sensed, would be the night she revealed the truth to all.

She nodded and Captain Staeli reached for the bowl of woad. He scooped up a wad of the doughy material with his forefingers and carefully and gently smeared it across half of her face. She closed her eyes, almost feeling herself transform into the persona of the Painted Knight. What the night would bring, she did not know. But she felt certain the battle would be momentous. If she needed to, she would bring Drew to another fortress and rally more defenders to them there. She felt a crushing duty to protect the king from harm. She was his shield, his secret protector. Fallon had been given the right to her father's seat, but it had been intended for her.

"I'm done, lass," Staeli said, wiping his hand on a rag and tossing it aside. "The Oath Maidens will fight to defend the king tonight. They've trained hard and they've trained well. So have you. I'd be lying if I said I wasn't worried about our fate, but we won't make it easy for them to take this castle. We'll put up a fight."

Trynne nodded to him. "I'm glad you are with me," she said. She dreaded losing anyone else she held dear.

There was a firm rap on the door. Trynne sighed and nodded to Staeli to open it. She used the power of the ring to summon the mirage of her face without the woad, her body dressed in the tunic of Averanche rather than the armor of the Maid of Donremy. She started toward the door as Staeli opened it, revealing Fallon's herald.

"The king is going to the wall with Lord Fallon," the herald said. "He wanted you to join them."

Trynne gave a final curt nod to Staeli and, gripping the hilt of one of her swords, followed the herald into the corridor. Even though it was the middle of the night, no one in the castle was asleep. The great hall was filled with the people from the town, mostly women and children. Every able-bodied man had been given a weapon and a shield and assigned a place to defend the fortress. The air was thick with fear, but people murmured that the king was there with Firebos. They would rally together to fight against the invader.

The torches affixed to the outer wall of Dundrennan cast light on the preparations that were being made. The drawbridge was up, revealing a jagged cleft of rocks separating the defenders from the attacking army. The bailey was crowded with knights, and many of the castle's braziers had been brought out to provide warmth. Trynne and Staeli followed the herald to a stone staircase leading up to the head of the gate. The king was pacing the battlements, wearing borrowed armor. The hollow crown was welded to his helmet. It was nearly midnight, judging by the stars overhead. The moon had disappeared.

Fallon stood there in his armor, the chain cowl up around his head, his arms folded imperiously. He nodded at Trynne as she reached the top of the wall.

The view filled her with dread. A veritable sea of torches filled the space below, and the golden armor of the warriors of Chandigarl glowed in the light. The ranks of Gahalatine's soldiers stood in perfectly ordered rows—spearmen, archers, and warriors with glaives. Row after row, phalanx after phalanx, with more coming still. There was no siege apparatus on display, no towers or ladders or ropes with grappling hooks. She knew from her own experience that they did not need them.

Their breath came out in puffs of mist. The night was bitingly cold and getting colder. Her eyes shot to the hollow crown.

Standing opposite Fallon was Duke Severn, wearing his black armor with the boar badge tunic, still bloodstained from the battle at Blackpool. He glared down at the host.

The king smiled when he saw Trynne. "We're outnumbered," he said to her. "But do not the rocks hold back the sea? I've ordered the maidens to occupy the heights along the inner wall. Fallon's knights hold this one. Do you approve?"

Trynne nodded, gazing down at the huge host, her throat stopped with fear.

Fallon approached. "The last Espion to make it inside said they found a treasure ship unloading in Blackpool two days ago. Another host of soldiers is marching to Dundrennan. They are converging here with suitable arms. Grand Duke Elwis crossed over from Brugia with an army of ten thousand and started attacking the supply lines. Some of this new army has diverted south to engage his. The war is happening in multiple places and across multiple battlefields. But this one is the largest."

"Thank you for the news," Drew said grimly. "We are hopelessly outnumbered. But one soldier with courage has always been worth a hundred men fighting for the wrong reason."

"My lord, look!" Severn said, pointing off the wall.

They all turned at once. The army before them was splitting in half. A black road appeared down the middle. Then Trynne saw Gahalatine striding through the ranks with Rucrius by his side and two other figures following behind them. She sensed the aura of their magic as they approached. It had become familiar to her.

Just a few days before, she had faced Gahalatine at the zenana in Chandigarl. Now he was approaching Dundrennan as a man of war.

The knights on the wall fell silent as he approached.

Drew's face twisted with animosity as he gazed down at the emperor. He was still looking at the scene below when flakes of snow began to drift down from the cloudless sky. There was an audible gasp as the soldiers noticed the flurry. A grim smile appeared on Severn's mouth. He knew, better than anyone, the special qualities of the hollow crown.

Gahalatine halted when he and his Wizr companions reached the front of the army. He held a sword in one hand and a blazing torch in the other. The wind was blowing hard still, thick with coin-sized flakes of snow that were quickly sticking to the ground.

The emperor of the Forbidden Court turned to Rucrius.

"*Bevah-kah-sha!*" Rucrius pronounced in words that trumpeted like thunder.

The wind instantly calmed. Silence fell across the wall, broken only by the hissing of the snowflakes as they hit the fires from the braziers and torches.

Gahalatine strode forward again, only stopping when he stood directly before the walls of Dundrennan. She knew that he had a way of amplifying his voice. And she felt his well of magic writhing inside him, a bowl full to the brim with power. He unleashed it.

"My name is Gahalatine, Lord of the Distant Isles. I see you plainly, Andrew, son of Eyric, son of Eredur. You wear the hollow crown. I have come to take it from you, to conquer your people and assert my claim to rule these lands as your emperor and protector. Before the bloodletting that will result if I am forced to earn my right by conquest, I give you this chance to surrender the crown to me and spare many innocent lives. But if you feel your duty is to preserve your crown by right of arms, then so be it. I did not come to kill you. Only to humble you. What say you, Lord of Kingfountain? Will you kneel before me?"

Trynne felt magic gush from Gahalatine as he spoke. He was using his words to try to cow Drew into surrendering. Faced with such impossible odds, another might have buckled and capitulated to prevent the violence of war. But Trynne stood near the king, and the magic did not shake Drew's confidence or his resolve to defy Gahalatine's claim. She saw the king's jaw clench and he leaned forward, putting one hand on a buttress of the battlements.

"Both of us worship and believe in the same Fountain, my lord. It was the Fountain that gave me the right to rule. And if it is the Fountain's will that I surrender it, then I shall. Be it according to the Fountain's will and not my own."

He did not have a supernatural way of lifting his voice, but Trynne did not doubt that he could be heard below.

After a moment of silent contemplation, Gahalatine lifted his head high. "Well said, sir. You are an honorable foe. I will grant quarter the moment you decide there is no longer hope. I have prepared for a year to carry on what I started. Tonight, we finish it."

"*He's* overconfident," Severn snorted under his breath.

"Rucrius, the gate if you please," Gahalatine said with a gallant gesture toward the castle, as if he were inviting him to dine.

Rucrius's smile was cold and humorless. He was gripping a different staff than the one Trynne had taken from him. It was black with a yellow-orange globe attached to the end. Trynne's pulse raced as the Wizr pointed it toward the castle.

"*Soontrybio!*"

The raised drawbridge jolted and exploded in a hail of splinters and debris that rained down into the black chasm below as if it had been struck from inside the castle instead of outside. The force of the explosion knocked them all to their knees. Trynne winced in pain, her ears ringing with the cracking noise as she watched small fragments of the drawbridge rain down with the snow across the bailey yard. Twisted and steaming hunks of iron littered the bailey yard too. The gate had been wrenched and snapped apart. Soldiers were scrambling to get away from the doorway.

Drew rose shakily to his feet, his eyes wide with shock. He gripped Fallon's shoulder and nodded. Trynne couldn't hear what he said, but she saw him mouth the word "Now!"

As if Gahalatine had heard the silent word, the first leaf-armored warriors began to land on the battlements as if catapulted from below. The din of clashing metal broke out all along the upper defenses.

It was just after midnight, and Trynne wondered in desperation if they would even be able to hold them off until dawn.

CHAPTER
THIRTY-ONE

Battle of the Kings

The thick flakes of snow obscured the onslaught against the walls of Dundrennan. Even though she could not see her enemies well, she sensed them through her magic and responded to their attacks. Trynne caught many of the warriors as they were unfurling and landing on the battlements, sending their bodies plummeting into the black abyss.

Fallon, holding a sword in one hand and a curved horn in another, pressed his lips against the end of the horn and let out a long, sonorous blast. From high above them, the noise was repeated as the watchmen on the tower began to sound their horns as well, signaling the commencement of the surprise attack.

Trynne was buffeted by a warrior landing near her, but managed to deflect his glaive with her twin swords. She rocked him off his heels, sending him into the abyss. After he fell, she saw something in the flurry below, movement coming from the warriors of Gahalatine's army. Not all were vaulting up to the walls. Then she saw it. That gap in Gahalatine's army was now filled with warriors carrying long wooden poles. No—they were the trunks of pine trees!

Trynne watched in horror as the soldiers carrying the trunks lumbered forward and she divined that the trunks had been prepared to clear the chasm. They hadn't brought siege equipment; they'd brought their own makeshift bridge, knowing that the Wizr would demolish the existing one.

The king brought the pommel of Firebos down on the helmet of an attacker, dropping him to the ground with a dented helm. The sword was a whorl of blue light as he fought, its magic adding strength to his blows. He threw himself into the fight with all the fervor of a man struggling to survive.

"Drew!" Trynne shouted, pointing down at the advancing men. Another leaf-armored warrior landed between them, facing her, and Trynne cut him down and then kicked him off the wall.

The king turned, followed her finger, and saw what was unfolding.

"They're going to cross!" he shouted, striking at another enemy who had fallen from the sky amid the flurries. He turned and shouted down to the bailey yard. "Severn! To the gap! Hold them!"

Trynne realized the danger. The aerial attack was a distraction. If Gahalatine could get his troops across the chasm, he could trap the defenders on the walls, isolating the king from the rest of Dundrennan's defenses.

"Aye, my lord!" Severn shouted back and growled at his knights to hasten and follow him down the stairs to join the battle below.

Groans of pain and surprise floated up from the ranks of Gahalatine's men as spears began raining down on them from the cliffs above. Trynne watched with triumph as the teeming mass of soldiers crumpled from the onslaught, dropping under a withering hail of spears. They hadn't expected the counterattack from their flanks.

"Well done, Fallon!" the king bellowed. "That will distract them a bit!"

Trynne flanked one side of Drew, Fallon the other. He was fighting with lethal skill, cutting down the warriors that still dared to land on the battlements. When Trynne flashed a look at him, she saw the determination in his eyes. This was what he'd always wanted: to prove himself.

The falling spears disrupted the attack on the battlements, and a whoop and a cheer started from the ranks of the knights who were defending the wall. There were only a few remaining pockets of fighting as multiple knights dispatched those who had landed and killed their comrades. Trynne knew the celebration was premature.

Gahalatine would not be defeated so easily.

Not long after the cheers rose from the wall, Trynne felt a sudden surge of power from below and saw a shimmer of light from the magic's aura. She sensed the danger an instant before it happened.

"Drop!" she shouted, grabbing the king's arm and yanking him down. A spear glanced off her shoulder and spun her around, but she managed to drop low. So did Fallon. A roar filled the air, loud as the thunder of a thousand charging horses, and the hail of spears began to fly at Dundrennan's walls. Knights who were slow to drop were impaled by spears and fell from the wall down into the bailey. She sensed the magic coming from Rucrius. He had invoked a massive whirlwind that had gripped the falling spears and hurled them against the fortress.

Spears sailed over Trynne's head, some cracking stone with the violence of their impact. Knights cowered behind shields as the storm shook and raged. The frozen sleet stung Trynne's cheeks, but her armor protected her.

Drew was flat against the stone wall, his eyes wide with terror as the colossal magic battered against Dundrennan's walls. Bodies dressed in the armor of the Pierced Lion began to plummet into the bailey, and Trynne gaped in horror as she realized Rucrius's spell was destroying Fallon's soldiers up on the ridge. He'd invoked a storm cloud, a whirling vortex of death. Trynne cowered from it, wishing her mother were there to counter it. Wishing Myrddin was there.

"*Keraunos!*"

It was a woman's voice. Morwenna's voice. It came from the middle of the bailey, where the poisoner was standing with arms splayed wide, hair whipping in the wind. Suddenly lightning began to streak across the sky from the enormous black cyclone roiling over the palace. The glittering forks of light were heading toward Gahalatine's army. No— they were striking repeatedly at Rucrius. They blasted into the ranks of the Chandigarli soldiers, leaving cries of panic in their wake.

The hail of spears subsided and the cloud began to dissolve and break apart.

"My lord, to the keep!" Trynne said, scuttling closer to the king. A chunk of rock whipped by her, barely missing her nose.

Trynne sensed Morwenna and Rucrius were locked in a duel of wills. Morwenna had an angry, defiant frown on her face, and her fingers were splayed as if she were digging them into something tangible. More lightning rained down on the enemy army, blast after blast of blinding fire. Trynne felt Morwenna's reserves decreasing by the moment. She could not sustain the attack, not against the combined might of so many Wizrs.

"She's right," Fallon said, rising to his knees. "This is our chance to hasten to the inner wall. We cannot survive this storm long if we stay outside."

Blood trickled from a laceration on the king's cheek. He nodded in agreement and gave the order to fall back. The brilliance of the lightning rippling through the disintegrating storm revealed the scene around them in flashes. Everywhere Trynne looked, there were fallen knights on the battlement. Her heart grieved at the losses, but she saw even more dead scattered in the field below. Gahalatine was taking heavy casualties as well.

A surge of power slammed into Morwenna—Trynne could sense the Wizrs had pooled their powers together—and the magic gushed from her like a punctured bladder. Her command of the lightning began to fail and the blasts became erratic.

"Flee to the keep!" the king shouted. As they reached the bottom steps, he turned to where Severn had rallied his soldiers. "Hold that gap until we've made it through the doors, then fall back and join us."

"I'll hold them," Severn promised. His voice full of fury, he yelled, "Men of Glosstyr! To me!"

Trynne hurried alongside the king as they crossed the rubble of spears and stone and dead men on the way to the hall. Morwenna's shoulders were slumped, her elbows pressed into her sides as she tried to fight off the combined will of the Wizrs. She dropped to one knee, her power nearly spent. Trynne ached for her, amazed that she was fighting for their side, wondering how she had broken free from her cell.

An angry voice carried on the wind. Trynne couldn't make out the words, only the sepulchral tones, and then Morwenna collapsed onto the cobblestones, unconscious.

"Here they come!" Severn shouted. "Stand fast! Stand fast!"

Trynne turned and saw the Chandigarli soldiers carrying the pine trunks toward the gap. Some of the logs were already in position. The men of Glosstyr rushed forward and shoved on the poles, successfully tipping some of them into the breach. The weight of the logs made them fall. But there were too many men behind each one, and soon Severn's men were outmatched and the gaps began to close. Leaf-armored warriors came swooping down into the bailey and began falling on Severn's men.

"For Kingfountain!" Severn roared in fury, leaping into the fray. Trynne felt tears prick her eyes as she watched him strike at the enemy. Warriors rushed over the makeshift bridge and began pouring into the bailey.

"We've lost it," Drew whispered, aghast, as he recognized that Severn's men were cut off.

Fallon scooped up Morwenna into his arms, grimacing from the burden.

Trynne watched as Gahalatine's men cut down the men of the White Boar. Drew shouted, "Retreat, Severn! We're almost through! Pull back!"

Most of the survivors of the outer wall hastened in through the door, shielding their eyes from the bright light of torches. Warriors of Gahalatine were already starting to charge toward the position where Trynne stood with the king.

Fallon arrived next, cradling Morwenna, whose head lolled. Her eyelids fluttered and she stared at the courtyard. "Father," she groaned.

Trynne saw Rucrius cross the bridge, holding his black staff and scowling in naked fury. He had the look of a man betrayed. His strange, catlike eyes glittered white from the torchlight. Then he extended his ringed hand toward Severn, who froze midstroke. He stood rigidly, a grotesque statue of a knight at arms.

He couldn't move.

Trynne stared in horror as Rucrius advanced on the helpless man. Severn stood frozen in place, his face twisted with fear and hatred. He spoke, lashing out with his words.

"Go on, slay me, you black-hearted villain! You coward! I fear you not. I fear no man. I'd rather die with my sword in my hand than cower like a pup as you do!" His Fountain magic dribbled from him, hardly grazing the Wizr, who gazed at him disdainfully.

"So be it," Rucrius snarled and whipped his staff around, cracking Severn's cheekbone with it. Trynne groaned in agony, wanting to save him but knowing that her duty was to protect and safeguard the king.

Gazing at Morwenna with hate in his eyes, Rucrius drew the sword belted at his waist and ran Severn through with it.

For a moment, Severn hung like a man fixed on a spike. Then his sword fell from his hooked fingers and clattered on the stone. Morwenna began to shriek and wail as Fallon bustled her into the fortress.

There was a look of open anguish on the king's face as he watched the awful scene. As soon as Morwenna disappeared from view, the magic ended and Severn collapsed in a heap.

Trynne felt her heart thump with agony. She knew the kind of pain that Morwenna was feeling. Knew the devastation of losing a beloved father. Grabbing the king by the shoulder, she pushed him through the gap into the doorway. Captain Staeli and the Oath Maidens were thronging the entryway, ready to fight. The last of the knights had made it through.

Destroy the Wizr, the Fountain whispered to her. *He is delivered into your hands.*

She felt a prick of fear, but it was quenched by a rush of confidence. Trynne looked Staeli in the eye. "Shut the doors," she said in a low, angry voice.

And then she turned and stepped back out into the courtyard, dropping the mirage from the magic ring on her finger.

The Painted Knight emerged into the gloom of the bailey.

CHAPTER THIRTY-TWO

Vengeance

The magic of the wellspring swept around Trynne like an embracing shield. Although it was invisible to the eye, it allowed her to sense and follow the movements of everyone around her. Time seemed to quiet and still to the point that she felt every throb of her heartbeat. Holding both of her blades, she charged toward Rucrius, sensing in him an impregnable magic—except for his neck. It occurred to her that in the game of Wizr, knight pieces were often sacrificed to claim an enemy's Wizr. Was that what the Fountain wished from her? Was that how she would best save her king?

Trynne saw the leaf-armored warriors rushing toward her, weapons lifted. The wellspring magic surrounding her made their movements appear lethargic, as if they were fighting in a field of mud. She sliced two of them as she ducked around, marveling that her speed was greater than theirs. She'd experienced the perfect weaving of her magic with the wellspring magic before in the training yard. It happened when she was totally focused and relentless. Nothing else mattered. Glaives swept toward her, but she had time to duck and counter, and she spun around and dispatched her attackers before they could even finish their initial strokes.

Rucrius's face slowly contorted with anger as he gazed at her. She saw his lips stretch and grimace as he formed words of power she couldn't hear past the thumping noises of her heartbeat. Two more foes went down before her, splaying on the snow as they clutched their wounds. She passed through the enemy ranks, untouchable, weaving between Gahalatine's warriors as they tried to strike at her, but none could match her speed.

Rucrius finished uttering the word of power and a blast of lightning struck at her from the wintry storm clouds. But Trynne was just ahead of it. Her skin tingled as if a hand were about to graze her neck, but the energy of the blast could not envelop her. Instead, several of Gahalatine's warriors were charred from their proximity to the strike.

A glaive blade came toward her middle as a knight squinted his eyes against the light while trying to strike at her. Trynne crossed her blades in front of her, catching the weapon, and it shattered on the impact. She buffeted the soldier with her elbow and he spun twice before collapsing.

Rucrius's eyes flashed with panic as she cut her way through the soldiers standing between them. Holding his staff and bloodstained blade, he positioned himself into a defensive stance.

Most of the soldiers were still blinded by the lightning, many of them covering their faces reflexively. She struck at several more Chandigarli warriors as she closed the gap, stopping only when she had reached the fallen body of Duke Severn, his eyes open, a gob of blood pooled by his mouth. Indignation filled her with new purpose.

Her magic was shrinking, drawing back into her. She had to conserve it. The strange becalming magic ended as she reached the Wizr Rucrius. The sounds and smells around her filtered back in—she heard the clattering of dropped weapons, the groans of agony from the injured and dying, smelled the singed, metallic odor of burnt stone. But she drove everything from her mind as she launched herself at the Wizr.

"I know who you *are*!" Rucrius gibbered with terror, swinging his staff toward her head. "And if you kill *me*, your father will die! It is not too late to save him!"

One of Trynne's swords deflected the arc of the staff's blow. She swung the other at his side, but he blocked it.

"I swear to you, he will live! Don't throw away your last chance to save him!"

She refused to speak to him. He was consumed with revenge. The only thing he feared was his own death. She swung at him again and again, but he blocked and parried, countering with attacks of his own. The warriors around them couldn't assist him; the blast had damaged their eyes.

Rucrius was full of life and power, and she sensed that he was resistant to aging, that he was one of the Wizrs of old who had lived for generations. Perhaps he was like Myrddin. But he knew he was vulnerable to her. She saw it in his pale cheeks, in his quivering lips as he sought to control his terror. When he decided to flee, she sensed his intention immediately.

Dundrennan was a nexus for the ley lines. It had appeared as such on every map Trynne had ever seen. The ley lines that passed through it went to Ploemeur, Kingfountain, and Edonburick. It seemed that his Tay al-Ard was not functional from overusing it, but he could still flee another way.

She couldn't let it happen.

As he was uttering the word of power that would launch him through the ley lines, she joined her mind to his. Dropping one of her swords, she gripped his tunic, and suddenly it felt as if she'd stepped into a rushing waterfall. She clung to the Wizr, feeling his thoughts buck and weave as he panicked. He kept changing destinations, trying to shake her loose. Images of fountains flickered through her mind, the noise of babbling waters of an endless variety mixed with the rush and roar of mighty waterfalls. They were passing swiftly, zigzagging across the continents, her insides wrenching with spasms, but still she held on to him. She sensed his weakness, his mounting desperation to survive. His magic was beginning to fail, and he was forced to carry her weight as well, which was only tiring him faster.

They finally appeared in a small alcove in a damp-smelling chapel. It was well past midnight and the waters of the fountain had been stilled. Trynne fell to her knees with exhaustion, her fingers still digging into Rucrius's robes. He fell as well, dropping his sword in the water with a loud splash and catching himself on his staff. His legs trembled violently. It was a familiar chapel—one she had been to recently. On her last visit, the twisting snakes carved into the walls had been illuminated by the orange light of torches. She recognized the old smell, a mildewy scent of water-ways and damp corners. This was the poisoner school in Pisan, the same fountain she and Morwenna had traveled to before going to Chandigarl.

"Don't," Rucrius said, his voice quavering. "Don't!"

It was considered the height of sacrilege to murder someone in a fountain. But she felt the murmur of the Fountain's voice.

Slay him.

Rucrius's eyes widened, as if he too had heard the command. His face twisted with grief and fear. Trynne slowly rose to her feet, her limbs feeling weak, her stomach roiling with nausea.

She had sworn an oath to obey the Fountain. She didn't have the desire to kill him. The idea repulsed her. But the Fountain demanded it of her, and she had sworn an oath to do its bidding.

"Please," Rucrius babbled. "I will tell you where your father is. I will serve you and no other. All that I have, all my wealth and power will be—"

She blocked out his words, grabbed a fistful of his tawny mane, and fulfilled the Fountain's will while standing inside the fountain.

◆　◆　◆

Trynne knelt next to the fountain, her shoulders heaving as she cried softly. The tears kept coming for a mixture of reasons. She had killed before but had never executed someone. She did not feel guilt—no, it was more a feeling of relief. But it anguished her to think her father might truly die because of what she had done. If Rucrius had left orders for his murder, she might have unwittingly sentenced him to death. That thought was unbearable to her, but she trusted the Fountain. She knew her father did as well. And perhaps the Fountain had seen to his protection somehow.

A noise coming from the outside corridor roused her moments later.

The light from a lamp appeared in the corridor, and she heard two men speaking in the language of Pisan. There was no need to utter the word of power that allowed her to understand all languages; she was familiar with this one from the merchants she had met in Ploemeur.

"I know I heard something. It came from the chapel."

"I heard nothing," muttered an angry voice.

Their footsteps drew nearer and Trynne rose, stifling the tears that were still fresh in her eyes. She stared down at the fountain water, expecting it to be clouded with blood, but the water was strangely clear. Rucrius's body was still and silent; all evidence of his magic and power had been snuffed out.

Then Trynne sensed something. It was an awareness, like the presence of another Fountain-blessed trying to remain concealed.

"What did it sound like?"

"I heard splashing."

There was a grunt of anger. "Maybe someone was taking a bath!"

"It's the middle of the night," hissed the other man. "Do you hear anyone now? No, I know what I heard. This way."

The light drew closer. Trynne knew it was time to return to Dundrennan. She couldn't be found there, and she did not want to leave the king so vulnerable.

Rucrius had brought her many places, rejecting each one, trying to break free of her grip. Of all the choices he could have made, he had brought her to the poisoner school of Pisan. The school where Morwenna had studied.

How long had Rucrius been involved in the affairs of the kingdoms? Had he played a role in keeping Ceredigion and Occitania and Brugia fighting each other? Was there more subtlety to the poisoner school than she or anyone had imagined?

But there would be time to explore her suspicions later. For now, she needed to return to the fight at Dundrennan. She straightened and invoked the word of power.

◆　◆　◆

Trynne emerged from the fountain in the midst of the castle and quickly invoked the magic of the ring, concealing the armor and streaks of woad on her face, looking just as she had before. The sound of fighting echoed in the stone hall. Trynne rushed out of the chapel and found the corridor filled with bodies, some wearing the tunic of the Pierced Lion, some the armor of Gahalatine. The corridors were lit by flickering torchlight.

"Gather near me!" she heard Captain Staeli bark. "Hold the doors. Do not let any of the wretches past!"

Trynne rounded the corner and saw a wall of soldiers facing off against Staeli and six Oath Maidens. They were outnumbered but defiant. The warriors of Chandigarl pressed forward and the Oath Maidens rushed to meet them, swinging blades and kicking out with booted feet. Trynne watched one of the girls fall. Then another, but for each one who fell, five or six of the enemy was killed.

She rushed to attack the Chandigarli from behind—the enemy soldiers were boxed in, and they seemed to panic when they realized it.

"That does it!" Staeli crooned, slashing at their foes with both hands. In moments, the rest of the attackers had fallen.

"Lady Trynne!" one of the girls said, seeing her.

Captain Staeli looked at her with surprise. "By the shroud, lass! Look at you!"

"It's Trynne!" said another girl. She had a cut on her cheek but looked hale otherwise.

"I told you she'd be well," Staeli grunted. She wanted to hug him, but there was too much going on.

"What is happening?" she asked.

"All the lads and lasses—save these, of course—are down in the dungeons and treasure rooms. The king is in the great hall. We've barricaded all the doors. This is the last one."

Trynne nodded, and Staeli turned and opened the door to the great hall. It was full of soldiers, both wounded and hale, and it was absolute mayhem. Some of the injured knights of the North were drinking from cups pressed into their hands, before rising once more to continue the fight. Groans and murmurs filled the hall, and Trynne saw King Drew talking to one of the maidens, giving instructions and pointing. He turned and saw her and his fierce expression wilted into relief.

"Get these doors barred!" Staeli ordered. "Use those water barrels, I don't care if they're full. They are going to fight us for every inch, by the blood. It's almost dawn. Hold steady. Hold steady."

As she hurried toward Drew, Trynne saw Fallon leaning over Morwenna, who sat slumped on the floor. The poisoner nodded her head slowly, her face ashen, as he took a cup from her. Then she caught sight of Trynne walking toward them, and she covered her face in her hands, her shoulders shaking with the power of her sobs. Fallon looked over his shoulder to see what had caused the reaction and then leaped to his feet.

He rushed up to Trynne, gazing at her like she was a ray of sunlight. "Where have you been? I've had everyone looking for you. Some said you never made it in from the courtyard. I've been worried to death you were trapped out there in the blizzard!"

"I used the ley lines," she told him, feeling pleased that he had worried, grateful to be back with him. Still, even though she knew Morwenna needed a friend now more than ever, she could not lie to herself. It bothered her to see them together. "I'm all right."

"Trynne!" Drew sighed, reaching them. He gripped her arm tenderly.

"I'm all right," she repeated. A part of her wanted to tell them what happened in Pisan, but she also wanted to block the memories forever.

"I have word from the Espion that Grand Duke Elwis and his army are on the march. They are rushing to Dundrennan. They bid us to hold fast. They're coming."

"I don't know how long we can hold out," Trynne said, shaking her head.

"My lord, they are coming!" someone shouted.

"Keep blocking the doors, then!" Staeli yelled. "They don't have battering rams."

There were three external doors leading into the hall. One of the far doors shuddered as something heavy struck it. Then something began to pound against the second door. The third led deeper into the castle, where the inhabitants of the city were hunkering down.

Drew turned and drew his sword. "This is where we stand and fight. This is where the honor of Kingfountain rests. Do your duty. I can ask no more."

Trynne's heart churned with worry. Should she take Drew somewhere else? If the Chandigarli soldiers broke through, should she flee with the king and leave Dundrennan to its fate? Leaving . . . Fallon? Captain Staeli? Her maidens? She covered her mouth, not knowing what she should do.

Then she spied Morwenna again, still slumped on the floor, gazing sullenly at the doors. The poisoner had helped them defend the castle during the storm Rucrius had summoned. Her reward had been to watch her father die at his hand. Although Trynne's feelings for the Argentine girl were complex, she did pity her.

Without thinking, Trynne left the king and Fallon and approached Morwenna. The dark-haired girl looked up at her, nearly cowering with shame and misery.

"You killed him," Morwenna said in a thick, haunted voice. Her eyes were red from crying. "You killed your father."

CHAPTER THIRTY-THREE

The King's Champion

Morwenna's words cut Trynne to her heart. It was her greatest fear that she would be responsible, inadvertently or not, for her father's death. The struggle to control and contain her emotions was challenging, but although the words had filled her with worry and misery, they did not ring of truth. There was no confirming whisper from the Fountain. Trynne dropped lower, putting her hand on Morwenna's shoulder.

"I don't say it out of envy or spite," the poisoner said with tears. Her face was ravaged with grief. "Rucrius left orders that Lord Owen was to be dispatched. Gahalatine doesn't know this. He's never known."

"Do you know where they were keeping him?" Trynne asked, letting herself hope. "Is there a chance to stop it?"

Morwenna covered her face. "I'm sorry, Trynne. It's all my fault. When I was at the poisoner school, I found a copy of *The Vulgate*. I told you this already. What I couldn't tell you is that Rucrius planted it there, seeking someone like me." She raised her tearstained eyes.

"What do you mean?" Trynne said, raising her voice. The noise from the besieged doors, shuddering on their hinges, was growing louder. Rows of knights and maidens were positioning themselves before them, preparing to defend the king.

"I was so fixed on it," Morwenna said, staring down at her knuckles. "On seeking revenge against your father. For his treason against mine. I think . . . somehow . . . my thoughts brought Rucrius to me. He was powerful. He taught me the ways of the Wizrs, even more than your mother did. But before he would teach me, he gave me a ring." Her eyes grew haunted. "A ring that would bind me to him, to keep me from betraying him. After I put it on, he . . . he had control of my mind. He could make me say things. He could compel my actions." She quivered and trembled. "He was arranging for me to marry Gahalatine. It would have given me everything that I wished for. But I fought against him the first chance I got. In the first surge of the battle, his will was so focused on his magic and maintaining the whirlwind that I broke free of his control and sought to counter him. He"—she swallowed miserably— "he murdered my father as punishment. When you killed Rucrius, I felt his control over me break. His thoughts faded like echoes. I've lost everything. Everything." Morwenna bowed her head and began to sob.

Trynne closed her eyes, her heart aching for the deceit and the manipulation. The eastern door cracked with loud snapping noises as the wood gave way.

"Stand fast!" Captain Staeli shouted. "Encircle the king!"

Trynne reached out with her magic and sensed that Morwenna's store was still empty. It was as if her cup had shattered and she was recognizing that Trynne's had not.

"You are powerful," Morwenna whispered, tears glistening in her eyes.

The door pieces came crashing down and the enemy warriors began wading through the debris to get inside.

Protect the king.

Gratitude welled inside her. The Fountain had whispered for her to defend the king, not spirit him away.

Trynne rose and reached her hand down to Morwenna. "Now is not the time to be enemies. Defend your brother."

Morwenna looked at her in startled surprise. "Do you trust me?"

Trynne chuffed. "No, not very much. But we're short on allies at the moment. If any Wizrs come through those doors, go for the neck." She drew her own dagger and handed it to Morwenna, who accepted it and then took her hand and allowed herself to be pulled back up.

◆ ◆ ◆

Trynne's throat was raw from thirst and her arms were weary from fighting. Both doors had been breached, but every time the Chandigarli soldiers tried to enter the hall, the knights of North Cumbria and the Oath Maidens of Averanche drove them out again. The sun had finally risen, but the situation had not changed.

Captain Staeli barked orders and improvised during the attack, constantly shifting the tactics and directing his maidens. His brow had been slashed by a blade, but he hadn't let the blood dripping down his face slow him. His leadership and fearlessness had inspired everyone.

There was a pause after the latest attack had been repulsed, and everyone was breathing and gasping for air. Trynne had watched Morwenna fight with all the savage fury she could muster. Though unarmored, she alone had killed over a dozen knights. Fallon had also performed feats of bravery and skill, showing the outcome of his training. Yet even King Drew, with the blazing magic of Firebos, had been unable to stop the relentless flood of attackers continuing the assault of the fortress. A biting cold wind came through the demolished doorways, speaking of the blizzard still raging outside. Drew's thoughts continued to power the storm that would unleash a mountain of snow on them.

"They're coming," Staeli warned, wiping a smear of blood from his cheek. "They'll run out of soldiers ere long. Keep up the fight."

Drew's voice was ragged. "I don't know how much more we'll be able to take," he gasped to Trynne.

She sensed the presence of other Fountain-blessed in the corridor. She recognized Gahalatine's presence. When she had first seen him at the Battle of Guilme, she had sensed his enormous store of magic—it was unmistakable. But his efforts to embolden his warriors to continue the fight during a ferocious blizzard had drained him. His magic was diminished, but his force of will was still incredibly strong. There was another with him . . . no, at least two other Fountain-blessed with him. How many Wizrs had he brought?

"I see them," Staeli snarled. He was in the front of the ranks alongside the maidens. "The emperor's come himself. How grand."

A disquieted murmur rippled through the hall. Trynne still tried to catch her breath, but she felt that the moment was coming. The fate of the kingdoms was about to be decided. She had no idea what it would be.

The Painted Knight must stand ready.

The thought throbbed in Trynne's mind—insistent—and she released the magic of her ring just as Gahalatine and his group came into sight. All eyes were focused on the doorway.

Gahalatine's fox-fur robe was thick with snow. He wore his armor and held a greatsword with one hand. Even though the ancient Wizr set had been destroyed, his presence in the castle filled her with the strange sensation that one of the pieces was moving across the board. There was something mysterious at work here, some magic she could not comprehend.

Gahalatine led the way, but this was not another wave of the attack. Not yet. Next to him was the same armored warrior that she had seen at Guilme. It was Gahalatine's champion, and he glared balefully at the enemies arrayed before him. There were two Wizrs behind Gahalatine, and when Trynne reached out with her magic, she saw that both were spent. They each had staves and rings and other magical trinkets to draw power from, but they looked haggard and weak.

Gahalatine paused at the threshold of the chamber. He looked at them in a condescending way, as if they were a group of children who had been caught at some mischief, and he—the ever-patient parent—had come to scold them. It made Trynne bristle with outrage.

"My lord of Kingfountain," Gahalatine said with a deferential nod to Drew. "You've fought bravely. You've summoned a winter storm that is as formidable as it is tedious. My men are cold and most have taken refuge in the town, where the greater bulk of my army is at their ease, eating and drinking and awaiting their turn to besiege the castle. You have withstood me with courage and honor, my lord. It does you credit. I came prepared for a winter siege, knowing the history of the crown you wear. You have surprised me many times, which does not happen very often." Then his voice turned more dangerous. "I come with this final plea to end the violence. You have an army marching here under the command of Grand Duke Elwis. Your snows have prevented them from reaching you, and I'm afraid he came unprepared for the inclement weather. I have an army awaiting his arrival and another one marching behind him. He's trapped either way. He cannot reach you and he cannot retreat. You are down to your bravest and most loyal supporters, and I tell you, my lord, that if I summon all my strength from the town, as I intend to do after breakfast, we will smite down this castle. You have no hope of victory. Yield to me, my lord. You've proven yourself both valiant and determined, and I will reward you for such competence as my noble guest in the Forbidden Court. We will fetch your wife and babe from the sanctuary of Our Lady, and together you may live out your lives in peace and prosperity."

His words hung in the air, crackling like icicles ready to fall.

Drew stared at Gahalatine, his cheeks flushing. "The Fountain gave me this crown," he answered thickly. "And it will help me maintain it. If you would have it, come take it from me."

Gahalatine looked disappointed but not surprised. He sighed and gestured to the armored man next to him. "So be it. You had your chance."

The armored knight charged into the room, his armor exuding a dustlike smoke as he moved. It was Fountain magic, and Trynne sensed the speed and agility it gave the warrior despite its bulk. He engaged Captain Staeli first, making Trynne's heart leap into her throat. Staeli, who had been fighting all night, was physically exhausted, yet he leaped at the warrior without hesitation. But the moment Staeli's sword struck the man's armor, the blade went red with cankered rust and then shattered. The impact made Staeli's face go slack from shock right before the knight backhanded him across the face with an armored gauntlet. As he struck the ground, the knight plunged his sword into Staeli's stomach, the blade shearing effortlessly through the hauberk. Staeli's legs began to twitch and then he went limp.

"No!" Fallon roared, rushing forward past the ring of Oath Maidens. The knight turned his hateful gaze on him, and Trynne felt her world tipping over like a huge vase, about to crash down.

Fallon did not repeat Staeli's mistake. He feinted with his sword and then kicked the knight in the chest. Fallon's boot shoved the man back a few feet, but it did not unleash the strange dustlike smoke. The knight returned and started swinging deliberately at Fallon, who countered with his own sword and gave ground to the opposing warrior's superior skill. Fallon focused on deflecting the blade and not counterstriking against the warrior. Trynne's hand clenched the pommel of her own blade, feeling helpless as she watched the knight come after Fallon.

Fallon's blade caught that of the other knight, their hilts locking together, and he kicked at the knight's knee. From Fallon's wince, the blow seemed to hurt him more than it did his competitor.

Fallon's face contorted with anger as his opponent tried to leverage him back. Reaching out, he grabbed the front of the knight's helm and yanked it sideways, trying to blind him. The trick worked, and Fallon managed to free his blade and retreat a step or two.

Gahalatine's champion unstrapped the helm, pulled it off, and threw it down.

The knight was a woman.

She was tall, only a little shorter than Fallon, and as muscular and strong as any man. Her resemblance to Gahalatine marked her as a relation. Beautiful and fierce, she had dark hair that was shorn short and features that were a slight bit more delicate than the emperor's. She came at Fallon and he defended, but Trynne saw the worry in his eye, saw how conflicted he felt about battling a woman to the death.

"He can't win," Drew whispered in despair. "He's already lost."

And then Gahalatine's champion sliced Fallon's leg at the knee, twirled, and brought her elbow into his nose. He teetered backward, trying to keep his footing despite the blaze of pain from his torn lip and the blood gushing from his knee. Then he went down, dropping his blade on impact. Trynne watched in horror as the knight maiden turned her sword toward his heart, gripping it with both hands.

Trynne saw what she must do. It opened in front of her like a vision.

"My lord, your sword!" she said to Drew, dropping her own and holding out her hand. She knew in her heart that Firebos would not be affected by the knight's armor. It was the only weapon that could pierce it unharmed.

Drew's eyes widened when he looked at her, seeing the smear of blue on her face, recognizing that she, Trynne Kiskaddon, was the Painted Knight. He obeyed her at once, handing the blade of the Maid of Donremy to her. Its magic felt familiar to her, as if she'd carried it into battle all along.

The enemy knight jammed the sword down toward Fallon's heart as Trynne invoked the wellspring magic once again. The room seemed to still and slow, as it had before, and she spanned the space between them with a few lunging steps, swinging Firebos around to deflect the blade. The two swords met with a clash of sparks.

Trynne continued her attack, driving the other knight backward, away from Fallon, back toward Gahalatine. Their blades met and rang, counter versus counter. Trynne did not limit her focus to the blade. She hacked at the other woman's armor, each blow sending splashes of dust into the air, but Firebos was indeed protected from harm. There was a screeching noise as the woman's armor was sheared open.

Trynne reached out with her magic, sensing for weakness, for vulnerability, and found plenty. The woman had trained in the arts of war for years, but she was so accustomed to the protection of her armor and her magic that she had mostly trained for attack, not defense. She was fearful now, recognizing that she was no match for Trynne's skill with a blade. She was full of Fountain magic, but there was something different about it . . . that was when Trynne realized that Gahalatine and his champion *shared* their store of magic. They were siblings.

And now Gahalatine's sister was in danger. Trynne attacked viciously, hitting her arm guards, shoulders, driving her back step by step, the shimmering blade of ancient kings like a storm in her hand. She felt the two Wizrs behind Gahalatine use their magic against her, but their spells simply shot past her, driven to the side. Trynne continued to push the woman farther and farther back and then made a quick strike at her wrist, sending her sword clattering to the floor.

"Stop!" Gahalatine shouted, his eyes blazing with panic as Trynne pressed her blade to his sister's bare neck. His hand was outstretched. His shout came with all the force of his magic, but it could not sway her. He stared at Trynne, stared at the smudges on her face, and slowly his eyes widened in recognition and surprise.

Trynne yanked down her chain hood, revealing her face, her hair.

"Yes," Trynne said to him, glaring at him. "It is I. Do you yield?"

An exultant smile spread on Gahalatine's face. His worry at seeing his sister murdered was ebbing. Perhaps he believed Trynne wouldn't kill her. He lowered his outstretched palm, but still held it out before him, as if coaxing friendship from an angry wolf.

"It is you," Gahalatine said. "I'd not suspected. Yes, I will discuss terms with you. After vanquishing your king's champion, I was going to insist he send you out to discuss terms of surrender."

Trynne gave him a glowering look. "We have no intention of surrendering, my lord."

A reckless sort of smile shone on his mouth. "Then treat with me, Tryneowy. My sister is your king's hostage. Come back to my pavilion with me, and we will broker a truce between our kingdoms. You and I. If we cannot come to terms, then I will exchange you for my sister and we will continue this war. But I believe—I dare even hope—that one word from you will resolve this. Will you come?"

Trynne lowered the sword deliberately and looked back at King Drew, seeking his orders.

There was a new look of hope in Drew's eyes when he met her gaze. "I empower you, Trynne Kiskaddon, to negotiate on my behalf."

CHAPTER
THIRTY-FOUR

Submission

It was like a river current was tugging her away. The scene was almost unreal. Captain Staeli on the floor, unmoving, his face turned away from her, his tunic soaked with blood. He was lost to her. Fallon was also one of the fallen, gripping his wounded knee as he stared at her in horror. He knew she was being swept away from him. Morwenna looked broken, defeated. Trynne gazed at them, one by one, and then walked to Drew and handed him Firebos. The king looked vulnerable, but there was still hope in his eyes. He was depending on Trynne to find a way to stop the violence from spreading further.

She took a deep breath, trying to steady herself, and then turned back and crossed the hall to Gahalatine, who stretched out his hand to her. His sister had risen, her armor broken and split from Trynne's attack. Her eyes were fierce and angry, but she had accepted her brother's decision. She remained behind.

When Trynne reached him, Gahalatine took her hand in his, gazing down at her with concerned but eager eyes. "Albion," he said to one of the Wizrs, "take us to my pavilion."

"It will be done, dread sovereign," the Wizr replied meekly. He withdrew a Tay al-Ard from beneath his tunic and rested his hand on Gahalatine's shoulder.

The rushing motion felt like falling, but it only lasted an instant. The dawn's light revealed the spacious and luxurious tent. The curtains were spun of a golden cloth that nearly glowed. There were embroidered curtains inside, separating the enormous space into rooms, well-appointed changing screens wrought of iron and plated with gold leaf, and camp chairs arranged around tables heaped with grapes, pears, and fruits with speckled skins that she'd never seen before. Garlands of flowers hung from poles, and there was even a monkey, tethered to an ornate padded pole, calmly eating one of the grapes. There was a throne-like chair in the middle of the room, showing this to be a makeshift audience hall. It was immaculately clean. The pavilion made her feel like she was in Chandigarl, but the air was cold and the wind gusted through invisible cracks.

Trynne felt a rush of vertigo and started to sway, but Gahalatine strengthened his grip on her hand to steady her. He turned to the Wizr and spoke, magic swelling behind his words.

"Albion, order a halt to the attack. Draw the warriors back to the outer wall and have them stand guard. Send the royal surgeons into the castle at once to tend to the wounded. There are many. Have them obey King Andrew in every whit. Send word immediately to Shigionoth to forestall his attack on the Grand Duke of Brugia. If the attack has already begun, cease hostilities and withdraw. Obey me, Albion. I don't know where Rucrius went or what mischief he may be up to, but if any of you defy me in this, I will have your heads."

The Wizr looked affronted. "I don't know where he is, my lord. He disappeared during the siege."

"He is dead," Trynne said in a low, meaningful voice.

The Wizr Albion stared at her as if she'd just uttered something beyond belief. His face twisted into a rictus of horror.

"He tried to flee the bailey, and I followed him through the ley lines. I will tell you where I left his body later."

Albion blinked, his cheeks growing pale. "You . . . *you* killed him?"

Trynne nodded.

Gahalatine looked pleased. In fact, he even looked relieved. "By the Fountain," he murmured. Then his eye grew sterner. "Secure the wards on the pavilion, Albion. No one comes in here unless I command it. On pain of death."

The Wizr touched his own lips fearfully. "My lord, the Mandaryn cannot allow you to be so *unprotected*. If this girl dispatched Rucrius, then—"

"I am not interested in your advice," Gahalatine snapped. "Invoke the wards and be gone! I'll have none of you eavesdropping while I negotiate with her."

"My lord," Albion said, shaking his head, but the fire in Gahalatine's eyes was such that the Wizr bowed meekly and turned without finishing his sentence. He began muttering words of power, making subtle hand gestures as he did so, and Trynne felt a blanket of magic descend atop the pavilion. The murmuring of the camp became distant and then hushed into quiet, like snow piling atop snow in a blizzard.

Albion ducked out of the tent, and Trynne felt as if a darkness had been lifted.

Gahalatine was still holding her hand. He grazed her knuckle with his thumb and led her toward one of the veils blocking the deeper interior of the tent. He parted the curtain for her, but he needed to duck himself to enter. The floor was covered in a massive tangle of fur rugs and cushions, and there were chests to one side and an empty armor rack to the other. Gahalatine unbuckled his sword belt and hung it on the rack. When he released her hand, she felt suddenly cold and very unsure of herself.

"My lord, am I correct in supposing that you still desire . . . what you wanted before?" she said, trying to keep her voice from quavering. "What you told me when I was in Chandigarl?"

He unfastened his cloak and tossed it to the floor before turning to face her.

"We are not going to start our negotiations yet." He gave her a lingering look and scrubbed his hand through his hair. "You're utterly exhausted. Come sit over here. Let me tend to you." He shut the lid of one of the chests and led her over to it by the arm, treating her with as much deference as a servant would. Though she was a little unsure of him, of the strange situation, she seated herself on the chest. He glanced around the room before retrieving a washbowl and carrying it over.

"Here, hold this in your lap," he said, setting it there. Then he dipped a cleaning rag fringed with gold into the water and started wiping the woad from her face. She saw the smudges of blue, brown, and even red leach into the fabric. He dunked it again, squeezing it hard with both hands, and continued to wipe her face. He was on his knees in front of her, treating her with tenderness and gentleness. She felt the shudder come a moment before it happened.

"Are you cold?" he asked her with worry.

"The water is a little cold," she said.

"It was warmer earlier." Then he rose, taking the bowl over to a stone column. There was a face carved into the polished stone, and she felt a murmur of Fountain magic as Gahalatine held the bowl beneath it. She almost gasped when the carving's eyes suddenly lit like red coals and steaming water began to stream out of them, as if the face were weeping hot tears, filling the bowl. It reminded her of the magic in the caves at the Glass Beach, the ancient crumbling faces carved into the rock that summoned light and protected the borders.

As Gahalatine carried it back to her, careful not to slosh the hazy water, she asked, "Is that magic from the Deep Fathoms?"

Gahalatine shook his head. "No, this came from another world. Useful, is it not? They are called 'leerings' there . . . after the word of power that summons light. *Le-ah-eer.*"

As he said the word, the carving began to glow, flooding the tent with more light.

"You know words of power?" she asked him, impressed.

Gahalatine knelt in front of her again and shrugged. "A few. When you are around Wizrs, you pick up on them." He set the bowl down on her lap. "Let me see your hands."

She pulled off the battle gauntlets that were part of her armor and he set them on the floor. The black tunic beneath her armor went down to her wrists. He gazed at her hands and then helped them into the bowl, washing them with the rag and the warm water.

"Thank you for sending your surgeons to the castle," she said, realizing that she hadn't thought to say it earlier. "That was kind of you."

She saw him smile in a self-conscious way. "Of course you would be worried. We will try to save as many as we can. I brought many surgeons with my ships for the purpose of healing your people after we'd defeated them." He sighed. "I'll admit that it was more challenging than I expected. A good fight. An honorable one." He gave her a tender look and set the bowl on the ground.

"First, you must eat and rest," he said. "In keeping with our traditions, I'd offer to bathe you completely, but I understand that your traditions and sensibilities are much different, and it would more likely embarrass you than do you honor."

Her cheeks flushed crimson at his suggestion and he laughed softly. "I thought as much. You will rest in here. I will bring you some food later, and then we can discuss terms."

She shook her head. "I am not going to rest while my people worry in anticipation. We will discuss terms now. We may well be at an impasse."

His brow wrinkled. "Surely not," he said. He put his elbows on the chest and looked up at her. "I've won the day, Tryneowy. Another quarter hour and every man . . . or woman . . . defending your king would have been struck down, except yourself. You were not counting on Grand Duke Elwis to save you? Or the soldiers in the mountains? They're both cut off from you, and I have even more reinforcements on the way by sea. Your king has my sister as a hostage. And I have you. I don't believe you are going to slay my sister any more than your king believes I'd slay you. As if I could! You are the prize I wanted, Tryneowy." He took her damp hand and brushed his lips against it. It sent shivers of fire up her whole arm.

He rose and pulled her up with him. "Rest. You are weary and tired. I don't want you to regret your answers. I don't want you to say later that you didn't have your full wits when you promised to be mine. That you were *forced* to be my wife, my queen, my confidante."

She looked him in the eye, seeing the earnestness in his words. "I will not have you," she said.

"Do not say that," Gahalatine said, shaking his head. "What must I do to *earn* your consent? I know you surely will not accept me without terms. I am prepared to make them." He stabbed his chest with his finger. "It was *you* at the Battle of Guilme. The Painted Knight. The king's best-kept secret. You are not just a wise maiden, but you are a warrior too! Do you not understand how intoxicating I find that? How much you intrigue me? Very little does that anymore. I wish to join with you, for you would shape me into a better man, I know it.

"I have faults and flaws, but a lack of honor is not one of them. I would never take you by force. Tryneowy, I am dazzled by you and all that you have accomplished. You've earned my respect and admiration. I had heard about your disfigurement, but in truth, I find you very attractive. Being with you right now is tormenting me in ways I hadn't anticipated." He turned away from her, perhaps to conceal or control his emotions. "I've been caught in a trap the Wizrs set. Brought perilously close to submitting, for there was no other choice. They sought to force me to marry another, the king's sister. Someone *they* could control. They promised me that she would be everything I desire in a wife. You are my chance to be free of them."

He pivoted on his heel to face her again. "I knew of you previously, of course. The Mandaryn said marrying someone from Kingfountain would help secure the peace quickly. I wished to marry you and invite your father to serve me, but they took him away. They've hidden him from me . . . from us.

"It was Rucrius's doing. He led the Mandaryn. They have more power than you can understand. Every emperor before has been controlled by them, but I will shake off the yoke. With our gifts merged together, we can do it. Now, do not tell me that you will not consent. I cannot accept that answer. What would it take to win you? Name it, Tryneowy. I would give you half of my kingdom. But truly, it is yours anyway! Name your terms and I will accept them. Only be *mine*."

His tone was pleading and passionate. There was ambition in his eyes, but it was not the only thing she saw there. There was open fascination in his gaze, as if everything about her intrigued him. She'd always felt so marred, so flawed. Morwenna was infinitely more beautiful. Yet he professed to feel passion for Trynne. But did he truly know her? They had only spoken twice. Was he in love with the idea of her? A conjuring of his own imagination?

He was so handsome, so self-confident. She was neither impressed with his wealth nor impressed by the opulence of his court. She could not imagine herself being the emperor's wife.

But this was the moment. Her heart told her *this* was what her mother had seen in a vision.

Gahalatine's look was so intense and imploring that she gazed down at the rugs beneath their feet.

"I cannot live apart from Brythonica," she said haltingly. "I have a duty to protect the people in my mother's absence."

"Done," Gahalatine said with a snap of his fingers. "My dear, as you well know, our magic is superior to yours. You can return to Ploemeur instantaneously every day if you wish it. I must rule from the Forbidden Court, but there is nothing to prevent me from joining you or you from joining me. Distance is not an obstacle to us. Please, think no more of it. What else? What are your concerns?"

Her heart nearly revolted at that moment, conjuring Fallon's face in her mind. She had loved Fallon for so long, even though she'd known they could not be together. Losing him permanently would be painful. She'd been preparing herself for it, but the moment was finally nigh. She pressed her face into her hands and breathed deeply, trying to quell the trembling of her limbs. She looked up at him, his expression so vulnerable. "You do not know me very well. There are many things we do not know about each other."

A smile quirked on his mouth. "Teach me, Tryneowy, how to please you. I *long* to tell you stories of my childhood, how I had to flee for my life. How I retook the city of my fathers and outmaneuvered the Wizrs at first. How I earned each of my wounds and battle scars. I *long* to hear the stories of your youth. Of the mischief you made. Stories of your father and how he outmaneuvered King Severn." He came closer and lifted her chin, gazing down at her. His thumb brushed against her mouth, at the frown that would not yield. "How *this* happened to you. And how you faced it with courage. You are so beautiful, Tryneowy, and you are even more desirable in your armor. What else do you fear? The fate of your king? You saw what I did with Sunilik. He is one of my greatest advisors. Surely I will honor such a man."

His mention of King Sunilik shifted Trynne's thoughts to Rani Reya. She had sent her to find Elwis and bring him and his men to Dundrennan. Was she trapped in the blizzard with him? Would she perish if Trynne did not come to terms with Gahalatine?

So many lives depended on her decision. The weight of it nearly suffocated her.

"What?" he said, growing concerned. His fingers stroked through her hair. "What concerns you? I cannot bear to see you in pain. Is it that you wish for King Andrew to retain his title? In most cases, I have replaced the rulers of the lands I've conquered. But that does not need to happen here. What are you worrying about? Tell me!"

She looked him in the eye and stepped away from him.

"Gahalatine," she said, shaking her head. "You have waged this war unjustly. We did not provoke you. Your Wizrs have been spying on us, I think, from the poisoner school in Pisan. That is how they met Morwenna and hatched Rucrius's plot. Our lands had united under King Andrew, and they saw we were becoming powerful, that we might, one day, pose a sufficient threat to the East Kingdoms. To their games. You are being used and manipulated, Gahalatine. Your advisors have tricked you. They've encouraged even more lavish spending so that you'll be beholden to them and their wishes." She clenched her fists before her. "They murdered my little brother and my father's parents in an attempt to destroy *me*. I saw Gannon plummet to his death and I had to commit his body to the Deep Fathoms. Rucrius admitted his hand was in it after I captured him." She lowered her fists. His eyes were wide with surprise and horror, but she did not give him time to respond. She continued, her manner fierce and bold.

"If that is not enough to harden my heart, I've also come to learn that your treasuries are nearly void of coin. Your kingdom is built on sticks that will come crashing down in a strong wind. We will hold out against you. Dundrennan may fall. But I have the power to take my king elsewhere. And you will be forced to chase us from one corner of his realm to the other. You've bribed your way to victory thus far. But King Andrew will not yield the hollow crown. It was given to him by the Fountain. He is the rightful ruler. Not you."

She swallowed, bolstering her courage. She looked him steadfastly in the eye, squeezing her fists until they hurt. "If you will kneel and swear fealty to him, to Andrew Argentine, as *your* rightful king and ruler, then I will marry you and help you repair the ruin you have nearly brought on yourself."

CHAPTER
THIRTY-FIVE

The Uncrowned King

Gahalatine endured her words with shocked silence. She had broken his perception of himself as a wise and benevolent ruler. She was also demanding him to surrender his ambition, to kneel before a man whom he felt was his inferior, to admit defeat. It was obvious her words had struck him to his core. He stared at her, measuring what she had told him, his eyes flashing from one emotion to another in rapid succession. His cheeks flushed. Would he fly into a rage? Would he challenge what she had said?

"I need some time to think," he said, his voice shaking. "Your words have cut me deeper than any sword."

Then he turned and strode out of the compartment, the curtain rustling as he vanished beyond it. Exhaustion settled over her. She went to the enormous pile of fur blankets and rugs and nestled amidst the softness to wait. They smelled of cinnamon and sandalwood, and as her muscles finally began to relax, she succumbed to sleep.

Trynne did not know how long she slept, but her dreams were peaceful. She was walking along the shore of the Glass Beach, hand in hand with Fallon. They spoke of childhood and their adventures together in Ploemeur. He reminded her of the magnolia trees and how he had caught her around the waist and twirled her around. His words brought back the memory and the dizziness, and her heart throbbed with love.

They sat down on the beach together, listening to the crashing of the surf. She loved that sound, loved everything about that place—the salty smell of sea air, the noise of gulls, the long wings of pelicans, and the little pips of sandpipers. She looked over at Fallon, but Gahalatine was sitting there in his stead, arms crossed around his knees, the wind tousling his hair. She was confused by the transformation.

Where had Fallon gone? She heard the sound of boots crunching in the sand and turned her head. Fallon was walking back toward the stone steps leading away from the beach. There was a woman standing in the distance, her black hair flowing in the wind. Trynne wanted to call out in warning, feeling a sudden panic in her heart.

Her eyes blinked open and she was instantly disoriented, not recognizing the furs and cushions on which she slept. Gahalatine was sitting on a cushion on the floor near her, head propped on one hand, writing with a quill and ink on paper. The sound of the quill head scratching the paper was soft as his hand moved swiftly across the page.

She blinked and lifted herself up on her arms. "When did you return?" she murmured, her voice quavering, her emotions still charged by the dream. She wiped her mouth on the back of her hand.

He glanced over at her. "You were resting so peacefully," he said, "I dared not disturb you. So I started writing up orders to be executed after we spoke again. My heart is burning in my chest, Tryneowy. You spoke the truth. You spoke of your pain. I'm honored that you would still accept me, even after all that has happened."

He cocked his head to one side, sighing deeply.

"Truth is like a double-edged sword. Is that not one of the teachings of the Fountain? It cuts through soul and spirit, joints and marrow. How did you know to strike me there, where I am most vulnerable?" He blinked rapidly, still not looking at her, his mind far away.

"As I thought about the things you told me, Tryneowy, I felt the truth of your words. I'm not certain I could have endured them had they been spoken by any other person." He looked at her then, his eyes full of sorrow and anguish. There were tears quivering on his lashes.

"Surely . . . surely you *are* right. About everything. There is no atonement I can make for the loss of your brother. Were Rucrius here right now, I would slay him myself for such a crime. I can still defeat this castle, even with the blizzard summoned by the hollow crown. But I cannot take the crown itself by force."

Trynne edged close enough to rest her hand on his shoulder. He jolted when he felt her touch and looked up at her shamefacedly. He covered his mouth with one hand, closed his eyes, and began stroking the stubble on his chin.

"My treasury is, as you say, depleted. The Mandaryn convinced me that this exploit would succeed, that our coffers would once again be overflowing." He shook his head slightly, then gazed up at her. "I assume Sunilik is the one who told you. He saw through the illusion. He has warned me repeatedly. I've relied on his counsel." He stared into her eyes. "Just as I would like to rely on yours. Is there anything else you learned about Chandigarl? Any other truths about my empire that I do not recognize?"

Trynne sat down beside him and smoothed some of her hair back from her face. "There is something about the zenana," she said. "When I visited it, I sensed . . . I'm not sure what it was."

Gahalatine sat up as well, crossing his legs and nodding encouragingly. "Go on. I have felt it as well."

"I don't know what it is. But I fear it comes from these Mandaryn. The men who wear the silver masks to hide themselves. Some of them have been sighted in our kingdom. Always secretly. They come and go in stealth."

He looked startled. "I've authorized no such incursions. Rucrius would have much to answer if the dead could speak. He was the ruler of the Mandaryn." He paused, then added, "They do not wear the silver masks as a disguise, but to hide the marks on their faces."

Trynne furrowed her brow. "What marks?" she asked, but even as she said it, she remembered the dark lines she'd noticed on the face of the man who'd confronted her and Sunilik.

"The Mandaryn use an ancient magic that causes sigils to creep from their chests up their necks and to their faces. Such markings frightened the women of the zenana, so the men were kept masked. Rucrius gave a special name to the Mandaryn assigned to the zenana. He called them the *Dokht Mandar*—or the *daughters* of the Mandaryn—for their duty was to treat the women as their daughters. They were in charge of finding a suitable wife for me." He pursed his lips and gave her a knowing look. "I was never comfortable with any of their selections. The women were all beautiful, skilled at conversation, music, and poetry. But they all felt . . . *wrong*."

Trynne felt something tugging inside her mind. "Something is not right about that place," she said again.

"Is that all?" he asked her gently.

She thought once more about her dream, the ache she'd felt as she watched Fallon walk away. Then she shook her head no. She was not ready to confide that part of herself yet.

"I have given this enough deliberation and careful thought. But it is my heart that persuades me I'd be a fool to reject your terms. I am ready to kneel before your king. I will swear homage and fealty to the Master of the Ring Table and the King of the Hollow Crown. You are a treasure worth more than crowns or rubies or palaces. Say that you will have me, and we will go this instant and declare peace. Will you be mine, Tryneowy Kiskaddon?"

She felt the warmth emanating from him, the tickle of his breath on her skin. Her feelings were as confusing as they were complex. She still loved Fallon. She always had. But in this man, in Gahalatine, she felt no trickery or deceit. What he truly lacked was discernment—and that was something she felt she could help him with. With it, she knew he could become a truly great man. She wished her parents could have been there to help her make her choice, but even though she believed this was what her mother's vision had bespoken, it was ultimately her decision to make.

"I will have you," she answered, feeling in her heart that it was the advice her mother would have given her.

He took her fingers in his hand and brought them to his lips for a kiss. "Then I will cherish you and protect you all the days of my life," he whispered huskily. He kissed her fingertips again.

Then he rose and helped her stand. She gave him one of her crooked smiles, feeling self-conscious at the way he was gazing at her with undisguised admiration. She didn't feel worthy of it.

"You are sixteen, are you not?" he asked her, but she could see he already knew the answer.

"I am, my lord," she answered with a small dip of her chin.

"Finding your father is my highest priority," he said. "We will do all that we can. I will enlist Sunilik's aid. He is responsible for my estates and manors. But your mother is living. I had expected her to be defending Kingfountain, but she was not there. Is she in Ploemeur?"

Trynne shook her head. "No. The Fountain called her away on a journey. She boarded a ship and seeks the Deep Fathoms. She is not here."

A troubled look surfaced on his face. "Indeed?"

"Yes," Trynne answered.

His look became more troubled.

"What is it?" Trynne asked.

Gahalatine sighed, looking down. "It is one of the customs of the East Kingdoms," he said, his brow furrowing. "A law, to be precise. It was done to protect women from being forced to marry against their will or from marrying too young. If a woman has no parents, her husband cannot consummate the marriage until she is eighteen. There are unscrupulous men who would do otherwise."

Trynne wrinkled her brow. "In this kingdom, a woman can be married at sixteen or seventeen. There are no such laws. And my parents are both alive, I hope. They are just not here."

Gahalatine nodded. "I understand the laws are different in Kingfountain. But I cannot overlook the customs and traditions of *my* people. I would bring dishonor on myself if I broke the law when it suited me." He smiled and sighed dejectedly. "If I had to wait a year or two for you, it would not change my answer. It will give me an even stronger motivation to find your father quickly," he said, raising his eyebrows meaningfully.

Trynne blushed. "I will have you, Gahalatine. I give you my promise."

He nodded and took her hands and kissed them again. "Until that time, we will be as brother and sister. I would not besmirch your honor for all the world."

"I know you would not," Trynne replied. It was obvious the law frustrated him, but it did not hinder his resolve to do the honorable thing. She felt acutely the relief that although she had to marry someone she didn't love—not yet—at least he was a man worthy of admiration.

He offered her his hand. "I think your king will be anxious to hear from us."

Trynne could hardly believe what she was hearing. She felt like the sunlight beaming through the curtain of the tent. Would the conflict end at last? With Gahalatine's help, would she be able to find her father? To save him and Drew and Genevieve? Would she herself be able to save the kingdom?

She was so exhausted, she only nodded. But she reached out and squeezed Gahalatine's hand. He looked so tender and mournful in that moment, she lifted herself onto the tips of her toes and grazed his cheek with a kiss.

♦ ♦ ♦

Trynne was amazed at how much the world had transformed since she had arrived with her army. The mountain Helvellyn was sheathed in heavy banks of snow with only a few gray crags visible. The roofs of the town were nearly buried under the drifts. The snow was falling in a continuous plume, threatening to bury the entire world in winter, and the air was so cold it burned her nose to breathe it. She saw Gahalatine's warriors patrolling the battlement walls, carrying torches and shoveling the paths.

The Wizr Albion brought them back to the great hall with the Tay al-Ard. The smell of blood and death hung in the hall and the place was full of commotion. Gahalatine's surgeons were hard at work tending to the wounded soldiers who had fought for Trynne and the king.

Her heart filled with grief at the destruction, especially the loss of Captain Staeli.

The crowd parted as she and Gahalatine started to walk, arm in arm, across the slabs of paving stone. She gazed through the crowd, and looking at those prostrate and receiving care, she finally spotted him on the floor by one of the support columns. She'd expected a body, cold and stiff, but he was *breathing*. They were slow, shallow gulps, but where there was breath there was hope. Haley knelt by him with tears in her eyes. Trynne, awestruck, released Gahalatine's hand and rushed over to where he lay.

Staeli's face was chalky gray, his mouth twisted into a rictus of agony. It was heart-wrenching to see her friend and protector in such pain, but he was conscious, and he blinked in recognition when he saw her.

"Hello, lass," he said with a groan. "We'll keep fighting. I'm feeling much better. Give me a moment . . . I'll be back on my feet. We'll drive these blackguards out of the North."

She reached out and touched his arm and invoked a word of power for healing. Her magic shrank and she felt herself grow dizzy at the discharge of power.

"You're alive, Captain," she said with relief, feeling tears trickle from her lashes. "I'm going to end this war. We won."

His brow furrowed. "Don't be rash, lass. We can hold them off longer."

"I know, Captain," she said, watching as the trembling in his body began to subside. "We didn't surrender. The Fountain knew this would happen. What I do, I do willingly." She gave him a tender smile and kissed his sweaty brow. When she rose, she saw Gahalatine standing nearby, speaking in low tones with the surgeon who had worked on the captain. His Wizr stood beside him.

"My sister wounded him," Gahalatine said somberly to Trynne. "He still lives?"

Trynne nodded, grateful that she had returned when she did. He had been going through the death throes, but her spell was taking hold and healing him on the inside. She offered a quiet prayer of gratitude to the Fountain that she had known the right word to use.

Then, taking Gahalatine's arm again, Trynne proceeded across the rest of the hall to the place where Drew, Fallon, and a few others were waiting. Fallon's leg was bandaged and he was leaning on a pike to hold himself upright. He looked anguished as he watched her approach, her arm linked with the enemy's. Drew's look bespoke his curiosity. Gahalatine's sister stood near Fallon. Her armor was gone and she wore a long, nondescript gray tunic. She was studying her brother and Trynne with interest. Off to the side, Morwenna was glaring at them, her eyes full of anguish and disappointment. *She* seemed to understand exactly what had happened.

They came to a stop when they reached the king, and the Wizr Albion bowed and stepped to the other side of Gahalatine. He seemed to emanate waves of nervous confusion.

Drew had a stern look as he glanced from one to the other. "Has an accord been struck, then?" he asked, his voice throbbing with worry. "What are the terms?" She could see he was dreading the news of what he had lost.

Gahalatine turned to Trynne and gave her a satisfied smile. Despite what he'd agreed to do, he did not look humiliated or nervous at all. She removed her hand from his arm, and he instantly stepped forward. Fallon gripped a dagger, as if worried the man was about to attack the king, but the Lord of the Distant Isles knelt before Drew and bowed his head. "I, Gahalatine, do hereby swear fealty and homage to Andrew Argentine, King of Ceredigion and Occitania, Lord of the Seven Kingdoms, and ruler of Kingfountain. I submit my will to yours and promise to rebuild what I have destroyed and to heal the breach between our empires. I recognize you as my sovereign lord." He remained there, kneeling before Drew, his head still bowed.

Trynne tried to conceal a smile as she saw the look of astonishment on the king's face. As if completely bewildered, he gazed at her and then at Gahalatine and then back again.

"What have you done to this poor fellow, Trynne?" Drew said, shaking his head. He stepped forward, still amazed. "Are there no conditions?"

Gahalatine shook his head. "None, my lord. My submission to you is unconditional."

"Rise, man," Drew said, gesturing quickly. He looked at Trynne again, seeking an explanation.

Gahalatine rose to his feet. He was a bigger man than Drew, and only a few years older. "You are surprised, my lord king, but you should not be. Anyone who knows the worth of this maiden would not underestimate her abilities. This was her suggestion. Her ultimatum, actually." He smiled wryly. "I have been led falsely by the intrigue of my court advisors." He glowered at Albion, who blanched and seemed horrified by what he had just witnessed. "You truly deserve to wear the hollow crown. I hope, one day, to deserve your pardon and forgiveness."

The king chuffed as if he was about to start laughing. He smiled at Trynne with such a look of regard and respect that she felt her cheeks grow warm.

"You did it," Drew said sincerely. "You did the impossible."

She bowed her head. "Please stop the snow, my lord," she told him. "Before Elwis's forces freeze to death."

"I think I can feel the sun shining already," Drew said triumphantly. "Send a group to rescue the men trapped in the snow. Bring them to Dundrennan at once and tend to them. By the Fountain, this is a day that will never be forgotten!"

◆ ◆ ◆

The war in the foreign land was not going well when our ship arrived. Some battles had been fought, and our king's forces had been beaten even though he outnumbered his enemy. We were ordered to help with the retreat to the ships when we were set upon by a fresh army from the enemy. I could see that we would be overrun and slaughtered if we did not act quickly. I told the captain how to turn the situation to our advantage. The captain, who had no ideas of his own and was near panicking, heeded my words, and we drove away the group attacking us. We were not as outnumbered as we'd supposed.

The captain was grateful for my quick thinking and recommended me to the captain of the king's guard, a man by the name of Carstone, when he arrived to inspect the new arrivals. He asked me about my training and background. I told him I couldn't remember who I was but that I knew the arts of war. Carstone said the king valued men like me and that I'd rise in rank quickly if I proved myself. The king had failed in his conquest and could expect swift retaliation from our enemy. I told him I didn't even know the name of our king. He was surprised no one had told me. He said the king doesn't go by his given name. He goes by the name of the duchy he once ruled. He's an ambitious man, an enemy to the King of Comoros he once served. His name is Dieyre and he's an expert swordsman himself. We'll be returning to Dahomey soon to defend it.

◆ ◆ ◆

CHAPTER
THIRTY-SIX

Reunited

The fire in the hearth in the solar roared and crackled, and Trynne warmed herself in front of it. She had changed from her battle clothes into a lady's gown and enjoyed the feeling of satin on her skin. There were bruises all over her body, but none of her wounds were serious or deep. She glanced toward the window seat, where Gahalatine sat with arms folded, watching her with an entranced smile.

Drew spoke in a low voice with one of the Espion, who would relay messages immediately to Kevan Amrein back at Kingfountain, alerting him of the truce and the sudden change of events. The Espion bowed and left the three of them alone in the solar. Drew clasped his hands behind his back and turned to face Gahalatine, giving him a probing look.

"Any news from your Wizrs?" he asked.

Gahalatine nodded. "Contact has been made with the Grand Duke of Brugia. The rescue is under way. Many of his soldiers are frostbitten, but we will treat them. Those who fell behind are being searched for. We will save as many as we can."

"Thank you," Drew said. "I was not in a position to offer much aid."

Gahalatine smiled and bowed his head. "I will do what I can to alleviate the suffering I have caused." He looked at Trynne, who felt a smile of gratitude tug at her lips. Gahalatine beamed when he saw it.

Drew noticed the subtle interplay between them and arched his eyebrow. "How will your people react to this news, my lord?"

Gahalatine leaned back against the window, looking thoughtful. "The Mandaryn will be violently opposed. They control the bureaucracy. But the military is loyal to me. I can also be very . . . persuasive, King Andrew. My people may need some time to accept this change. But I do not doubt that they will come to see the advantages as I have. I would like to invite you to visit us in the Forbidden Court. To see for yourself what the East Kingdoms offer to your splendor."

Drew arched his brow again. "You used the word *us*. And I've noticed the way the two of you have been looking at each other." He scratched the corner of his mouth as if trying to subdue a grin. "You said your surrender was unconditional. But is there an understanding between the two of you? I sense that there is."

Gahalatine said nothing, but he looked at Trynne with a pleased and humble smile. She stroked the warm fabric on her arms, savoring the sensation and the feeling of calm assurance in her heart. She walked over to the window seat and sat next to Gahalatine, taking his hands in hers. He caressed her fingers with his thumb, and she gave him a shy glance.

"When I went to Chandigarl," Trynne said, looking over at the king, "Gahalatine promised me his troth and I declined it by fleeing his presence. My first loyalty and duty has always been to you and your wife. But I did promise him, when we were discussing terms, that I would be his wife if he swore fealty to you. Truly, my lord, he has no guile. He trusted my word just as I trusted his." She heard the door open as she turned to Gahalatine and spoke the next words. "I do accept your troth."

Drew turned at the intrusion, and they all saw Fallon standing in the doorway, leaning on a crutch. The look in his eyes filled Trynne with pangs of regret. He did not look startled. He did not look angry. He looked defeated. But he rallied himself, putting on a complacent mask.

"My timing is always infallibly, imperturbably, and impressively punctual," Fallon said, forcing a chuckle. "I nearly missed the best part." He hobbled inside, wincing at the pain in his leg, and shut the door. His mask of affability was firmly in place, but Trynne knew him well, and she saw the pain in his eyes. "Well, my lord Gahalatine, let me be the first to wish you both well. When are the nuptials? Did I miss that part?"

"No, Fallon," Drew said, giving the duke a surprised look. "I only just found out myself." He turned back to the couple at the window seat. "And so," Drew said, encouraging her to continue, "you've accepted him?"

"I have," Trynne said, gazing into the king's eyes, not daring to look at Fallon again. She could feel the concern in Drew's words, his unspoken question. He was wondering if she had sacrificed herself to save his kingdom. She rubbed Gahalatine's arm with one hand. "My lord, my mother once had a vision of my marriage. Even though she is not here, I believe this fulfills it. I've . . . been expecting something like this. For some time."

Drew nodded, pursing his lips. "If this is your decision, Trynne, I will not countermand it. Regarding the nuptials, has anything been decided? I will honor any terms you both agreed on."

Gahalatine smiled and leaned forward slightly. "Urgently would be my desire. I explained to Lady Tryneowy that the laws of my realm forbid a man from consummating a marriage with a lady who is not of age if her parents are dead or cannot present her. In your kingdom, she is of a suitable age to marry. But in mine, we cannot be man and wife in truth until she turns eighteen or until one or both of her parents grant their consent. It would be wise, therefore, if some distance separated us in the interim. There is much that I must do to repair the injury I've done to Ceredigion. There are troubles in my own lands that I must address. But I would marry her this very day at the sanctuary of Our Lady if your lordship will permit it."

"Our Lady," Drew said, nodding as he thought on the words. "My own dear wife has been in hiding there. I should like to see her again."

"Perhaps we can all go there together?" Gahalatine suggested. He rose from the window seat and brought Trynne, who was still holding his hand, up with him. "I will happily surrender the castle back to you, and we can end this conflict."

"I think that would suit us all perfectly well," Drew said. He turned to Fallon and raised an eyebrow.

Trynne risked a look at him, and part of her was relieved to see his mask still in place. "I'm unfit to travel at the moment," Fallon demurred. "While I would regret missing out on the marriage, I think it would be better if I stayed behind. I do have some news for you, my lord. Lady Trynne may wish to hear it also?"

"Go on," Drew said.

"It concerns the thief Dragan," Fallon said. He was looking at Trynne as he spoke. "I heard a report before the battle that he was dead." He shook his head. "It wasn't true. He awakened, but he was a changed man when he did. He began raving. He didn't know who he was, he said. Or why he had been jailed. The man cannot remember his own name."

The king wrinkled his brow, full of doubt. "He can no longer remember?"

Fallon nodded. "I've spoken to him myself, my lord. He looked at me as if I were a complete stranger. He doesn't know the name of our kingdom. He doesn't know why he was captured. His memories have all been stolen."

"But it is a jest, surely?" Drew asked.

"Perhaps," Fallon offered with a shrug. "But if it is one, it doesn't make sense. What would he have to gain by pleading amnesia? Surely it does not pardon his many crimes. He was frightened, earlier, about being killed. Do you remember?" he added, looking intently at Trynne.

"I do," she said, feeling cold despite the heat of the hearth. "He was afraid of Morwenna."

"Yes, but she was locked inside her cell," Fallon said. "When the battle grew fierce, she used her magic to rip the cell door open. That was the first time she left . . . *after* he was already found unconscious, presumed dead. My lord, what will you do with them?" He had a strange edge to his voice, one of strained concern.

Drew's face twisted into a frown. "They will both face the Assizes," he said sternly. "Justice will be done." Then he softened. "I will have Lord Amrein interrogate them both. There may be mitigating circumstances. Morwenna may have been under the sway of the Wizrs."

"This is the king's poisoner you speak of?" Gahalatine said.

Drew nodded. "My blood-sister."

"Before you condemn her," Gahalatine said, "let me see what I can discover about her involvement. There may be more evidence I can bring to bear."

"Thank you," Drew said to Gahalatine. Then he turned to Fallon. "Can I trust her to your custody for now? She must be guarded night and day."

"Of course, my lord. But I ask that I not be the judge in the matter. Assign Lord Amrein or someone else, if you would. I will hold her until you send for her."

Drew sighed and agreed. "To Kingfountain, then. Shall we?"

Trynne's stomach twisted with excitement and dread. Soon she would be married to a capable and kindhearted king, but she sorrowed for Fallon, both for the suffering she saw in his eyes and for what might have been.

Without Morwenna's help during the battle, things would have been worse for them, but she did not think it terribly wise to keep her in Dundrennan. Trynne would suggest to Genevieve that she be moved elsewhere, like Beestone castle.

As they started to follow Drew out of the solar, Fallon blocked the way. He looked at Gahalatine, a half smile on his mouth. "Congratulations, my lord," he said, closing his eyes and bowing his head in a gesture of respect. "You will not regret your decision. You have won you the best that our shores have to offer." Then he gave Trynne a heartbreakingly sweet smile. "Farewell, *Cousin*."

He stepped out of the way and extended his hand gallantly for them to pass. But he did not follow them out of the solar.

◆　◆　◆

The only hint of winter was the sharp feeling of the air. The sky over the city of Kingfountain was the deepest, clearest blue without even the hint of a cloud. The three of them emerged through the fountain in the side chapel of Our Lady.

The sanctuary was crowded with citizens offering coins and prayers. It was obvious that word from Dundrennan had not yet reached the city. Their murmurs filled the air as Drew came to a stop in the threshold leading to the main audience hall. Light from the sky filled the huge windows and painted dazzling colors on the black and white marble tiles.

No one had noticed them yet.

Trynne's stores of magic were depleted, but when she reached out to probe for threats and dangers, there weren't any.

"There's Lord Amrein," the king said, sighing in relief. "Who is that woman at his side?"

Trynne followed his gaze. It was the widow Mariette, whom Trynne had assigned as the queen's bodyguard. She was exceptionally tall compared to Lord Amrein, but they were speaking in confidential tones. There was an intimacy to it that made Trynne smile.

Then she noticed the king was staring at her. She turned and gave him a quizzical look. He reached out and took one of Trynne's hands, cupping it between his own. When he spoke, his voice was low and thick with emotion.

"Thank you, Trynne. I cannot thank you enough. You saved my kingdom. You saved us all. You were my silent shield, my unseen protector. You were my true champion. Until your father returns, I would have you take your rightful place at the Ring Table. In his chair."

Her throat thickened and she felt a spasm of surprise at his words. "But what of Fallon? He is your champion."

Drew shook his head. "He was defeated, Trynne. *You* were not." While holding her hands, he turned to Gahalatine. "I offer you a seat at the Ring Table as well, Lord Gahalatine. I would value your wisdom and leadership. I would trust you as an emissary to act on my behalf."

Gahalatine smiled, pleased. "It would be an honor, my lord."

But then someone saw them in the alcove, and the quiet moment ended. Word began spreading like wildfire. "The king! The king is here!"

"The hollow crown! It is him!"

"Wait for me here," Drew said, smiling with chagrin. He released her hand and marched into the huge room, one hand on the hilt of Firebos. The crowd parted before him as he strode toward the fountain from which he had first drawn the sword. And then Trynne saw that Genny had joined Lord Amrein and Mariette, and a tingle of warmth went down to her toes. Her throat caught with delight as she watched Genevieve, holding baby Kate in her arms, rush forward and embrace her husband with laughter and tears.

"The war is over!" Drew shouted to the assembled crowd in a loud, triumphant voice. "We have peace!"

A chorus of cheers and exultant shouts thrummed throughout the vast chamber. Within moments, the bells of Our Lady began to ring, adding to the frenzy. A few children began dancing with reckless abandon inside the fountain waters. Having heard the stories of her father and Lady Evie playing in that very fountain as little ones, Trynne started to laugh through her tears. She pressed her hand against her nose, trying to stifle the sobs.

Trynne felt Gahalatine's arm wrap around her shoulders and she leaned into him. He pressed a kiss into her hair.

Genevieve presented the baby girl to Drew, who picked up the lass and smothered her cheek with kisses. A pang of longing filled Trynne at the sight. While she was pleased that the Fountain had used her to bring peace to the realm, she missed her own father dreadfully. Seeing the scene unfold before her awakened feelings she'd suppressed. Would her father and mother come home again? Would they be a family together once more? She remembered something Genny had said, the memory as sharp and piercing as a thorn.

"What sort of world will she inherit? Will it be Gahalatine's? Or her father's?"

"She'll inherit the world we leave her," Trynne had said.

"And what kind of world will that be?"

Trynne looked up at Gahalatine, saw him staring down at her with a look of affection. It awakened a hunger inside her, a longing that could not be denied. She couldn't imagine anything changing that look. He was firm and constant. He was to be her husband. She stared up at him, wanting him to bend down and kiss her.

And almost in response to her contented thought, a shadow passed over the sunlight outside as a cloud drifted by. And with it came the memory of Fallon's kiss.

EPILOGUE

Into the Deep Fathoms

Sinia Montfort Kiskaddon gazed at the map of ley lines she was painstakingly crafting in her cabin. In the months she had been at sea, she had adjusted to the pitch and sway of the ship. There were times when the wind had blown them steadily westward. On other occasions, the ocean was flat as glass and the crew labored with oars and dinghies to drag the ship onward.

Staring at the map, she touched the various islands that they had visited along the way, looking at the markings she had made in her elegant script with the assistance of the ship cartographer. They had encircled the islands to collect the shapes of the coves and inlets.

Each one they had found contained a carved boulder—a boulder with a face engraved into it. The boulders contained the magic of the Fountain—asleep and waiting to be awakened. Whenever she reached out and touched one, she could see blazing in her mind the location of the next stone on the next island. There was also script carved into the rocks, an ancient language, which she had used her magic to decipher. The markings had been left by a Wizr from Chandigarl centuries before, and they documented his search for the Deep Fathoms.

With each visit, Sinia had felt something beckoning her onward.

She sighed, mopping sweat from her brow with a nearby towel. The journey had been both thrilling and dangerous. Storms had threatened them and damaged the ship, and they had encountered a treasure ship not long after leaving Ploemeur. The Wizr on that ship had sought to hunt them down, but Sinia had conjured a mist to hide their escape. Still, all their adventures could not banish her sense that something terrible was happening back at Kingfountain. She'd had a vision of a runaway wagon barreling down the switchbacks from the castle atop the hill in Ploemeur, but the vision was frustratingly short on details. They so often were.

Sinia leaned back in her chair, staring at the map but not seeing it. The urge to turn the ship around was nearly overpowering. There was a war in her heart. She was determined to exercise faith in the Fountain and where it was leading her, but her instincts as a mother were powerful and omnipresent. She would do anything to safeguard her children and protect her people. She had trained Trynne in what to do, how to reset the wards and preserve Brythonica. She thought back again on the vision she had seen of Trynne's marriage. She had never met the man before. Judging by his clothes, he appeared to be from the East. King Andrew had been there. So had Genevieve and Lady Kathryn. She herself had not been there, so she had taken the vision as a blessing from the Fountain. It allowed her to be there even though she could not be.

Go back, the thoughts tormented her. *Abandon this silly quest. You are no longer of the Deep Fathoms. You are mortal now. You do not belong among them.*

She forced the thoughts away. Leaning forward again, she retraced the series of islands they had encountered amidst the vast ocean. Each carved boulder was a link to a ley line, and each was close to a small natural fountain. They'd used the fountains to replenish their supply of water aboard the boat. Fruits from the native lands had been harvested to restock their supplies.

They were getting closer.

Sinia heard the footsteps coming toward her chamber before the knock sounded. It was a firm, commanding sound. She recognized it as Captain Pyne's knock.

"Come in." She watched as the captain opened the door.

"My lady," he said, his eyes wide with wonder. "I know not how to describe it. I didn't believe the sailor in the crow's nest until I saw it for myself, so I climbed up the rigging just to be sure." He had a scraggly beard from their months at sea. The dome of his head was covered in stubble as well as a healing gash from an injury he'd suffered during a storm.

"To be sure of what, Captain?" she asked in confusion.

"My lady, we're approaching the island you directed us to. It's a beauty, I tell you. Green as the spring and full of vegetation. There's a hump of mountain on the southeastern side, showing a cliff and such. It's an odd-shaped crook of land, to be sure. But my man in the crow's nest saw something. There's an undersea waterfall."

Sinia knit her brows in confusion. "I don't understand, Captain."

"That's the only way to describe it, my lady. There's some sort of underwater breach. You can see it from high above. The current is pulling us toward it. Do we go around the other side? I'd like you to come and look at it, my lady."

"Of course," Sinia said, pushing away from the table and hurrying after him down the cramped corridor. The crew members, still dressed in their Raven tunics, were hard at work, but many of them were pointing at the island with enthusiasm. It had been two weeks since their last stop. She could smell the difference in the air. Being aboard a vessel for so long had awakened new senses she'd not realized she had.

"Up the rigging this way, my lady," Captain Pyne said. He let her go first and followed behind. She had climbed up the rigging more than once and loved the feeling of being up in the crow's nest at the apex of the mast. Gripping the ropes one by one as she climbed, she felt exhilarated as the wind streamed through her hair. When she reached the top, the sailor in the nest gripped her wrist and helped her climb up.

"Over yonder, my lady," the sailor said in a rough but respectful manner. "I don't quite know what to make of it. I've seen naught like it in all my years at sea."

Sinia waited for Captain Pyne and swept the hair from her face as she gazed at the horizon. The island was a verdant paradise, and she could hear the noise of birds even from the distance. To her amazement, though, much of the island was partially submerged. She could see the rocks and reefs below the clear blue water. There was a whitish outline in the water, marking the boundaries of the island.

That was when she saw it.

There was a deep gulf off the western sprit of land, and what appeared to be a massive underwater waterfall, as if the entire ocean were draining into that singular point. The waters in the chasm were an astounding shade of blue and green with white-capped foam. It was like staring off a cliff at a waterfall, except it was all beneath the surface of the sea. If she had not seen it with her own eyes, she wouldn't have understood that such a thing was even possible.

"Do you see it, my lady? Do you see it?" the sailor said.

"It's the entrance to the Deep Fathoms," Sinia whispered, feeling her heart sear with the truth of the words. The underwater trench was wide enough to sink a ship much larger than theirs.

"What do we do, my lady?" Captain Pyne asked her. He wiped his mouth on his forearm, looking down at the scene they were drawing toward.

She closed her eyes and listened to the quiet deep inside her. The current was dragging the ship toward the gulf.

"That is our destination, Captain," she said, opening her eyes and fixing him with her gaze. "We take the ship into it."

"Going in is the easy part," he said nervously. "But my lady— how . . . how do we get *out*? Isn't the Deep Fathoms the land of the dead?"

She stared at the surging surf and the gaping breach. She felt drawn to it, pulled inexorably to the land of her prebirth.

"It is more than that, Captain," she said softly, giving him a comforting touch on his arm. "It is much more than that. The Fountain is calling me home. I can hear its music. Will we not obey its summons?"

The captain swallowed. "Aye, my lady. If you say so."

By the time they reached the bottom of the mast pole, the rest of the crew had caught sight of the otherworldly waterfall. A hush of reverence came over the crew as each man stood watching the spectacle. Sinia stood by the captain at the helm, staring at the waters, listening to the crash and noise of the surf. The ship was bobbing in the waves, rising and falling in yawning pitches. She felt her stomach thrill with anticipation.

"Steady, Captain," she said as he heaved his muscles against the helm to steer them. She could hear the music growing louder. The crew was silent, some biting their fists to keep from crying out in fear. She saw the looks on their faces, saw the terror mingled with hope.

Sinia gripped one of the sturdy peg spokes of the helm, squeezing it as the ship lunged down and up. The roar of the gulf was deafening, but she still heard the music of the Deep Fathoms.

A small *Sinia* butterfly flew before her face, catching her gaze. She smiled at it, feeling serene.

The ship dipped into the yawning gulf of water and lurched into the chasm.

AUTHOR'S NOTE

While doing research for the Kingfountain series, I came across several ideas that helped inspire the plot. First, there was a belief in the late fifteenth century of a mythical land of Nestorian Christians ruled by an ageless king named Prester John. There are many legends and books written about this person, which I studied, tales of rivers that could flow backward and mysterious items of magic. But it was reading some of the Arthurian legends within the Merlin Vulgate texts that I became acquainted with the details of the legend of Galehaut and how he invaded Arthur's realm and sought to make himself king. Lancelot, in disguise, had helped Arthur prevent a crushing defeat. Galehaut was so impressed by Lancelot that he willingly gave up his conquest and submitted himself to the king.

I loved this story idea and retold the legend, shaping the character of Gahalatine off this "uncrowned king." But I also came across a wonderful book by Gavin Menzies called *1423: The Year China Discovered America*. It's an amazing history of a period of discovery that I had never known about, and it inspired the treasure ships and the armada and the construction of the Forbidden Court. I based the East Kingdoms on the emperors of China during this period of our world's history.

Our world has an interesting and rich history of female warriors who became legends. I've always been inspired by Joan of Arc, but have since discovered many other women warriors who were known to be the best fighters in their respective kingdoms. Women like Turandot, Khutulun, and Brynhildr. Their stories have been told over and over throughout history, much like Owen's observation that history seems to keep repeating itself.

But there is another famous woman from the Arthurian legends, one who has a story that rivals and conflicts with Lancelot's. Morgan le Fay is the one who helped destroy Arthur in the end. Interestingly, according to the legends, the wounded Arthur was carried away on a boat to the Isle of Avalon. Legend says he is still buried there. That spot today is known as the ruins of Glastonbury Abbey. I learned this studying the lore of Glastonbury while writing *The Wretched of Muirwood*. Muirwood Abbey was based on that place.

Stay tuned for the adventure to continue and the secrets to be revealed at last in *The Forsaken Throne*.

ACKNOWLEDGMENTS

There are so many people involved in the production of my books. I literally cannot do this without the help and support of my brilliant editorial team (Jason, Angela, Wanda), my early readers (Robin, Karen, Shannon, Emily, Sunil), and my friends and family who have supported me over many years and many books (way too many to list them all!). Thank you. But I feel especially blessed to have the career I always dreamed of. I'd like to thank the Lord for helping make this all happen in ways I could never have imagined. I too am a great believer that "as [a man] thinketh in his heart, so is he" (Proverbs 23:7). I hope you continue to enjoy what I think about!

ABOUT THE AUTHOR

Wall Street Journal bestselling author Jeff Wheeler took an early retirement from his career at Intel in 2014 to write full-time. He is, most importantly, a husband, a father, and a devout member of his church. He is often seen roaming hills with oak trees and granite boulders in California or in any number of the state's majestic redwood groves. He is also the founder of *Deep Magic: The E-zine of Clean Fantasy and Science Fiction*. Find out more about *Deep Magic* online at www.deepmagic.co, and visit Jeff at www.jeff-wheeler.com.